THE BROKEN VOW

LUISA A. JONES

Storm

This is a work of fiction. Names, characters, business, events and incidents are the products of the author's imagination. Any resemblance to actual persons, living or dead, or actual events is purely coincidental.

Copyright © Luisa A. Jones, 2024

The moral right of the author has been asserted.

All rights reserved. No part of this book may be reproduced or used in any manner without the prior written permission of the copyright owner.

To request permissions, contact the publisher at rights@stormpublishing.co

Ebook ISBN: 978-1-80508-327-6
Paperback ISBN: 978-1-80508-329-0

Cover design by: Sarah Whittaker
Cover images by: Alamy, Shutterstock

Published by Storm Publishing.
For further information, visit:
www.stormpublishing.co

ALSO BY LUISA A. JONES

The Gilded Cage

Goes Without Saying

Making the Best of It

"A woman is like a tea bag. You can't tell how strong she is until you put her in hot water."
— attributed to Eleanor Roosevelt

This book is dedicated to Sam, Ben and Anna, with my love. You make me proud every day.

PROLOGUE
MARCH 1915

Rosamund

Rosamund was alone in the Dower House when her pains started. A low griping at first, as if her insides were gears, grinding into a slow but inexorable motion. Fumbling with a taper, she adjusted the wick on the small oil lamp that sat on the table next to her chair, as if light could banish pain and fear. If only the telephone was working, but the gales of the past week had brought the line down. Even if it worked, she could have summoned the doctor, but she couldn't have reached her lady's maid, Nellie Dawson, who was away on another of her regular visits to her ailing mother. Nellie had promised to be gone for no more than a day and a night, arguing that there was plenty of time yet. Except, it now seemed, there wasn't.

Distraction was what she needed. These pains might yet turn out to be a false alarm; she'd felt her swollen belly tighten several times in recent days. A pang of hunger reminded her she hadn't eaten for hours. Taking care to keep it level, she carried the brass lamp into the chilly, blue-painted kitchen. In the larder she found a piece of pork and egg pie Ethel, her maid of all work, had left on a plate covered with a napkin. A spoonful of piccalilli and some slices of vinegar-soaked cucumber from the jars on the shelves made it feel almost like a meal. Rosamund set the plate on a tray with a glass of milk and the lamp, and carried it back to the parlour, not bothering with a tray cloth; there was no one to witness her lapse of decorum.

Anxiety and the increasingly intense contractions squeezing her abdomen made each mouthful an effort, and despite her hunger it was a relief to finally lay down her fork and put the tray to one side. Picking up a book, she read a few chapters, pausing now and then to catch her breath. After an hour or so, the pains became too intrusive. When she had read the same paragraph three times and was still unable to recall what it had said, she tossed the book away.

Pacing the floor didn't help, either. Against all her hopes, the pains had not reduced. Rather, they were building in strength and frequency. Her mind raced with terrifying imaginings. Without help, she might die, and her baby along with her. It wouldn't be an unusual occurrence, after all. She'd bled badly at her last miscarriage and spent hours barely conscious. What if that happened this time?

Even if she and the baby could get through the birth without help, there was still the danger that she might die of complications afterwards, as her own mother had done. Since her husband's death had spared her the fear that she might perish at his hands, she had striven not to dwell on her vulnerability. Now, though, it was impossible to ignore.

Perspiration darkened the silk under the arms of her green housecoat, even though the room was only warm near the fireplace. She twisted the wedding ring she still wore only for form's sake. Women were open to so many risks: not only from their husband's fists, but also to the charms of amiable seducers and the subsequent danger of ruin. Not that she had been seduced. On the contrary: she had been the seducer.

So much depended on this baby. Sir Lucien's will had stipulated that she should receive an income and be allowed to live in the main house on the Plas Norton estate should she bear him a son to inherit the baronetcy. If the baby should turn out to be a girl, Rosamund would receive only the annuity from her brother's estate, a mere one thousand pounds a year to live on and to cover the wages for two servants. She couldn't depend on her stepdaughter Charlotte for financial support, either: the girl had always despised her, and the baby was a threat to her inheritance.

If this baby was a daughter, then Rosamund pitied it, and would be sorry to have to rear her in straitened financial circumstances. Poverty is poverty, however genteel. If it was a son, she hoped to live long enough to influence the man he would grow up to become. She would certainly bring him up to be kind, to treat women with courtesy, and to be a good husband when the time might come for him to take a wife. She would encourage him to be a generous landlord and employer, and to deal with people fairly. She could only hope his character would be more like that of his true sire, Joseph Cadwalader, than Sir Lucien Fitznorton whom the world believed to be his father.

Joe had loved her, but his dreams of a future together had been impossible. He was only her late husband's chauffeur, yet to her mind the ostensibly rough working man had been more of a gentleman than the cruel Sir Lucien, who had died as a result of her own desperate act of self-defence. She had lived with fear for years as a wife; as a widow, her constant fear was that someone might guess her shameful secrets. It would be dangerous enough if her baby grew up to look like its real father, as they could both lose their place in respectable society. But if anyone realised that her husband's death had not been an accident, she could hang.

Whether a son or a daughter, her only prayer was that she would live long enough to see it reach adulthood. So many mothers were suffering the agony of outliving their children in these dangerous times. How awful it must be to rear a son past the hazards of infancy, only to send him away to war and never know how he died or where he lay buried. Hopefully this war, which had swept so many nations into its ravening jaws, would end in victory and an everlasting peace, so her child would never go off to fight.

Would she be a good mother? She hadn't succeeded in making her stepdaughter love her. But she'd have this child from the start. She'd pour out upon it every drop of the love she'd been storing up for all those years when she'd longed for a baby. Whether in riches or in poverty, she'd bring it up with gentleness and kindness, to feel the same safety and security Rosamund had known as a child. It would be a gift far greater than money. It would be her legacy.

Another pain, stronger still, brought her back to the present with a groan. If only Nellie were here, to go and fetch the midwife from the village. Not for the first time this evening, she berated herself for allowing her maid to leave her. She'd been trying to be kind, knowing how much she needed Nellie on her side to keep her secrets. Nellie knew Cadwalader must be the baby's father, and surely suspected the true cause of Sir Lucien's death. Rosamund had realised months ago that she would have to do whatever it took to keep Nellie happy in her post and guarantee her discretion, to safeguard her child's future. Only tonight was the potential cost of this generosity becoming clear.

Without Nellie, she would have to obtain help herself. She made for the doorway to fetch a coat and boots, but a pain so strong it took her breath away made her put aside any idea of attempting to walk to the village. If she collapsed on the road she would be in even greater danger than she was here, where at least she had warmth, light, clean sheets and towels. Fear had her in its grip now, as all-consuming as the waves of pain that left her moaning softly and clutching the back of a chair. It was a struggle to keep from tumbling headlong into panic, to remember to breathe in and out slowly.

The curtains in the parlour were open, giving a clear view of the lane. It was early enough for someone to pass by. She would wait, rest on the window seat, and pray. Not for herself: she was too great a sinner for God to pay her any regard. But her unborn child was innocent of any wrongdoing. Perhaps God would take pity on it, and not visit the sins of its adulterous parents upon it. So she knelt upon the soft cushion in the bay window, her breath fogging the cold glass, and whispered her pleas for mercy.

It seemed an age before anyone passed, and they were on a bicycle, speeding by oblivious to her frantic tapping at the windowpane, gone before she could even cry out. It was past eight o'clock now, and the lane was shadowy. Most people would be ensconced in their houses. Surrounded by loved ones, they would be discussing the day's events, or perhaps reading or sewing by the fire before getting ready for bed. They could have no idea of the drama unfolding at the Dower House near the edge of the Fitznorton estate. Having chosen to keep to herself and live quietly for so many years, Rosamund could not expect to be remembered in any one of her neighbours' thoughts.

At last she spied a movement and heard the scuff of boots on the lane. Rapping on the glass, she was flooded with relief to see two faces turn in her direction, half hidden by woollen scarves and hats. The footsteps faltered and she called out.

"Please, stop! Help me."

Her knees were stiff from waiting so long, and she staggered to the front door, her calves and feet tingling. The bolt drew easily, and she swung the door open, leaning upon it half-bowed as another searing pain seized her.

"Help me," she gasped again.

The passers-by were two young women, staring dubiously at her with large eyes in pale faces, as if they couldn't believe what they were seeing. The nearer one pulled down her scarf and spoke.

"La-lady Fitznorton, is it?" the woman stammered in the melodious Welsh lilt of the local working class. "Are you alright, m'lady?"

Rosamund shook her head, dumb with relief that the girl was listening. The perspiration on her forehead cooled rapidly in the night air.

"Is it your baby? Is it coming?" Leaving her companion out on the path, the girl swung open the metal gate and crunched up the frosty gravel path towards Rosamund, eyeing her belly and then glancing beyond into the stillness of the house. "You're not on your own, are you? Where's Miss Dawson? Or Ethel?"

"Not here," Rosamund managed to say. She frowned, confused as to how the girl could know so much about her, but before she could ask, the girl had caught hold of her arm.

"You'd better get yourself back inside in the warm. I'll come in with you," the girl said before turning to her friend. "Jenny, you go and get my mam. She'll know what to do. And then fetch the midwife. Quick as you can, now."

With a nod, the other girl spun on her heel and took off back along the lane the way she had come, her boots clattering on the cobbles and her shawl flapping behind her.

Rosamund sank onto the bottom stair, her teeth clenched against the pain. It took every ounce of willpower to stop herself crying out. Behind her, the girl had closed the front door and hung her coat and hat on the newel post.

"Come on," the girl said, her voice gentle but firm as she ducked under Rosamund's arm and lifted her up. "We'd best get you upstairs. My mam won't be long. She's had eight – no, *nine*

THE BROKEN VOW

– babies in all, so she'll know what to do. There's no need to worry."

Each step was a struggle, but somehow they managed to reach the top. The girl kept up a cheerful prattle all the way, as if Rosamund was a child to be petted and soothed. "That's it, you're doing really well," and "Nearly at the top, now which room is yours?" and "Ooh, there's a lovely bedroom, isn't it? Let's pop you into bed now."

Slumped against the pillows, catching her breath before the next onslaught of pain, Rosamund watched her, assessing this stranger she had invited into her home. She could be anybody; a thief, even. But what choice had she had but to bring the girl in?

Despite the jolly reassurances, the girl's eyes were wide and frightened, as Rosamund imagined her own must be. The girl's face was pretty: slender, but not with the thin, consumptive look of some of the young women Rosamund had glimpsed about the town on her rare excursions. Her blouse and skirt were clean and respectable. She clearly wasn't from a wealthy family, but if she was poor, she wasn't desperately so. Her sensible, kindly manner suggested a level of intelligence, even though her accent marked her as uneducated. When she glanced quickly about the room, it was as if she was wondering how best to proceed, not what might be worth stealing. And she was strong, with steady, roughened hands marked with red welts like burns.

"What's your name? And how do you know me?" Rosamund asked, just as another woman's voice called up the stairs.

"Maggie? Jenny said her ladyship's baby is coming. Are you up there?"

"In here, Mam!" The girl, Maggie, who had been sloshing water into Rosamund's glass, blazed out a relieved smile.

The door was pushed open and a solidly-built woman with

straight, salt-and-pepper hair caught up in a bun entered the room. Dark eyes took in the scene as she unwound her shawl.

"My lady, this is my mam, Mary. Even though you don't know us, we know you because my dad is your driver: Joseph Cadwalader."

ONE

THREE MONTHS EARLIER: JANUARY 1915

Charlotte

The trouble with war, Charlotte Fitznorton was beginning to realise, was that it was utterly, mind-numbingly and apparently interminably *boring*. Once one had grown accustomed to the glamour of an officer's uniform and the cheery chaps marching off ever-hopeful to save poor little Belgium, there was little excitement and endless ennui. Turgid teas on dull afternoons, a miserable litany of reported losses that made one almost afraid to enquire after anybody's loved ones. No balls, no parties, for fear of accusations of frivolous insensitivity. The dashing young men who could enliven a gathering were away, or dead; the only males left in her milieu were either too young or middle-aged to be of any interest. Mostly she spent her hours with women, doing good works for the war effort, and where was the fun in that? How she missed the social whirl of last summer with her fiancé Eustace!

"Is it really necessary to sigh quite so often, or with quite so much gusto?" became Aunt Blanche's frequent remonstrance, quite unfairly in Charlotte's view. That was the trouble with old people: they forgot how it felt to be young, with a need for a little dancing and flirtation to lend colour to the days.

Tears stung at the corners of her eyes; she wiped them away surreptitiously with her black-edged handkerchief. They were not tears of sadness, but from the eye-watering strain of preventing her jaw from stretching wide in a cavernous yawn. The other ladies at the table seemed not to have noticed, their attention fixed on their knitting and sewing. All except Aunt Blanche, whose gimlet-hard gaze had settled upon her. Charlotte's hand froze momentarily before she tucked her handkerchief back up her sleeve and focused again on her task. The murmur of soft voices, the ticking of the clock, the click of needles and the occasional dull clatter of scissors being laid back down on the table... it was difficult to imagine a less interesting way to spend an afternoon.

If only knitting trench caps wasn't so tedious. Not merely tedious, but difficult: she had dropped another stitch and would have to fumble to pick it up before continuing. Try as she might, she couldn't achieve a consistent tension with her yarn, and she was constantly in a muddle with the decreases. Still, this was proving easier than her earlier abortive attempts to make socks, and she supposed the soldiers would be too busy shooting Germans to care what their woollen hats looked like, as long as they were warm. As a young woman, she may not be able to help her country in its hour of need by fighting the enemy, but she must nevertheless make herself useful. At this rate, poorly crafted, ill-fitting woollens were destined to be her sole contribution to the war effort.

Amidst so many people making such great sacrifices, it would be unthinkable to voice her wish that being useful could be more pleasurable. Sometimes her shoulders and neck became stiff from spending too long seated in one position. Her fingers were sore from the horrid, scratchy yarn. Frowning, she stifled yet another yawn and shifted in her chair.

The black crepe of her mourning garb was thrown into sombre relief against the light, feminine surroundings of Aunt Blanche's drawing room. She hated wearing black: it made her complexion look pale and drawn, and her fair hair mousy. Its plainness was so depressing. A constant reminder of the agony of losing her darling Papa, she had only to glance down at her clothing to be stabbed with guilt if ever she should forget herself so far as to laugh or smile.

How she longed to be able to wear something pretty again, even for a few hours. To dance with a handsome fellow, wearing jewels and ostrich plumes and a fine gown, as she had done last summer, when she had stayed up late and smiled and flirted and captured Eustace's heart. It seemed so long ago now. Another lifetime, one in which fun was permitted and idleness was normal. Now, such frivolity would be frowned upon even were she not in mourning. Gatherings must be purposeful, and every spare hour must be filled with useful deeds to support the war effort.

Still only nineteen, she felt like an old woman sometimes, bowed under the weight of the mixture of her concern for Eustace and their future together, her grief; and bewilderment at the momentous events going on in the world.

Sometimes she had to look at Eustace's photograph to remind herself what he looked like. She had spent so little time with the man she was destined to marry, and almost none of it alone. She must cling to the hope that they would soon have decades to get to know each other better. When her thoughts trespassed into depressing territory, she would cheer herself up by telling herself that by this time next year they might even be wishing for some time apart.

Five months after Papa's sudden death, his loss was hardly less painful than it had been when the terrible news first reached her. A constant throbbing ache under her breastbone, his passing had blown a hole in the very fabric of her previously happy existence. Perhaps one day she would be accustomed to living a life in which his towering presence was no longer a vital part; but this was surely a long way off. For now, thoughts of him still brought sorrow as sharp as it had been in those early days. How she missed the way she could make his booming laugh erupt from his broad chest. In Papa's presence, she had known she was adored. Her guardian Aunt Blanche was fond of her, but that fondness could never match the light of love and pride she had seen in her father's eyes. Eustace was a dear, but he didn't give her that same feeling of safety and of being protected that she had felt as a little girl on her father's knee.

As thankful as she was to be able to live in London with her aunt, rather than with her sour-faced stepmother Rosamund – whose chilly presence had always been a source of resentment – it was not always easy to focus on her blessings. At times her orphaned state made her want to howl.

She hadn't been back to her childhood home since Papa's funeral in August. There was a part of her that missed Plas Norton's oak-panelled rooms, its lichen-spotted, slate-capped turrets, and the great emerald sward of verdant Welsh grass, sprinkled with deer and sheep, which surrounded it. The funeral had passed in a haze of unreality. She hadn't attended the interment, of course. It wasn't considered suitable for women to attend the burial, which was probably a good thing in her case as she had sometimes pictured his great oak coffin being lowered into the earth and imagined throwing herself after it.

She had felt a swell of pride at the number of people who attended the marking of his passing. And even though their praise highlighted the magnitude of her loss, it had offered Charlotte a little comfort when the mayor and other local dignitaries spoke of his many achievements and talked of setting up a statue of him in the town. Scores of workers from his factory, mine and tinworks had lined the route his cortège took through the town after the procession set off from the house. All the domestic staff and estate workers stood by, their heads bowed in the respect due to him as the most notable landowner and employer in the district.

Her father had been her all for as long as she could remember. Several silver-framed photographs of him now stood along with a miniature of her mother on the dressing table in her room at Aunt Blanche's house in Belgravia. One of them looked a little narrow for its frame, due to her cutting the image of her gaunt, unsmiling stepmother off, but apart from its lack of proportions, it was her favourite. It captured Papa just as she liked to remember him: tall, solid, and broad as a bear, with a bristling beard and a fierce gaze. Feet planted wide apart and his chest puffed out, for all the world like one of those powerful portraits of the old Tudor King, but wearing plus fours and a shooting jacket instead of doublet and hose.

She had no memory of her mother, and only her portrait and her jewels to connect her to the woman who had given birth to her. When Papa married Rosamund and brought her to Plas Norton, Charlotte hated her from their very first meeting. She could still recall the day they were first introduced, and the bolt that had shot through her stomach at the way her father was looking at the woman beside him on the sofa.

Instead of reaching out with a laugh to pinch Charlotte's cheek, then tossing her up exuberantly into the air, the way he usually did on returning home from one of his interminable business trips, he had barely glanced at his daughter. She had received only the briefest of smiles by way of greeting before he turned his gaze back to linger upon Rosamund's mournful face. It was almost as if Rosamund had captured him with a spell. It made Charlotte's mouth fill with water, as if she was going to be sick.

Rosamund was pretty – little Charlotte had seen that immediately. Rosamund had worn a gaily striped dress with puffed-out sleeves. The fabric had a silky sheen that should have brought out a glow in her cheeks if she wasn't so dark-eyed and wan. She'd remained seated while Papa moved behind the sofa and rested his big hands on her shoulders. Charlotte resented that grip. She wanted Papa's hands to hold her, to lift her up high over his head the way he used to, when he would pretend to drop her and she would be filled with a heady mixture of fear and excitement.

"Come in and greet your new Mama," he had said, and Nanny prodded her back with a bony finger, propelling her forward.

"Good afternoon, Charlotte. I hope we shall be friends." Rosamund had spoken so softly, Charlotte barely heard her, but the words filled her with fury. How could she ever be friends with this woman who had interposed herself between her and Papa?

Scowling, Charlotte had clenched her fists and stamped her foot. The frown that instantly darkened Papa's brow made her feel hot; she lunged towards him, suddenly desperate to reclaim her place, but Nanny seized her arm in a rough grip and dragged her back to the nursery.

Over the years, her fears that her stepmother would supplant her in Papa's affections had receded. Even as a child, she had sensed the tension between the two adults. Some days it hung in the air so heavily she could taste it. Rosamund rarely spoke unless directly addressed, and Charlotte was only too happy to ignore her and focus on her father instead.

"You are the apple of my eye," he would say. Or, at breakfast, "How is my little princess this morning?" It made her feel complete. She basked in the warmth of his approval and revelled in recognising his growing dislike for his wife, which confirmed her own opinion that Rosamund was nothing more than an interloper who got in their way.

While Papa spent months away from home in London, attending to his business interests, Charlotte would mope in the nursery or schoolroom, the time dragging. In the early days, her stepmother would try to read to her or to tell her stories, but she resisted listening and scrambled down from the sofa to play with her dolls, until at last Rosamund gave up. She'd had no interest in spending time with the insipid wraith of a woman who haunted the library and music room of Plas Norton like a ghost. It should have been Papa spending time with her, Papa telling her stories in that powerful voice which made the servants jump to attention and Rosamund flinch. When he returned from his trips, the contrast between his daughter's enthusiastic welcome and his wife's frosty reception made it obvious who was more worthy of his affection. Eventually, when she came to realise that Rosamund was not even trying to compete against her, Charlotte had come to feel more secure.

There had been times when she wished Rosamund would leave, or even die, so that she could have Papa to herself. It was doubtless a shameful admission, and therefore one made only to herself and her aunt. It rankled that events hadn't transpired that way. Instead, it was Papa who had vanished from her life, and soon afterwards came another sickening blow when Rosamund wrote to her with the momentous news that she was expecting a child.

Charlotte no longer had the letter: she had torn it into tiny pieces and thrown them into the fire. She hated to think of Rosamund possessing anything of her father's, and nothing could be more closely connected to him than a child. The anticipated birth could spoil everything. Instead of automatically inheriting the whole of her father's estate, she might now only receive a portion of it. If the child should arrive safely and prove to be a boy, the infant usurper would inherit almost everything that had once been intended to be hers.

Charlotte's knitting needle snagged, snapping her out of her thoughts. The stitches were too tight again, and no wonder: even thinking about Rosamund and her brat had set her foot tapping with suppressed rage.

Her aunt looked up, ever alert to any sign that Charlotte's behaviour might be less than impeccable. Blanche raised one eyebrow in reproof, and Charlotte gritted her teeth. In a few months' time, she would be a married woman. Her aunt shouldn't treat her as if she were still a little girl.

The light at the window was fading already, the thick, sooty London fog filtering out the weak January sun. Garwood, the butler, came in, treading silently on the deep carpet as he circled the group of ladies and lit several lamps dotted about on side tables. Not so long ago this task would have been performed by the footman, but he had joined up and Blanche said they must all make do, including the staff.

A warm glow illuminated the gathered faces. None of the other ladies seemed to be having difficulties with their knitting; all appeared content to let their fingers fly whilst sharing morsels of gossip. Lady Bramford, plump and pigeon-breasted, was telling the other matrons about her four sons, all away fighting at the front. One of them had been injured and was being treated in hospital in France. Charlotte listened with only half-hearted interest.

"You may imagine how thankful we were to receive a letter from him this morning, a sure sign that his hand is healing. He told us that he expects to make a full recovery. Our medical units are marvellous, of course. The best in the world. They'll soon have him fit again."

"That is excellent news," replied Mrs Cutler, an elderly woman with surprisingly fleet fingers considering her swollen, arthritic knuckles. "You are quite right that there is none to match us. Do you know, I heard the most extraordinary thing yesterday... The French have established a hospital staffed entirely by *women*. Can you imagine? I never heard of anything so outlandish. Even the surgeons are female. Operating on *men*, would you believe?"

All eyes around the table widened, and one or two of the ladies sniffed or gasped. Charlotte supposed it did seem rather odd, to have a woman in charge of an operating theatre. Odder still for a woman to want to cut into men's bodies. She had only the vaguest sense of what this would involve, and no desire to picture it vividly. She had always been a little squeamish, and the sight of an injured animal would give her a strange, rushing sensation in her head until she looked away. It must be horrid even to look upon wounded human beings, and to hear their ghastly cries of distress, let alone to have to perform gruesome surgery upon them. Perhaps knitting caps or even socks was not so troublesome, by comparison.

One or two of the older ladies were muttering that it was indecent for females to perform surgery on men, which evoked an altogether more interesting series of imaginings. Did their outrage mean that the men were naked during such a procedure? But would they not be unconscious, unable to act upon any improper urges that might overcome them at the prospect of being in such proximity to a woman?

"I suppose we must move with the times. It is perhaps equally indecent for young girls to go off unchaperoned to be nurses," Aunt Blanche said with a sigh. "Thank goodness you are engaged to be married, Charlotte, and shall soon have an establishment of your own to run; children too, God willing, in the fullness of time. You won't have time then to go running off to war."

"Don't worry, Aunt. Even if I had not accepted Eustace's hand, I should hate to wear an ugly uniform, or to tramp up and down hospital wards with a lamp all night. I fear I'm not cut out for mopping fevered brows or plumping up pillows."

A few of the ladies tittered, but Mrs Hartley-Rolfe's pursed lips were an awkward reminder that her daughter had recently joined the Voluntary Aid Detachment and would soon be heading off to foreign shores to do just that.

"My Sarah told me about that hospital in France," said Mrs Hartley-Rolfe. "It's run by the British, you know. Set up by a Scotswoman. I gather she is quite well-known. A suffragette before the war, as so many of the women thrusting themselves forward these days are. It strikes one as quite peculiar that women who only recently carried hammers up their sleeves to smash windows and cause mayhem up and down the land should now claim to want to serve their country."

A murmur of agreement followed.

"There's no one quite like a Britisher, whether male or female, for getting a job done. Our girls, your daughter included Mrs Hartley-Rolfe, have gumption. Our friends on the Continent cannot match us for pluck," said Lady Bramford.

"We all must serve in our own way, whatever that means," Aunt Blanche said. "Those who lack the patience or selflessness to care for the sick and wounded may still contribute to the war effort, as we are doing here. My goddaughter Venetia Vaughan-Lloyd, whom I think you all know, is a prime example. She has been fundraising tirelessly since the beginning of the war, and organising a whole host of committees and activities. She would have joined us this afternoon, as she usually does, had she not already volunteered to help at a bazaar in aid of injured servicemen. And Charlotte has been selling flags, as well as knitting, of course. I see you have almost completed that hat now, dear."

Charlotte had almost reached the crown of her cap. "Yes, Aunt." She held up her knitting and sighed. "If only we could make them in nicer colours, instead of drab grey or khaki. I'm sure our chaps would find that wearing cheery red or blue would lighten their spirits."

The other ladies' reaction to this made Charlotte's cheeks heat up. Pouting, she stabbed the needle through the yarn. It was unfair of them to think it a ridiculous suggestion. If anyone should understand the depressing effect of wearing dull colours, it was she. Was it so wrong to want to make the world feel bright again, the way it used to be in that wonderful time less than a year ago, before the war spoiled everything?

TWO

Charlotte

A letter arrived from Eustace in the third post the next morning.

Dearest girl,

I received no letter from you yesterday, and how I longed to hold in my hands a note from you. Please do write every day, even if you feel you have little news. Tell me about home, and how life is in London. I miss the walks we took in Hyde Park last summer, before all this, when you would take my arm and the brightness of your gay chatter made the sunshine seem dim by comparison. Sweet girl, I wish I could hold you in my arms and tell you aloud how I long for us to be married. Of course we must wait until you are no longer in mourning, but the time passes slowly.

Days are mostly dull here, but now and then we get a trifle hot under the collar, and sometimes it is pretty frightful, I'm sad to say. I am thankful to be safe, and sorry for those chums who have not been so lucky. We lost six yesterday, but despite some narrow squeaks you'll be glad to know I didn't suffer so much as a scratch. We are hitting the Germans hard, and gaining ground, and keeping our spirits up with thoughts of home. It is my memories of you that remind me to always be careful, so that nothing might prevent us being together again when this ghastly war is over.

If you are still knitting socks, do send me some. They wear out quickly when marching, and it is terribly chilly here. Wearing something made by your little hands will keep my heart warm as well as my toes. The Christmas cake Mother sent is all gone now, so I have written to ask her to send a Dundee cake and some more smokes.

Please pass on my fond regards to your aunt. As always, I remain

*Your devoted,
Eustace*

Charlotte smiled. Eustace wrote such lovely letters, much better than those she sent by way of reply. She was too impatient for writing, needed the immediacy of face-to-face contact. Then, grammar and penmanship didn't matter and she could express herself without thinking too hard about what she wanted to say. Admittedly her habit of saying exactly what she thought could lead to accusations of insensitivity or impetuousness from Aunt Blanche, but surely, Charlotte felt, being honest was a good thing? At least people knew what she was thinking and feeling. She would hate to be all closed-in and buttoned-up like her stepmother, who had a reputation for being cold and inscrutable. No one would ever tiptoe around Charlotte wondering if she even had a heart in her breast, as they did with Rosamund, for Charlotte wore hers on her sleeve.

She looked again at Eustace's photograph where it stood on

her dressing table in its heavy silver frame. His parents had it taken last summer, and an identical version of it stood in pride of place in their drawing room. He wore his cavalry officer's uniform and a serious expression, which Charlotte supposed was to be expected considering he was about to go off to war for the first time with the British Expeditionary Force. She tried to picture him writing his letter, but it was difficult to imagine what the trenches were like. He had given snippets of information, and now and then someone would murmur about how ghastly and muddy they were. It struck Charlotte as odd, because she had always thought that the cavalry would carry out heroic charges on horseback across open fields, swords held aloft. The idea of them hunkered down in a hole in the ground seemed somehow unnatural. Inhuman, even – like badgers in a sett, not like men at all.

They must have rooms, surely? Camps with buildings and warm, cosy rooms in which Eustace could fold himself into a comfortable chair, tuck his long legs under a proper desk, and settle himself to write. She imagined him dropping his hat on the desk, then picking up a piece of paper and laying it on a blotter before taking out his pen and deciding what to say. This would be in a library, she decided, in one of those pretty French manoirs or châteaux like the ones Papa had planned to send them to for their honeymoon if he hadn't been so cruelly taken from her and if the war hadn't made holidaying on the continent impossible.

Eustace had referred to the war as ghastly, and yet on their last meeting in August she had been struck by how much he was looking forward to getting stuck in. He had smiled that broad smile, his eyes bright and eager, and reassured her that it would all be terribly jolly. He'd be surrounded by chums and it would all be the most marvellous adventure. Yet his recent letters didn't make it sound marvellous at all.

THE BROKEN VOW

Charlotte sighed. It seemed nothing in life was as she had expected to be. Adulthood had seemed a light on her girlish horizon, a time when she had imagined she would emerge from childhood like a butterfly bursting out of a cocoon, unfolding beautiful wings to universal admiration. And she had sparkled in that first season; she knew she had. She had caught Eustace's eye from their first meeting, when their eyes had met across a candlelit ballroom and he had murmured something to his friend whilst still fixing her with an unwavering gaze. Later, he told her what he had said: *She's the one for me.*

Charlotte found it remarkable that he had known so soon. Even now, with their engagement sealed by public announcement and the approval of both their families, she sometimes felt she had been picked up by a whirlwind and dropped down in unfamiliar territory. This was what she had been born to, of course: to win the hand of a man of equal or greater social standing. She had done well to bag herself the son of a viscount, even if he was only the second son. Papa had told her quite bluntly that Eustace might outlive his elder brother Freddie, who had a consumptive look about him and who had not been accepted for active service.

She liked the idea of being a viscountess and perhaps even wearing a coronet to the next coronation, although of course that would mean Freddie and King George would both have to be dead. She brushed those thoughts aside; Charlotte wasn't one for dwelling on the unpleasant aspects of her dreams, preferring to think positively. It was an attitude that helped her when thinking about the war.

Apart from an occasional glance at the society pages, Charlotte didn't care for reading newspapers. Nevertheless, she couldn't remain unaware of the casualty figures, given that several families she knew had lost loved ones in the conflict. Most of the young people she knew had expected the war to be over by Christmas, and the troops on their way home, yet here they were in January and no one seemed to think it was going to end any time soon.

It was all so frustrating. London was changing around her, with shortages in the shops. Suddenly, things which had been expected of young women before – like endless shopping trips, buying fripperies, wearing pretty things out to tea and to evening parties – were frowned upon. One must be seen to "do one's bit", filling long days with good works. The war restrictions affected her less than they would have done, given that she would be wearing black for months yet; but still the need for restraint chafed when she wanted to pour her energies into planning her wedding.

She had pictured all the details. She would wear a white silk gown with a long train, and a veil edged with Honiton lace, held in place with a crown of white, fragrant flowers. She would carry a large bouquet of lilies. Eustace would turn at the altar, and gaze at her, rapt at the vision she would present as she glided down the aisle on— No, wait – not her father's arm. All at once, the vision vanished, like a balloon being popped with a pin. Perhaps Eustace's father would lead her down the aisle. But it wouldn't be the same. Nothing was as it should be.

Plumping down into a chair, she resolved to write back to Eustace. There was nothing she could do about the wedding for now, except to try to keep his spirits up.

Dearest Eustace,

Thank you for your letter. Life at home is awfully dull. There are no parties and very little fun. I will pass on your good wishes to Aunt Blanche. Her goddaughter Venetia Vaughan-Lloyd is going to take me to a meeting later. She was quite insistent. It is called "What Women Can Do for the War". Of course I am already doing what I can. I have had to stop trying to make socks, but I will send you a scarf or a hat instead.

I hope you are keeping warm and I am glad to hear that you are being careful. I spend my days dreaming of our wedding.

With fondest wishes,

Charlotte

THREE

Charlotte

"Find something useful to do, dear, would you? You can't be forever sighing and moping about the house," had become Aunt Blanche's frequent exhortation these days. If it wasn't too foggy, and they had no prior engagement or charitable activity planned, she would urge Charlotte to venture out for a stroll around the local gardens or to a park with her bossy goddaughter Venetia Vaughan-Lloyd, who was a frequent visitor to the house in Belgravia.

Having been thrown together so often, Charlotte had come to appreciate Venetia's openness and good-humoured zest for life, but she couldn't help feeling they had little in common. Whilst Venetia enthusiastically supported charitable works and had often suggested that Charlotte might like to join her in supporting the Girls' Friendly Society by offering to read to the working-class girls at their sewing classes, or by speaking at one of their teas, she had so far resisted. It didn't sound much fun, either for her or for the working-class girls.

Still, twenty-six-year-old Venetia was interesting enough for

Charlotte not to mind spending several hours of each week in her company. Although Charlotte couldn't share in her enthusiasm for volunteering – thinking it must be frightfully dull to spend afternoons writing letters or filing documents for local charities – she couldn't help but admire the other woman's energy. Unlike Charlotte, Venetia had little interest in pretty clothes, romantic novels or parties. Nor had she much fashion sense, dressing in a style that Charlotte could only describe as *practical*.

At nearly six feet tall, with a commanding presence, Venetia never stooped the way Charlotte had noticed other tall women often did, but unapologetically held her head high. A bout of polio in childhood meant she wore a brace on her right leg and walked with a pronounced limp, yet she seemed full of restlessness, and could never stay still for long. It was impossible to imagine her ever enjoying a day of indolence or relaxation. In fact, Charlotte suspected Venetia would find it torture to stay in bed late or to laze on a chaise longue with a book – unless it was a terribly serious tome about female suffrage or child welfare. In that case, she would probably sit at a desk, making endless notes in the margin and dashing off irate letters to her many contacts in political circles.

Considering Aunt Blanche's determination to see Charlotte married well, it was surprising that she had not also pushed Venetia towards marriage. Perhaps she feared that men would be less keen to wed a woman with a physical handicap – even though Venetia could by no means be called ugly, and Charlotte wasn't aware of any reason why she might be unable to bear children. She certainly appeared to be as strong as an ox. But with the brace on her leg, and her frumpish, almost masculine clothes, not to mention her unusual height and forceful manners, Charlotte secretly thought it unsurprising that she'd failed to attract a husband.

Even if Venetia had managed to find a man who could overlook her unusual looks and forceful nature, Charlotte suspected many men would be put off by her infamous past. As a suffragist before the war, Venetia had attended countless parades and rallies, and had even been accused of deliberately damaging public property. Smashing windows struck Charlotte as monstrously unfeminine and deeply unattractive, and she could not accept Venetia's argument that vandalism was justifiable as long as people were not harmed, only property.

In the course of her political activism Venetia had been manhandled by police officers, spat upon by strangers in the street, and even arrested at least twice. At one parade a ruffian had molested her, leaving, Charlotte had once heard in a shocked whisper, *bruises on her breasts*. Charlotte had never understood the passion that could drive a woman to suffer such outrageous indignities. Aunt Blanche had grave reservations about it, and when Venetia announced her intention to take Charlotte along with her to a women's meeting that evening, she immediately spoke up, sending her goddaughter a severe look down her aristocratic nose.

"I hardly think it proper for Charlotte to become embroiled in your suffragist activities, my dear."

"You need have no fears on that score, Aunt. I've no interest in politics, so if that's what it's about, I'd really rather not go," Charlotte said.

Venetia threw up her hands, exasperated. "It's no such thing. You know very well that campaigning has stopped for the duration of the war. The meeting will be perfectly civilised, merely an opportunity to encourage and inspire women to do whatever they can to support the Empire—"

"Aren't we doing that already, with our knitting? And I sold flags last week," Charlotte protested.

Aunt Blanche cast Charlotte a withering look. "Venetia, I should be *most* displeased if you allowed my niece to be exposed to radical or militant views. Do I have your word that there will be nothing untoward at this meeting?"

"I give you my solemn promise. Besides, even if suffragist meetings *were* still taking place, there'd be little point in my taking young Charlotte here. I can't imagine any girl less likely to be swayed to join the cause or to become a firebrand. Why, she might break a fingernail or get a smut on her blouse, and that would never do." Venetia's intelligent eyes twinkled, and Aunt Blanche had relented.

Charlotte was less convinced, however. She tried pleading a headache at the last minute, but this was immediately pooh-poohed.

"You'll feel better once you're out of the house," Venetia said in her strident way, making it impossible to refuse. "As my cousin Doctor Havard always says, mental stimulation is almost as good for the soul as fresh air and exercise."

Trusting in Venetia's admittedly unimpeachable integrity, Aunt Blanche had agreed, on this point at least, and so Charlotte had been swept away in Venetia's wake.

There were worse people to have as friends, Charlotte supposed. She didn't tend to enjoy the company of girls her own age all that much. While it was sometimes fun to go shopping and to gossip, she often detected undercurrents of malice in their gay chatter, and that was something which could never be said of Venetia, who was straightforward and honest in all her dealings.

"I do hope you're right about there being no talk of politics or voting at this meeting. I really don't see the point of it," Charlotte grumbled in the back seat of Blanche's motor car as they made their way to the meeting.

Venetia stared. "What on earth do you mean, you don't see the point?"

Charlotte suppressed a huff of annoyance. She was growing tired of other people looking at her as if she were stupid.

"Do you really imagine that one vote makes any difference to what happens in the country, or in the Empire?" she retorted, matching Venetia's brusque tone.

"One vote won't, no. But given that women make up more than half of the population of said Empire, collectively their votes add up to rather a significant expression of political will, wouldn't you say?"

Charlotte shrugged and looked away. It was hard to debate against practised arguments when she had given the matter so little thought.

"You must have inherited a tidy sum from your father," Venetia continued, rather rudely Charlotte thought. "He was a wealthy man, wasn't he?"

"Yes, he was. But as a matter of fact, I'm not altogether clear yet about what I will inherit. Matters are uncertain due to my stepmother's... condition." She pursed her lips, lest she should say something indelicate and earn even more disapproving looks.

"Ah. Blanche mentioned something about that. Well, let's speculate anyway, about what would have happened if not for the impediment of a sibling. You'd be a wealthy woman, given the charge of a wide range of industrial interests. You could, potentially, run those businesses yourself—"

Charlotte cut her off. "Don't be silly. I couldn't do that."

Venetia's piercing blue eyes regarded her with genuine curiosity.

"Why not? You have a brain, even if you haven't had the training."

"But it wouldn't be my place. As a woman, I mean."

"Tell that to Amy Dillwyn. Tell it to Margaret Haig Mackworth. Both are your countrywomen; both have proved themselves very capable in running their family's enterprises. Every bit as capable as their fathers, and equally successful."

Charlotte shifted uncomfortably in her seat under the weight of Venetia's forthright gaze.

"You'll pay tax on whatever you inherit, you know. You'll pay tax, and yet you'll have no say in how that taxation revenue is spent. Lunatics and prisoners will have more rights than you, purely because their bodies are different. By sheer accident of birth, they may exercise power, while *you* may exercise only influence, or at least attempt to do so if you are fortunate enough to know someone who holds an important post. All very well for women like us, but not so helpful for those of the lower classes who have no such important connections.

"Even for women like us, relying on our potential to influence men is like expecting a tiger to be gentle, simply because one has stroked it and called it a good boy. It may choose to be nice, or it may eat one's arm. The outcome of one's efforts depends upon its mood at the time. I'm sure everyone of sense would agree that it is folly to rely on a tiger's good nature. Only when we get the vote will we get protection from the vagaries of the tiger's whims."

Her manner of speaking made Charlotte feel as if she was on the receiving end of a public address, rather than engaging in simple conversation. It left her feeling fatigued, and often confused, with an uneasy sense that Venetia's radical views might actually be right. Perhaps it wasn't entirely fair for women to have to give the government money if it wasn't going to give them a say in how it was used. But then, she wouldn't have any notion of how the country should be run.

"Don't you think that men are better placed to understand things like how to run a country? These are complex matters far beyond my comprehension. I wouldn't know what to vote for, and I'm sure many other women would feel the same. Our fathers and husbands are more knowledgeable and experienced, not to mention more educated…"

"That argument might stand if there weren't quite so many stupid men, and so many clever women. Do you think the world would be in the mess it is in, if women were in charge of it, or if we at least had a say in the decisions made at the top? Would we, or the women of Germany, be sending our sons and brothers off to murder one another? Would husbands be allowed to beat their wives and children with impunity? Would there be women and children dying malnourished in Britain's towns and cities? Did you know, many of the lads who try to join up have to be turned away because they are so undernourished, their growth is stunted and they haven't the strength to fight? The country must change, and women must have a place at the table, to be a part of that change. We should be entitled to a share in power, not merely to try to persuade our menfolk to do the right thing. What we have is not enough. But we *will* get the vote, mark my words."

"I thought you said the suffragettes had agreed to stop campaigning for the vote now that there's a war on."

"For the duration, yes. For now, the need to defeat Germany and her allies must take precedence. But don't make the mistake of thinking we are giving up the struggle, Charlotte. Slowly, the government is coming to understand that victory cannot be achieved by the men at the front on their own. They need our help, even if not all of them want to acknowledge it yet. We'll help the men win their war, and in return we'll expect to be given the rights to which we should have been entitled all along."

To Charlotte's relief, Venetia seemed satisfied at last, and they subsided into contemplative silence until the chauffeur found a place to pull alongside the kerb and they alighted. Fog hung thick and cold around their heads, stinging Charlotte's eyes. Blackout restrictions for fear of Zeppelin attacks meant that most windows had been covered. There was nothing more than a murky, sulphurous glow from the front door of a tall building further along the road, but it was easy to see by the stream of women flowing towards it that that was where they were bound.

Charlotte huddled into her fur collar and followed Venetia, almost having to trot to keep up with the other woman's long stride, which was barely hampered at all by the brace holding her right leg rigid.

It seemed as if every class of women was represented in the throng threading along the rows of wooden seats. Venetia marched down the central aisle to the front of the hall, where she shook hands with an efficient-looking woman in a sensible hat who directed them to their reserved seats. Further back, women of all ages chattered, a hubbub of high voices. There was an atmosphere of eager interest, almost like the palpable excitement before a theatrical performance, and Charlotte wouldn't have been surprised to hear an orchestra strike up. But there were no musicians present, and no more than a few men. Having resigned herself to the prospect of finding the meeting interminably dull, she was struck by the other women's enthusiasm for it.

Soon, a small, round woman with a kindly face took her place at the lectern, and the noise faded to a murmur, then an expectant silence.

"Good evening, ladies – ladies and gentlemen, I see – and welcome to our meeting on the subject of *What Women Can Do for the War Effort*. It may seem to some, including the potentates in the War Office, that the role of women in the war is merely to wave off our boys with a tear in our eye, then to sit quietly at home to wait and pray and knit. However, there is much more we can do to bring this campaign to a swift and decisive conclusion. The more we do, and the sooner we do it, the more lives will ultimately be spared on all sides. Now, it is my great pleasure to introduce our speaker..."

A rustling buzzed around the hall as the audience around Charlotte sat up even straighter and more alert. A woman swept onto the rostrum: with deep-set, striking eyes, dark hair threaded with grey, and an elegant bearing, she drew every eye.

In the seat beside Charlotte, Venetia thrummed with excitement. "Mrs Pankhurst," she whispered, ablaze with anticipation. Charlotte nodded, suitably awed by the appearance of such a famous figure, and not a little alarmed. Surely Venetia wouldn't have lied to Aunt Blanche in an attempt to lure Charlotte to a gathering of radicals? It would be completely out of character for the young woman she knew to act dishonestly.

Her thoughts were so distracted that she hardly heard the notorious suffragette leader's opening words. A few moments passed, then Charlotte shook her head slightly. She must refocus. Against all her expectations, she didn't want to miss a moment. This had the potential to be the most diverting thing she'd done in weeks.

"Women of Britain, your country needs YOU," Mrs Pankhurst declared, pointing Kitchener-like around the room with her fierce gaze seeming to pierce every soul. "Let none doubt our courage, or our willingness to serve. Already, this conflict has threatened the lives of British women. In Hartlepool, in Whitby, in Scarborough and, only days ago, in Great Yarmouth and Kings Lynn, civilians, including innocent women and children, have died in German attacks. I say, if we are not safe in this war, if we must risk our lives, then let us serve. We demand the right to offer ourselves in the struggle."

The audience, Charlotte included, was rapt.

Mrs Pankhurst paused to allow her words to sink in. "Let none doubt our courage, or our fitness," she went on, lowering her voice so that every head craned forward. "We know that women are, by nature, creators and nurturers, not destroyers. So let us create the munitions our lads need. Let us prepare the food and launder the linen and clean the barracks, to free the soldiers who are doing those tasks today, and to play our part in keeping our boys fit to fight. Let us drive the ambulances and tend the wounded until they are ready to return to the front. But know this: we are more than ministering angels. Even as we urge our menfolk to join the fray, we recognise that just as they must fight, we women must work.

"Every fit young man working for the post office, or on the tram, or in a factory or shop; every lad working on a railway line or in a bank; every labourer on a farm; every driver, could be set free to join the battle. Every manly worker released to do his duty at the front by a willing woman worker or volunteer will bring us a step closer to victory, and a step closer to bringing our loved ones home safely.

"I call upon you to volunteer. Offer your talents, your skills, your willingness to work hard. We will see this great task through. We will make ourselves indispensable. We will show ourselves worthy of the vote. For what good is a vote, if we lose the country in which we would cast that vote? May it never be said that the women of this proud nation failed to rise to the challenge in its hour of need."

There came an explosion of applause. Murmurs of approval, and louder exclamations of assent rippled around the room. The clapping continued as Mrs Pankhurst nodded acknowledgement, shook the hands of the other ladies on the stage, and then disappeared from view.

"Isn't she marvellous?"

Charlotte turned to Venetia, whose cheeks were as pink as she guessed her own must be after such a rousing speech. "Yes, she is. Utterly, *utterly* marvellous."

In the wake of such a charismatic speaker, the other speakers failed to maintain Charlotte's interest. It seemed to take an age to leave the hall, as Venetia's impressive connections meant a whole host of introductions. Charlotte had no hope of remembering all the names of the ladies whom her seemingly indefatigable friend greeted. Venetia's memory, on the other hand, appeared limitless.

"How on earth do you know so many people?" Charlotte murmured when they finally hailed a hansom cab for the ride home.

Venetia gave a dry laugh. "I make it my business to. One never knows when one's associates might prove useful. It's a mutually beneficial exchange, you understand. There are occasions when I am able to help them. We are a sisterhood, Charlotte. Women must help each other, for you may be sure that men will do precious little on our behalf unless forced to do so."

"I suppose I should do more," she said, in a small voice. "But I'm not sure what I *could* do." She couldn't bring herself to express her doubts, for fear of earning Venetia's scorn, but she suspected she wasn't brave enough to go off to the front like the First Aid Nursing Yeomanry even if she knew how to drive an ambulance or nurse the wounded. And she hated the idea of wearing a uniform. So unattractive.

Venetia smiled at her for the first time that evening. "Why don't you start by coming with me tomorrow afternoon, to roll bandages for the troops?"

FOUR
FEBRUARY 1915

Maggie

Maggie Cadwalader staggered to her feet, her knees aching from her time scrubbing the kitchen floor on all fours. The cold seemed to leech into her joints from the flagstones and as young as she was, she could understand why her mother moved so stiffly in the mornings. As she lugged the bucket of dirty water to the scullery and tipped it down the sink, then rinsed the gritty water away, she sent up a quick prayer of thanks for the indoor plumbing that had only recently been installed. Dad would no doubt argue that it was Lady Fitznorton who should be thanked, not the good Lord, as her ladyship had ordered the work to be done in all the estate workers' cottages; but Mam had brought Maggie up to give thanks in all things, and she felt it was a good habit to be grateful for her many blessings when so many people in the town were experiencing hardship.

She set the block of red carbolic soap on its wooden cradle to dry, rinsed the stiff bristles of the scrubbing brush under the new tap, then turned the zinc bucket upside down in the corner before wiping her hands on her apron and hanging it up on a peg. She'd need to go to the village for some groceries before she could start preparing dinner. Shopping and cooking were both tasks she enjoyed much more than cleaning. Most chores around the house struck her as little better than drudgery, but at least shopping was sociable, and cooking tasty food was satisfying. It gave her pleasure to see the smiles on her family's faces when they ate meals she had prepared. There was a measure of joy to be found in looking after other people.

Maggie missed her job at the factory since it had closed in the autumn, as she had enjoyed being able to chat with the other workers on the way to work and after their shift. She also missed earning her own money, even though most of her wages went straight over to her mother as her contribution towards the housekeeping. She could only hope that the factory would soon reopen, else she might have to resort to finding a job in domestic service, something she had always resisted despite her mother's view that it was the most suitable job for a young woman. Unfortunately, since Sir Lucien Fitznorton's death there had been uncertainty about the future of not only the factory but his other businesses in Pontybrenin. His widow's pregnancy meant it wasn't clear who stood in line to inherit his industrial interests. If she had a son, the boy would be unable to take charge for many years, and his daughter Miss Charlotte Fitznorton lacked experience. It seemed most likely that the rest of his businesses would be sold and the proceeds shared between his children.

The factory had been sold first, fuelling rumours that the proceeds had been used to pay off debts or death duties. The workers had completed the outstanding orders and then the gates had been shut. It was a tough time to be out of work. Many of the men had decided their best option was to join up: a soldier's pay was less than they had earned doing heavy work in the factory or coal mine, but it was better than nothing.

Maggie put on her stout boots and donned her coat and hat, then gathered up a basket before reaching for the tin on the

THE BROKEN VOW

kitchen shelf which contained the housekeeping money. Her brother Len's photograph was propped against the tin, and she picked it up and smiled fondly at it before counting out a few coins and dropping them into her purse. She could only hope that they would be sufficient to buy what she needed today. The war was causing shortages, and there were often queues in the shops for staples such as butter and flour. Prices had risen, too. It seemed the world was conspiring to make ordinary people's lives even more difficult than they had been before. The rich would be alright, of course: they could afford to hoard whatever they needed, or get it through the black market.

Carefully, she propped Len's photograph back up against the tin. He looked so smart and proud in his suit. He'd had it taken just days before leaving for his military training, knowing how much their mother would treasure it. He wasn't one for writing home much, and Maggie supposed he wouldn't get many opportunities for posting letters once he was away fighting. Often, when she sat at the kitchen table to eat with her parents, she would see Mam's eyes fill with tears as she gazed at Len's picture, and wished he would send word home more often to let them know he was safe. At least he was still only training for the time being, with hopefully several months to go before he would be sent off to fight. Perhaps it would all be over by then.

Maggie had thought her mother's heart would break when Len joined up after losing his job in the factory closure. Mam was inclined towards pacifism, but it didn't do to express such unpopular views too much in public. And, as Dad had told her, taking her by the shoulders, Len was old enough to make his own decisions.

"I need to do my bit for King and country," Len had said, over and over, until at last Mam and his sweetheart Jenny gave up trying to convince him to stay. "How can you expect me to hang around here doing nothing when boys younger than me are willing to take the King's Shilling? I've seen the way people look at me, and I can't blame them for it."

"Then ask to be a stretcher-bearer, or train to drive an ambulance," Mam pleaded. "You don't have to fight. Thou shalt not kill, Len."

"Tell that to the Belgian refugees who arrived in town today, who've been driven from their homes and seen their countrymen murdered. I'm sorry you don't like it, but I intend to help them get their country back."

Maggie sighed, thinking back to her mixed feelings of pride for Len's courage and determination to do what he felt was right, and her wish that he would spare Mam the worry and sleepless nights waiting for him to come home.

The road from the estate cottages to the village was rutted and slippery with a mulch of dark, wet leaves. Maggie picked her way swiftly but carefully, avoiding the puddles for fear of turning her ankle in a hidden pothole. As the wind began to bite, she huddled into her coat and wound her woollen scarf more tightly around her neck. Here and there, snowdrops strained to show their faces under the bare trees: a sign of hope, perhaps, in the midst of the bleakness of a Welsh winter. Hope was something they all needed these days.

As she approached the village, Maggie's heart skipped at the sight of a black-edged card in a window, declaring: *A man in this house has given his life for his country.* Six months of war had caused so much heartache. How much longer would it go on? She sent up another swift prayer, for Len and for Uncle Wilf, before joining the queue outside the grocer's shop.

"Ah, I thought it was you, Maggie, when I saw you coming down the road. You not with your mam today? How is she? I haven't seen her since Chapel on Sunday." Mrs Evans sent Maggie a cheerful, toothless grin from beneath her moth-eaten red shawl.

"She's well, thank you, Mrs Evans. Now that I'm home so

much, she's over Auntie Peggy's a fair bit. With Peggy's youngest one toddling she needs eyes in the back of her head, so she's glad of the help."

Maggie was pleased to have a chance to chat. It could be lonely at home, with her younger siblings out at school most days and Dad out at work maintaining Lady Fitznorton's motor car and driving her maid around on her errands. Now that she could rely on Maggie to share the housework, Mam would often go to help her sister Peggy, who had started taking in sewing to earn a few bob. Peggy's husband Wilf had been laid off from his job as a groom at Plas Norton after the government requisitioned the Fitznortons' horses, so they'd had to move to a smaller two-up, two-down cottage in the village, and Wilf had gone off to use his skills in the army.

Mrs Evans seemed equally glad of the opportunity to talk, and by the time Maggie had reached the door of the shop, she had learned all the latest gossip: which of the young lads in the village had been sent to Borstal for stealing; which of the women was rumoured to have a man on the go while her husband was away fighting; who had fallen ill. She made a mental note to report back to her mother, especially about those members of the chapel congregation who were unwell, as she knew Mam would want to call in on them with some soup and bread. They didn't have much to spare, but Mam would always offer charity where she could. As Dad's specialised skills as a chauffeur meant he was paid more than most of the other staff, Mam was particularly conscious of the need to be charitable.

"Faith, hope and charity," she'd say, quoting the Bible as she so often did. "And the greatest of these is charity."

Maggie had always been proud of the way her mother helped other people as a point of principle. "It's your family, friends and neighbours that get you through the hard times," Mary often said, and she should know, having suffered griefs aplenty in her forty-five years, with the loss of two children and both parents being particularly hard to bear.

By the time Maggie reached the shop's counter there was no dried fruit left, and she quickly revised her plan to make Welsh cakes. It would have to be rice pudding instead, she decided, and bought as much sugar as she could afford, knowing from recent experience that the grocer might have none by the next day. There was little to choose from in the butcher's shop, but they had some bacon left, so it was soon sliced and wrapped in paper and tucked into the bottom of Maggie's basket. She headed to the greengrocer next for some potatoes and leeks, as their own supply from their little vegetable plot had been used up. On impulse, she also asked for a small bunch of parsley. She'd add it to their leek and potato soup for some extra flavour.

As she took out her purse, the greengrocer nudged a couple of slightly wrinkled apples across the counter towards her. "Here, take these for those young brothers and sisters of yours. They're good enough for stewing with a bit of cinnamon." He shrugged off her offer of an extra penny.

"Have you heard what people are saying about the factory?" he asked, knowing Maggie had worked there.

"No, what news is that, Mr Harries?"

"It's only a rumour, mind. But I've heard talk that the government will be taking it over for making munitions. It makes sense, when you think about it. We can't afford to have good factory space standing empty and idle when our boys at the front need all the shells and bullets they can get."

Maggie nodded, her spirits lifting. "That's wonderful news, Mr Harries. Do you think it'll create a lot of jobs? A lot of people around here would be glad of it."

"Who knows? But if you're looking to get back to it, you should get yourself down there tomorrow morning and ask. The Lord helps those who help themselves, petal."

Beaming, Maggie pocketed her purse and hefted her basket

over her arm for the walk home. It was weeks since she'd felt excited about anything, but this was news to gladden her heart. Unwilling to wait any longer than necessary to share this hopeful titbit of news, she called in at Aunt Peggy's house and found her mother and aunt sitting near the window with their sewing, making the most of the natural light before it faded.

"Wipe your boots!" Peggy called out by way of a greeting as Maggie let herself in at the back door, then added: "Oh, it's you Maggie. I thought it must be the children coming in. Put the kettle on, would you? I'm parched. I say, what's happened to make you look so pleased with yourself?"

Mary looked up at that, but her nimble fingers barely stilled, and she quickly turned her attention back to her neat row of hemming. She did stop, though, when Maggie shared the news she'd learned in the greengrocer's; Mam's face fell and her hands dropped to her lap.

"Why do you want to go back to that horrible, dusty place, love? And to make *munitions,* of all things?" She said it as if it was a dirty word. "That's no job for a young woman. Let the men make their tools for killing, not girls like you."

With a sigh, Maggie slid the kettle across to the hottest plate on the kitchen range. She hated seeing the disappointment on her mother's face, but if she let it stop her she'd end up scrubbing on her hands and knees, only to earn a pittance and be spoken to as if she was no better than filth on the mistress's shoes. No, the factory wouldn't be easy: it meant heavy work and long hours on her feet, but at least she'd be contributing something more valuable to the world than she ever could by cleaning up someone else's dirt.

"I know you don't like the war, Mam, and I can see why it would bother you for me to make weapons. But look at it this way: every shell or bullet I can make is one step closer to bringing Len home. We have to get ahead of the Germans, and if I can play a part in that *and* earn a respectable wage doing so, then I'm all for it. I'll be going to the factory tomorrow to see what I can find out, and if I get the chance, I'll be signing up."

She measured a couple of teaspoons of tea leaves into the warmed pot. Mary had opened her mouth to protest again, but snapped it shut when Maggie played her trump card.

"Dad will agree with me. You'll see."

FIVE

Charlotte

Dearest girl,

Things have been a trifle sticky, so your note was especially welcome today. You cannot imagine how much we rely on news from home when all around us is utter madness. We are mired in mud, swarming with lice, infested with rats. As I sit here scratching, hardly daring to taste what passes for tea from a chipped enamel mug, I can scarcely remember what civilisation is like. We no longer know what it is like to be clean, or dry, or comfortable. I cling to my memories of you, and picture you drinking tea from a china cup, with a saucer on the table, and dainty cakes and sugared almonds. I think of you on our walks, shading your delicate, perfect skin with a parasol. I imagine the softness of your hair, and the loveliness of your smile.

Yesterday was a trying day. We attempted an advance and it went badly. The chap beside me was hit. It took half of his face off in an instant. There was nothing I could do for him, and he died before my eyes, choking on his own blood and shards of tooth and bone. We lost so many good men, cut down in agonies, and there is no reason why I should still be here when they are not.

You say in your letter that your life is dull. Send me news of dull things, that I might think of them instead of what I have seen, and remember that I am,

Ever yours,

Eustace

SIX

MARCH 1915

Charlotte

Charlotte stamped her foot and tossed the proffered frock back into her maid's arms.

"Not that one! I need something better than that to visit the Chadwyckes. Fetch me the one with the white lace collar. You'd have me go there looking like some drab crow!"

She fussed with her stockings while Sharp, her lady's maid, hastened to locate the correct dress. Visits to her future in-laws always filled her with a maelstrom of nerves. Knowing how keen Papa had been for her to marry into the aristocracy made it even more important not to give the Viscount and Viscountess of Westhampton any reason to doubt her suitability as a future bride for their son. The very thought of making any kind of bad impression was terrifying.

If Papa had not died when he did, she and Eustace would probably have been married by now. She would have had her society wedding, her position would have been secure, and she might even have been expecting the viscount and viscountess's first grandchild. But here she was, stuck under the guardianship of Aunt Blanche, and still dressed in sepulchral black. Thankfully, her dreary garb could be relieved by a little white and a few items of unostentatious jewellery besides her diamond engagement ring, now that the first six months of mourning had passed. But even half-mourning made it impossible to appear as effervescent and delightful as a young woman should.

Perhaps it was not such a bad thing that Eustace had been away for most of the period of their engagement: he wouldn't have to witness how the drab colours she wore drained the rosy glow from her cheeks. He could keep an image in his mind of how she had looked when they first met, in those halcyon days of her first Season, when she wore pastels and feathers and frills, and they danced at her first Court ball.

Once her dress had been arranged to her satisfaction, it seemed to take an age for Sharp to get her hair right. Her incompetence made Charlotte long to scream and jab at her hand with a hat pin. She restrained herself, but couldn't help venting a measure of her frustration and anxiety as she swept out of the room, leaving a muddle of discarded clothes for the maid to sort out.

"Smile, dear," Aunt Blanche said, observing the way Charlotte stormed down the stairs towards her. "That scowl of yours is deeply unappealing."

"You would scowl too, Aunt, if you had to wear such ghastly things at my age. How is one to make a good impression, looking like this?" She swept her hand across her bosom, earning one of her aunt's chilliest glares.

"One can always make a good impression with a semblance of dignity, a pleasant smile and a sunny disposition. Really, did that stepmother of yours teach you nothing?"

"Indeed she could not have taught me anything about that, for as you well know, Rosamund has quite the *least* sunny disposition of anyone I ever met. She's as pleasant as a wet weekend in Bognor!"

Blanche turned towards the front door, but not before Charlotte had seen her lips twitch. Her amusement at this description of Rosamund made Charlotte smile too, in spite of her bad temper, and by the time they had completed the short journey by motor car to the Chadwyckes' Mayfair residence, she had calmed down and was ready to be charming. They were quickly shown to the drawing room and announced by the butler.

"Mrs Ferrers, what a pleasure to see you. And Charlotte, my dear. I'm so pleased you could come."

Lady Westhampton had been reading a letter, but now laid the correspondence down and indicated that they should join her at the tea table. The ladies settled into polite small talk until the tea had been poured. Charlotte nibbled at a parchment-thin piece of bread and butter, casting envious glances at the viscountess's elegant tea gown of eau de nil silk.

"I received a note from Eustace today," Lady Westhampton said. Her voice was as soft and well-modulated as ever, but Charlotte caught a hint of strain in the way she spoke. "Have you heard from him recently yourself, Charlotte?"

Charlotte flushed, unsure whether she should admit that she received a letter from him most days. "One arrived yesterday," she said.

"And what were your impressions?"

"My impressions?" She paused, not knowing quite how to respond, and took a moment to wipe her fingertips delicately on her white linen napkin. She sensed that Blanche's ears had pricked up, as sensitive as her own to the unspoken tension in their hostess's demeanour.

Lady Westhampton's eyes did not leave Charlotte's face.

"Was the tone of his most recent letter in the same vein as his previous letters to you?"

"It was – perhaps – a little gloomier."

"Go on."

"He mentioned someone who died." Again, she paused. It

seemed cruel to speak of a man being shot so close to her son. Was it fair to offer such a stark reminder of the dangers he must face every day?

"And did he... Forgive me, dear. Did he describe what happened?"

Blanche had set down her cup and shifted uncomfortably in her chair, looking fixedly at the tablecloth. Charlotte felt pinned under the weight of Lady Westhampton's attention; she wished she could wriggle away, rather than recall the gruesome details from Eustace's letter.

"Yes. He did."

Lady Westhampton nodded, fidgeting distractedly with her napkin. "One cannot help feeling a measure of concern, given the awful stories one hears... of men brought to the brink of despair. When they're witnessing such ghastly sights, it is a wonder any of them can bear it." Her hand seemed to tremble, and she quickly set her cup back in its saucer.

Charlotte had intended to take a scone from the top tier of the cake stand, but felt now that anything she could eat would taste like ashes in her mouth. This visit was not at all what she had expected.

"He had obviously had a difficult day when he wrote his letter," Charlotte allowed. "But he is as brave as a lion, and he knows where his duty lies. Of course you know him better than I, my lady, but please allow me to say that I really feel you mustn't doubt him. I'll write to him this evening and urge him to have courage, and you must do the same. We must remind him of his loved ones, and his home in England, to bring to his recollection all that he is fighting to protect. I don't believe for a moment that he would waver; but if he has, even for a second, our combined efforts will steady him."

She stopped, surprised at her own sudden burst of passion on Eustace's behalf. She hadn't realised he could evoke such strength of sentiment in her, yet here she was daring to challenge the one woman she could not risk offending for fear of her potential influence over her son.

It had been so many months since she had been able to look upon his cheerful face and hear his laughter, there had been moments when Charlotte had wondered if she even loved her fiancé at all. She couldn't remember what his voice sounded like. They had not spent many hours in each other's company before he had asked her the question that fulfilled all her father's and her own ambitions for herself. If not for his frequent letters, she might have felt that she barely knew him, beyond thinking him an amiable sort of fellow, with a pleasant and charming disposition.

It didn't trouble her, as she would have years in which to get to know him. If they should eventually tire of each other's company it would hardly matter, for by then her future as a wife would be assured, and hopefully there would be an heir or two, and they would each have their own interests to occupy them. She didn't expect much more from marriage than a chance to occupy the role to which she had been brought up. Certainly, she did not expect to feel any depth of affection for her husband. Respect would be nice, and mutual liking; but if the latter did not happen she would not be overly disappointed. Yet her defensiveness now on Eustace's behalf struck her as an indication that she might, perhaps, have fallen in love with him after all.

Lady Westhampton nodded, and Aunt Blanche gave a tight smile. As their conversation turned towards lighter topics, Charlotte was left to brood on her thoughts.

SEVEN

Maggie

The best part of Maggie's day was her walk to work. Up with the lark to stoke the range and lay the fire, she allowed herself no more than ten minutes to wolf down a couple of slices of bread and butter with a boiled egg to set her up for her day's labours. Leaving the washing up to her younger sister Dolly, she set off in the damp morning air, huddling into her collar to stop the cold biting at her cheeks. Her breath was misty about her face, dampening the woollen scarf she kept across her nose and mouth for warmth. Dawn glimmered above the hedgerows and a flock of sparrows chirped a cacophonous alarm as she passed, maintaining a brisk pace and swinging her arms to keep warm. She had to make sure she arrived at the factory in time: to be even a couple of minutes late would cost her a chunk of her precious wages.

Jenny Gittins, her older brother Len's sweetheart, waited at the crossroads, beating her arms against her sides to warm herself. Thin as a hat pin, Jenny's pinched face always lit up at the sight of her friend approaching.

"Here," Maggie said, holding out a waxed paper package. "I tried a different recipe this week. See what you think."

Jenny tucked her mittens into her pockets and tore off the paper as they walked. Her brown eyes widened at the sight of the Welsh cakes, dotted with sultanas and glistening with precious flakes of sugar. She wolfed them down, murmuring her appreciation of the flavour.

"What do you reckon? Some of my best, Dad said."

Maggie knew Jenny's pride would never allow her to admit she hadn't had breakfast. By suggesting she needed her to test her cooking, she could help her without affronting her dignity. Jenny's mother was a widow with a brood of children to feed and precious little money for bread or coal. Some mornings Jenny looked wan with hunger and would walk with her skinny arms hugging her empty belly, as if pressing on it could make it feel full.

"Mmm, he's right. They're delicious," Jenny said, licking the last remaining flavour from her red fingers before shoving her chilblained hands back into her mittens.

"I'm glad you like them. I might try adding a bit of chopped orange peel next time, too, if I can get it."

It warmed her to know her cooking had given her friend such enjoyment. Now that she was working twelve-hour shifts, with an extra hour a day walking to and from work, Maggie didn't have a lot of time for baking, but she liked to keep her hand in on Saturdays. Her mother wouldn't allow it on the Lord's Day, although Maggie thought it ironic that Mary called it a day of rest when she and her children tramped to the chapel and back three times to worship.

"Have you had any letters from Len?" Jenny was always eager for news, and her face fell when Maggie answered in the negative, as Jenny relied on getting news of Leonard second-hand. Maggie suspected the cost of stamps, paper and ink was too much of a stretch, with Jenny's wages from the factory the only thing saving the Gittins family from penury. Not only that, but her friend admitted that she wasn't much good at reading and writing, having spent most of her childhood kept home from school to look after her younger siblings. Len had stopped writing to her directly when he realised she had to take his missives to Maggie to be read aloud. It made Maggie's cheeks burn to remember the things he had written, things that had made Jenny snatch the letter from her with a scarlet face and a fit of the giggles.

It was light by the time they arrived at the factory gates to join the throng of women already waiting. One or two stragglers only just made it as the gates closed behind them, and joined the dash to the long room where they stripped down to their chemises and threw on coarse grey tunics and trousers. Each woman removed her hair pins and gathered up her long hair in her hand to wind it into a twist or bun before tucking it into a mob-cap. Corsets, boots or shoes were left behind with their clothes, and they filed along in wooden clogs. Maggie had found it strange wearing trousers at first, especially knowing how much her mother would disapprove. Now, though, it was second nature; she could even say she found them comfortable.

On their way to the factory floor they paused for inspection. Some of the women invariably took the opportunity to vent their spleen at the supervisor, whose hoity-toity demeanour annoyed them.

"Look at her, thinks she's a cut above us. Stuck-up bitch."

"Yeah, go on, have a good search. I bet you live for this, you ugly sow – a chance to go fumbling in another woman's unmentionables is all the excitement you'll ever get."

Their remarks were accompanied by a good deal of cackling and whooping, not to mention crude gestures and winks. It was a revelation for Maggie. Before she entered the working world she had never encountered women who swore, and she still hadn't got used to it. It was something she could never discuss at home: Mam would find the prospect of her facing such bad influences even worse than her wearing trousers.

Maggie would never dream of being so disrespectful towards the supervisor, whom she knew was a volunteer doing her best to ensure the factory produced as many shells as possible for the war effort. Her heart pounded as she ran through a swift mental checklist. Were there any metal buttons or hooks and eyes fastening her underwear? Had she accidentally left any pins in her hair? At least she knew there was no risk of forgetting to remove jewellery, as she had none. The older woman ahead of her was hastily wrapping thread around her wedding ring, trying to cover it before the supervisor spotted it. Maggie guessed the woman had worn it so long it would no longer come off.

"Do you want to go after me?" she whispered. The other woman nodded, glad of the extra few moments to complete her task. The consequences for failing to completely cover it could be far more serious than just having her wages docked: they had all been warned over and over that any metal object or flammable items such as matches taken onto the factory floor could cause a spark that would lead to an explosion. It was a sobering thought.

Having passed inspection, each woman was handed a cup of steaming cocoa, and Maggie gulped hers down gratefully, glad of the comforting warmth and the way it bolstered her energy before she took up her post.

Someone had obviously reached her bench before her: black oil was splattered across it, coating the handles of the tools in a sticky mess. Exclamations from other women around the room suggested their workstations had been similarly sabotaged.

"Those bastards! I'll wring their bloody necks if I get hold of them!" came a cry from one of the coarsely spoken women who had insulted the supervisor earlier.

"What's going on here?" The supervisor bustled towards them and was soon apprised of the situation.

"It's the men on the night shift again. They think we're taking men's jobs, so they've spoilt our benches. Look at the mess! It'll all have to be cleared up before we can start work."

The supervisor's eyes narrowed. "You'd better get some cloths and start mopping it up," she said. "I shall have something to say about this. Taking men's jobs indeed. We're freeing them to do the work they jolly well *should* be doing – at the front!"

The other woman caught Maggie's eye. "First thing that posh cow has said that I agree with," she muttered.

EIGHT

Charlotte

Charlotte had been unsure what to expect when she heard that her future mother-in-law was to visit, but it certainly hadn't been this. Lady Westhampton looked ghastly pale, with purple smudges under her eyes. Their blueness, so like Eustace's bright, clear sea-blue eyes, was intensified by her puffy, reddened eyelids which suggested she hadn't slept in days. In contrast with her usual effortless calm and elegance, she fixed her attention on the tea table, as if couldn't bear to meet anyone's gaze.

Charlotte stared at her. The sight of her ladyship's tightly controlled expression made an icy needle of unease slide down her spine. Something must be dreadfully wrong with Eustace for her to come to visit in such a state of repressed emotion. The only faint glimmer of hope was that he couldn't be dead, or else his mother would have had the curtains drawn closed and stayed at home dressed in black.

Aunt Blanche offered tea, which Lady Westhampton

declined. Charlotte swallowed hard; her mouth had gone dry. At last, her aunt took charge.

"Might we ask if there is something wrong, my lady? It is always a pleasure to see you, but I hope you won't mind my observing that you seem somewhat troubled."

The other woman finally looked up. Her mouth was set in a downward turn that made her look years older.

"What's happened to Eustace?" Charlotte blurted out, unable to hold the question in any longer. She gripped the edge of her seat, wanting nothing more than to jump up and shake the truth out of Lady Westhampton. Whatever may have occurred, not knowing and imagining the worst couldn't be any more painful than the news her ladyship had come to deliver.

Lady Westhampton sighed. "My husband and I received distressing news earlier this week. You may imagine how much it pains me to have to tell you... Eustace has been wounded."

Wounded. The word was like a dagger blow.

Charlotte gasped. "Is he dying?"

"Charlotte!" Aunt Blanche exclaimed, her mouth an O of disapproval.

"Lady Westhampton wouldn't have come to tell me if it wasn't serious." She wasn't sure whether Aunt Blanche found her directness rude, or if she was concerned that Lady Westhampton was too delicate for plain speech, but this wasn't a time for hedging about with niceties. Despite the prickles of sweat breaking out beneath Charlotte's clothes, she had no intention of dashing out of the room or falling down in a faint, and she was pretty sure Eustace's mother was sufficiently stoic to cope with a blunt question, given that she had come out specifically to deliver the blow in person. She could easily have sent a note, or picked up the telephone, if she had been unwilling to provide more than the most essential details.

Lady Westhampton shook her head. "No, dear. He isn't likely to die. But, just to be sure, his father is speaking to his contacts in the War Office. We intend to ensure that anything that may be done, *is* done."

Charlotte frowned. "But you're worried, I can tell. If his wound is only slight...?"

Aunt Blanche interjected again. "Charlotte, dear, no mother wants to think of their son being hurt or in danger. I'm sorry, my lady. Charlotte means no offence; of course it is only natural for you to be concerned. We do hope Captain Chadwycke is expected to make a full recovery?"

"His physical wounds are minor. It isn't entirely clear what has happened, as the reports give precious little information. My husband did not want to tell me at first." She hesitated, bunching the fine silk of her skirt in her hand as if oblivious to how it would crumple. "It appears Eustace was hit by a blast from a shell which knocked him unconscious for a time. Apparently he was... he was buried by debris from the explosion. His men had to dig him out."

Bile rose in Charlotte's throat. She covered her mouth with her hand.

"My poor boy," Lady Westhampton continued, her voice thin and strained, threatening to crack. "My poor, poor boy, buried alive. I haven't slept since I heard. I keep picturing him – his beautiful face – *smothered*. Cut and bleeding, and crushed by filthy mud." She blinked, her proud face taut with the effort of maintaining her composure, and sucked in a gulp of air as if she, too, had been struggling for breath under a weight of earth.

The room seemed airless. Looking around in a daze, Charlotte could no longer remain seated. She stumbled to the window, her eyes blurred by tears, and pressed her forehead to the cool pane. The London street looked drab and grey in the dusk of early evening, reflecting the warm glow of the room back in the glass and emphasising how safe the indoor world of home was compared to the frigid brutality of the world outside. Droplets of rain had gathered against the glass and were trickling down, joining together in swollen, glistening beads where they met. *Even so, he is alright*, she told herself. Then, louder and firmer, to the room at large: "He *is* alright. He will recover."

She barely heard Lady Westhampton's next words. "He did suffer some shrapnel wounds which cut him up a bit. Not badly, so he should make a full recovery from those, provided they don't fester. But with all that mud... And we've been told he can't speak properly. He keeps shaking. They're saying he's suffering from blast concussion which has had a temporary effect on his mind. A *hysterical* effect – although that is a word I struggle to accept being applied to a man. His doctor described him to my husband as 'shell-shocked', whatever that means."

"Shell-shocked? Then he is stunned in some way following the explosion?" Aunt Blanche's face must have reflected Charlotte's own confusion.

"It's a term being bandied about in the press. It must mean nothing more than a temporary incapacity in my son's case. Whatever it means, we must assume he will require a period of rest before being well enough to return to his post. We'll need to send him somewhere quiet, where he can forget what has happened. He'll need to recover from the physical wounds, of course, but they are not the primary concern. His doctor is optimistic that he can be restored to health, provided he is well cared for. He will be as fit for duty as ever he was, with our help."

It was a lifeline to cling to. "Of course he will recover! He will be coming home soon, then?"

Lady Westhampton shook her head. "He most certainly cannot come home. That is out of the question."

"Did you not hear Lady Westhampton say that Captain Chadwycke is shell-shocked?" Aunt Blanche interjected.

"Yes, but I don't understand. You said he will recover...?"

"He needs to go somewhere peaceful and restorative: a sanctuary, if you will, where he can receive the very best of *specialised* medical care. Going home is impossible. He is too well known there, and people will talk. I won't have people gossiping about my son, saying he's a shirker."

Charlotte flinched at the way she almost spat out the word.

"The difficulty is: where to send him? Our home in London is too busy for him to find a moment's peace; even at our country home he may not be afforded a level of privacy conducive to his recovery. This is a situation of the utmost delicacy, Charlotte. His reputation, his future... there is so much at stake." Her tone was unexpectedly forceful, revealing a strength of will Charlotte had not previously detected in her.

With her mind racing, Charlotte gripped the windowsill. As far as she was concerned, the main thing at stake was her future marriage into the aristocracy. Papa had been determined that it would happen, and so was she. Whatever this "shell-shock" was, she wasn't about to let it stand in the way of her future. It must mean some kind of blow to the head which had left Eustace stunned or dazed following the explosion in battle.

She recalled hearing some years ago about a boy from the village who had fallen from a tree and landed on his head. He had been utterly changed afterwards, transformed from a bright and cheeky lad to an imbecile. Papa had referred to him as a *cabbage*, an idea which seemed so ridiculous at the time that it had made Charlotte giggle behind her hand. Her blood ran cold at the momentary thought that Eustace's head injury could be in any way similar. His mother seemed to see it as potentially damaging to his future and reputation – something shameful, to be hidden away where no one who knew him would see how he suffered. But she also believed that he would recover.

It made no sense. Charlotte had seen a few injured war veterans on the streets of the city, some of them maimed. People passing by would look uncomfortable, yes, or sometimes disapproving if the men were begging or cursing. They might look away, perhaps unwilling to look at any reminder of the potential dangers their own loved ones might be facing. But people didn't behave towards them as if their wounds were something to be ashamed of. They didn't send them off to the countryside.

It was the thought of the countryside that gave her the idea, dropping into her brain like a coin falling into a slot. It was a brilliant way to get her wedding back on track.

"Plas Norton is standing empty," she said. "He could go there."

Lady Westhampton's expression lifted hopefully, but Aunt Blanche immediately shook her head.

"Haven't you been listening, dear? Lady Westhampton has explained that Captain Chadwycke needs specialist care. It isn't *only* a case of resting out in the country. He will need... well, if not exactly a hospital, at the very least a convalescent home, if he is so... unwell."

She had picked her words with great care, darting uneasy looks at Lady Westhampton while addressing her niece. It was annoying, the way she hedged about it so tactfully, as if Eustace was having some sort of breakdown.

Impatiently, Charlotte ignored her and addressed Eustace's mother directly, detecting in her an air of desperation that might make her consider what seemed to Charlotte an eminently reasonable suggestion.

"Plas Norton is as comfortable as you would expect, my lady. Although it is shut up at the moment, with no one living there, I could soon have it aired. We could get some of the staff back without much difficulty, I'm sure, or take on new people. And Eustace will find the scenery around Plas Norton most pleasant. He could ride in the deer park, or hike in the surrounding hills once his wounds are healed. No one knows him there; he would have perfect privacy, with not a soul to trouble him."

Despite Charlotte's enthusiasm, Lady Westhampton's frown suggested she still had doubts. "I appreciate that this is a kind offer, and it would afford him privacy; but if anything, being alone in a large and unfamiliar country house might be *too* isolating. I think we shall have to look for somewhere small and discreet where he can go to recover alongside other wounded officers."

Charlotte pressed further, convinced that she had found the perfect solution. "Give me a day," she urged, wishing she had paid more attention to Venetia's charitable endeavours. "I'm sure I remember Venetia telling me about a friend whose house has been converted into a Red Cross military hospital. Let me speak to her about it."

Eyes bright with excitement, she turned next to her aunt. "You know you have been encouraging me to devote my time to worthy pursuits in service to the war effort, Aunt. What better cause could I give my energies to than the recovery of my future husband?"

NINE

Charlotte

That night, sleep proved impossible. Despite staying up later than usual with her knitting, trying to tire herself until she was almost cross-eyed with fatigue and with shoulders as stiff as her knitting pins, Charlotte's brain whirred into action the moment she slipped under her blankets. She allowed herself half an hour of rumination before summoning a sullen Sharp to light an oil lamp and fetch some warm cocoa. Hopefully, the milky drink would soothe her. It seemed to take an age before the maid returned.

"There you go, miss." She plonked the tray down on the bedside cabinet, making little effort to smother a yawn. "Can I go back to bed now?"

"Yes, off you go." Irritation flared briefly, but Charlotte resolved to address her maid's attitude in the morning instead of rebuking her immediately. She'd heard several ladies complaining about the difficulty in replacing domestic staff due to factories offering them better wages, so it wouldn't do to push

Sharp too far. Still, servants should execute their duties with good grace.

An unappetising greasy film had formed across the surface of the cocoa on its long journey from the basement kitchen to Charlotte's room. Grimacing, she flipped it into the saucer with her spoon before taking a sip. The cocoa was so sweet it made her teeth hurt. Not soothing at all: if anything, she felt even more on edge. At last, she hopped out of bed and donned her dressing gown and slippers before seizing the lamp and padding downstairs to the library.

The fire had gone out in the grate, but the room was still cosy with lingering warmth. The lamp's yellow glow created a soft halo where she lifted it towards the shelves, seeking distraction. She'd already read her latest fashion magazine twice from cover to cover; although she wasn't usually one for reading books, she needed a way to unwind. Surely there must be a lightweight romance here somewhere? But her perusal of the length of the shelving revealed only serious volumes, their titles picked out in stamped and gilded lettering on the dark leather bindings. In the end, she settled for *Oliver Twist*. Not too long, and she could skim past the lengthier descriptions.

Back in bed, with her feet tucked under her knees and her back propped up with pillows, she didn't progress further than a couple of pages. Her mind was filled with thoughts of Eustace. She was convinced that her idea for him to convalesce at Plas Norton was a good one, but how would she convince his parents, or Aunt Blanche for that matter? Blanche would continue as her guardian for another year, so there was little she could do without her permission. Tomorrow she would speak to Venetia and together, hopefully, they would come up with a proposal that would win Blanche over.

She was sure her idea of turning Plas Norton into a hospital could work. Eustace would be lonely there by himself; having other soldiers around him would surely be helpful in speeding his recovery. But how on earth might one go about setting up a hospital? It sounded like a mammoth undertaking, even for someone older than herself with experience of committees and letter-writing and with a web of contacts in important positions who could provide advice and support. A hospital would require nurses – real, qualified ones to supervise, as well as unpaid women helping as part of the Voluntary Aid Detachment. They'd need medical equipment and proper hospital beds. Beds would need linen, and lots of it, she guessed, if the men had wounds which bled or if they were sick. They would need doctors and an ambulance with a driver to transport the patients from the local railway station. The more she thought about it, the more complicated the idea seemed.

She rubbed her eyes and abandoned her attempts to read. The concerns of a fictional Victorian orphan had no meaning for her when there were real problems to think about. Back downstairs she went, this time to hunt for a pencil and some notepaper to jot down her thoughts. She found some in the library desk and laid the paper on the blotter, tapping her bottom lip with the pencil before setting down a title: *Plans for Plas Norton.*

Somehow her previously wild and tangential thoughts made more sense written down, and seeing the words on the page made her ideas seem more concrete. Her list of all the things a hospital might need was so daunting, it made her heart sink. How could she ever fund it all, never mind organising it? She couldn't afford to make a mess of this, with Eustace's recovery at stake, not to mention the recovery of perhaps a number of other serving soldiers.

Her footsteps slowed as she carried the paper and pencil back upstairs to bed. She was finally starting to tire, her energies spent in the flurry of writing. Now that she had captured the essence of her plans, she was more doubtful of their potential for success, yet she was reassured that her notes provided something to build on. Somewhere in the scatter of jottings, the essence of a realistic idea would surely be found. Venetia was clever; Venetia knew important people. If anyone could help her pull the random threads together, she could.

The sheets had cooled by the time she slid back into bed, making goose pimples stand out on her limbs. She contemplated summoning Sharp again, to fetch a hot water bottle this time, but decided against it. She'd faced enough dumb insolence for one night. For a while she remained curled up, but then forced herself to straighten her legs out, little by little, keeping her feet together for warmth until the chill had gone from the bed. With the lamp extinguished, and the tension in her cold muscles gradually easing, darker thoughts began circling like crows, wheeling about her head and occasionally darting in to peck at her.

What if Eustace's injuries had changed him? The prospect of marrying him had always pleased her, and not merely because she was keenly aware of her father's ambitions for her future connection to the aristocracy. Eustace was a handsome boy, dashing in his captain's uniform – or at least he was before he went off to the trenches. A picture of his face swam before her mind: warm eyes and fresh, rosy cheeks; a boyish moustache that she knew disappointed him in its sparse fluffiness. How would it feel to look upon that face if it had been marred by shrapnel wounds? If he was scarred, or even disfigured, would she still experience the same frisson of shy excitement when he looked at her and smiled? Would she find his scars repulsive? Photographs she had seen in the press of men with empty sleeves, or trouser legs pinned up, had invariably sent a bolt of shock through her and made her look away.

Thankfully, Lady Westhampton's report suggested that Eustace was not at risk of losing any limbs, but if his physical wounds festered, could she bear to look upon a husband who was so afflicted? Would he see through any attempts to reassure him with a less than genuine smile? She was very much afraid that she wouldn't be able to put a brave face on her feelings.

She didn't want to be the kind of girl who would abandon a man who'd suffered a misfortune, especially when it had resulted from noble self-sacrifice. She liked to imagine herself as a woman who would be loyal and true, a worthy wife for a hero. If she ended their engagement, society would condemn her for her failure to stand by him. She could never face the shame of it. And what would be her chances of finding another eligible bachelor of sufficient social standing willing to make her an offer? Greatly reduced, if not negligible. Not only would she lose the specific marriage her papa had wanted and planned for her, she might lose the chance of any marriage at all. The prospect of ending up an old maid was enough to make her goose pimples return. More than anything, Charlotte craved the security of a guaranteed position in aristocratic society and a man not old or ugly or poor to provide for her.

Tears stung the backs of her eyes, making her nose prickle and her throat sore. The loss of Papa was like an old wound that had reopened under the strain of this problem. If only he were here, he would know what to do. She wept into her pillow, too ashamed of her fears to go to Aunt Blanche, with loneliness pressing down on her as if she was being smothered by a great weight. For her, there would be no one to come and dig her out or tend her wounds. She would have to come to terms with her changed future as well as she could, and cling to the hope that Eustace would be alright.

TEN

Charlotte

"Crikey, you look positively dreadful!" Venetia exclaimed at the sight of Charlotte's swollen eyes the next day.

Charlotte looked away, her pale cheeks colouring with embarrassment. "I slept badly," she murmured.

"Really? I never would have guessed if you hadn't said."

The arch tone caught her by surprise; she couldn't help a rueful smile.

"I recommend a dose of fresh air and exercise. A walk in the gardens will do you the power of good, and you'll probably sleep better for it tonight. It's mild out, and for once it isn't raining. So, what do you say?"

She hesitated. "I can't let anyone see me like this…"

Venetia was already on her feet, dusting her palms together in readiness for action. "Nonsense," she said. "Who do you imagine will be looking at you? They'll all be much more interested in the former suffragette beside you, who may still carry a hammer or Mills bomb up her sleeve." The gleam in her eye as she gestured towards the door was impossible to resist, and Charlotte found herself summoning Sharp to help her change into walking clothes and sensible shoes.

Primroses and crocuses brightened the borders out in the garden square, their bursts of yellow and purple between the lawns lifting the grey city environs in a way that made Charlotte's energy levels rise. She found herself breathing more deeply and taking in more of her surroundings: the details of knotty bark on the still-bare trees, the branches with their early buds showing the promise of spring.

"Tell me what's troubling you," Venetia said in her customary brisk manner.

Charlotte sighed and paused at a bench, sinking onto it and gazing about the garden square as if an answer to her problems might be laid out for her to read in one of the formal beds. Still at a loss, she focused on examining the showy stamens of the crocuses beside the path, their flashes of orange lively amongst the delicate lavender-coloured petals.

Venetia perched beside her and folded her gloved hands in her lap, sticking her lame leg out in front of her. If anyone passed, they could easily trip over it, but they were alone in the gardens. There was something about her companion's intelligent gaze that invited confidences, and Charlotte found herself telling Venetia about Lady Westhampton's news and her fear that she may no longer be able to marry Eustace.

Venetia let her speak at length, then finally sniffed. "One thing that always strikes me about you is the way you talk about your forthcoming nuptials as if marriage is your only ambition in life. Should your fiancé recover, you'll be married at – what, twenty or twenty-one? And then, what? What will you do with the subsequent fifty-odd years?"

Charlotte had been expecting to hear murmured platitudes, reassurances that all would be well and that Eustace would make a full recovery. She stiffened at the implication that her ambition was somehow lacking.

"I'm sure I don't know anyone who has the next fifty years mapped out ahead of them," she retorted.

Venetia's lips twitched annoyingly, as if she was amused by Charlotte's defensiveness.

"Five, then."

"I suppose I shall have children, if we are blessed."

"Yes, but if you are *blessed*, as you put it, you won't devote any time to looking after them. You'll have a nursemaid for that, won't you? The little angels won't give more than an hour's trouble each day, I don't suppose. What will you do with the other twenty-three hours, I wonder, when you are Eustace Chadwycke's wife?"

Venetia's candour made Charlotte want to squirm. She gripped the handles of her bag, resisting the urge to jump up and stride away at a pace Venetia couldn't hope to match. How dare she be so rude? What gave her the right to make assumptions about another girl's future, or to judge her for following the path she had been born to? It wasn't as if her own life had been a success, unless one could count committing criminal damage and landing oneself in a police cell for a protest that had never achieved its aims as *successful*.

"You don't seem to have a very positive opinion of marriage," she said, her tone sharp. "I take it you've never considered wedlock to be a suitable ambition for yourself?"

There was a long pause, until she had almost given up on ever receiving an answer.

"I loved someone once. A long time ago. But it wasn't possible for us to marry."

Charlotte's interest was piqued. She stared, intrigued by this unexpected titbit of information. Venetia's face was shuttered and blank; presumably this mysterious lover had disappeared from her life some years ago. What could have been the obstacle? Had he been, perhaps, already married to someone else? What a scandal that might have caused, worse even than her suffragette activism.

Her mind raced through the exciting possibilities that had suddenly made Venetia seem much more interesting. Had there been an age difference, perhaps, or a disparity in their social class that forbade marriage? It was tempting to ask for more details, but Venetia had risen and was limping towards the next flower bed. Eyeing the ugly brace just visible at her ankle, Charlotte speculated whether that had been the real reason Venetia had been unable to snare her perfect match. It would take a remarkable man to look past a physical infirmity.

It was a shame, though. Venetia wasn't bad looking, for a woman of her age. She might still be able to marry and have children of her own, if she could find someone else who might disregard her lame leg and her strident views. Although she didn't give the impression of caring much for fashion, her appearance was always neat and her clothes well-cut. Her hair was a deep shade of honey blonde, and when she smiled, especially when she unleashed the impish grin she occasionally displayed when making a teasing or ironic remark, her face was quite pleasant, even if her front teeth were a bit prominent and horsey. Charlotte knew several much uglier women in her aunt's acquaintance who had succeeded in finding husbands, which suggested perhaps Venetia hadn't tried hard enough to snag one after her initial disappointment. It was enough to make Charlotte feel quite sorry for her.

Clasping her bag, she hurried along the path, forced by her fashionably narrow hobble skirt to take short, rapid steps to catch up with her companion.

"Don't give up hope. You may still find a husband in the future," she said, with what she hoped would be an encouraging smile. It soon faded when Venetia threw back her head and laughed.

"I have many hopes, dear girl, but finding a husband certainly isn't one of them. I'm fortunate enough not to need one to provide for my financial security, and I have no desire to bear children, so why should I want one? What possible use would a husband be to me?"

Stunned into a temporary silence, Charlotte's face fell as she tried to picture a future for herself that didn't involve marrying Eustace. She simply couldn't imagine what else she would want to do. Marriage was what she had been brought up to. It provided a happy ending for all the heroines in the novels she occasionally read. Why would any woman prefer to be a spinster? There could surely be no fate worse for a woman than to end up an old maid, dried up and alone, living on the charity of her relatives. The very words used for unmarried women were ugly.

"I find you awfully strange," she blurted out. "Anyone might think you believe I'm *wrong* to want to marry Eustace, even though you know very well that it was my father's last wish, and that it will offer me security for the future. It will give me back a family, and I haven't had one since last summer, apart from Aunt Blanche of course, who is a dear but is getting old and won't be here for ever. Once she's gone, I shall need someone else to take care of me. I should hate to be alone, and I can't understand why you – or anyone – would deliberately choose to be so."

Venetia took her by the shoulders as if she would dearly like to shake her. Her expression was one of patient amusement, though, as if she viewed Charlotte as a foolish child in need of education.

"You silly goose. I didn't say you were wrong. I hope and trust you'll be perfectly content as the financially secure Mrs Chadwycke, and I'm sure the Westhamptons will gladly welcome you into the bosom of the family. I wasn't implying that your ambitions are misguided; I only meant for you to realise there are other destinies that may offer a woman fulfilment."

"What would you see as a more worthy destiny, then?"

"Heavens, who am I to judge? You are in charge of your own path. I can only speak for myself."

"Go on, then. What would you like to do?"

"Well – I should like to be able to look back upon my life and feel that I have made a difference. To leave a legacy, and hopefully even to change the world for the better. I have tried, in small ways, but I wish I could do more."

"Like what?"

"I'd dearly like to join the Women's Emergency Corps and serve in France, driving ambulances or looking after the wounded, but with this dratted leg I think I should be more of a hindrance than a help." Her face fell, and she slapped the thigh on her lame leg as if she wanted to knock it into shape.

It must be hard for someone with so much drive to be held back by a physical handicap, Charlotte supposed. She reached out to give Venetia's arm a tentative squeeze.

"Oh, enough of all that. It can't be helped, and there are other tasks that need to be done. I can write letters, and I'm a born organiser. I can be as bossy as the next woman – as you've no doubt noticed – so I'm sure I shall be able to make myself useful. As will you, in whatever way you see fit. It's clear that your young man is terribly important to you, so come: as it's your most pressing concern for the moment, let's discuss what may become of him. You said he is suffering from shell-shock, the poor fellow?"

Charlotte nodded. "I don't really know what that means."

"Well, I presume they mean war neurasthenia. Nervous attacks," she added, no doubt perceiving that Charlotte was still no less confused. "I've heard my cousin Doctor Havard mention this kind of thing. From what he's said, a lot of our chaps are showing signs of being quite debilitated by it, although naturally there's a reluctance to mention it publicly, for fear that it might encourage others to claim they also have it. In my cousin's view, it's hardly surprising that a chap's nerves might be put under strain when an unseen foe is constantly endeavouring to blow his brains out, and when he witnesses daily the ghastly injuries of his friends. The army would like us to believe that such things are perfectly normal, I suppose, or else it might make it tricky to persuade more and more men to join in. We can only hope that Fritz is suffering equally badly. And that your beloved will make a full and swift recovery, of course. Will he come home to London?"

"Lady Westhampton said he needs quiet in order to rest, so she'd like him to go to the country. Somewhere he isn't known."

"Is that so?" Venetia raised an eyebrow, as if speculating as to the reasons for this, but she said nothing more.

"I suggested Plas Norton. You've visited us there, Venetia: do you agree that it could be the perfect place? It's quiet, surrounded by fields and woodland. He could walk or ride and start to feel well again."

"You're not proposing to be alone there with him?"

Charlotte's eyes widened. "No, of course not. Besides, his mother says he will need somewhere discreet where he can recover alongside other wounded officers. I was wondering... Didn't you say you know someone who has converted their home into a military hospital?"

"I know of several." Venetia paused, her eyes narrowing with interest. "Is that what you have in mind?"

"Do you think it could work? I don't think Eustace needs a *hospital* as such, just somewhere like a rest home..."

Venetia had seized her arm and was beaming as proudly as if she had just made a fabulous new discovery. "My dear girl, of course it could work. We shall make it work! You have long been in need of something more useful to do than winding bandages or knitting, and I should enjoy nothing more than to help you in your bold endeavour. We shall devote our energies to creating The Plas Norton Convalescent Home for Officers: it has a marvellous ring to it, don't you think?"

ELEVEN

Maggie

As much as she enjoyed her work at the factory in many respects, especially the camaraderie among the women and the sense of making a valuable contribution to the war her brother was training to fight in, Maggie had started dreading what she might find each morning as she approached her workbench. Her eyes would dart over the equipment as she made a speedy inspection; after finding it sticky or filthy more than once, she had learned to examine the drawer handle from underneath before touching it. On most mornings, someone's bench would have been interfered with in some way. Sometimes tools would have gone missing, and work would be delayed while she hunted for replacements, her heart pounding in case she was blamed for losing them and her wages docked.

For the past three days, though, there had been nothing amiss, and she dared to hope that perhaps the men had grown bored of their pranks, although it was probably too much to hope that they might have come to value the women's efforts. A few of them had taken to lingering at the factory gate and cat-calling as the morning shift arrived.

"Proud of yourselves, are you? Knowing you're taking work a man should be doing."

The women marched past with their noses in the air, only a few returning insults as they went by. Maggie linked arms with Jenny and tried to ignore them, but one man nudged his friend and pointed to her.

"Hey, she's a looker, Bill. You wouldn't kick her out of bed. I know I wouldn't, anyway."

The pock-faced one they called Bill had straightened and pushed off from the wall with one booted foot before slipping in between the ranks of women to stand in front of Maggie and Jenny. The acrid smell of sweat and halitosis filled Maggie's nostrils and she couldn't help but flinch and sidestep to avoid him, lowering her eyes with her heart thumping. Had he nothing better to do after a long night shift than accost young women who had done nothing to encourage him?

"Leave us alone," she tried to say, but her voice cracked and came out as a feeble whisper.

"Ooh, leave us alone," he repeated, mocking her. He grasped her upper arm in a harsh grip and she jerked it away, her voice rising with her temper.

"Get out of our way. We're trying to go to work."

"She's feisty, this one. What're you doing after work, flower?" He rubbed his crotch and laughed at her expression of disgust as she shoved past him, dragging Jenny along with her. She pretended she hadn't heard as he called after her: "I'll wait for you after your shift, shall I? Show you a thing or two."

Jenny's eyes were wide as Maggie shepherded her through the factory gate and across the yard to the entrance. "You don't think he'll wait for us, do you? I wouldn't like that. I don't think Len would like it either."

That was true. Len would probably thump him if he were

home. Maggie's jaw was still clamped tightly shut, and she slowed her steps deliberately, realising Jenny was stumbling to keep up. In the changing room she practically tore off her outer clothes and bundled them carelessly instead of folding them as she usually did. Such was her fury at being spoken to so crudely, she donned her work uniform quicker than she had ever done before and marched to her workstation with fists still clenched after passing the supervisor's dress inspection.

She glared at her bench suspiciously, casting her eye over the equipment and the surface. Nothing appeared to be amiss. Everything was where it should be. Yet she had a feeling something was wrong, a prickling at the back of her neck that made her uneasy. Other women had started picking up their tools and there were no exclamations of dismay, just the usual sounds of banging, hammering, and machinery starting up that would have made conversation impossible even if it were permitted. Crouching, she looked upwards to examine the handle of her drawer from a different angle. It appeared to be clean. She grasped it and pulled the drawer out, then immediately let go to clasp her hand over her mouth in a silent scream.

Curse words filled her mind – words she couldn't permit herself to voice aloud. Her mouth filled with saliva, bile rising in her throat as she retched into her hand. It was too revolting, too horrible. Catching the supervisor's eye she beckoned the older woman over and pointed towards the drawer. She kept her gaze averted, unwilling to look again at the sight that made the supervisor recoil with a gasp. With the drawer open, the smell made her gag and wrinkle her nose. She breathed through her mouth to try to avoid it, but it was so strong she could almost taste it.

"Who could have done this?" The supervisor's face had turned an alarming shade of puce.

"I don't know, miss."

"Well, don't just stand there. Fetch a bucket and a shovel, or something. Clear it up, there's work to be done." The supervisor stalked away, shaking her head as if to clear her mind of the disgusting sight.

If only Maggie could forget it so easily. Someone must really have it in for her, to leave a turd in her drawer for her to find. She scraped it up, heaving, trying not to think about where it had come from. Was it human? She could hardly believe it possible. More likely that someone had scooped up a dog's faeces with the specific intention of putting it in her drawer, but what kind of person would do such a thing? With her arm outstretched, she carried it on the fireside shovel past the curious faces of her workmates.

"That was a shitty thing to do," one of the older women said, cackling at her own joke. Some of the women laughed; some gasped as she passed, reflecting her own shock and outrage, while others merely grimaced and continued their work.

After disposing of her revolting burden in the toilets, she scrubbed her hands and found they were trembling.

It was just a prank, she whispered to herself. *No harm done.* But she was left sickened. For the whole of the rest of the day she withdrew into herself, barely uttering a word to anyone during their brief meal break, when they ate their sandwiches at their benches. Only Jenny came over to give her a reassuring pat on the arm. The simple act of solidarity made tears spring to her eyes, but she wiped them away unshed, determined not to be cowed by whichever rotten bully had targeted her bench.

She tried to tell herself it wasn't a personal grudge, but what had she or any of her fellow workers done to deserve such unkindness? Why did the men resent the female workers so much when they were making a valuable contribution to the war effort? They had been promised jobs only for the duration of the war, so would be out of work as soon as the troops came home. What's more, they were earning less than men would be paid for similar tasks, as the women were deemed to be 'unskilled' labour.

As always, the noise on the factory floor was deafeningly loud as Maggie and the other women bashed broom handles with wooden mallets to stem powder, packing it tightly into each shell case from bottom to top. Maggie worked as quickly as she could, but took care, knowing the shell would be a dud if she didn't pack it tightly enough to fit all the powder in. Even though it was boring and repetitive work, and her arms and feet ached every day, she knew the importance of doing the job right.

Her thoughts churned over the events of the morning. By the end of her shift, her spirits were as weary and sore as her feet. It was out of the question to mention what had happened at home, as she knew her parents would be furious. More than likely they'd forbid her to go back; Mam would go on more than ever about how she should go into domestic service instead of the factory. She already worried about the colour of Maggie's face, which was turning yellow. In the mornings, when she got up, the bed sheets had a yellowish tinge to them, too, as if the powder she handled seeped into her skin during the day and then leached back out at night.

The hot, milky cocoa they were served at the end of the shift scorched her throat as it went down. With their energies revived, she and Jenny joined the others to strip off their clogs, overalls and mob caps, and pinned up their hair ready for the walk home. The weather had turned milder and Maggie unwound her scarf, finding she was warm enough without it. The women streamed out of the factory gate, turning in various directions for home, but Maggie held back, waiting for Jenny to emerge from the red-brick building.

"Are you alright?" she asked, noticing that Jenny's shoulders seemed to be hunched over and she was hugging her arms around herself more than usual, even though it wasn't cold.

"Just got a bit of a cough, that's all. It'll settle once I've had my tea."

Their boots clattered on the cobbles as they followed the path of the river, its fast-flowing water dark and discoloured from the factories further upstream. A knot of children played marbles in the gutter, some barefoot and all in patched, ill-fitting clothes. The Bridge Inn lay ahead, its windows still darkened, and men loitered in the yard waiting for it to open, voices loud and harsh. One of them hammered on the door and shouted out, presumably to the publican:

"Come on, Ned! It's nearly half-past six. I've got a raging thirst here!" He looked around as Maggie and Jenny passed, and nudged one of his friends. "Look who it is, Bill. Those girls from this morning."

Maggie's heart thumped as he and the man called Bill took off their caps and sauntered out to walk beside them.

"Evening, my little canaries," Bill said, quickening his pace to match Maggie's.

She and Jenny exchanged glances. Her mouth had gone dry, and Jenny's saucer-round eyes showed she was equally nervous.

"You not got nothing to say to us? There's rude, isn't it?" said the other man, moving to block their way as they reached the other end of the bridge.

"Please let us pass," Maggie said in her Sunday voice, hoping she sounded more confident than she felt. The physical bulk of the men looming in front of them made her feel small.

"You should be ashamed of yourselves, taking up jobs that belong by rights to men. Taking a man's wages to spend on what? Ribbons and bows and hat pins." His top lip curled in a sneer, showing a row of crooked brown teeth.

Maggie felt Jenny's hand squeeze hers. She lifted her chin defiantly.

"Let us pass," she repeated.

The one called Bill looked her up and down, then hawked up a gobful of phlegm and spat it out onto her skirt. All four of them stared at it clinging greenish, gleaming wetly against the brown wool. No one spoke, but when she tore her gaze from it to look at the man's face, she saw he was grinning.

It was too much. All at once, something inside her flipped. She'd had enough of people trying to stop her doing her bit, picking on her and treating her like dirt. She'd give him hat pins, alright. Almost before she knew what she was doing, she'd whipped the pin from her hat and jabbed it towards his throat, livid with fury.

He backed up against the parapet of the bridge, his acne-pitted face sallow with fear.

"I've had enough of people like you!" she exclaimed, her voice coming out like a roar. She was dimly aware of Jenny shrieking at her side and tugging at her arm, but she shook her off like a dog shaking a rat, pressing forward with the six-inch hat pin aloft, eyes blazing. "How dare you spit at us! Filthy, disgusting animal that you are. Don't you *ever* come near us again, or I swear I'll take your eyes out with this, do you hear?"

"Leave 'em, Bill. There's a copper coming, look."

As Maggie took a step backwards, the men seized their opportunity to take to their heels.

"Mad bitch!" one yelled from the safety of the other end of the bridge, before running off down a side street.

A dozen yards away, the policeman paused and stared. Maggie nodded acknowledgement, then slid the pin back into her hat, sinking it into her topknot. She was still breathing heavily, her nostrils flared with temper. Jenny stood back, wringing her hands. Perhaps she had gone too far in the heat of the moment, Maggie thought, but a glance at her friend's face revealed she was grinning in unabashed admiration.

"I never thought you had it in you, Maggie. You really saw them off. What a pig, spitting on you like that... But you made him sorry. He'll think twice before he tries that again!" She flung her thin arms around Maggie in a hug.

"Careful, you'll get it on your skirt." Maggie felt curiously flat now that her rush of anger had dissipated. She was left enormously tired, her limbs so heavy she wasn't sure how she would pick up her feet to go home. More than anything, she wanted to get the man's phlegm off her skirt, but she couldn't bear to touch it, or to spoil her handkerchief with it. Twisting her mouth in disgust, she gathered up a fold of the woollen fabric and wiped it against the rough stonework of the bridge until only a tiny, darkened patch remained.

TWELVE

Charlotte

It was strange to be back, arriving in the damp chill of a Welsh spring having left in the glow of early autumn. After changing trains in Cardiff, leaving Sharp to arrange for the transfer of their luggage while she settled into the warm first-class compartment for their onward journey, Charlotte hadn't wanted to miss a moment of drawing nearer to her childhood home. The vivid emerald hillsides, some dotted with heavy-fleeced sheep and their eager lambs, and others with the occasional herd of cows, were a tonic to the eyes after the drabness of months spent surrounded by city smog and tall buildings.

Now and then they passed through industrial areas, with ribbons of squat terraced houses and blackened valleys where man had scarred the land indelibly in his lust for wealth. Goods trains loaded with stone and glittering black coal lumbered past or waited in sidings to snake towards factories and ports, sending Wales's riches on their way across the world. In every station they passed through, uniformed soldiers jumped from the train to fling themselves into the waiting arms of their sweethearts and families: a reminder that soon Eustace would return to British shores and would make his own way to Pontybrenin on a hospital train. There was no way of knowing yet whether he would be capable of walking, or whether his wounds would mean he had to be stretchered off the train to be transferred to Plas Norton.

Every soldier she saw made Charlotte's resolve firmer. She wasn't yet clear how she would do it, but she would make the convalescent home a reality somehow. In doing so, she would save both Eustace and her own future prospects as his wife. The Westhamptons would be forever grateful to her.

By the time the train drew in to Pontybrenin station, Charlotte's stomach was growling and her eyelids were heavy with fatigue. It had been a long day, and she wanted nothing more than a cup of tea, a light meal, and a hot bath to wash the grime from her face. She'd feel better once she'd eaten and dressed in fresh clothes. The sooner she could get back to her comfortable room in Plas Norton, the better. Sharp had sent a telegram in advance to ensure that her father's chauffeur, Cadwalader, would meet them from the train. Alighting onto the platform, she scanned the throng of passengers for a glimpse of his peaked cap.

Sure enough, he was threading his way towards them. She nodded, grateful to see he was flanked by a porter who could fetch their luggage. He had grown a beard since she last saw him, the dark brown streaked with white. She wasn't sure she approved of it, and frowned a little, but decided to say nothing for the time being. Better to address it in the privacy of the motor car, rather than draw unwanted attention to her servant's appearance in public. His uniform looked smart enough: his navy-blue wool coat and trousers had been freshly brushed, and his leather boots were as shiny as his brass buttons. He would pass muster for now, she decided.

"See to the bags, would you, Sharp?" She threw the instruction over her shoulder to the grim-faced maid, who had looked sullen all the way here from London and now flinched as the train released a burst of steam and a shrieking whistle before heaving its way out of the station. No doubt she would have preferred to remain in the city, rather than here in the depths of Wales where there were no modish shops or theatres to visit, and the local picture house was frequented by workers from the nearby factories rather than the fashionable set. Well, it was too bad: Charlotte hadn't come back for a life of excitement, but to perform an important task. Sharp would have to play her part, if she valued her job.

Cadwalader stepped aside for her to precede him, and she picked her way through the thinning crowd towards the station entrance. Disappointingly, only a few people seemed to have noticed her return to town by nudging their companions or whispering behind their hands. One or two acknowledged her presence, but she felt the lack of attention keenly. It had been so different when she travelled with Papa. Beside him, she had seen the effect of his presence on the townsfolk, many of whom would have worked in his factory or mine. Without him, she felt small and insignificant. The thought of it made her want to shrink inside her fur coat, but she set her chin to a proud angle. It would all change when she was Mrs Chadwycke, she told herself. She would hold the arm of her handsome war hero and bask in the reflected warmth people would bestow upon him.

She waited beside the car for Cadwalader to open the door to the rear compartment, then sank into the plush grey cord interior with a sigh. This, at last, was familiar. Papa had enjoyed owning this car, at least until her stupid stepmother crashed it into a ditch and injured him. Charlotte had little doubt that the blow to his head in the accident had contributed to his death that night, even though Doctor Sheridan had implied that a surfeit of brandy was more likely to blame. It had given her all the more reason to despise Rosamund. She supposed she would have to see her stepmother now that she was back, if only to discuss arrangements for sharing the motor and driver, but she was determined to put it off for as long as she could. Perhaps a note would be sufficient to communicate her requirements: she would send one in the morning, straight after breakfast.

As soon as Sharp was safely seated in the fold-down maid's seat, Cadwalader closed the door on them and started the engine, before sliding into the driving seat. Charlotte settled back to enjoy the journey of a few miles, anticipating the first glimpse of Plas Norton's four stone towers that would greet her as they rounded a bend in the deer park.

Pontybrenin was little changed since her last visit, apart from a few straggling queues of shawled women outside the grocers' shops and occasional uniformed men on the streets. There were, perhaps, more men wearing black armbands than might have been expected before. It was a reminder that she could consider herself fortunate that Eustace had only been wounded, as it was becoming impossible to be unaware of the high price the empire was paying in its struggle against the Kaiser's ambitions.

Soon Eustace would be here, settled in comfort in one of the bedrooms at Plas Norton. She could picture it so clearly. He would gaze gratefully into her eyes, tired no doubt and a little pained from his shrapnel wounds – perhaps with his arm in a sling, or walking with a crutch until he was better – and he would tell her how proud and thankful he was to be back with his darling girl. She would make herself look as pretty and bright as her mourning clothes would allow, and plump up his pillows to make him comfortable. She'd cut up his food and feed him with delicate forkfuls, and they'd laugh at how clumsy he was with his arm bandaged up. Being with her would help him forget the trenches. In a few weeks, when he was fit again, they might even be married. Perhaps, by then, the war would be over, although at the moment everyone seemed determined to be pessimistic about the potential duration of the conflict. If it hadn't ended, perhaps Lord Westhampton would be able to use his connections to secure his son a desk job at the War Office. Eustace had already done his bit for King and Country. Once his wounds had healed, someone else could take his place on the front line.

Charlotte's thoughts continued in this happy vein as the motor car purred past the fields and hedgerows outside the town, and her reverie was only disturbed at last when she realised they had passed the main gate to Plas Norton and turned towards the Dower House. Immediately, she sat up and grasped the speaking tube, holding the mouthpiece to her lips.

"What's this, Cadwalader? Why aren't you taking me to the main house?"

His head inclined towards the horn where her voice emerged, but he had already eased the car to a halt outside the Dower House before he had time to reply. Charlotte's temper rose as he hopped out and brushed his gloved hands down the front of his coat, ready to open the door. She was tired and hungry, and wanted only to get back home. The prospect of paying a visit to Rosamund now, before she had had time to wash and eat and compose herself, was insupportable.

"You'd better get back in, Cadwalader, and take me to Plas Norton directly," she said with a glare, the moment he opened the door.

He paused before addressing her in his lilting Welsh accent, as if he was explaining a simple concept to a child. "Miss Fitznorton, Plas Norton is closed."

"Miss Sharp has sent a telegram to Mrs Longford to send her to open up the house. Haven't you, Sharp?"

The maid fumbled nervously with her handkerchief, avoiding Charlotte's stern gaze. "I did send a telegram, miss, but I didn't get a reply. And there was so much to do with getting everything ready, I forgot all about it..." Her voice tailed off, leaving Charlotte fizzing with anger.

"How could you—?" she spat, then sat back in her seat, her fists clenched. If her housekeeper had not responded to the message, and the house was still shut up, then she would have no means of getting in. The heavy oak front door would be locked, the rooms still covered in dust sheets. Her bed would not have been aired, and there would be no one waiting with a pot of tea and a comforting meal. She squeezed her eyes closed, unable even to look at her maid's scarlet face for fear that she would be unable to restrain herself from slapping it.

"I'm s-sorry, miss," Sharp stammered, earning herself such a fierce glare that she clamped her lips together and hung her head like a petulant child.

"Lady Fitznorton is expecting you, miss," Cadwalader said. If he was shocked by Charlotte's seething fury, he knew better than to show it.

With a huff, Charlotte seized her bag. It seemed she had no alternative but to accept her stepmother's no-doubt grudging hospitality. She would go along with it for one night, or until another housekeeper could be found, but she wouldn't spend a moment longer with Rosamund than she had to.

THIRTEEN

Charlotte

Fuming, Charlotte stomped up the gravel path and swept through the front door of the Dower House as if she owned the place, which she indisputably would if not for Rosamund's inconvenient pregnancy casting a shadow over her inheritance.

It was years since she had last entered this house, long ago in her childhood when her grandmother held court here and Nanny had brought her on occasional visits to be inspected and made to speak in French. She had a sudden, vivid recollection of Grand-mère's thin hands, gnarled like the claws of the stuffed raptor in its glass case in the hall at Plas Norton, and how they shook as she reached for her sherry glass. She recalled her hawk-like beak of a nose, and her nasal way of speaking to Nanny, ignoring Charlotte except to sweep a disdainful glance over her and criticise her clothes or manners or lack of height. The memory left her strangely shaken, and her step faltered at the threshold of the parlour even though she knew Grand-mère was long dead and could no longer make her feel small and inadequate.

A stout, middle-aged maid she didn't recognise had gone ahead into the room. "Miss Fitznorton, m'lady," the maid announced.

Taking in a deep breath, Charlotte followed her into the room and, for the first time in months, saw her stepmother.

Rosamund was seated in a chair beside the fire, putting aside a small linen garment she had been embroidering, purest white on white. She looked up, and if she didn't quite smile, she didn't look unfriendly either. Charlotte had never seen a woman in such an advanced stage of pregnancy at close hand before – certainly, not one of her own class. It was considered not quite decent for a woman in such a condition to be seen in public, for reasons Charlotte couldn't explain, except that she gathered it was something to do with whatever husbands and wives did in private. The sight of Rosamund's body, so changed, came as a shock and she hugged her arms defensively around herself, staring at the other woman's grossly swollen abdomen. It looked impossibly large, grotesque even, as if pregnancy had made her stepmother somehow deformed.

She was transformed, too: one glance at her face was enough to see that. The frigid, pallid emptiness Charlotte had been accustomed to through her childhood was gone. Now, Rosamund's features were more rounded, softer and livelier than Charlotte had ever seen them. It was as if a soul had moved in to inhabit her body, where there had been no reason for one to dwell before.

Was this what pregnancy did to a woman? Charlotte felt a stab of resentment: she couldn't remember her own mother well enough to know if she'd ever worn this look, and Rosamund had made such a poor replacement. How much had she missed out on in her infancy through having no opportunity to know a mother's affection? And she stood to lose out on more, yet: Rosamund's baby, the child their father didn't live long enough to know about, would rob Charlotte of at least half of her inheritance.

They had not parted on good terms. Colour flooded Charlotte's cheeks as she recalled the last time she returned to Plas Norton, after receiving the news of her father's death. She had hurled accusations at Rosamund, who had been present when Papa died. In a fit of grief she had even shoved her so hard Rosamund fell to the floor. Grudgingly, she had to acknowledge to herself that it was generous of the woman to welcome her into her home at all, let alone with an offer of tea and accommodation.

"Do sit down, Charlotte. Ethel will bring us some tea directly and arrange for your luggage to be taken upstairs. I imagine you must be tired and hungry after such a long journey?"

The maid sidled discreetly from the room, carrying Charlotte's coat. The door closed behind her with a soft click.

"This room has changed since I was last here," Charlotte said, taking in the pretty blossom-sprigged wallpaper, vases of fresh flowers, and plump armchairs.

"For the better, I hope?" Rosamund's tone was mild, almost amused.

"Yes, I would say so. I used to hate it." She sat down in the chair opposite and smoothed down her skirt, meeting her stepmother's frank gaze.

"Your Fitznorton grandmother was rather beastly, wasn't she?"

Charlotte's eyebrows flew up. Finding herself sharing common ground with Rosamund was a new experience. Shifting uncomfortably in her seat, she was glad of the distraction when the tea tray arrived, bearing a selection of cakes and dainty sandwiches of thinly-shaved ox tongue. The maid poured each of them a cup of tea before leaving them alone. They nibbled at their sandwiches, Charlotte's stomach rumbling so loudly at the prospect of food that she was afraid Rosamund might hear.

"I'm surprised to see that you're not wearing black," she remarked after a few minutes. It made a flare of anger rise in her chest to note that her father's memory was being so disrespected. Rosamund should be wearing widow's weeds for at least another year and a half, not that blue housecoat.

"I would still dress in full mourning if I ventured out, but in the privacy of my own home, with only Ethel and Nellie to see me, I believe this will suffice. My condition is not conducive to comfort, and wearing crepe could only make me feel worse."

Having set down her plate and leaned back in her chair with her hands cradling her belly as if to shield it, Rosamund was watching Charlotte intently. "I must confess to some curiosity as to the purpose of your visit," she said at last. "Last time we met, you were only too glad to return to London."

"I had hoped to return directly to the main house, not to trouble you by staying here, but it seems Mrs Longford may not have received my maid's communication, and the house is still shut up."

"Indeed. I have the keys, should you wish to go there tomorrow. I fear it will be a somewhat cheerless homecoming for you."

Charlotte's mouth turned dry, and she forced the morsel of cake down, fearing she might choke on it. "My father is dead. Of course it will be *cheerless*." She couldn't keep the bitterness from her voice, especially as Rosamund's poor driving might have been the cause of her grief.

Rosamund's expression froze. "My apologies," she said, avoiding her gaze.

"As it happens, my return is not for sentimental reasons, or for my own pleasure. I have plans for Plas Norton. Many country houses are being turned into military hospitals and convalescent homes; it's only right to make use of Plas Norton when our country is in need, instead of leaving it to stand empty."

"Why, Charlotte – that is truly laudable." Rosamund wasn't even attempting to conceal her surprise. Was it really so unexpected for Charlotte to do something altruistic?

"Thank you. Now, I need to speak to you about Cadwalader."

To her surprise, the healthy colour drained from Rosamund's cheeks and her brown eyes widened, fixing on Charlotte as if she were an animal caught in a trap. Puzzled, Charlotte let the silence hang for several heartbeats, then cleared her throat.

"Cadwalader. Papa's driver. I realise he has been working for you, but I shall need to make use of him myself. For the patients."

"The patients?"

"They'll arrive in Pontybrenin on the hospital train, but we can hardly expect them to walk from the station to Plas Norton, can we?"

Rosamund nodded and stroked a finger across her top lip. "Of course. I'm sure he will be glad to assist you. His eldest son has volunteered for the services."

Charlotte swallowed her irritation along with her mouthful of cake. "I have no interest in his personal life. I meant only to make you aware of my expectations." It made no difference to her whether the chauffeur would be glad to help her or not: he should expect to earn his wages, and no doubt his job had been a very easy one recently, given that Rosamund had a reputation as something of a recluse. He probably had very little to do.

She dabbed at her mouth with her napkin, noting as she did so that Rosamund's tense expression had softened. She was gazing at her stomach, caressing it in a dreamy way; then, as her hand stilled, a private smile spread across her face like a ripple on a pond. Aghast, Charlotte observed as her stepmother's belly shifted, heaving towards one side as if it was some kind of monstrous growth entirely independent of her body. She stared at it with horrified fascination, her knees drawing up as if her legs were screaming at her to get away from the unnatural spectacle.

Rosamund had caught her looking. "Baby is active this evening. He always seems to wake up when I have cake."

She couldn't hide her revulsion. Nor could she bite back the words that sprang to her lips as she rose and crossed the room to put some distance between herself and the horrible sight.

"He? You believe it is a boy, then? The son and heir you failed to give my father when he was alive. Some people might find it suspicious that you've managed to do so now that he is dead and unable to protect my rights to his estate."

Rosamund's expression darkened. Gripping the arms of her chair with both hands, she struggled to her feet and faced Charlotte, straight-backed and fierce. "As you well know, my child was conceived several weeks before your father died. If I failed to deliver a child before, the fault is not with me. You can see for yourself that when I am left unmolested, when I am not threatened or beaten or kicked or abused, I am perfectly capable of carrying a baby to full term. Your beloved father, your Papa whom you always idolised, destroyed all the others. Yes, Charlotte. There were others. You may turn your face from me, but you *will* hear me out."

She reached the door surprisingly swiftly, barring Charlotte's way. Her eyes glittered, whether with fury or with unshed tears Charlotte could not tell.

Charlotte looked away, unwilling to read the agony on display in her stepmother's features, and put her hands over her ears. But Rosamund grasped her wrists and pulled them down.

"It is my sincere wish that you will never, *never* experience the kind of marriage I had."

"Let go of me," Charlotte whispered. Hot tears coursed

down her cheeks. She had despised Rosamund before, but now... In that moment she loathed her for saying such terrible things about her father. Allowing her loathing to show, she bared her teeth in a grimace and almost spat out her words. "Let me go, or so help me I will shove you again, like I did before."

Loosing her, Rosamund took a step back. Her shoulders slumped.

"I don't believe you," Charlotte cried. She wanted to pummel the door and scream. "Papa was a good man. It was you – *you* who let *him* down. He always said so. He said if you were a brood mare he would have had you shot..."

Rosamund's head snapped back up. "He did. I remember." She gave a bitter, dry laugh, then waved her hand. "Well... if you choose not to believe me, you are free to go. But ask yourself what kind of man speaks in such a way about his wife, Charlotte. Would a good man say, in front of his daughter and his servants, that his wife should be shot for not producing an heir? How would you feel if Eustace spoke to you in such a way? Search your heart and ask yourself why I would humiliate myself by speaking of those years of torture and shame to you, if it weren't true."

Charlotte reached past her and wrenched the door open, spinning on her heel to lash out in anguish one last time before running to the stairs. "Don't you dare besmirch Papa's good name in front of me! If he was unkind to you, you must have deserved it. You were never what we needed. I was just a child when you came, a child who needed her Papa. But he changed after you arrived. All he could see was you. Even though I could tell he disliked you, you drew all his attention – I had to work for it. I had to charm him, amuse him. But not you, even though you were cold from the start. I was so young, and you didn't even try to like me. So don't you dare to complain about your life with us. You had everything, but neither Papa nor I were good enough for you."

FOURTEEN

Charlotte

Having nowhere else to go, Charlotte stormed upstairs, dashing the tears from her cheeks on the way. She almost bumped into the stocky figure of Ethel on the landing and half expected the maid to turn to face the wall, as the staff had been trained to do at Plas Norton when encountering a member of the family. Instead, the older woman stood her ground.

"My, you're in a hurry, miss. Your room is along there, second door on the right. Nancy's just unpacking your things. There's a bathroom at the end of the corridor; best not to lock the door, it sticks." With that, Ethel gave a peremptory nod and clumped down the main staircase as if she was perfectly entitled to use it.

Charlotte stared after her, tempted to ask if there was a reason for her not to use the back stairs, but held her tongue. She didn't have the energy for another argument, and it wasn't her problem if Rosamund's servants showed so little regard for their proper station.

The bedroom was warm and cosy, the late afternoon sun

lending a rose-gold glow to the pale yellow furnishings. A fire burned in the grate and a vase of fresh flowers stood on the dressing table. Sharp was arranging Charlotte's silver hairbrush, comb and accessories beside it. She straightened, bobbing a curtsy, when Charlotte entered.

"I expect you'll be wanting to change out of your travelling clothes now, miss?"

"Yes, of course. You could hardly expect me to keep them on all evening." She pinched the bridge of her nose and turned her back on the brightly lit window. "I have *such* a headache. I wasn't expecting to have to stay here instead of the main house. I shall go to bed, I think; you can bring my dinner on a tray. And in the morning, as I won't be down for breakfast."

The pause Sharp left before drawing the curtains bordered on insolence. Without saying a word, she helped Charlotte with her buttons, shook out a clean nightdress, and gathered up the discarded clothes from the floor. There was no offer of a hot water bottle or warming pan, and as she sank against the downy pillows, Charlotte winced at the way the maid allowed the door to slam behind her. An overwhelming sensation of loneliness fell on her, like a stone weighing her down. She lay under it as if paralysed.

In London she had mostly been kept too busy to be lonely. Aunt Blanche had so many friends and acquaintances that there was a stream of visitors to the house, and they in turn made frequent calls. Lately they had filled their time with their charitable efforts.

As the afternoon blurred into evening, she tossed and turned under the blankets, missing Venetia's common sense and good humour. She was probably the nearest thing Charlotte had ever had to a best friend. How she could do with her now, to talk over that awful, shocking conversation with Rosamund.

She had said such beastly things about Papa. It really was insufferable, the way her stepmother had behaved. She had sat there, with that self-satisfied smile, caressing that grotesquely shifting mound of a stomach, no doubt congratulating herself at the thought of her own child supplanting her stepdaughter by claiming the lion's share of the Fitznorton fortune.

Charlotte's nanny and governess had raised her on stories of wicked stepmothers: she had known what to expect from the moment Papa's new wife arrived at Plas Norton. Fairy tales had taught her that stepmothers entered previously peaceful homes and subverted the natural order by promoting the interests of their own horrid children over any poor, motherless first daughter. They were bound to exploit the affection of the man of the house, making him turn against his first wife's children. Stepmothers were dangerous, manipulative creatures, and not to be trusted. Charlotte had learned this when she was little, and saw little reason to change her opinion.

Yet she had to admit now, however grudgingly, that Rosamund had not exploited her father's affections by attempting to turn Papa against her. Perhaps this was only because she had never succeeded in presenting him with a child of her own. Being a mother might make a woman much more ambitious, Charlotte imagined. Papa had always been open about his longing for a son to take over his businesses, maintaining that there was no point in trying to teach a girl about them so he would teach his future son-in-law instead. Venetia might insist that women could run their own enterprises, just because she was familiar with one or two who had done so; Papa had known better.

Rosamund had never loved Papa. She'd been too icy to show him any affection. Sometimes Charlotte had been able to smell the tension in the air, like an animal scenting fear. She'd hated Rosamund for that, too. How could a child feel safe or at ease around a woman who always seemed coiled and ready to run? She had instinctively understood the need to endear herself to the more powerful parent. The weak one didn't count.

If Papa had loved Rosamund, she might have earned herself some favour by showing fondness towards her stepmother, but she had always understood that his feelings for his wife, whatever they were, were not love. At least, not the kind of tender, affectionate love that Charlotte had felt for her nanny, who had left when she was six. Nanny had been replaced by the vain, idle governess Mademoiselle Boucher, who had shown little interest in her charge but spent her days reading novels with her feet up, dangling a cigarette out of the window while Charlotte amused herself creating tea parties for her many dolls.

The more she remembered, the more her head pounded. Rosamund's allegations about Papa seemed to echo in her brain, tainting her good memories of him. He had been an indulgent father when he was at home, and she had delighted in her brief opportunities to spend time with him, when he wasn't either away or working. He'd allowed her to buy whatever she wanted when they were in London, and acquiesced when she protested that she couldn't bear to be sent away to school. He had never told her off for being unladylike when, as a little girl, she hurled herself into his arms or clambered onto his lap.

There was nothing she had loved more than his attention: she craved it the way he had craved his cigars and brandy in the evenings. She remembered standing beside him while he read the newspaper, patting his bristly, whiskered cheek, chattering to him and even interposing her face into his line of vision until he shook his newspaper and carried it into another room, locking the door behind him.

"Your father is busy. He's a very important man with much to do," her governess would say, grabbing her wrist and dragging her off to the nursery despite her whining protests, while Rosamund watched them in silence.

Could it really be true that he had beaten her? That he had

kicked and abused her, as she claimed? She couldn't imagine it. Didn't want to imagine it. But there had been times...

No, she couldn't believe it of him. There must be another explanation for the way Rosamund used to stiffen as if she was bracing herself when Papa approached her. And if there wasn't, and he had hit her, then it must have been Rosamund's own fault. With her infuriating lack of spirit or energy, and her bloodless frigidity, she must have brought it upon herself.

Telling herself this was comforting at first, but as she tested the thought, it seemed to settle as uncomfortably as bile in her stomach. She recalled the slender delicacy of Rosamund's limbs, and Papa's powerful size, the strength in the meaty hands that could crack walnuts without a nutcracker. The image conjured in her mind made her nauseous. Those hands on Rosamund's shoulders, showing his possession of her, holding her still, which had thrown Charlotte into a jealous tantrum as a little girl, now seemed to hold an altogether different meaning. One of his power and Rosamund's helplessness. His strength and her frailty.

Charlotte curled into a little ball, resisting the terrible thoughts that challenged everything she'd ever believed about Papa and Rosamund. If she had been wrong all those years about the two people who'd lived with her, how could she ever trust her judgement again?

When at last Sharp brought the steaming dinner tray, the smell of cabbage and gravy made her duck her nose under the blankets. She waved the food away, insisting she wanted nothing more than water, and was too pained to object when the maid tutted and stomped from the room.

A tear dribbled down her nose and she let it flow unchecked. She supposed Sharp *was* cross, after she had made that pointless trip upstairs with the heavy tray. On reflection, the maid was probably just as tired after their long journey as she was herself. Perhaps Sharp was even more fatigued because she'd had to buy their tickets and deal with the porters. Then she had unpacked Charlotte's things and helped her into bed, with no time to unpack her own personal items from her much smaller, battered valise.

This unprecedented attack of empathy aroused a sob of self-pity. With Rosamund and Sharp taking against her, there was no one in the world to care about her any more, apart from Aunt Blanche and perhaps Venetia. Not now that Papa was gone.

The next morning, when Sharp arrived with the breakfast tray, Charlotte roused herself to sit up.

"Thank you, Sharp," she said, pretending not to notice the maid's surprise. "I'm sorry I was out of sorts last night." By now Sharp's eyebrows had climbed almost to her hairline.

"Are you feeling alright, miss?"

"Yes, thank you. My headache has almost gone. I hope to be able to go over to the house and make a start on things today. That is..." She hesitated, unused to feeling the need to treat her staff as if they had emotions and desires like her own. "That is, if you feel up to it after your busy day yesterday?"

"Yes, thank you, miss."

After pouring a cup of coffee, Sharp fished in her pocket and pulled out an envelope and a large metal ring bearing a score or more of keys, large and small. She tucked them at the side of the tray, next to the toast rack and boiled eggs.

"Ethel asked me to pass these on to you, miss. A letter from Lady Fitznorton and the keys to the big house." After a quick, bobbed curtsy she left Charlotte alone.

Charlotte's stomach gurgled as if she had not eaten in days, and a sip of the coffee sent a rush of light-headedness over her. The letter's contents would have to wait until she had eaten. She wasn't sure she wanted to read anything from Rosamund, anyway. Last night Charlotte had threatened her with physical violence – the thought of it made her wince. Admittedly, she had been dreadfully upset, but she was uncomfortable at the memory of her own behaviour towards a pregnant woman who had opened up her home to her. A woman whose food she was now swallowing in a lump that seemed to have stuck in her gullet. She rubbed her breastbone and took several more sips of coffee to wash it down.

With the plate cleared and her cup empty, the letter still waited, biding its time like an oracle anticipating the arrival of a supplicant. Heaven only knew what judgements it might contain. Unable to put it off any longer, she threw down her napkin and tore it open to slip the sheaf of thick white paper out. She unfolded it to reveal Rosamund's familiar, neat handwriting.

Dear Charlotte,

Of all my many regrets when I reflect upon my life, possibly the greatest is that I was not a better stepmother to you. I particularly rue the moment last evening when I allowed myself to be provoked to excessive candour. Please be assured that I had not planned to share with you such intimate details of my life with your father. I do not expect my indiscretions to change your opinion of him; your experiences with him were entirely different, for which I am thankful.

Like you, I grew up blessed with the love of an indulgent father. Mine did not remarry after my mother passed away, and we lived a quiet life, not even visiting relations; consequently I had no experience with young children when I first met you. Nor had I any knowledge of what to expect from marriage, and my initial experiences of it came as such a shock that I spent months too overwhelmed to offer you the attention you needed. In time, with maturity and greater experience of the world, I hope you may begin to comprehend the difficulties of my situation.

Perhaps it would be asking too much to request your forgiveness for either my inappropriate disclosures or for my failure to bond with you when you were a little girl. I should have tried harder to win your affection. Last night, I should not have allowed myself to be provoked. However you think of me, please know that I wish you to be happy, especially in your own forthcoming marriage. I hope you will recognise this as sincere.

Your intention to set up a home for convalescent officers in Plas Norton is commendable, and I wish you every success in your endeavours. If I may be of any assistance, you need only ask. Cadwalader will be pleased to drive you or the officers at any time. I have asked him to convey you to the house at eleven o'clock this morning, and hope this accords with your wishes.

With my sincere regards,

Rosamund

Charlotte folded the letter back up and tucked it back into its envelope. What was she to make of it? Rosamund's expressions of regret certainly appeared genuine. The bitter flood of her lifelong animosity ebbed away, leaving her lost and numb. Having sailed upon it for so long, she was unsure what to feel.

Of one thing she was certain, though: Eustace would be bound for British shores soon, along with several other similarly afflicted officers, and now that she had the keys there was no time to be lost in preparing Plas Norton for their arrival.

FIFTEEN

Charlotte

The air outside the car was cool enough for Charlotte's breath to fog the windows. Leaning forward in her seat, unwilling to miss the first glimpse of Plas Norton, she wiped an area of glass clear using her handkerchief. It was too breezy for frost: clouds of varying shades of grey scudded across the sky, revealing patches of blue here and there like flashes of a jay's wing. On the edge of the woodland across the valley, the reddish-brown fallow deer cropping the grass in the deer park lifted their heads as the car purred past, but remained where they were, too far away to feel threatened. When a pheasant burst from the hedgerow, startled by the passing vehicle, Charlotte started back instinctively before putting a gloved hand to her breast and exchanging a rueful glance with Sharp.

Her next glance out of the window revealed the house, squatting at the end of the valley as if pinned down at the corners by its grey, slate-topped towers. Charlotte's heart gave a lurch.

"I'm back," she breathed, greeting the house which had

been awaiting her return. Although it was hidden at intervals by clumps of oak and wych elm, she took in its details: the triple gothic arches of the front porch, the pointed windows and the crenellations along the roof line. Cadwalader drew the car up just outside the ha-ha and slid across the front seat, leaving the engine running while he climbed out and opened the front gates wide. The metal hinges screeched like an eagle's cry, welcoming Charlotte home.

She half expected to see Phelps, the family's portly butler, waiting inside the porch, but of course there was no one waiting to greet them. It was the first time she had ever seen the house entirely empty. Without any signs of human activity, the grey stone seemed cold and bleak, the windows blank and dark. Weeds had sprung up in the gravel with no gardeners to remove them, and when Charlotte descended from the car she stepped carefully to avoid the rabbit droppings scattered everywhere. She approached the porch, hunching her shoulders against the wind, which whipped through it with seemingly renewed vigour. The largest and heaviest key fitted the lock in the oak front door, and she crossed the threshold into the darkness of the hallway.

Sharp made no attempt to conceal her dismay at the gloominess of the interior. With a shudder, she looked about her and folded her arms against the chill. Charlotte sympathised: she wouldn't be taking her hat or coat off any time soon.

Its emptiness made the hall feel unfamiliar. There were no flowers on the table, only a heavy white sheet to protect it. The chairs serried against the panelled walls were covered in a film of dust, and the air smelled stale and musty. It was so quiet, Charlotte could hear herself breathing: the clocks had stopped ticking without Phelps or the footmen to wind them. She spun on her heel. Had she imagined the sound of tiny, scurrying feet along the corridor? Probably not, to judge by the way Sharp had turned pale. It seemed her first task would be to find mouse traps or get a cat.

A rhythmic squeaking from outside grew louder, then stopped; Charlotte ventured outside and saw a boy on a bicycle handing an envelope to Cadwalader, who had been lifting luggage down from the roof of the car. Leaving the trunk on the gravel, he brought the envelope to the door. She hesitated before accepting it from his outstretched hand, unaccustomed to having things handed to her directly. Servants had always passed things to her on a tray or salver before now.

She gave herself a little shake. This was not a time to stand on ceremony: there was too much to be done. But she fancied she saw an ironic gleam in Cadwalader's eyes before he turned back to the suitcases.

While Sharp directed him to their rooms with the luggage, Charlotte took the envelope to the library. A few chinks of light shone at the edges of the thick velvet curtains, and she strode across the room to open them, surprised at the effort it took to pull the heavy fabric. Weak sunshine flooded in through the panes, which were spotted with long-dry sooty raindrops. She had never before seen any aspect of the house appear less than spick and span. Cleaning the windows would have to be added to her mental list of things to be done before the officers arrived.

Like the hall table, the desk was swathed in cloth, and she dragged it aside to rummage in a drawer for her father's letter-knife. Holding it in her hand, she felt closer to him. How many times must he have opened correspondence, sitting at this very desk? She let her fingers glide along the smooth polished wood of the chair-back, then sank into the seat.

Would he be proud of what she was doing? She couldn't be sure. Perhaps he would have laughed, or dismissed it as a ludicrous girlish notion. He had rarely given her his full attention, but usually listened with only half an ear; a useful trait when she wanted something and he capitulated without thinking, but hardly designed to reassure her of his interest in what she had to say. When he spoke about girls or women at all, it was generally to dismiss them as silly or ignorant. Contemplating the task that lay ahead of her, she felt both to be true in her case. But then, when had she ever had an opportunity to prove she could be something more?

Her discarded gloves lay on the tooled-leather top of the desk beside the envelope. She turned it over, poking the letter-knife into the corner, then stopped, dropping it as if it could combust. Her heart skipped. What if it was bad news? So many telegrams were, these days. It could be a message to inform her that Eustace had died of his wounds, and then what would she do? She drew up her knees in the chair and hugged her arms around them, wanting to put off the moment of truth.

Now you really are being silly, she admonished herself, squaring her shoulders. If it was bad news, better to have it out in the open than to sit imagining the worst. She slit the envelope open with one swift movement, and unfolded the telegram with her breath stuck in her throat.

Arriving Pontybrenin six p.m. with nurse. Send car. VVL

Letting out her breath in a rush, she closed her eyes and tipped her head back with a broad smile. Venetia was on her way – and she was bringing a nurse to help run their hospital. Charlotte's mood lifted: it was as if the sun had come out and given her a new burst of energy.

Delving again into the desk drawer, she pulled out a notebook and pencil and began a list on a clean page, quickly realising it would make more sense if she grouped the tasks under headings. Impatiently, she tore out the page and screwed it up before starting again. Turning the book on its side, she scored bold lines, then added a heading at the top of each column; DO for the practical tasks such as cleaning and airing beds; GET for items they needed to buy or acquire, such as dressings; *DECIDE* for things she hadn't worked out yet. She could discuss these last with Venetia later, such as whether the soldiers should share bedrooms or each have their own. She had made a fair start, frowning with concentration, and was tapping her lip with her pencil when she heard a knock at the door.

"Ah, Cadwalader. How timely. I shall need you to take me to collect Miss Vaughan-Lloyd from the station at six. She's bringing a companion. Given the state of the house, we'll all book into the Station Hotel for the night."

He nodded acknowledgement. "The doctor has just arrived to see you," he said.

Puzzled, Charlotte straightened in her chair. "How odd. I haven't called him. Did he give a reason for calling?"

Cadwalader was no Phelps: he merely spread his hands as if he had no answer, then beckoned down the hallway. "Miss Fitznorton is in the library, Doctor."

Within a moment Doctor Sheridan marched past him, looking short and rotund beside the chauffeur's lean figure. His ginger whiskers and balding pate were exactly as Charlotte remembered them. He had seen her through all the usual childhood illnesses: measles, whooping cough and chicken pox. It was he who had been called to examine her father's body immediately after his death in Rosamund's bed. In those first days afterwards, shocked by grief, Charlotte had sought his advice. Could Papa's death have been anything other than an accident, she had demanded to know. Knowing her stepmother had so little love for him, she had been almost convinced that something untoward must have occurred.

But Sheridan had patted her hand. "I'm afraid your father was not in the best of health. After his head injury in the car accident earlier that day, and, I fear, several glasses of brandy, we should not be surprised that he suffered a fall. His gout had been troubling him, remember, and his blood pressure was high.

The fall may well have been caused by a stroke, even before the fatal injury occurred. It may comfort you to know that he would not have suffered."

Cold comfort at the time, and even now. She pushed the memories from her mind and focused on her visitor, wishing there was a footman who could be summoned to fetch refreshments; it was odd having no help at hand. She could, perhaps, summon Sharp or Cadwalader, but they were busy with their duties and could hardly be expected to rustle up tea when the kitchen range hadn't been lit in months.

"Good morning, Doctor Sheridan. This is an unexpected pleasure." Charlotte reached out her hand and the doctor shook it. The smell of tobacco surrounded him like an aura, another reminder of Papa.

"Good morning to you, Miss Fitznorton. I was passing the Dower House, so called on Lady Fitznorton. She informed me of your return. I fear you find your former home much changed."

"Indeed. But I shall soon make it feel more welcoming again."

"Do you intend to stay long, or is this a fleeting visit?"

"Didn't my stepmother mention the reason for my return?" She leaned her elbows on the desk and steepled her fingertips the way she had seen her father do in the past.

"No. I did think it curious, you coming back before the staff..." He looked pointedly at the dust sheet which still covered half of the surface of the desk, then around the room. She supposed it did feel cold and unloved, with most of the curtains still closed, and no fire in the grate or tea tray to greet guests. Even her father's Tantalus with its twin crystal decanters of whisky and brandy was empty and smothered in a layer of dust.

"I'm surprised she didn't mention that I'm planning to open a hospital for officers." She couldn't help a small, smug smile, but it vanished in the face of his chuckle. Although he quickly stifled it, it felt to Charlotte like a slap. With an effort she swallowed the burst of temper that had sparked in her breast for fear of appearing even more foolish.

"A hospital? What could a delicately raised young lady know about running a hospital?"

"Very little. I shall have to learn."

"Forgive me, but I fear that in your natural enthusiasm to support the war effort, you may have underestimated what is required."

"That is why I am not doing it on my own. I have an admirable source of support in Miss Vaughan-Lloyd, whom you may remember. She has recruited our first member of the medical staff today, a nurse who will be able to guide our endeavours."

"A nurse, or some silly young VAD who thinks she can win us the war by donning a uniform and emptying slops?"

She paused, unsure of the answer. If Venetia had meant a VAD, she would doubtless have said so. "A nurse," she said firmly, then couldn't resist embellishing it, just to assert herself. "A well-qualified nurse, at that."

Leaning back in his chair, he crossed his ankles and fished in his jacket pocket, pulling out his pipe. It seemed he had settled in for a long conversation – one she didn't have time for.

"Do you mind if I smoke?" he asked, his tone suggesting he assumed she could have no objection.

"Actually, I do."

"Oh."

Ignoring the inner voice that quailed at the idea of contradicting a man so bluntly and whispered to her to relent, she held her tongue. It was *her* library now, and he had pooh-poohed her idea, so why should she care if he was annoyed?

"What kind of hospital are you proposing to set up, might I

ask?" His beady gaze fixed upon her, as if assessing her chances of success.

"A convalescent home, rather than a hospital. No operating theatres or… or…" She stopped, realising she wasn't sure what else might be found in a hospital. "Somewhere peaceful for the officers to rest and recuperate."

"I'm glad you've specified officers, not the ordinary Tommies."

"Naturally, and only a few at any given time. But perhaps in the future, who knows?"

"I'd stick to officers if I were you. You don't want any old riff-raff let loose in a house like this. Chaps who know how to behave, that's what you want, if you really are keen on pressing ahead with your scheme. You'll need a doctor in charge, of course." This last was added almost casually, he picked at an imaginary speck of fluff on his trouser leg, then looked directly at her.

She met his gaze. "Do you know of one who might be interested in helping us?"

"Well…" He huffed and puffed a bit, shifting in his seat. "It would be a shame for your scheme to fail due to a lack of experienced personnel. And it is for the war effort, of course. One must do what one can to support the troops. I, for instance, would not be averse to considering the role."

Charlotte folded her hands in her lap. It would not be a bad idea to have Dr Sheridan on board. He was a capable enough doctor, and he was local. They wouldn't need to have him living in, interfering, as would be the case with someone who had to be brought in from elsewhere; and he was old, so there was no risk of him being called up. They could use him as much or as little as they liked.

"Thank you, Doctor," she said. "I shall commend your proposition to my colleague Miss Vaughan-Lloyd and inform you of our decision in due course."

She rose and held out her hand.

He lumbered to his feet. "Very well, Miss Fitznorton. If you are truly set on this proposal, then I shall be interested to follow its progress. Still, if you want my advice, I recommend going back to your aunt and not troubling yourself with making plans which can only cause you a great deal of bother." He had paused in the doorway and looked back, perhaps surprised that she hadn't moved from behind the desk. "Don't worry, I can find my own way out," he said, adding a little more volume than necessary.

"Jolly good!"

Picking up her pencil, she plopped back into her chair and made a show of perusing her notepad until he had gone.

SIXTEEN

Charlotte

Charlotte shivered. The weather had turned dull, and there was very little sunlight to warm the room, despite the tall windows. Her conversation with Doctor Sheridan had left her thirsty, too: a cup of tea was long overdue. Out of long habit, she reached for the bell pull near the fireplace, then remembered it was unlikely that anyone would answer it. Still, she knew where the kitchen was, and how difficult could it be to make a pot of tea? Even quite stupid people were capable of it.

She marched out of the room and along the servants' corridor, past the butler's pantry and the bells high on the wall with their rooms individually labelled, past the doors out to the courtyard with its central iron pump, and into the kitchen. It was light in here, compared with the library: the white tiles reflected what little sunshine there was from the row of high windows, and the pale blue walls above were reminiscent of a springtime sky. It was odd, this room being so cold. Usually there would be a fire in the enormous range at the end of the room, and Charlotte had hardly ever seen Mrs McKie, the former cook, without beads of perspiration on a face flushed red from its heat while working. Now, though, the room was as chilly as the slate slab in the pastry room next door.

Her footsteps echoed on the flagstones as she passed the long, scrubbed pine table and the racks of copper saucepans in a bewildering array of sizes to approach the ranges. The bigger one was impossibly complicated, with chains and bars hanging over it. She could almost smell the roasting pork, its juices dripping into the trough below. Beside it, a smaller range looked no less intimidating. There was an iron kettle, as black as the range, and surprisingly heavy even without any water in it. But the kettle wouldn't be any use if she couldn't get it hot. How would she ever light the range? It was obvious where the coal should go, but even she knew getting a fire going wasn't as simple as throwing a bucket of coal in and tossing a match on top. Besides, she'd get filthy.

Disappointingly, the idea of tea would have to be abandoned. A glass of water would have to do. In the scullery next door, one wall was taken up with a row of three sinks, set into a wooden shelf with smaller shelves above. A rack for plates and bowls stood nearly six feet tall on the adjoining wall. She tried one of the taps. It was stiff, but at last, using two hands, she got it to turn. Nothing happened. She tutted and tried the next one along, but again, not a drop of water came out.

"What on earth...?" Hands on her hips, she glared at the taps. How would she be able to move back into Plas Norton, let alone set up a hospital here, if she couldn't even manage a task as simple as getting water to come out of the taps?

Swift footsteps approached, then Cadwalader appeared in the doorway. "You having trouble, miss?"

"Something's wrong. There's no water. I wanted a cup of tea."

He came to stand beside her and watched as she demonstrated the uselessness of the tap.

"They'll have turned the water off to avoid the pipes freezing over the winter," he said, as if this was obvious. "The last thing you'd want to come back to is a load of burst pipes." He ducked under the sinks and shifted some buckets. "What you want is to turn it on at the stopcock... Try that, now."

A fearsome groaning sound was followed by a series of bangs, a dramatic splutter, then the tap spewed a deluge of brown water into the deep sink below. Charlotte staggered back with a squeal and Cadwalader hurriedly turned the tap down, reducing the flow to a steady, dirty stream.

"We can't drink that! It's disgusting. Whatever has happened to it?"

"Don't worry, miss. It'll be fine. Just let it run for a bit and it'll soon clear."

She was only partly reassured, and still thirsty. "I'll do that, then. Thank you. And then, do you know how I can get the stove going?" Her frustration must have shown, as his face softened, his eyes crinkling at the corners. It was a kind face, one that made her want to lean her head on his shoulder and be comforted.

"If you want to find yourself a cup, and another one for Miss Sharp of course, I can brew up in the motor stable. I've got a little stove in there, and a separate supply of water."

"Really? Oh, thank you. That would be marvellous."

Having located two cups and saucers, she crossed the courtyard towards the motor stable, being careful where she trod as a carpet of slippery green moss had sprung up on the flagstones. There, in Cadwalader's domain, where the smell of hot coals, grease and oil lent the space a distinctively masculine atmosphere, a much smaller kettle was already humming faintly on the stove. Charlotte set down the cups in a clear space on the workbench.

The motor stable was surprisingly large without the car, which was still parked outside the porch, but with the heat from the stove it wasn't as cold as the house had been. Tools hung from rows of nails, and shelves bore various jars, bottles and oilcans. A broom stood in the corner, where brown overalls hung on a peg. Everything seemed neat and in order, much like the driver himself.

Cadwalader seemed unperturbed by her presence in his working environment, even though she was so obviously a fish out of water. As soon as the kettle began to sing, he grabbed a cloth and poured a splash of water into a brown earthenware teapot, swished it a couple of times, then tipped it out onto the floor and spooned in a couple of scoops of tea leaves.

"Hope you don't mind drinking it black, only I've no milk," he said as he agitated the pot.

"You mean you don't have any slices of lemon?" She couldn't suppress a mischievous grin when his expression suggested he thought it a serious question.

"Not quite what you're used to, I daresay," came the dry response as he handed her a cup.

"Heavenly nevertheless."

He seemed to appreciate her enthusiasm. "Help yourself if you want another cup. I'll take this one over to Miss Sharp. Warm yourself up by the stove, if you like."

He had spoken to her as if they were equals, but she was surprised to find she didn't mind. By the time he returned to pour some for himself into a dented, tannin-stained enamel mug, she had made a decision, one that came to her whilst gazing into the glowing coals in the stove and sipping the strong, bitter tea. She had to be realistic about what she and Venetia could achieve before Eustace was due to arrive. She had been thinking the rooms downstairs should be stripped back and turned into hospital wards, but as she cradled the china cup, warming her hands, she realised that wasn't what was needed at all.

After time in the trenches, Eustace and his fellow officers

would need the house to be warm and welcoming, with a plentiful supply of home comforts. Good food, milk puddings, pies and broth, such as they might have had in the nursery, and as much tea, coffee and cocoa as they could drink. A glance across the stable yard made her think about the outdoors. It was a shame the horses had all been bought up for the army and the grooms had gone with them; riding would have been fun.

Fun. That was what their officers would need. A place to enjoy themselves. Recuperating shouldn't be dull and miserable when Plas Norton had all the facilities to make their stay feel like a country house party from pre-war days. With the nurse on site to see to any medical needs, she and Venetia would be free to play the role of charming hostesses. To make it work, she would need to re-engage a number of household staff, ideally people who were already familiar with the house and its workings. But she had no idea where any of the previous servants might have gone.

"Do you think Mrs Longford and Mrs McKie would come back?" she asked Cadwalader, hoping he might know more than Sharp had done about the former housekeeper and cook's whereabouts.

"Your guess is as good as mine, miss. Miss Dawson might be in touch with Mrs Longford. Last I heard she'd gone to help a friend who has a boarding house in Newport."

"If we can't get Mrs Longford or Mrs McKie, do you know of anyone who might be willing to take their place? And we shall need at least one kitchen maid and housemaid. I'd offer the going rate, naturally."

She didn't actually know what the going rate was, this being new territory. Nor was she sure how much money she had, and of course her situation might change soon when her half-brother or half-sister was born. But she'd worry about the financial implications later; Aunt Blanche could help if necessary. Her focus for now must be on getting the house ready for Eustace. She'd make him better if it was the last thing she did.

Cadwalader stroked his chin, reminding her that she hadn't yet spoken to him about shaving off the beard. "You could put up a notice in the post office in town, or advertise in the *Herald*. You might find someone local that way. My daughter Dorothy is nearly thirteen, so I'll mention it to her if there could be a housemaid post going. Not sure if she'll want it, though. Margaret and Stanley work in the factory, so she might want to follow them instead."

Charlotte's face fell. She had forgotten about having to compete with the factory for workers.

"You have a son at the front, I understand. Is it the same son who used to work here with you?" she asked.

"My eldest has joined up. He's not at the front yet, but still training in north Wales. Last I heard he hadn't been given enough food or kit yet; some of the volunteers have threatened to go back home. The one who worked here with me was my second boy, Stan. With only Lady Fitznorton using the car, and that not very often, there wasn't enough work for him here any more. Once we'd finished the repairs on the car after… after the accident… it made more sense for him to find work somewhere else, with more to learn and with people his own age."

His brows drew together in a brooding expression, and Charlotte looked away, remembering the day Rosamund crashed the car. Her father's last day of life.

It still made her jaw clench to think that he might still be here if her stepmother had not driven recklessly that day. She was startled to find that she must have voiced her thoughts aloud, as Cadwalader set down his mug and regarded her coldly.

"You can't think that was *her* fault? I mean, it's hardly surprising they had an accident, given the way he behaved just before they left."

"What are you talking about?"

He turned away, picking up a small brush and sweeping a few specks of dirt off the bench.

"What do you mean?" she asked again, sharply this time.

"He was knocking her about," he said, eyeing her with that frank, cool gaze. He tapped the brush against his other hand for a couple of heartbeats, then shook his head and resumed his sweeping. "He pulled her hat off in the yard. Nearly pulled her hair out with it, mind. He mocked her, made her put my cap on, and threatened her until she agreed to get in the car and drive. Not my place to try to stop him, and not my place to speak about it now, really, but fair's fair. I'm sorry you lost your father, but you're mistaken if you think any of it was her ladyship's fault."

Charlotte took a step back. "Who told you all this?"

"No one told me. I saw it with my own eyes."

Tears threatened. She felt as if she were choking on them. Fumbling, she tried to put her cup down on the bench, but her eyes were stinging too much to see clearly. It teetered on the edge and fell onto the brick floor, smashing into a dozen pieces. She fled, feeling her heart had suffered the same fate.

SEVENTEEN

Maggie

Maggie loved Sunday evenings, once the family was home from the third and final service of the day at Chapel, and their simple tea of sandwiches and cake was cleared away. She and her mother Mary would sit near the fire and knit or sew, or write letters to Leonard. Sometimes Mam would read aloud from the Bible while Dolly practised her neat hemming stitches on a petticoat or chemise. It was the quietness that Maggie appreciated: the soft voices, the scratch of a fountain pen on note paper, the tumbling of burning coals in the grate. Sometimes Dad would join them, sitting in his armchair to read a book by the light of an oil lamp, its warm glow lighting the lines and contours of his face and highlighting the threads of silver in his hair, little Miriam on his lap sucking her thumb while Teddy and Jack read picture books or played with toy soldiers on the rag rug.

With gusts of spring rain lashing against the windowpane, it felt all the more warm and cosy indoors. When her ears caught the sound of tapping at the front door, she paused in her darning and cocked her head, but decided she must have been mistaken. No one in their right mind would be out visiting at this time, not in weather like this. But her instincts were proved wrong when the door opened a crack and Stanley beckoned her, putting a finger immediately to his lips and checking with a sideways glance towards their parents that he hadn't been seen.

Maggie put down her sewing and slipped out of the door.

"It's Jenny," Stanley whispered. "She's soaked through – I've put her in the kitchen. She's asking for you."

Only one lamp was alight in the kitchen. Jenny stood in the shadows, rainwater dripping from her skirt onto the flagstone floor as she held out shaking hands towards the faint warmth of the range. She hung her head, wet tendrils of hair sticking to her cheeks. Realising she was weeping, Maggie crossed the floor in a few short strides and gently took hold of her by the shoulders. The door closed softly behind them as Stan left them alone.

"Whatever is the matter?" Maggie asked, filled with concern.

Jenny gulped down a sob and shook her head. Her eyes were red and swollen, almost shut, her nose scarlet and running. She wiped it on a corner of her sopping wet shawl, and Maggie fished a handkerchief from up her sleeve, pressing it into her friend's cold hand.

"Jenny, you're shaking and soaked through. Let's get this shawl off and get you dry, shall we?"

Jenny nodded, her teeth chattering.

Maggie fetched a towel from the scullery to wrap around her head, rubbing her hair and face. No doubt Jenny's skin would make the towel yellow, as Maggie's own did, but no matter. Maggie's mind was racing with more important concerns as she tried to imagine what could have caused her friend such distress.

"Stay there," she said. "I'll fetch something warm for you to wear, and then I'll make us a pot of tea to get you warmed up.

What were you thinking of, out in this weather without even a coat? You'll catch your death of cold."

Quickly, she helped Jenny out of her threadbare clothes and into her own spare nightdress, then wrapped a blanket around her and sat her down in a chair next to the range. Kneeling, she peeled off Jenny's wet stockings and towel-dried her feet, rubbing briskly to get some warmth into them. Tears poured down Jenny's cheeks all the while and she looked so hopeless and dejected, Maggie's heart went out to her.

By the time she had a cup of hot, sweet tea in her hands, Jenny had stopped weeping, although she still shuddered now and then with the effort of holding in her emotions. She looked drained of energy, and pale despite the yellow tinge from the factory and the blotchiness that had been brought on by crying.

Maggie cut a heel of bread and spread it with dripping, guessing Jenny must be hungry, and felt a fresh wave of sympathy at the speed with which her friend ate. It was criminal how little Jenny got to eat, considering she handed over every penny of her wages to her mother.

"Mam has thrown me out," Jenny whispered at last, hanging her head as if she was ashamed.

"But why? What's happened?"

"It's my fault. I've been stupid."

Tears threatened to spill over again; Maggie crouched beside her chair and caught hold of her hands.

"Whatever it is, things will look different in the morning. You can stay here tonight, and then go and talk to her. She'll see sense once she's calmed down, I'm sure."

But Jenny shook her head. "She won't. And your mam wouldn't want me here either, if she knew. The workhouse is the only place for the likes of me."

"Nonsense! I won't have that kind of talk. What would Len say if he could see you like this?"

THE BROKEN VOW

A bitter grimace crossed Jenny's face. "It's Len who got me into this fix."

Maggie rocked back on her heels. "Are you saying what I think you're saying? Jenny, are you...? Are you having a baby?"

Jenny nodded, then buried her face in her hands. "What's to become of me, Maggie? We only did it the once. If I'd thought this would happen... But I knew how much I'd miss him, and he talked about us getting married. So on the last night before he left, I let him..." Her voice tailed off.

Rising to her feet, Maggie took in a deep breath. Jenny had been foolish, but there was nothing to be gained in saying so. Being thrown out of her home, and the shame that would be cast upon her reputation once her pregnancy started to show, would be punishment enough. She paced the floor, wondering what to do. How would her parents react at the news that their son had fathered a baby out of wedlock? Should she and Jenny try to keep it a secret for a bit longer?

Before she had reached a conclusion, the kitchen door swung open and her mother entered the room, one hand fluttering to her breast as she started in surprise.

"There you are!" she exclaimed. "I thought I'd make a cup of tea. Is that Jenny?" Her face fell as she took in the scene.

"She needs somewhere to stay."

To Maggie's relief, her mother nodded without hesitation.

"Of course. Have you had a falling out with your mam, Jenny love?"

The two friends exchanged a glance; Jenny's eyes brimmed with fresh tears, and Maggie sighed. There was no way they'd be able to keep Jenny's disgrace from Mam now.

Sure enough, Mary pressed them to know what was wrong. Maggie held her tongue, not knowing how to break the news. In any case, it wasn't her secret to tell.

"She's that ashamed of me, Mrs Cadwalader. And I don't blame her. I've brought it on myself. But me and Len... I do love him, you see. And I didn't think it would do any harm. But now I've brought disgrace on my family, and I'm so sorry for bringing it to your door, but I had nowhere else to go and I didn't know what to do."

Maggie saw the moment of realisation in the way her mother's eyes widened and the colour drained from her cheeks. Mary groped for a chair and sank into it, leaning on the table for support. For a minute or two, maybe longer, the girls waited with bated breath while she sat and stared at nothing.

"We have to help her, Mam. She's got nowhere to go. And it's Len's baby. Your grandchild. You have to let her stay – please, Mam."

Mary's eyes refocused, meeting Maggie's gaze.

"Does Leonard know about this? Have you told him, Jenny?"

Jenny shook her head, and Maggie closed her eyes, cursing Mrs Gittins again in her mind for depriving her daughter of an elementary education. Jenny wouldn't have been able to write to Len to tell him. She couldn't imagine how desperate her friend must have felt, bearing the burden of her secret shame alone.

"Let her stay, Mam. I'll send word to Len in the morning. And then, next time he's home on leave..."

To her relief, her mother nodded. But she could tell from her grim face that she shared Maggie's own fear. As one, they both looked up at the photograph on the mantelpiece: Len in his suit, looking so proud of himself, so keen to go and serve his country.

Mary jerked her head towards the door and Maggie followed her into the hallway.

"How far gone is she?" Mary whispered.

"She said it happened the night before Len left, so she must be four months gone, or near enough."

Mary covered her mouth with her hand, looking this way and that as if she couldn't think what to do.

"How could he have been so stupid? To go off and leave a girl to face the consequences of his actions, when he might not —" She broke off, unable to bring herself to say the words, but Maggie knew what she was thinking. Len might not come back. "He'll have to marry her. Tell him that, when you write. I'm too disappointed to write to him myself. Stupid, stupid boy. And she should have had more sense. Has that mother of hers taught her nothing? The first leave he gets, he'll have to make an honest woman of her."

"She can still stay though, can't she, Mam?" Maggie caught hold of her mother's hand. "I don't suppose she'll eat much."

"We'd better hope she does – have you seen the state of her? She looks as if she hasn't had a decent meal in months. It's a wonder she even caught for a baby, she's that thin. And the colour of her – she's even worse than you, Maggie. It can't be good for you girls to be working in that place, with those poisons turning you both the colour of daffodils. Heaven knows what effect it will have on the babe."

"Don't keep on about the factory, Mam. We've gone over it a hundred times. I'll share my bed with Jenny – we'll top and tail, or just squeeze in together. At least that way only one set of sheets will end up turning yellow. I know it'll be a bit awkward—"

"Awkward!" Mary hissed. "It's more than just *awkward*, Maggie. How will we be able to show our faces in Chapel? She and Len could both be cast out for this."

Maggie nodded grimly, knowing this to be true. There had been an unwed girl a while back who'd got herself in the family way, and she had been cast out of the fellowship. "Well then, Mam. We had better pray even harder that he'll come home on leave soon, so he can save the poor girl from ruin."

EIGHTEEN

Charlotte

For the first time in her life, Charlotte threw herself into work as a distraction from her problems. She couldn't change what her father was alleged to have done, but she could change things for Eustace, and thereby for herself. Her powerlessness to rewrite the past didn't preclude her from creating a good future.

Several times each day, the thought of Rosamund nagged at her. She hadn't responded to her stepmother's letter, and hadn't been back to the Dower House. Charlotte, Sharp, Venetia and Nurse Boyle had taken rooms in the Station Hotel in Pontybrenin until more staff could be recruited to make Plas Norton habitable once more.

In one respect, at least, they were lucky. Through Cadwalader and Rosamund's lady's maid, Dawson, they'd managed to contact Mrs Longford, who had readily agreed to resume her duties as housekeeper the following week. In the meantime, there were decisions to be made, and housework to be done.

"You won't be able to stay in your old room," Venetia declared over dinner at the hotel on their first evening.

"Why ever not? It was my bedroom for nineteen years, I see no reason to change it now."

"Because, my dear Charlotte, if the men are fit enough to sleep upstairs, there is the question of decency. You cannot spend your nights in a room adjoining a soldier's bedroom and expect your reputation to remain unchallenged. We'll have to take rooms in the attics with the maids."

This hadn't occurred to Charlotte. Annoyed, she stabbed her pork chop with rather more force than was necessary, making her fork screech against the plate. "I'm surprised to hear you, of all people, worrying about what anyone else thinks. Presumably you weren't concerned about *your* reputation when you got yourself arrested for smashing a window."

"As *I* was not desperate to catch an eligible husband, my participation in political protest was hardly likely to ruin my future prospects."

"I'm not desperate. That's a horrid thing to say." Charlotte laid down her knife and fork, and dabbed at her mouth with a napkin. If she hadn't still been so hungry after a day shaking and folding dust sheets, she would have flounced off in a huff.

"Don't get on your high horse. The point stands: you can't sleep in your old room. Besides the not inconsiderable matter of your reputation, it isn't safe. What if the men sleepwalk? What if they have bad dreams and go wandering about in the night? It's out of the question. What do you say, Matron?"

Nurse Boyle had already finished her meal, having wolfed it down like a starving orphan. She had excused herself earlier by telling them in her broad Irish brogue: "I'm accustomed to being called back to my duties at short notice, so I take as little time as possible over my meals."

Now, she pursed her lips and lowered her chin towards her chest in a most unflattering manner. Irritatingly, she agreed with Venetia. "I see no need to damage any young woman's future prospects when there are serviceable beds in the attics. Your friend has offered you excellent advice, Miss Fitznorton. You'd do well to heed it."

So that was how it was going to be. Recognising she was outnumbered, Charlotte shovelled another forkful of meat into her mouth and fixed her gaze on her plate. However filling the plain wartime fare of meat and boiled potatoes might be, there was a different hunger in her which could not be so easily assuaged: the desire for her life to be normal again. Not the dull, boring life of recent months, but the life she had known a year ago, when she'd been so eagerly anticipating her first glittering Season and everything ahead of her had seemed likely to be good. When her home had felt like home, and Papa had been the backbone of everything.

She needed to be her own backbone now. Doubtless it meant she would need to bend sometimes, because even the strongest spine could snap if pressure was applied too brutally. Swallowing her pride and disappointment along with the last morsel of her dinner, she set her knife and fork down and reached into her bag for her notebook and pencil. They might as well make plans while Venetia was still eating.

"I'd better add moving my possessions into the attics to Sharp's list of tasks," she said tartly, ignoring the way Venetia held up her napkin to conceal a grin. After adding the note, she looked up. "Now, then. Tomorrow, I suggest we give Matron a full tour of the house. The dining room, billiard room and gun room will need to be cleaned..."

"Gun room?" The nurse's eyes had widened in alarm. "We can't allow shell-shocked men to have access to guns, Miss Fitznorton."

"They're only shotguns. For deer-stalking, shooting wood pigeon, rabbit and so on."

"Mother of God, no."

Charlotte tapped the pencil against the page, annoyed at the way her every move seemed to be blocked.

"The men will benefit from fresh air and exercise, provided their physical injuries permit it."

"I agree wholeheartedly with exercise, to be sure. But not with guns."

Charlotte leaned forward. "They are soldiers, Matron, trained in weaponry. I hardly think we need have any concerns as to their competence to handle shotguns."

The nurse did not look reassured. "If I'm to understand this situation correctly... You've decided to establish a convalescent home for shell-shocked officers, with the first of them due to arrive from France on a hospital train in a little over a week. The house is not currently habitable, there's no fresh food yet on the premises, and no medical supplies. The only other medical support currently engaged is a local doctor who's never seen military service. You yourselves have no nursing or even administrative experience. These factors are concerning in themselves, but in the light of this conversation I feel I must ask: how much do you actually know about shell-shock, ladies?"

Venetia shrugged. "How much does anyone know? I wrote to my cousin Doctor Havard about it, and in his return letter he suggested it may be a kind of damage to the brain caused by shell blasts. Which rather leads one to imagine that it is not dissimilar to concussion."

"Sure, you're right. Up to a point," Boyle added, causing the smug expression to drop from Venetia's face as swiftly as it had appeared. "But this isn't a topic suitable for discussion in a hotel dining room, ladies."

Rising, Nurse Boyle picked up her bag and motioned towards the door with a look that would brook no argument. It seemed Charlotte and Venetia would have to forfeit their pudding.

NINETEEN

Charlotte

The three women took the hotel's wide stairs to Charlotte's room. It was larger than Venetia's, and would afford them some privacy.

Charlotte stood beside the window, trying to ignore the cold air seeping in through the cracked pane. Someone had stuffed paper into a gap in the peeling painted frame, but there was still a draught. When her toe scuffed against a threadbare patch of carpet, she sniffed and pursed her lips. Although the room appeared to be clean, it was annoying that Sharp had not managed to secure better accommodation, given the Fitznortons' standing in the locality. She hoped Venetia's room was less shabby: Pontybrenin could never compare with London, of course, but she didn't want her friend to be dismayed by her stay in the town.

Nurse Boyle pushed the door closed behind them and leaned against it for a moment before pushing off to face them with the doleful expression of someone who felt obliged to share bad news.

"Lack of moral fibre. That's what they mean when they talk about shell-shock," she said.

"Lack of moral fibre?" Charlotte repeated. She must have misheard. She looked at Venetia, whose thick fair eyebrows had risen in an expression that mirrored her own.

The nurse nodded. "Don't mistake my bluntness for a lack of sympathy, Miss Fitznorton. Most of them can't help it. I'm not saying they can. Some of them are simply not cut out for fighting, and even if they genuinely want to serve, they find, when push comes to shove – when things start to get a bit too close for comfort – well, they go to pieces, some of them. There's all this talk now of how it might be due to concussion, but if you've been around soldiers for long enough, you'll have seen it before. Leastways, that's what I've heard."

Venetia cleared her throat. "Heard from whom?"

"In medical circles. The hospital where I worked in London was run by a matron who served in the Boer War. She saw it then: men unmanned by what they'd seen, turned into gibbering wrecks. All this new talk, calling it 'shell-shock' – it's just a fancy name for a lack of character. That's what she said, and she should know after all."

Charlotte stood rooted to the spot, as motionless as if she had been paralysed.

"That's why you can't let them near guns. Nor razors, nor knives, and we'll have to watch them with belts or anything else they could use to hurt themselves, because more than likely they won't want to get better if it means they'll be declared fit to serve again. They'll be hoping to convince everyone that they should be discharged on medical grounds so they can go home and let others do the fighting for them. If they can't go home, they may just decide to end it all rather than risk going back."

It made no sense. Why would a fear of being shot make a man shoot himself?

"Are you suggesting these men are cowards?" Venetia's rough use of the word made Charlotte flinch.

"I wouldn't use that word. I don't see that as a helpful word at all, to be sure. It isn't for me to judge. Some men just break down more easily than others, I imagine. They reach the limit of their capacity and they go to pieces because they don't have the stomach to go on."

Her eyes flickered from one to the other, and she wrung her hands a little, as if she sensed the impact her words were having on her stunned audience. "I daresay we'll all be able to make up our own minds about it soon enough, if that's what we're going to be dealing with at your convalescent home. I for one shall treat them the same as any other patient, regardless. Under my care they'll receive rest, good food, hot drinks and plenty of sleep, the same as any man who has actually been wounded in action. No mollycoddling. Sympathy won't help them shape up, and there's no sense in pandering to their weakness by dwelling on their problems. Our focus must be on chivvying them along, brightening their spirits through common sense and good humour, and getting them back on their feet to be useful again."

She paused. "I'll bid you a good evening now, if you don't mind. From what you've told me about the house, we'll need all our reserves of energy for the task ahead. An early night won't do any of us any harm. I'll write some letters and then turn in."

Charlotte merely nodded. She couldn't trust her legs to hold her up much longer; the garish pattern on the carpet seemed to swirl dangerously, but still she didn't move. At the edge of her consciousness she was aware of Venetia closing the door, then felt her hand warm on her shoulder through her black silk blouse.

"It can't be right," she murmured, looking up at Venetia's troubled face. "Eustace is a hero. They gave him a medal a month ago. He can't be both a hero and a coward, can he? And don't try to tell me that isn't what she meant. She may not think it a 'helpful' word, but you heard her. What else would she mean by *lack of moral fibre?*"

The hand on her shoulder gave a squeeze, and she found herself being propelled across the room to plump down inelegantly on the edge of the bed. The mattress dipped as Venetia sat beside her, her lame leg outstretched; Charlotte wondered fleetingly if it troubled her after her day of travelling.

Venetia spoke slowly, as if thinking aloud. "Nurse Boyle advised that we should apply our common sense, so let's do that. If it's cowardice, then it seems odd that the newspapers should suddenly be reporting an epidemic of it amongst our officers and men who, after all, volunteered to serve. The article my cousin Doctor Havard referred to spoke of wounded minds: I think that sounds like a much more plausible explanation than simple fear, don't you? If they really were afraid, too cowardly to go on, then they'd simply run away, not get ill. Or at least, that's what logic tells me. It must be something more: an illness, or some kind of wounding or injury to the brain, just as Doctor Havard said."

Grateful for her friend's reasoning, Charlotte felt some of the tension flow out of her chest, enabling her to breathe again. Venetia had often spoken of her cousin, Doctor Havard, a medical man whose opinions Venetia seemed greatly to value. Charlotte had conjured a mental image of him: balding and rotund like Venetia's father, and perhaps a little stooped from too much time spent hunched over medical textbooks and operating tables. If he considered shell-shock to be a genuine injury, then that was good enough for Charlotte.

"Don't fret, old girl," Venetia continued, draping an arm around her shoulder. "No one shall utter a word against your Eustace in my hearing without getting a very considerable ticking off, of that you may be sure."

The hug brought a lump to Charlotte's throat. "You are a brick, Vee." She leaned her head against Venetia's shoulder, resisting the urge to bury her face there like a child. It was surprising how comforting her friend's simple gesture was, but then Charlotte couldn't remember the last time anyone had put their arms around her, apart from Eustace when he said farewell and kissed her cheek frustratingly close to her mouth, and that had been quite different. That had been exciting and had left her flustered, not comforted.

"Gee up now, Charlotte. What she said is no more than repeating another person's opinion. No one really knows what shell-shock is, not even the army doctors who should be best placed to understand it. We shall apply our womanly intelligence to the problem. There now, that's better. I'm glad to see you smiling again."

Charlotte straightened, allowing her friend's arm to drop. Venetia was right: the nurse's pessimism wouldn't derail her.

"Thank you. You're right, of course. And in one respect, so was she: we *shall* be able to cheer our officers and brighten them up. In a couple of months everything will look different. Eustace will be better after a rest, and the war may even be over. We'll be able to pack up the hospital and use Plas Norton for our honeymoon instead…"

"A few months? Charlotte dear, nobody believes any more that the war will be over that quickly. Many of our people in government believe it could take years."

"Years?" The word fell on her like a body blow, making her want to double over and groan. "I can't wait for *years*. I could be left an old maid if he goes back to fight and something even worse happens to him. He's been buried alive once. What's to say he might not fare worse if he goes back a second time?"

Venetia nodded glumly. "Must you wait until it's over to be married? People do marry whilst they're still in mourning – just without all the folderols. The question is, could you accept a quiet, simple wedding? One without fuss? Knowing he would have to return to the front before you've had the chance of a proper honeymoon?"

It gave Charlotte a hollow feeling to picture it. She'd always wanted a grand society wedding, with a beautiful gown and her mother's pearls, a big church filled with guests, and lavish floral displays filling the air with fragrance. But Papa had always been a key part of that vision. Without him to walk her down the aisle, did all the rest of it really matter? The main thing was for her future to be secure. Her future as Eustace's wife, the fulfilment of all Papa's hopes.

"If it means Eustace is properly mine, then I could. Nothing is as it used to be, in any case. It seems half the world is wearing black these days, and life is too short to wait for what one wants. A simple wedding would be a small price to pay to be Mrs Chadwycke."

"That's settled, then. All you have to do is convince Eustace to bring things forward, as soon as he's well enough." Venetia's cheeks dimpled with the mischievous smile Charlotte had grown fond of. "I'm sure it won't take much effort on your part to charm him into compliance, dear girl."

Stiffly, with a muffled gasp of discomfort, Venetia rose and hobbled towards the door. "I'm going to turn in. You'd better do the same. When Eustace arrives you won't want him seeing bags under your eyes like those: they're so big you'll need a porter to carry them for you in the morning if you don't get some shut-eye."

TWENTY

Charlotte

Charlotte had never used a duster before, or a sweeping brush, or mopped a floor. She'd never realised how much her arms could ache from buffing furniture with a mixture of beeswax and turpentine, nor how the smell would seep into her sore, roughened hands. She hadn't even noticed the housekeeper's cupboard on the corridor upstairs before, with its special sluice for emptying and rinsing chamber pots.

Never before had she climbed a ladder to unhook heavy curtains or flung them over a line to beat out clouds of dust. It had never occurred to her that cleaning was heavy work, that it would involve lifting and bending and moving heavy furniture, or picking up rugs to beat them, or that scrubbing could make her back and knees ache even more than her arms. And yet she was only assisting Mrs Longford and the new housemaid; her main tasks each day were not cleaning but administration, making lists of vital supplies needed for the "Plas Norton Home for Convalescent Officers". She had found that this newly-invented title smoothed the way and made the task of acquiring items much easier than using her own name.

Venetia had been allocated the task of placing orders and calling in favours, a job for which she was eminently well suited. It would have been pointless for her to attempt heavy work, given her infirmity. The telephone proved invaluable to Venetia's efforts, offering a speedy if expensive link to Aunt Blanche and her network of contacts in London, many of whom were married to men of influence, as well as to Venetia's own, more bohemian and politically minded circle.

Soon, deliveries started arriving, bringing medical supplies and foodstuffs as well as special white armbands embroidered with red crowns for the convalescing patients who were due to arrive within days. Mrs Longford made a doughty quartermaster and with her knowledge of the building from her years as housekeeper, she had everyone well organised. Cadwalader was their man on the spot for more local purchases, and for heavier lifting. When a wheelchair arrived broken, it was he who calmly took charge and spirited it away to the workshops to effect repairs.

The arrival of Mrs McKie cheered everyone as it meant they were treated to hot meals instead of managing with cold cuts for lunch, and they were able to move out of the hotel. Charlotte found it strange to climb the servants' stairs to the attics at night, to the room she now shared with Venetia. The floorboards were bare except for a small rug between their beds, and there was hardly any space to store clothes. Each of them had a narrow iron bedstead and they shared a washstand with a bowl and an ewer of water that was icy cold in the mornings, and thus highly effective at waking Charlotte up.

Miss Sharp's role had changed almost overnight. The hectic pace of Charlotte's days and the lack of opportunity for dressing up meant she had little need of a lady's maid. Instead of spending half an hour each morning brushing and pinning up

Charlotte's hair into an elaborate style, a simple chignon or a braid wound around her head was all that was needed. She and Venetia helped each other with any fiddly buttons, so the maid was left with little to do other than mending and dispatching dirty clothes to the laundry. She seemed to resent being asked to help with housework.

"I'm not happy about all this," Sharp complained at the end of the week, while braiding Charlotte's hair ready for bed. Her timing was ill-considered, as Charlotte, exhausted after a long day of unaccustomed physical labour, was too preoccupied with her own aches and pains to feel much compassion for her maid's grumbling.

"Not happy about what?" Charlotte's voice betrayed her impatience. She longed for a soak in a hot, scented bath in a bathroom she didn't have to share with anyone else. She kicked off her shoes, flexed her toes and rolled down her stockings.

Sharp faced her squarely, her hands on her hips. "Miss Fitznorton, you know as well as I do, this isn't the job I signed up for. It strikes me you want a skivvy, not a lady's maid. It's fashion that interests me, and city life, not spending my days in the back of beyond while you dress as plain as a Quaker and ruin your hands doing manual labour. There's no satisfaction for me in working for a woman who never goes anywhere and who dresses little better than I do."

"I can easily give you more to do if you're bored, Sharp. There's no shortage of work to be done, with our first patients arriving tomorrow." Charlotte was acutely conscious of the pungent smell of her own sweat as she unbuttoned her blouse and shrugged her arms out of it. "There are five beds to be made up, for a start..."

"No, miss. I left my housemaid days behind four years ago."

Charlotte raised an eyebrow at the maid's tone. It bordered on insolence, as did her sullen pout. She bit back a stinging rebuke, lacking the energy for a fight.

"You do understand what I'm doing? The task we are trying to achieve here isn't for recreation or amusement. There are war-weary officers depending on us to help them recover from injuries and experiences we can barely imagine. I will admit to being less concerned with fashion in the past few weeks than has been my wont, but given that I'll be wearing mourning for another six months, and the war means there's precious little variety in the shops, there's scarcely any pleasure to be gained from clothes these days even if I had the time to think about them – which I don't."

"Do you intend to go back to London once the men are here and everything is up and running? Miss Vaughan-Lloyd is going back in a couple of weeks, I think, to carry on her committee work. Will you do the same?" Sharp picked up her clothes as Charlotte discarded them.

"No, I don't believe I shall be returning to the city for a while. My place is here."

After everything she had done to make Plas Norton a haven for Eustace, she had no intention of leaving any time soon. Her future prospects lay with him, not in London. And besides, despite her daily frustrations and her protesting muscles, she was enjoying herself far more throwing herself into their new initiative than she had ever done when selling flags or attending tedious bandage-rolling afternoons or knitting parties. She could never have anticipated the satisfaction to be gained from tasks such as cleaning or organising people, but the visible results that could be achieved spurred her on to do more. Seeing the improvements around the house as it was brought closer to readiness each day was surprisingly exciting. She wasn't about to give it up to return to fund-raising or knitting, when the outcome of such efforts was less tangible. Here, at least, she would be able to see how her work benefited Eustace and his fellow officers.

The door creaked open and Venetia limped into the room, looking every bit as weary as Charlotte felt.

"Ah, Miss Sharp. Would you be an absolute treasure and fetch some cocoa, please? I'm quite done in. I'm sure Miss Fitznorton would appreciate some too, after her busy day," Venetia said, flopping backwards onto her bed with a heartfelt groan. "Those stairs will be the death of me," she grumbled as the maid departed, closing the door behind her. "Whose idea was it for us to sleep in the attics?"

"Yours," Charlotte replied drily, padding over to the washstand. The washcloth was cold enough to make her catch her breath as she washed her face, then scrubbed her armpits and rubbed them with bicarbonate of soda while they were still damp to combat the smell of physical exertion. When Sharp returned with cocoa, Charlotte barely noticed, as she was still intent on examining her complexion in the mirror to check for spots. She swept glycerin and rosewater on her face to complete her ablutions.

Venetia stretched out on her bed, leaning her back against the wall. "It amuses me watching you preening yourself in the mirror," she remarked, her blue eyes twinkling over the rim of her cup.

"I hope you're not suggesting I'm vain?" Charlotte protested. She couldn't help chuckling at the way Venetia's lips twitched. "Oh alright, I suppose I am a little. But you must admit I'm not as vain as I used to be. Look at these hands!"

She held one out for Venetia to inspect. Her nails were cut short and the cuticles flaking. The pads of her fingers were roughened and dry, despite her nightly applications of cold cream and lanolin.

Venetia patted Charlotte's hand indulgently. "You poor, downtrodden wretch. No one will ever love you with hands like those."

"Then I shall have to rely on my face to make my fortune."

"If a pretty face is required for that, I should count myself lucky that I've been blessed with independent means."

Charlotte frowned. Did Venetia really see herself as unattractive? It was true that she had once thought of her friend as rather plain, but now that she knew her better, she had come to appreciate the warmth in her eyes and the humorous quirk to her mouth. She might not be conventionally pretty, but she glowed with an intelligence and energy which were in themselves appealing. "I think you're a jolly attractive woman, and any man would be lucky to have you," she declared loyally.

"Oh, dear girl. You are too kind, but I shall never think of myself in those terms. I realise it may seem strange to you, but sometimes I feel I'm not like most other women. I don't really want what they want. The things you want, and most other girls I know. Call me an oddity, if you will. I'm sure plenty of other people do."

Charlotte had finished her cocoa; she set down the cup on the nightstand and burrowed under her blankets, frowning. She had always been utterly sure of her own femininity, and her ability to play on it to charm men, from the time of her infancy when she had been able to get what she wanted from her papa by pouting or flattering him.

"What do you mean, you're not like other women?"

"It isn't that I don't *like* women. On the contrary, I do. I love them. Their softness is beautiful – your awful hands excepted, of course." She smiled. "I especially love how that softness so often conceals toughness and resolve below the surface. Men are the opposite, don't you think? They must appear hard, yet the best ones have a core of tenderness. My cousin Kit Havard is like that, except that he isn't one of those men who tries to appear brave or manly. He is perhaps the most at ease in himself of anyone I know." There was a pause while she sipped her cocoa.

Charlotte was still puzzled. As much as she wanted to

understand Venetia's meaning, she wasn't sure she could. "If you don't feel like other women, why are you so concerned about women's rights? Why should you even care?"

"Perhaps it's precisely because I don't feel I fit the world's general conception of a woman that I can say with a level of rational detachment that it can't be fair for one half of the population to so control the other, without any sensible reason that I can see. Look at you: you didn't have the opportunity of a proper education. Who knows what you might have achieved if you had? There's still time, of course. If you studied hard, you could go to university. Although most of those venerable institutions won't give you the degree you've earned, of course. One must possess a penis for that."

After choking on her giggles, aghast that her friend could say something so shocking with such nonchalance, Charlotte shook her head. "I'd hate to go to university, even if they did give me a certificate. I'm not suited to poring over books. One thing I'm starting to realise, since we began all this, is how energised I feel when I'm *doing* things. I couldn't spend my days reading dry textbooks or writing essays. It would drive me to despair, even if I were clever enough, and I'm quite sure I'm not."

It was the first time she had articulated her feelings about how stimulating action was proving to be, and she felt the words settle comfortably. Even when she made mistakes or things went wrong, she had felt for this past ten days or so that she was moving forward. This was the kind of learning she wanted, the kind that came from experience and observing others, not the academic sort that came from dusty books or pointless debate.

When faced with a situation she was unsure how to handle, she felt her pulse ratchet up and a cold sweat break out between her shoulder blades. She was frequently frustrated by her own lack of knowledge, and there was so much that could go wrong. But often, things went right, and each small success made her feel as if something good was growing inside her. As if, little by little, step by sometimes painful step, even allowing for her failures, she was growing into the person she was really meant to be. A person she'd never imagined she could be, or ever wanted to be until recently. Like a hound chasing a fox, she was chasing the scent of her own potential.

"You're cleverer than you know." Venetia's voice was low and firm. With a grunt she heaved her braced leg back to the floor and clumped towards the doorway, shrugging into her thickly quilted dressing gown. "You know the biggest problem with women?" she asked, silhouetted in the light from the corridor.

"No. But I'm sure you'll tell me."

Venetia turned in the direction of the bathroom along the corridor, tossing her opinion over her shoulder as if it meant little, when in fact it landed heavily and pressed on Charlotte's mind long after she laid her head on her pillow and the light went out.

"The biggest problem with women, my dear, is how vastly they underestimate themselves."

TWENTY-ONE

Maggie

Maggie tucked Jenny's thin arm in the crook of her elbow and kept her voice bright, trying to raise her friend's spirits. Their visit to Jenny's mother had been fruitless, as Mrs Gittins had refused to allow her daughter across the threshold. Immune to Jenny's tearful pleading, she slammed the front door in their faces, and they were left to traipse back to the Cadwaladers' cottage without even being allowed to collect poor Jenny's meagre possessions.

"Try not to fret, Jenny. It will be different once you're married. Len must be due some leave soon; he'll be able to get a special licence, and once you've got a ring on your finger, your mam will change her tune. He'll be extra careful to stay safe now he knows he's to be a father."

Jenny nodded and attempted a quavery smile. She must have known as well as Maggie that everything depended on Len staying alive. At least he wasn't in much danger for now, while he was still training. The worst was yet to come, when he'd be sent to France, or perhaps even Turkey. Maggie was still musing on the frightening possibilities when she heard a sharp tapping sound, as if on glass. She looked around, and realised it was coming from the Dower House.

"Did you hear that?" Their steps faltered by the gate.

"Please, stop! Help me." A faint voice could be heard from inside the house, then the scrape and thud of a bolt being drawn. The front door swung open, revealing the silhouetted figure of Lady Fitznorton, her father's widowed employer.

"Help me!" Wrapped in a robe as if she had undressed for bed, with her brown hair in a braid hanging down her breast, Lady Fitznorton appeared to be almost doubled over in pain.

Maggie's eyes were drawn to the woman's swollen stomach as she took in the scene.

"Are you alright, m'lady?" she asked, pulling down her scarf.

The other woman only shook her head, as if speaking was difficult.

"Is it your baby? Is it coming?" Maggie swung open the metal gate and crunched up the frosty gravel path towards the house, glancing beyond her ladyship into the stillness of the house. "You're not on your own, are you? Where's Miss Dawson? Or Ethel?"

"Not here," Lady Fitznorton managed to say before gasping as if she was gripped by pain.

Maggie sucked in a deep breath. She couldn't leave her ladyship alone in this state; nor could she allow Jenny to witness the distress of labour or childbirth. She knew it would be hard, remembering the sight of her mother's strong labour pains, but at least she, unlike poor Jenny, wouldn't be faced with it a few months from now.

"You'd better get yourself back inside in the warm. I'll come in with you. Jenny, you go and tell my mam. She'll know what to do. And then see if you can fetch the midwife. Quick as you can, now."

Jenny spun on her heel and took off back along the lane the way they had come, her boots clattering on the cobbles and her shawl flapping behind her.

Lady Fitznorton staggered to the foot of the stairs and sank onto the bottom step, her face taut with pain. Following, Maggie hung her coat and hat on the newel post and closed the front door, leaving it on the latch so that Mary and the midwife would be able to come in.

"Come on," she said, trying to keep her voice gentle but firm as she ducked under the other woman's arm and lifted her up. For a slender woman, she was surprisingly heavy and awkward to manoeuvre in this helpless state. "We'd best get you upstairs, I think. Mam won't be long. She's had eight – no, *nine* – babies, so she'll know how to help. There's no need to worry." She hoped this last was true.

Each step was a struggle, but somehow they managed to reach the top of the stairs. Maggie guessed from Lady Fitznorton's wide eyes that she was frightened, as well as in pain.

"That's it, you're doing really well. Nearly at the top; now, which room is yours?"

Lady Fitznorton released her grip on Maggie's arm and indicated the first room on the left before clutching at her again.

Maggie had never seen a room like it. The amount of space in here would probably accommodate most, if not all the upstairs rooms in their tied cottage. Below a painted wooden picture rail, the walls were papered with twisting designs of leaves and flowers in peaceful greens and pink. In the centre of the wall opposite the large window was a wooden four-poster bed hung with pretty chintz drapes. At its foot was an elegant chaise longue, while a dressing table stood to one side with a neat array of crystal bottles, jars, and a silver-backed hairbrush, hand mirror and comb lined up on its polished surface.

"There's a lovely bedroom," Maggie said. She didn't like to

say it was the kind of room she had only ever seen in a book of fairy stories, or in a moving picture.

She hesitated, unsure what to do as the other woman let out a groan that seemed to come from the depths of her soul. When Mam was last in labour, they'd carried on trying to finish the family's ironing before giving up when the pains made work impossible. Maggie had been shut out and given the task of fetching the midwife and an elderly neighbour. Her own role in the proceedings that followed had been to care for the younger children, distracting them with stories and slabs of bread and jam when the animal sounds from upstairs proved alarming. She hadn't seen her mother until an hour or two after little Annie had been born, when she and each of her siblings had been invited to tiptoe into the room to kiss Mam's pale cheek and gaze upon the baby in her crib. Poor Annie, who had been such a delightful baby, and such a dreadful loss to them all, especially her parents.

Things hadn't been the same since Annie died. Mam and Dad only recently seemed on better terms with each other instead of snapping and circling one another like fighting dogs. She pushed the thought away. Lady Fitznorton needed encouragement, not the gloominess that would inevitably result from such painful thoughts.

"Let's pop you into bed now," she said. She wasn't sure if it was the right thing to do, but her ladyship did look tired, and after all Mam was tucked up in bed for days after Annie was born.

Soon Lady Fitznorton was lying back against the pillows, catching her breath before the next onslaught of pain. Her brown eyes were watchful, and well they might be, given Maggie's ignorance of what to expect. Maggie glanced quickly about the room, hoping there might be something to inspire her next steps. A carafe of water stood on the nightstand beside the bed, and she pounced upon it, sloshing it into the accompanying glass. Doubtless childbirth would be thirsty work: people called it labour, after all. And besides, it gave her hands something to do.

"What's your name? And how do you know me?" Lady Fitznorton gasped out.

There was no time to reply, as a familiar voice was calling up the stairs.

"Maggie? Jenny said her ladyship's baby is coming. Are you up there?"

"In here, Mam!" She felt her shoulders drop with relief as her mother entered the room.

Mary's dark eyes took in the scene as she unwound her shawl and dropped her carpet bag in the corner.

"My lady, this is my mam, Mary. Even though you don't know us, we know you. My dad is your driver: Joseph Cadwalader."

To her surprise, her ladyship appeared more alarmed than reassured by this introduction. She rolled onto her side, trying to push herself up on her elbow and swing her legs out from under the bedclothes.

"Please don't trouble yourselves," she panted in obvious agitation. "I'll be quite alright if you can fetch the midwife. There's no need for you to stay."

Maggie and Mary exchanged puzzled glances before Mary put a calming hand on Lady Fitznorton's shoulder.

"Getting up is probably a good idea. Things will slow down if you lie down for too long." Mary's kindly eyes crinkled in response to the other woman's expression. "If that sounds like a good thing, believe me, it isn't really. You don't want to be in pain for any longer than you must be." Putting her hands on her hips, she surveyed the room. "I expect Miss Dawson has put some different sheets aside for your lying-in, m'lady? No sense in spoiling these good ones, is there?"

Lady Fitznorton mumbled something indistinct. It seemed

to Maggie that she had withdrawn into herself, entirely focused on the pain racking her body. Swaying, she gripped one of the bedposts. Her knuckles whitened as her breathing quickened.

Mary, whose gaze had fixed upon the dainty mantel clock, nodded with an air of satisfaction that mystified Maggie.

"Seems to me you'll have that babe in your arms by morning, m'lady. We'll stay until the midwife gets here, if you don't mind. Now, Maggie: let's have a look for some old sheets and towels, shall we? Perhaps there'll be a linen cupboard out on the landing." With a jerk of her head, she indicated for Maggie to follow, then closed the bedroom door softly behind them.

"What's she doing on her own in this state? Nellie Dawson needs shooting, going off and leaving her so late on." She sighed and dragged her hands down her face. "Why did you have to send for *me*, Maggie?"

"Who else would I have sent for?"

"I know, I know, but... Your father was beside himself when Jenny came and told us what was happening. I thought he was going to be sick, he went so green."

"Why would he be upset about her ladyship having her baby?"

Mary cut her a sideways glance, then opened a door further along the landing. It was a bathroom, tiled in sparkling white; she stuck her head in, looked about, then shut the door again.

"He likes her, doesn't he? He used to... used to have hopes in that direction." Mary's face flamed and she bit her lip.

The revelation hit Maggie like a dash of cold water to the face, making her jaw drop.

"But... she's his employer! And he's married to you, Mam."

"Yes, but he's a man, and they don't always think with their heads, do they? Sometimes other parts are in charge."

It was Maggie's turn to blush.

"Oh, there was no harm done in the end. He tried it on the once, but she sent him off with his tail between his legs. We can all count ourselves blessed that she kept him on as her chauffeur. But it feels a bit uncomfortable, me being here. Knowing about all that."

Maggie imagined it would probably feel a whole lot more uncomfortable to Lady Fitznorton. No wonder she'd tried to tell them to go. Following her mother's lead, she started opening doors along the landing until one of them revealed a walk-in cupboard containing a sluice and cleaning materials on one side. On the other, smelling strongly of camphor and lavender, was a linen press with neatly folded bedlinen, towels and, to Mary's obvious relief, a stack of muslin and rough cotton squares, as well as binding cloths, which must have been put aside for the baby. Mary fingered the snow-white linens, frowning, before selecting some sheets and towels, draping them over her arm.

"I was hoping to find some old sides-to-middle ones, but they're all better than anything we've got at home. Criminal to ruin them with a birthing, but what can we do? It looks as if this one has been darned once or twice, so we'll use it and hope Miss Dawson hasn't put some others aside. Right, Maggie: while I remake the bed, you go and put the kettle on. Make some nice, sweet tea: three cups, as we'll all need our energy tonight. And make sure there's plenty of hot water in the copper." She took a deep breath – as if she would rather be anywhere but here – before crossing the threshold back into Lady Fitznorton's bedroom.

Downstairs, Maggie found the kitchen and set about stoking the range and heating the copper. She set cups and saucers on a tray: the best bone china for her ladyship, and a plainer set, presumably used by the maids, for herself and Mam. In normal times she guessed Mam would think it presumptuous to put their cups of tea on the same tray as the gentry, as if they were on a level; it made her smile grimly to herself as she carried the tray carefully up the stairs. Judging by the moans coming from her ladyship's room, aristocratic ladies' bellies were no different from those of working women, and Lady Fitznorton would have more important concerns than sharing a tea tray with the working class.

She was right. Her ladyship didn't even notice the unusual arrangements. Having stripped the embroidered counterpane from the bed and replaced the sheets, Mary had taken a seat near the window with her carpet bag at her feet and her knitting in her hands. Her fingers moved swiftly and deftly, knitting needles tucked under her armpits while her eyes only occasionally dropped to the jumper she was making for one of the younger children. Mostly, she watched Lady Fitznorton, who shifted restlessly, sometimes clutching a towel Mary had tied to the bedpost, sometimes pacing the patch of floor between the bed and the door, often doubling over and groaning or gasping in pain.

Half an hour or so passed before the front door knocker rapped, heralding Jenny's return. Maggie dashed downstairs to let her in.

"Where's the midwife?" she demanded, feeling the blood drain from her face as she peered past her friend into the darkness of the lane.

"She's out at another birth over in Pontybrenin. I left a message with her neighbour, and they'll try to find her and fetch her."

Poor Jenny looked fit to drop; Maggie led her to the kitchen and sat her down with a cup of tea. There was a loaf of bread in the larder, so she sawed off a thick slice and buttered it, trusting Lady Fitznorton wouldn't mind. By her reckoning Jenny had earned it – and a wedge of cheese and a dollop of chutney to go with it, too.

"How is she?" Jenny asked with her mouth full.

"I'm sure she'll be right as rain. Mam says the baby will be here by morning. What about you? You look done in."

"Oh, I'll be alright. I'll go back to yours in a minute. Your dad was pacing the floor when I left. You'd think it was *his* wife having the baby, not Sir Lucien's. He'll be frightened of losing his job, I expect. If she dies, I mean."

Maggie stared. How could Jenny be so matter of fact about death in childbirth? Yet she chewed away with no sign of fretting. Maggie wasn't sure if she would ever face those risks as calmly.

"She won't, though, will she? She's rich; healthy."

"Old, though. Got to be nearly forty, having her first baby. And if the midwife can't come…" Jenny shrugged and licked her fingers, then used the moistened fingertip to pick up and eat the last crumbs from her plate.

"You look like you enjoyed that."

Jenny grinned. "I never ate so much as I have since I've lived with you. Thanks, Maggie. I'll head back now, help your dad and Dolly with the little ones."

Maggie ascended the carpeted stairs with a heavy tread, dreading the moment she would have to tell Lady Fitznorton that the midwife wasn't here yet. She sent up a hasty prayer that Jenny's message would somehow get through.

TWENTY-TWO

Maggie

An hour or more went by. Lady Fitznorton had barely spoken, apart from incoherent mumblings about the pain. Maggie did her best to provide some comfort by talking to her in a soothing voice, patting her hand, and helping her clamber on and off the high bed. She couldn't help but be fascinated by the way her ladyship seemed completely absorbed in the agonising work of her body: sometimes rocking, sometimes swaying or clutching any nearby means of support. A sheen of perspiration made her nightgown stick to her back, and wispy tendrils of chestnut hair that had escaped her braid clung to her face.

Maggie was conscious of her mother's expression growing increasingly solemn as time went on. Now and then Mary paused from her knitting to watch the clock. At one point, she rummaged through some drawers and pulled out a pair of bed socks.

"I'll pop these onto her feet while you fetch some cool water and a cloth for her forehead," she said.

She remembered glimpsing a bathroom in the adjoining

room earlier, and went in. What a room! There was no indoor bathroom in Mary and Joe's cottage on the Fitznorton estate, and it was only in recent months that a tap had been plumbed into the scullery downstairs at Lady Fitznorton's behest. How wonderful it must be to have running water and a private bathroom upstairs: no need to carry jugs of steaming water from the copper to the zinc bath in front of the kitchen fire. Here, there were even taps for hot water as well as cold, and an indoor toilet, as well as a gigantic bathtub that must take gallons of water to fill. At last, she shook herself. She couldn't stand here gawping all night.

As she bathed Lady Fitznorton's forehead, she wasn't sure which of them was more comforted by her ministrations. Certainly, she appreciated feeling helpful, even in a small way. Witnessing the suffering of another human being was surprisingly hard. It tugged at her heartstrings to see a woman go through such torment, with no way of knowing how soon it might end. Her ladyship was pathetically grateful, murmuring thanks as Maggie dabbed her face with the cloth, refreshing and wringing it every few minutes to keep it cool. How Maggie wished she knew how to do more to help.

When the sound of the door knocker echoed around the hall, Maggie started up.

"Perhaps the midwife got our message after all," Mary said. Renewed hope blazed in her eyes. "Go and answer it. I'll watch her."

Maggie raced downstairs as quickly as her long skirt would allow, and wrenched open the front door.

"Dad! What are you doing here? We hoped it was the midwife."

He looked as anxious as she felt. "How is she? Jenny's with the kids, so I thought I might be able to do something to help. I can fetch the doctor, if the midwife still isn't here. But is she... Is she alright?"

"Fetching the doctor would be a good idea." Mary's voice travelled down to them from the top of the stairs as she descended to join them in the hallway, her brow furrowed with concern. "We're looking after her as best we can, but things aren't moving as I thought they would. When the girls first found her, she was already a fair way in, but that was hours ago and although the pains are worse, she's showing no signs of pushing yet."

Her father looked bewildered, as well he might. Maggie sympathised, feeling ignorant of how these things should go.

"The Fitznortons have had Sheridan as their doctor for years. I know where he lives – I can be there in less than an hour if I walk fast." He already had his hand on the garden gate, but looked back to Mary as if wanting guidance.

"Go," she said. "And while you're walking, pray."

Her expression was unreadable as she closed the door behind him, then leaned against it.

"Are you alright, Mam?"

Mary's smile seemed to take a great effort.

"We'd better get back upstairs to her. I just hope Doctor Sheridan knows what he's doing. Oh, and Maggie..." She pulled her close and Maggie laid her cheek on her mother's shoulder, her heart lifted by the fleeting contact.

"Yes, Mam?"

"You're doing well, *cariad*."

As Maggie reached the top of the stairs, she heard the harsh sound of retching, and entered the room to find her ladyship on all fours, throwing up bile into the chamber pot. It took both of them to help her back to bed. Lady Fitznorton had started to shiver, her whole body shuddering even though she was bathed in perspiration. Maggie sponged the trail of bile from her face, her throat choked with pity; Mary gently wrapped her in a shawl.

"I can't go on," Lady Fitznorton wailed brokenly. "I can't..."

She shook her head and cried out, tears rolling down her cheeks and her legs jerking. "The pain," she managed to croak out.

Maggie realised her own cheeks were wet. The night was like a terrible dream. Swept along as if on a tide that threatened to drown Lady Fitznorton in excruciating pain, it was no longer possible to imagine a sweet little baby as its result. Were they going to witness her ladyship's death tonight, and the baby's along with her? Could a human body suffer such tortures as these and recover? She went on dipping the cloth into the basin of cool water, wiping and dipping, all the while holding in her own sobs and longing to run away, to pretend it wasn't happening and forget she had ever seen a woman experience such agonies. If not for her mother's soft, calm voice, she might have bolted.

"I know it hurts, my lady. But every pain brings the end of pain closer. It's desperate, I know. I remember. Your body is opening up. Have faith: your baby will be in your arms before you know it."

Maggie took the chamber pot and rinsed its contents down the sluice in the housekeeper's cupboard, then washed her hands and dried her eyes with a handkerchief. How had her mother suffered so much with her own labours, and then gone on to do the same again, not just once more but nine times in all? A rush of admiration filled her, making tears threaten to flow again. It gave her the courage to return to Lady Fitznorton's side and offer what comfort she could.

It was the middle of the night by the time the doctor arrived. He strode into the hallway as if Maggie was invisible, pausing at the foot of the stairs only to hand her his hat and coat, then puffed and heaved his stout bulk and his leather Gladstone bag upwards, like a steam engine pulling out of a station.

"Let's get you into bed, shall we?" he boomed, setting his

bag down on the chaise and opening its mouth wide. "Bathroom?" he directed this at Maggie, sweeping past her when she indicated its location.

For the past few hours, she and her mother had taken it in turns to support Lady Fitznorton as she heaved and groaned. Mary had insisted she would be better off upright, so Maggie wasn't surprised now to see her mother raising a sceptical eyebrow on hearing the doctor's instructions. Nevertheless, they obeyed, helping Lady Fitznorton into bed, pulling her nightdress down over her calves and then tucking the sheet around her.

In the quiet space between her ladyship's birth pangs, they clearly heard the rumble, then dribbling, of the man pissing next door; the flushing of the toilet, then the rush of tap water as he washed his hands. Maggie had a sudden, hysterical urge to laugh, but forgot it as Lady Fitznorton needed the chamber pot again and was retching into it when the doctor returned.

"Now, whom do we have here?" he asked, his dour glance sweeping over Mary and Maggie.

"I'm Mrs Cadwalader, and this is my daughter Margaret. We've been here since the evening."

"And where is the maid?"

"Visiting her mother, unfortunately." Mary reached for Lady Fitznorton's hand and squeezed it, adding: "Her ladyship has been very brave. She's been pushing for the past three hours or so, but..." She shook her head, and Maggie guessed she was unwilling to say more in front of Lady Fitznorton, who lay with her head flopping against the pillows like a swan with a broken neck.

Dr Sheridan grunted, then delved into his bag to pull out a canvas roll and a pair of thick rubber gloves.

"Lift the sheet and pull her down to the foot of the bed, would you? I need to examine her."

While they manoeuvred Lady Fitznorton as gently as they

could, he pushed the chaise away from the bed and sat upon it, holding up his gloved hands and pursing his lips impatiently.

"Knees up, now. Hold her legs, will you? Keep still, my lady, if you would."

The indignity of it made Maggie hot and cold all over. She held on to one juddering bare thigh while her mother held the other, but kept her eyes on Lady Fitznorton's face. It had contorted in a rictus grimace as she arched her back, crying out in another paroxysm of pain. It made Maggie want to shout at the doctor to stop. Somehow she held her tongue.

"Hmm," he said at last. "Put a large saucepan of water on the stove to boil, would you? And fetch a basin of hot water, and carbolic. We'll see if we can help this baby along."

Maggie had been helping Mary pull her ladyship's nightgown back down over her legs, but at the doctor's words she froze, seeing how the colour had drained from her mother's face.

"What are you going to do?" Mary demanded in a tone that earned her a contemptuous glance.

Doctor Sheridan rose, removed his gloves and barked out his reply. "I shall use my medical expertise to assist my patient, madam. But first I shall wait while you sterilise my instruments in boiling water. Be quick about it, now."

"You go, Margaret. I'll stay here to help make Lady Fitznorton comfortable."

Maggie nodded dumbly and went to the kitchen in a daze. Once more she stoked up the range, adding more coals, then lifted a large copper saucepan down from its hook. Heaving it onto the hob, she filled a couple of enamel pitchers with hot water from the copper and poured them in. While waiting for the pan to boil, she found soap, a basin and towel, and delivered them back to the bedroom.

The doctor had unrolled the canvas package from his bag, revealing a terrifying set of gleaming metal tools. He pulled out a pair of scissors and a peculiar instrument that looked rather like a pair of shiny silver spoons. They had only rims, no bowls, and were joined with a hinge.

"Boil these for at least ten minutes before using tongs to remove them. Fold them into a clean cloth – a pristine cloth, mark you, one that has been boiled and pressed – and bring them back to me."

By the time she had carried out his instructions, her stomach was rebelling against the thought of any of his gruesome instruments being used on Lady Fitznorton. She took comfort, though, that he had not asked her to clean either of the hooks she had glimpsed in his canvas pack.

Wearily, dreading what was to come, she dragged her aching legs back up the stairs. She held out the linen package containing the doctor's device and he took it without acknowledging her before resuming his seat at the foot of the bed.

"Now, then. I'm sure we all could do with some sleep, so let's get this baby out without any further ado, shall we? I shall need you flat on your back, knees up, as you were before, my lady. Then I shall give the little one a helping hand, and you'll be glad to hear it will all be over in a few pushes."

Feeling sick, Maggie stepped forward to take hold of one of the woman's legs, but Mary held up a hand.

"You're not going to just put those inside her. Not without giving her something for the pain." The dark shadows under her eyes showed how the past few hours had wearied her, but her voice was strong and forceful.

"I beg your pardon?" The doctor's cheeks grew livid above his beard. Maggie guessed he wasn't accustomed to being challenged, but then he hadn't met her mother before. No one could defy Mam and get away with it.

"You heard me. Give her something for the pain, or so help me, you'll be needing medical attention yourself."

He spluttered into the shocked silence.

Lady Fitznorton's brown eyes, sunken and hollow, were

fixed on Mary as if she was her saviour. "Oh God, help me," she cried as another contraction took hold and made her gasp and writhe, legs pedalling in her fruitless travail.

"Chloroform," Mary insisted, louder now. "Do you have it with you?"

"Of course I have it. But I cannot administer it effectively without an assistant, and the longer we delay, the greater the risk."

"Maggie will help you. She's a bright girl; tell her what to do, and she'll do it."

He blustered, but pulled a small metal cage and a roll of gauze out of his bag. Maggie watched, fascinated, as he unrolled a length of gauze and formed it into a ring, then made a pad out of some more and used this to cover the cage.

Crossly, as if he were being inconvenienced, he snapped out instructions. "You'll need to cover your nose and mouth with a handkerchief, and hold your breath as you drop the chloroform onto the gauze. We don't want you passing out and giving us two patients instead of one. Now, stand aside and I'll show you what to do."

She felt strangely calm as she watched him lay the rolled gauze and cloth-covered cage over Lady Rosamund's frightened face. Using a bottle with a dropper, he began dripping a sweet-smelling liquid onto the cloth at intervals. Despite her exhaustion, Maggie felt a fresh burst of energy. She could do this. After all these hours, this was something practical she could do: something that would make a difference.

Gradually, over the course of a couple of minutes, Lady Fitznorton's eyelids fluttered closed and her breathing calmed. Doctor Sheridan nodded to Maggie to take over, and she accepted the bottle with a heavy sense of responsibility.

"Not too much," he said. "It's better if she can still push, and besides, too much is dangerous."

He resumed his seat at the foot of the bed and glared at Mary. "I take it I may proceed?"

"Yes, thank you," she said, not sounding the slightest bit cowed by his sarcasm; but Maggie could see by the way Mam's hands trembled where she squeezed the barely conscious patient's hand that she was not as unaffected as she pretended.

While Mary watched the doctor, who had once again lifted Lady Fitznorton's night gown and started fumbling about with his strange, jointed spoons, Maggie kept her attention fixed on her patient. There was a rhythm to it, she discovered, dispensing the drops at regular intervals while holding her breath. Her focus was complete, until she was jarred out of it by the doctor's harsh voice.

"Damnation!" he swore, bending to reach for something on the floor.

Mary's eyes widened in dismay, before closing tightly. Maggie knew she would be praying.

"Slow down now," the doctor growled at Maggie, then raised his voice. "Lady Fitznorton, can you hear me? On the count of three, I need you to push with all your might. One. Two. Three!"

Maggie stroked Lady Fitznorton's damp hair from her brow, murmuring words of encouragement. Her ladyship gave a low, animalistic groan, and soon after Maggie's nostrils flared at the metallic scent of blood.

Doctor Sheridan wiped his forehead against his shoulder and counted again, then as her ladyship gave one last, desperate cry, Mary dived forward with a towel.

Maggie dithered, not knowing what to do. It was as if time had stopped. She bent her head, unable to watch whatever was happening at the foot of the bed.

"Oh, the poor little mite!" Mary exclaimed after what seemed an age.

Maggie's head jerked up. Mary had wrapped the baby in

the towel, and now stood wiping its face. A thick, pulsating blue cord hung down and, as she watched, the doctor's gloved hands, slick and scarlet, clamped and cut through it.

A thin wail sounded and Maggie saw her mother's weary face shine with a smile dazzling enough to light up the room, though her eyes glistened with tears.

Maggie realised she was sobbing with relief.

"Did you hear that?" she whispered against Lady Fitznorton's ear. "Your baby cried."

The doctor nodded, his forehead shiny with perspiration, and sat back.

"Will you stay to deliver the afterbirth?" her mother asked.

"I shall, and then Lady Fitznorton will require sutures," the doctor said, making Maggie wince at the thought of it.

Mary cradled the baby in her arms, murmuring softly and tenderly as she wiped it clean. "Poor little thing is all grazed from the forceps," she said. "But you'll be alright now, *bach*. You and your mammy will be right as rain, you'll see. God be praised." She turned her face heavenwards and rocked the baby in her arms until Maggie had settled the new mother against her pillows.

"Where's my baby? Is it alright?" Although her eyes were still glassy, and her words slurred, the new mother seemed fretful, and Mary hurried forward to show her the baby.

"Here she is, m'lady. You have a daughter. Don't worry about those grazes on her face, they'll soon heal."

"A daughter?" she repeated, smiling though her lips were dry and cracked.

"She's beautiful, isn't she? What will you name her, my lady?" Maggie asked.

She saw Lady Fitznorton's lips move, and leaned closer to listen again, straining to hear.

"Say it again, my lady. I didn't catch it. Ah, Josephine, did you say?"

In the corner of her vision, Mary put her hand to her throat and turned away towards the window. Maggie sat up straight and fussed with the fabric around the baby's chin. "That's lovely. Welcome to the world, baby Josephine. May the Lord bless you and keep you."

"Congratulations, my lady," Doctor Sheridan said, stepping forward to feel for the pulse in his patient's wrist before pulling down her lower eyelids. Apparently satisfied, he declared his intention to step outside for a cigar, and instructed them to call him when her ladyship commenced pushing again.

Maggie couldn't tear her eyes from the baby, wrapped up and blinking in her arms. A girl. Chestnut haired, like her mother, and perfect but for the injuries to her puffy little face.

No doubt Miss Charlotte Fitznorton would be pleased by the news. The whole village had been agog to know whether Sir Lucien's daughter would be usurped by the birth of a brother. But with the arrival of another girl, Miss Charlotte would get half of her father's fortune, which did seem fairer to Maggie than losing nearly all of it to a baby boy. It was extraordinary to think that this little scrap of humanity, with only her squashed, grazed face visible from within the tightly wrapped white towel, would one day be rich beyond Maggie's wildest dreams.

TWENTY-THREE

Rosamund

Rosamund was burning. The pain in her abdomen had worsened each day, an insistent ache that frequently intensified into a sharp stab like a knife in the guts. Her private parts were swollen and stinging, making her flinch every time she was helped to use the chamber pot. Her breasts throbbed only a little more than her head, and any attempt to sit up made her dizzy. However much Nellie or Ethel sponged her down and supported her neck to help her sip water, nothing could cool her or take away the sour, dry taste in her mouth. Her body was unfamiliar, as if it had been switched for this broken one when her baby was delivered.

Her mind was tormented by nightmarish memories. For the first time in years, her worst dreams were not of her husband, but of recollections of Josephine's birth: the tearing, terrifying agony and the helplessness of it. She'd believed she was going to die that night. She'd survived, but from what she'd been told today, confirming her own darkest fears, she wouldn't live long.

Death had only loosened its grip temporarily. It would close its fist to crush her within days.

Perhaps her sufferings were a means of easing her towards an acceptance of the inevitable by making her glad to die. The exhaustion, the physical pain, the mental tortures... would they come to a merciful end when her final moment came, or would she then be condemned to an eternity of agonies as a punishment for her sins? It could be argued that her transgressions in life merited such harsh justice after death. But there was still a quiet voice in her head which whispered that others had done worse. And the greatest punishment that could be meted out to her had already been pronounced, when Doctor Sheridan took a seat beside her bed and told her, without once looking her in the eye, that she must put her affairs in order, for she would not live to see her daughter grow up.

She'd wanted to contradict him, but her body told her he was right: not only the worsening pain, but the intolerable heat and cold, the way her mind slipped into delirious, mad dreams, and the foul stench that seemed to have become a part of her. Deep inside, even without the faint sound of Nellie's weeping from the corner of the room confirming his words, she knew he was telling her the truth.

It was a relief when he left. The sight of him was too great a reminder of the night when he had dragged her child from her body. Her thoughts turned back to it again and again, against her will, probing her mind's wounds. Reminding her of her shame.

Of all the people who might have passed by the Dower House on that terrifying night, why did it have to be Maggie Cadwalader, her baby's half-sister? Would Maggie have treated her so kindly if she'd known? Would Mary, if she'd realised that her husband had betrayed her and that the child she helped to deliver was his secret by-blow?

The irony of it gnawed at her as fiercely as the physical

pains. Providence must surely have been indulging in a joke at her expense that night, to make her feel such an obligation, such gratitude, to the two women who had saved her and Josephine: the two women who had perhaps the most reason to hate them. The guilt racked her.

She owed the Cadwaladers everything, and had tried, discreetly, to explain this to her friend Ewart Rutledge when Nellie sent for him. He'd come all the way from Rosamund's childhood home in Yorkshire to sit at her bedside, his hand refreshingly cool where it held hers. Tears brimmed in his guileless, sensitive blue eyes, sparkling on his lashes.

"Help the Cadwaladers," she'd said. "If not for them, I wouldn't have my Josephine. I might even be dead already."

He'd nodded and squeezed her hand, assuring her that their services would not go unrewarded.

Dear Rutledge. His face was an open book, with his feelings for her on display for anyone to read. His letters over the past six months had been full of reminders of the charms of Ambleworth Hall, as if he hoped to tempt her to return one day. He'd written to her of the future, how he hoped to remarry and make the house they both loved a happy family home once more. He'd never explicitly told her of his feelings or asked her to marry him, but she'd understood. No doubt he'd intended to wait a suitable time, until her baby was born and she could leave off her widow's weeds. Now, that time would never come. If it was a punishment for her sins, to deprive her of that future, it was a harsh one. Not only would Rutledge suffer the pain of missing out on the happiness he had dreamed of, but Josephine would be deprived of the loving care of the mother who had so longed to be there for her.

The question of whether Josephine should know the truth of her origins ran through her mind over and over. What would be the right thing to do? If she had the strength, she could compose a letter to explain everything, and seal it to be opened on her daughter's twenty-first birthday. But she'd struggled even to append her signature to the new will her solicitor had brought to her bedside. She'd never have the strength to write a letter.

Part of her had longed to tell Rutledge, but her exhausted brain couldn't find a way to form the words. How could she ever make him understand what it had been like for her, the loneliness and torment that had driven her into Joe's arms to seek solace? She couldn't rely on anyone's understanding. Moreover, Josephine's security could be destroyed if her true origins were revealed. Her daughter would be better off believing herself to be a Fitznorton, with no evidence to cause the world to doubt it.

They'd brought Josephine to her at intervals, the baby instinctively rooting towards the heat of her mother's body. Perfect, she was – peachy soft with downy dark hair. Even the bruises and rapidly healing grazes from her traumatic entry to the world couldn't spoil her beauty in Rosamund's eyes.

Brokenly, Rosamund had tried to whisper how much she loved her, how she had longed for her and now treasured her; her hopes for Josephine's future happiness; her regret that she'd succumbed to this fever and weakness. When she sobbed too bitterly, they took the child away.

Of all the many tortures she had experienced in her lifetime, the pain of having to leave her daughter was the greatest agony of all.

TWENTY-FOUR

Charlotte

Charlotte hung the earpiece of the telephone back in its cradle, then permitted herself the indulgence of a stifled squeal before looking along the hallway to check no one else had heard.

Eustace was on his way.

At last, everything she had worked towards was coming to fruition. She had to squash her excitement, lest it should cause her to do something foolish in this gleeful moment. Grinning, she felt an urge to pirouette with happiness, or dance a polka. A joyful, exuberant, flamboyant polka, down the hallway and out through the front door. For a dizzying moment, she pictured how it would feel to dance out of the porch, around the side of the house and across the stable yard. She stifled a giggle with her hand, picturing how everyone would stare.

For now, though, she contented herself with a glance around the room, wrapping her arms about herself and giving herself a little squeeze. The Plas Norton Convalescent Home was going to be a triumph. After all their hard work, the house was ready to receive the five officers due to arrive at Ponty-

THE BROKEN VOW

brenin station later that day on a hospital train direct from Southampton. Everyone involved, with the regrettable exception of Sharp, wore an air of pride along with their tired eyes and aching limbs. The large blue and white vase on the central hall table was once again filled with hothouse flowers, and every surface shone. The windows had been washed, and bright sunlight poured in, heralding the hope of warmer spring days to come. Every room was scented with calming lavender; every surface shone. Mrs McKie had been preparing soups and baking bread so the men could be comforted with tasty, nutritious meals, and Nurse Boyle had given them all instruction in rudimentary first aid.

Not that it had been easy. Nurse Boyle had an abrasive manner that tended to rub Charlotte and Venetia up the wrong way, and many an eye roll had been exchanged between the younger women in silent protest against her domineering tone. Given their comparative lack of experience, they'd had to concede on most points, but it hadn't always been easy for Charlotte to hold her tongue. She found she was proud of herself for this unexpected ability to exert self-control where previously, with less at stake, she might have shouted or flounced out of the room in a huff. There hadn't really been time to exercise her temper, though, with such a limited window of opportunity to prepare for the officers' arrival. For once, Charlotte's feelings had had to take a back seat.

It was a shame that the stables were empty now, and the shotguns had been locked away for safety's sake. Still, there was a plentiful supply of fishing tackle for the men to while away hours outdoors. During inclement weather they would be able to distract themselves from their troubles in the billiard room, or they could avail themselves of stacks of notepaper, art materials and packs of cards, as well as the books in the library. Rosamund's piano had been recently tuned, and there was a gramophone, so there would be no shortage of ways for them to fill their time.

Charlotte had expected to feel nervous once the arrival schedule had been confirmed, yet she felt strangely calm. She'd done everything she possibly could to provide a sanctuary, and now the worst was behind them. From this evening, Eustace's recovery would begin. Her future as his bride was assured.

Venetia had suggested a couple of hours of afternoon rest for the whole household, as a reward for their efforts and to freshen them for whatever they might need to do once their patients arrived. Charlotte's initial reaction had been to scorn the idea, but then she saw the sense in it. Who knew when they might get another break? And now that she came to think of it, with the initial rush of giddy excitement wearing off, she was rather tired. Stifling a yawn, she made a final check in the morning room, swiping a finger along the picture rail to satisfy herself that there was not a speck of dust to be found. Satisfied, she stumped, weary but happy, to the foot of the main stair.

A noise in the servants' corridor behind made her turn, and to her surprise, Cadwalader appeared, still wearing his cap. He doffed it hurriedly, seeing her frown, but didn't wait for her to address him first as he should have done.

"Miss Fitznorton, I'm glad I caught you," he said urgently. "You need to come with me at once, miss."

"Whatever for?"

"It's Lady Fitznorton, miss. You're needed." As she tutted with annoyance, he added: "It can't wait."

"I'm afraid it must," she said. Presumably this would be about the baby. She swept aside a pang of guilt that she hadn't yet visited her new half-sister; she had been much too busy for social calls, and it wasn't as if she and her stepmother were close. She had sent flowers and a message of congratulations – even allowing for her reservations about Rosamund's difficult relationship with her father, it was the right thing to do. A note arrived a couple of days ago, requesting that she come to meet Josephine, but she had been too busy to respond. She would visit, of course she would. When Eustace was settled, and she could find the time.

"No, miss. It has to be now."

She arched a brow at his insistent tone.

He faltered, turning his cap over in his hands. He had lifted his gaze towards the ceiling and she noted how his Adam's apple bobbed in his throat. When he looked back at her, there were anxious lines furrowing his brow and his eyes seemed to glisten. His lilting Welsh voice sounded strangely hoarse.

"She's in a bad way, by all accounts. Things didn't go right after the birth, and she's developed a fever. If you don't come with me now, you might not get another chance to make your peace. And I don't believe you'd want that on your conscience, knowing how she did her best to do right by you, even if you didn't always get along."

Charlotte blinked and grasped the newel post, grateful for its solidity.

"Is this a joke?" she demanded. But his expression told her it wasn't. "I'll fetch my coat," she said, and fled upstairs with her heart hammering.

Venetia sat bolt upright in bed as Charlotte burst into their room and dashed to fetch a coat, gloves and hat.

"Where's the fire?" she asked in her characteristically dry voice, brushing a stray strand of hair from her eyes.

Charlotte squashed her hat onto her head and muttered under her breath as she struggled into her coat. "No fire. It's my stepmother. It sounds as if she's..." She covered her mouth with her hand, as if stopping the words could prevent the unthinkable. She didn't like Rosamund, and couldn't deny feeling some resentment towards the sister with whom she would have to share her inheritance; but she didn't wish her stepmother dead, whatever she might have said once or twice in the heat of an argument. Knowing as she did how painful it was to grow up without a mother, and having now lost her father, she certainly wouldn't wish for the baby to be orphaned.

Leaving Venetia to make of it what she would, she hastened to rejoin Cadwalader, who had brought the motor car to the front door and was waiting with the engine running. He was already in the driving seat, not waiting to hand her in to the rear compartment, so she had no choice but to slide into the passenger door beside him and close the door herself. In the circumstances, looking at the grim set of his jaw, she'd overlook this incivility.

He set off at once at a pace that made the tyres skid on the gravel. Tension made her shoulders feel as if they were being wound tightly upwards towards her ears.

"I know things have been difficult between the two of you in the past," Cadwalader began, and her eyes widened at this further breach of protocol. "But if I might presume to offer you a word of advice, miss, I'd suggest you let go of all that now before it's too late. Life's too short to hold a grudge, and she's a good woman. The best kind of woman."

He broke off, his voice catching in his throat. She had the sense that he was holding back a storm of emotion. Of course: he'd be concerned for his future, and for his family, if Rosamund no longer needed a chauffeur.

"You needn't fear losing your job. I've already told you, we'll need a driver for the hospital."

He didn't respond, merely increased their pace. She gripped the leather handle attached to the door, nervous at the speed with which they were rattling past the deer park and woodland. Small stones pinged against the car, and she tried not to think about the damage they could be doing to the paintwork.

Compared with the imminent death of a family member, it was hardly important.

Within a few minutes they had reached the Dower House, pulling to an abrupt halt within a few inches of the doctor's car, which was parked outside. Cadwalader faced straight ahead, his usually pleasant and amiable face now haggard and rough-hewn like a crag of Welsh slate. Neither of them spoke.

There was something unreal about the idea that Rosamund could be dying. Harsh words had passed between them on so many occasions in the past, mostly uttered by Charlotte, admittedly. But the thought of this woman, who had known her since she was small, ceasing to exist... It felt like another blow to Charlotte's world, especially coming so soon after the loss of her father.

Would Rosamund's death be a loss? If she'd been asked a few months ago, when the idea would have been nothing more than a distant possibility, and she'd had no understanding of her stepmother's viewpoint, she'd have said no. Now that she knew more and it might be a reality, perhaps it would be.

The front door of the Dower House had opened, revealing the stout, sombre figure of the maid in her grey dress, starched white apron and lace-trimmed cap. She hurried forward to open the car door, and Charlotte nodded acknowledgement. The maid's name escaped her: Edna, was it? Enid? She still hadn't recollected it by the end of the short gravel path, where she crossed the threshold and was immediately ushered towards the front parlour.

"Isn't my stepmother upstairs?" she asked, confused. Surely, so soon after childbirth, and especially if she truly was dying, she should be in bed?

"I've been instructed to direct you to Mr Rutledge first, miss."

Charlotte frowned, trying to place the name. Who was this Rutledge fellow? She'd never heard of him. Another doctor, perhaps, come to assist Doctor Sheridan? Or a lawyer, come to administer Rosamund's last wishes? There was no time for pondering, as the parlour door closed softly behind her and she found herself facing a stranger. Middle-aged, with fair hair and a grave expression on a lined face, he stood beside the window with his head bowed, but looked up when Charlotte entered. His faint smile of greeting seemed a triumph of good manners over despair.

"Miss Fitznorton, I am glad you came."

"You're American," she said, surprised, before adding as she shook his outstretched hand: "I'm sorry, I don't believe we've ever met."

"No, but I've heard a great deal about you from your stepmother. Won't you take a seat?"

"No thank you. I've come to see Rosamund. They told me..." Her voice trailed off at the twist of pain that crossed his face.

"I'm afraid the news must have come as something of a shock to you, as it did to me. You've been very busy, I understand, fitting out your hospital? She was impressed by that, I hope you know. She thought it a selfless and generous thing to do."

"Did she?" Charlotte faltered. The idea of Rosamund saying such gracious things about her was somehow more troubling than if she had been unkind. "But... Might I ask how you know her?"

"I live in Ambleworth Hall."

"Her childhood home?"

He nodded. "I travelled here yesterday after receiving a telegram from Miss Dawson. Lady Fitznorton and I are friends."

This was surprising. Charlotte hadn't realised her stepmother even had any friends. His shoulders had slumped a little, as if he was fighting exhaustion. No wonder, though, after travelling all the way from Yorkshire.

"I'd like to see her."

"You shall, of course. But first, I must discuss the future with you. Your sister Josephine's future, I mean. I'm afraid your stepmother's condition has worsened rapidly since last evening. It does, in these cases." His face clouded, and she had a feeling he was speaking from past experience.

"Is there nothing that can be done?" Realising she was wringing her hands, she flexed them, willing herself to hold still even though her instincts were telling her to march upstairs and see for herself. She didn't want to hear this bad news from a stranger. Yet if she did go upstairs, and faced Rosamund in her sickbed, she would be forced to confront her feelings about her. She didn't want to do that, either. Not now, when things had been coming together so perfectly at Plas Norton. Perhaps not ever.

"I'm afraid nothing can be done. She is gravely sick," he murmured.

"I think I will sit down after all."

"That might be wise." He scrubbed his hands over his eyes and cheeks, making them rasp softly against his beard. "You're almost twenty-one, is that right? And your father's sister is your legal guardian, along with Lady Fitznorton?"

"I'll be twenty-one in April next year. But what has that to do with—?"

"They had to tell her that she's dying." He paused, emotion twisting his face, then pressed on. "It was the right thing to do, allowing her to set her affairs in order, for the sake of her daughter. Your sister Josephine has no living relative on her mother's side, you understand."

Charlotte nodded. It was a pitiable predicament for any child.

He was watching her with a strikingly direct gaze, the deep

cobalt of his eyes heightened by their reddened lids. "You are Josephine's closest Fitznorton relation, but as you haven't yet attained the legal age of majority, I approached your aunt with regard to Josephine's guardianship. I'm afraid when I spoke to Mrs Ferrers this morning she was unwilling to take responsibility for the child."

"Oh." What could she say? Aunt Blanche had no liking for Rosamund, but she was Josephine's aunt every bit as much as she was Charlotte's. If she wouldn't take the child, then who would?

"Miss Fitznorton, while you are young, you *are* old enough to marry and to have a child of your own. Might I ask if you would be willing to care for your sister?"

Instinctively, she shook her head. It didn't escape her that he didn't look at all surprised by her refusal, and she felt the need to justify it. "I couldn't care for a baby. I wouldn't know where to start. And the hospital takes up every hour of my time. I couldn't be..." She stopped before the word *saddled* could come out of her mouth, unwilling to say it to this sad-eyed stranger. The spring sunshine streaming through the window made a halo of light around him, and this, together with the intensity of his candid gaze and deep voice, made him seem like an angel imparting some holy task or quest. It was as if they were characters in one of the stories Rosamund used to like so much.

"It is unfortunate that your stepmother is not well enough to express her wishes with regard to this matter, but I know from the letters we've exchanged in recent weeks that she believes you to be loyal and loving at heart, as evidenced by your devotion to your father. She told me about your hospital, which suggested to her that there is kindness in you, and determination and dedication. Having lost both of your parents so young, I think you'd know better than most how to rear an orphan with care and understanding. I realise this proposition will have come as a shock to you, but if you and your aunt both refuse to take your sister, there will be no alternative but to have her adopted outside the family. Is that really what you want for her?"

She had been shaking her head throughout his speech. She felt hot and cold; her mouth filled with water as if she was going to be sick, and she swallowed hard, looking instinctively towards the door as if seeking escape.

"I can't do it," she repeated, louder this time, folding her arms defensively.

His disappointment was written clearly in his face. He nodded, as if giving her permission to go. "Then you'd better go upstairs now and tell your stepmother to send her child to an orphanage."

She felt the implied condemnation like a wound; it made her catch her breath even before he turned his back to resume his silent station at the sash window. She wanted to shout at him, to stamp her foot and scream for putting her in this position. It was intolerable. She was too young and inexperienced – legally, still a child herself. She didn't even *like* her stepmother, so why should she assume responsibility for the woman's newborn infant? It wasn't fair.

Assuming he had nothing more to say, she rose and marched to the door, but before she could wrench it open he addressed her again, in that same disappointed tone.

"If you won't look after her child, will you at least ensure Nellie Dawson's years of loyal service are rewarded? Lady Fitznorton has left some financial provision for her servants, of course, but I thought you might offer Miss Dawson a position?"

She nodded. That, at least, did not seem unreasonable. Perhaps Dawson would be willing to help in the hospital, or if not then Charlotte could settle a few weeks' wages on her and provide a glowing character reference.

In the hallway, the maid of all work was waiting, dabbing at her eyes with a handkerchief which she stuffed into her apron pocket when Charlotte appeared.

"She'll see you now, miss." The woman pointed to the stairs.

Unable to refuse, Charlotte climbed upwards with leaden feet. By the time she reached the top, her heart was thudding, but not from exertion. She had never before seen anyone who was dying, and an intolerable weight of expectation and guilt had just been laid on her shoulders.

Only one door on the landing stood open, and as she reached it, Doctor Sheridan emerged, a heavy frown weighing down his familiar features.

"Ah, Miss Fitznorton. Good." He seemed on the verge of saying more, but stood aside and gestured for her to enter the room, then descended the stairs as if he, too, longed for nothing more than to escape.

She tiptoed in, unable to stop herself wrinkling her nose at the foul, sickly smell in the room. Her collar felt too tight; she swallowed hard and adjusted it with her index finger.

Rosamund lay in the bed at the centre of the room, her face sallow against the white sheets. If she hadn't known who she was, Charlotte wouldn't have recognised her. Her cheeks were hollow, her skin blotchy and covered with a sheen of perspiration. At her side sat Nellie Dawson, dipping a cloth in a bowl and wringing it before laying it tenderly on her mistress's forehead. As she approached, Charlotte realised that the maid's face was streaked with tears.

Beside the bed was a wooden crib. Curiosity got the better of her, and Charlotte peered in, her heart thumping as she glimpsed the baby for the first time. Josephine lay with her head turned to one side, her cheek like peaches and cream above the pure white blankets, smooth apart from an angry, hoop-shaped red weal. A knitted white bonnet covered her scalp, so it was impossible to tell what colour her hair was. Her eye was closed and puffy, with a dark bruise to the side. What had she gone through to arrive in this world, to have those visible signs of injury? Despite her previous feelings at having to share her father's property with a girl who had never even known him, Charlotte's heart softened.

Her senses pricked as if someone was watching her; sure enough when she looked up her stepmother's dark eyes were open, bloodshot and sunken, smudged with shadows as dark as the bruise on the baby's cheekbone. Her lips, cracked and dry, moved soundlessly, but Charlotte made out the words: *You came.* Rosamund's eyes fluttered briefly closed, as if in relief.

It was hard to swallow a lifetime's dislike and resentment, but in the circumstances there was little choice but to put aside her pride.

"Congratulations on the birth of your daughter. She's beautiful," Charlotte said, gesturing towards the crib.

She was rewarded with a grudging nod of approval from Dawson. Rosamund attempted a smile. Strangely, she found that their favourable opinion felt good. She had never much cared before whether or not her stepmother liked her. But now her conscience pricked her that she hadn't always made it easy.

"Rosamund, I've come to understand recently that things were, perhaps, difficult for you... I failed to appreciate it when I was younger, for which I owe you an apology." The words seemed to stick behind her teeth; she licked her lips before continuing. "It's too late now, I know that. But I wish things had been different between us."

Rosamund's mouth opened as if she wanted to speak, but before she could utter a sound her eyes rolled back and closed. Her limbs started to shake beneath the bedclothes, and her teeth chattered. Dawson leaned over her mistress, whose slurring and incomprehensible attempts to speak made a lump of emotion wedge in Charlotte's throat. She bit on her gloved fist and squeezed her eyes closed to blot out the distressing sight, turning away and blundering against the crib as she did so.

Two little hands sprang open like starfish above the blankets, and Josephine's head swivelled from side to side. Her pursed pink mouth seemed to be questing. Rosamund had stopped trying to speak, but now lay still and insensible, her breathing rapid and somehow unnatural, it seemed to Charlotte. It was a relief to focus her attention on the baby, whose face had crumpled as she released a surprisingly fierce cry.

"She'll be hungry, poor little lamb," Dawson suggested over her shoulder as she bathed Rosamund's forehead again. "Ethel went down to fetch a bottle of milk a few minutes ago. When she comes back with it, you can give it to Miss Josephine."

Charlotte opened her mouth to protest that she had no idea how to feed a baby, but stopped when another burst of squalling came from the crib. Josephine's cheeks were turning scarlet. Her swollen eyes were screwed up and her chin wobbled as she cried, a harsh sound that tightened the tension in Charlotte's limbs. Instinctively, she reached in to stroke the baby's head, then drew back her hand, remembering the bruises and grazes on each of her temples.

Rosamund roused at the sound of her daughter's cries, her head tossing against the pillow as if some instinct made her want to soothe her child. Dismayed, Charlotte looked to Dawson, who was murmuring reassurances and patting Rosamund's hand where it plucked vainly at the blanket. Rosamund's teeth had started to chatter again; in the moments when Josephine paused for breath, the sound seemed disconcertingly like the rattle of bones.

Dawson tucked the blankets more tightly around her, a desperate look on her face. "Pick the baby up, would you?" she snapped.

Charlotte's mouth fell open at the discourtesy, but she had to let it pass. The baby's fretful cries were harsh enough to make every nerve jangle, even without the strain of witnessing Rosamund's fitful breathing and chills. Feeling all fingers and thumbs, she reached down into the crib and peeled back the soft white blankets before pausing, unsure how best to lift the squalling infant.

"Support her head and hold her close to you, so she can hear your heartbeat. It's alright, she won't break."

Charlotte did as she was told, gathering the baby up and clutching her tightly to her breast for fear of dropping or hurting her. Instinctively she jiggled up and down, relieved as the volume of Josephine's cries diminished a little.

"What happened to her head? It's bruised."

Dawson's lip wobbled. "It was a difficult birth, by all accounts. She got those grazes when the doctor pulled her out. I can't imagine how her ladyship suffered. Then, I'm told, the afterbirth didn't come in one piece. The midwife came not long after the baby was born, but although she did her best, she couldn't prevent the infection taking hold. This – this is the consequence." Choking on tears, she stroked Rosamund's hair back from her forehead.

As if she had realised Charlotte had no milk for her, Josephine's frantic rooting against her breast paused just long enough for her to summon another furious burst of crying.

"Give her your finger to suck. It'll keep her quiet until Ethel brings the milk."

Obediently, Charlotte crooked her little finger and watched, marvelling, as Josephine's mouth latched onto it with determination. The tension in her chest gave way to an overwhelming tenderness that took her breath away. Bending her head towards the baby, she took in the sweet, warm scent of her.

Ethel appeared at her side with the bottle and gave a satisfied nod at the sight of Charlotte nursing the baby.

"Give her this, miss. No, no – keep it tilted up, to stop her swallowing air. You don't want her getting trapped wind."

With the teat safely plugged into Josephine's mouth, Charlotte allowed herself to be guided to a chair where she sank down, unable to tear her eyes from her baby sister. Ethel hovered at her elbow, and Charlotte was glad, anxious in case she did something wrong and inadvertently caused harm. At one point Josephine spluttered, as if the milk was flowing too quickly, and Charlotte pulled the bottle away in alarm, then laughed softly at the way the little mouth pursed up again, seeking more.

She's lovely. The thought came unbidden, and she tried at once to fight it. One brief moment of closeness didn't mean she could care for an infant the way a mother would. There would be someone else out there, someone older and more experienced, some lonely woman who'd longed for a child of her own, who would do a much better job of it. Josephine could be adopted into a family and grow up knowing nothing of the loss she'd suffered as a newborn.

A low, indistinct murmuring came from the bed. Charlotte tore her gaze from Josephine and watched as Nellie Dawson leaned forward to put her ear close to her mistress's lips.

"Say it again, m'lady. I'm sorry, I can't make out the word."

For a moment, the only sounds were the baby's soft gulping and Rosamund's rasping, irregular breaths. Then came a groan, more incoherent mumbling, and at last, just as Charlotte had almost given up straining her ears to understand, a single word.

Joe.

Dawson sat back, startled, and threw a quick glance at Charlotte.

"Did she say Joe? Why would she say that?" Charlotte asked, confused.

The maid seemed flustered. "It's obvious, isn't it? She means Josephine." Her next words landed heavily on Charlotte's shoulders. "She'd be glad to see you taking care of her, miss. Has Mr Rutledge spoken to you about it? You'll know about your aunt..." Nellie sent a sidelong glance towards

Rosamund, clearly reluctant to say more for fear of causing her further distress.

"Oh, no... I don't think I can. I didn't even know how to pick her up, until you told me."

"It isn't as if you'd have to do it on your own, miss. You'd hire a nanny, wouldn't you?" She said it as if it was simple. Charlotte supposed it must appear so to her, and to Mr Rutledge, but still the idea of having responsibility for another human being – for their welfare, for providing for them, ensuring they would be educated and cared for – loved, even – because that would be the most important thing... Could she do all that?

"You plan to have children with Mr Chadwycke, don't you?"

"Well, yes. I suppose so, eventually."

"Then what's the difference? It's just a bit sooner than you'd planned, that's all. That's the way I see it, at least. And I reckon you owe it to her ladyship to at least try, seeing as she tried her best with you when you had no mother to care for you." Dawson sighed, turning to gaze at Rosamund as if the cares of the world were on her shoulders. Charlotte supposed that must be how she would feel, facing the prospect of losing the life she had known for the past decade or more, along with the employer she had served loyally.

Josephine's suckling had slowed; her eyelids closed drowsily and a thin stream of milk flowed from the corner of her mouth. Charlotte lifted her head higher, frightened that she might choke, and mopped her chin with a handkerchief. She was a darling little thing, with that snub nose and her downy skin. So tiny, so vulnerable and in need of protection.

How cruel life was, to steal away her mother before she could form any memories of her. Knowing the void it would leave, Charlotte's heart ached. She sniffed, her eyes and throat smarting with unshed tears. Still, however much she pitied her,

Josephine wasn't her problem. She hadn't asked for a sister, and wasn't even legally an adult herself. With the hospital to run, and Eustace to look after, a child would be a responsibility too far.

She didn't dare look at the baby again, for fear of changing her mind.

"Take her," she said to Ethel, whose face fell as she reached to take the baby from her arms. "I have to go back to Plas Norton. Our first patients will arrive in a few hours."

Cadwalader must have heard her rushing down the stairs, for he appeared in the hallway, squashing his cap down onto his curls before she could don her coat. Wordlessly he held it while she slipped her arms into the sleeves, then followed her out to the car. She didn't look back, for fear of seeing Mr Rutledge's disappointed face at the window.

If Cadwalader could read her inner turmoil in her face, he hid it well. To her great relief his expression was closed, and there was no repeat of his earlier rush to give advice. More than anything, she wanted to put this afternoon aside and focus on her dreams of an unencumbered future with Eustace. She would apply the same determination that had enabled her to set up the hospital to blotting out any lingering thoughts of Josephine's sweet face.

TWENTY-FIVE

Charlotte

It was unusual for hospital trains to travel as far as Pontybrenin. Generally they would disgorge their load of wounded men at the bigger towns. There they could be taken to hospital, if there were sufficient beds for them, or cared for in large marquees which had been set up to accommodate the steady influx of men from the front. As Pontybrenin had only a small cottage hospital, and was further from the main centres like Newport or Cardiff, there had been little need up to now for local volunteers to meet the newly-arrived men from the station. The local St John Ambulance Brigade had offered to provide transport for the officers, but Charlotte had turned them down. The officers were walking wounded; Cadwalader and Nurse Boyle could fit three in the rear passenger compartment of the Wolseley, and Doctor Sheridan could bring two more in his car, with the assistance of a volunteer from the Voluntary Aid Detachment.

For the third time in five minutes, Charlotte checked her wristwatch. Her ears strained for the sound of approaching cars. The days had flown by recently, with a myriad of tasks to complete, and then that painful hour at the Dower House earlier, which had left her with the haunting image of Rosamund's hollow eyes and the memory of her irregular, rattling breaths, as well as the gnawing, bitter feeling that Charlotte had let down not only her dying stepmother, but also her baby half-sister.

A distant rumble made her rush to the window, peering into the darkness. Yes, there it was – the unmistakable growl of the Wolseley, and a lighter, clattering noise that must be Doctor Sheridan's car following behind. The crunch of wheels on gravel, like the sound of the sea on pebbles, told her they had arrived. Which car would Eustace be in? Would he be exhausted after his long, slow journey from France? She ran to the doorway, then paused and dashed to the mirror. Her face glowed with excitement, despite the tired smudges under her eyes after the strain of the past few days. She patted her hair, tucking some stray strands behind her ears, and took some deep, steadying breaths.

By the time she returned to the hall, the other staff and volunteers were assembling to greet their patients. All were wide-eyed and expectant, despite their fatigue. Catching Charlotte's eye, Venetia nodded and gestured towards the front door.

"It's only right that you should be the first to greet them, Charlotte. None of us would be here if not for you." Pulling the heavy oak door open, she stood aside and with a grateful smile Charlotte moved past her into the covered stone porch.

The doctor's car had drawn up behind the Wolseley, illuminating it in a glare of headlights that made Nurse Boyle shade her eyes with her hand. Its rear doors were already open, and Charlotte's breath caught in her throat as she moved closer, unable to see past Cadwalader's broad back as he waited to assist his passengers. Which car had Eustace travelled in? Did he even know yet that Plas Norton was his destination, or that his fiancée was there waiting for him?

The sight of the first patient emerging from the Wolseley made her blood run cold. He was dressed in a stained, crumpled uniform, and one arm was in a sling. But it wasn't his dishevelled state that startled her. It was the way he walked – if the strange, jerking, shambling movements of his limbs could even be described as walking. With every shuffling step, his uninjured arm flung out, and his head twitched as if he had no control over it. It wasn't Eustace, thank God. Surely Eustace wouldn't look like that?

Nurse Boyle had taken hold of his good arm and was steering him towards the door, making slow progress given the almost drunken way he lurched along. Fleetingly, her gaze met Charlotte's, burning into her as if to say: *This is shell-shock. This is what you get when you bring them to your home.*

"Look lively," Venetia hissed into her ear. "There are four others, remember."

Half-dazed, Charlotte realised she was right: she must pull herself together.

Cadwalader was helping a second man out of the car. There wasn't a mark on him to suggest he was injured in any way, but his hands flailed, then grabbed Cadwalader like a shipwrecked man clinging to a mast.

"Step down now. That's right. Keep hold of my arm, I'll lead you in. There are no more steps until we get to the porch; I'll give you warning," Cadwalader murmured.

It hit her like a blow to the sternum: the man was blind. Yet how could he be, when his face didn't appear to be hurt? As if in a dream, she stepped forward to greet the third occupant of the car and peered in to see if he might be Eustace.

The man was huddled into the corner with his chin on his chest, mumbling something incomprehensible to himself. His limbs trembled visibly in a manner she had only ever before seen in the very old and frail.

"Hello...? Are you alright?" She could have kicked herself

for asking such a stupid question. He wouldn't be here if he was alright. She pressed on. "I'm Charlotte Fitznorton, and this is my family's home in Wales. You're safe now. You can stay until you're feeling better. Would you like to come in? We have tea and toast. Or soup, if you'd prefer?"

A pair of haunted blue eyes peeped at her as the man raised his chin.

She gasped. "Eustace! Is it really you?"

His limbs jerked in response, his head seeming to shrink back involuntarily into his shoulders as if he was ducking to avoid something above.

Charlotte reached out. "Take my hand, won't you? Let's get you inside, where it's warm. You're safe here."

Despite his trembling, and the way his head twitched so strangely, he grasped her hand and emerged warily from the car, sending darting glances about him as if to check for hidden dangers. He leaned his weight on her, draping his arm around her shoulders, and she braced herself against the scratchy wool of his uniform, breathing through her mouth to avoid the offensive smell. Due to his twitching and apparent physical weakness, it was surprisingly awkward helping him through the porch and up the shallow step. She decided to lead him into the library, where a welcoming fire had been laid in the grate. He was sure to start feeling more like his old self with a cup of tea to refresh him. But as they stepped into the hallway, Nurse Boyle passed on her way back out to the doctor's car.

"I wouldn't get too close to him if I were you," she said, in that tart way of speaking that always made Charlotte purse her lips. "Follow the others – the VAD and I will get them all stripped and bathed, and their uniforms sent for fumigation. Riddled with lice, they are. The way you've got yourself tucked under his armpit there, it might be advisable to check your hair later, Miss Fitznorton."

TWENTY-SIX

Charlotte

"Now, Miss Fitznorton, this simply won't do."

Charlotte gritted her teeth before turning back towards Nurse Boyle. The matron's constant criticism was wearing thin. It seemed that no matter what she did, or how she did it, Boyle always knew a better way. Did it really matter precisely how a bed sheet was folded, or whether her hair was covered, or whether she wore earrings or a wristwatch? It wasn't as if this was her job, so she didn't take kindly to being treated like an employee. She was a volunteer, and this was her house – well, technically hers and Josephine's, she supposed, but her baby sister wouldn't be able to stake a claim to it for years to come. Straightening, she put her hands on her hips.

"Thank you, Nurse, but I think it works perfectly well. And I'm sure you have much more important concerns than my poor bed-making skills. Like checking Captain Reynolds' dressings, for instance."

They faced each other. If this was going to be a battle of wills, Charlotte had every confidence she would win. Sure enough, it was the nurse who looked away first, and stalked off muttering something about checking on Ambrose. Strangely, though, the moment of victory afforded little satisfaction.

Nothing was as Charlotte had expected it to be. When Eustace had arrived the previous evening, she had been shocked by how changed he was. Perhaps she should have anticipated it, after Boyle's warnings; and of course he wouldn't have been sent back to Britain if he hadn't been in a bad way. But she'd expected him to be a bit melancholy, that was all. She hadn't expected him to twitch and avoid her gaze or to look so – well, so *broken*. He was no longer the charming young man she had met last spring. It was as if the spirit had been drained out of him, leaving him a shattered husk of his former self.

Making her way to the library, where she had glimpsed him earlier gazing vacantly through the window at the intermittent blustery showers shaking the budding magnolia trees, she gave herself a talking to. There was no reason to give up on him. He was tired, that was all, and in need of rest and feminine kindness. Being with her, back in Britain and in a safe and comfortable environment, would reignite the spark that had made him seem so dashing before the war.

Hoping he would be alone so that they might converse privately, she poked her head around the door. He was still there, dozing under a blanket in an armchair, but he wasn't by himself. Hastily, she recomposed her features to avoid showing her disappointment in front of Major Brooks, who was scrutinising the contents of the bookshelves with his back to the door, and the blind Lieutenant Hitchens, who sat slumped in an armchair like a sack of potatoes that had been dropped from a height.

"Good morning, gentlemen." Affecting a bright smile, she pretended not to notice the way all three men jumped at the sudden sound of her voice and her footsteps on the polished wooden floor.

Eustace struggled to rise, as if it cost him a great deal of effort, and she gestured to indicate he shouldn't get up. Crouching at his feet, she patted his hand; her face fell when he pulled it away.

"Don't," he said. In the thin grey daylight from the window he appeared five years older, at least, than the fresh-faced young man he had been when she saw him in August.

"What is it, Eustace? You don't know how glad I am to see you here, safe, after everything you've been through."

His expression was cold, as if he were so worn down by fatigue that he didn't care where he was.

"I shouldn't be here. Why have you brought me to your house? I should be with my men, not with you." His head jerked with agitation.

"But you're not well, dear heart. Your parents wanted to make sure you had somewhere safe to rest and recuperate, so we've rather pulled out all the stops to make Plas Norton as welcoming as we could. You can all stay here for as long as you need, to get yourselves better again."

"Don't lump me in with that lot." Eustace's chin jutted forward mulishly as he tipped his head towards Brooks and Hitchens.

Hitchens gave no response, but it was obvious from Brooks' raised eyebrow that he had heard and took the remark amiss.

"You should have seen some of them on the train," Eustace went on.

Her eyes widened at the way his previously pleasant voice sounded harsh with resentment.

"Nothing but a bunch of maniacs, twitching like puppets. There wasn't an ounce of sense between them. Couldn't get a wink of sleep at night with them all shouting out and screaming: anyone would have thought the Hun had come charging through the carriage, with all the fuss they made. And him – Hitchens, over there – he's barking mad. I heard the doctor saying there's nothing wrong with his eyes, and yet he claims to be struck blind. It's just an excuse for shirking, if you ask me."

Major Brooks had tossed his book onto the table and now sent an arch look in their direction. His hands rested on the tabletop, the fingertips bouncing due to their constant trembling, and Charlotte made herself look away, embarrassed at the thought of being caught watching.

"I say, Chadwycke," Brooks drawled in a low voice. "If you'd seen your brother's brains blown out and splattered all over your face and chest, perhaps your eyes would pack up, too?"

"We've all seen more than our fair share of horrors," Eustace muttered, avoiding Brooks' frank gaze.

"Poor Eustace was buried alive, weren't you, darling?" Charlotte said, trying to help Brooks understand why he was so out of sorts. She reached again for Eustace's hand, but he snatched it away.

"Leave it," he growled, then pinched the bridge of his nose. "My head is pounding again. Leave me alone, would you Charlotte? This constant fussing doesn't help anyone." Throwing off the blanket she had tucked more firmly over his lap, he shoved past her and stalked out of the room.

She rose, taking a moment to fold the blanket again before placing it carefully on the chair, glad of the chance to hide her consternation from Major Brooks. How could Eustace be so changed? The fun young man she had known in London had been ruddy-faced and jolly, with a dazzling smile and eyes that sparkled. They'd had the time of their lives in that brief London Season, drinking champagne and attending glittering parties. She hadn't hesitated when he proposed marriage: Papa had wanted it for her even more than she did, and she had felt it would be the easiest thing in the world to please him. Their future happiness had seemed assured. But this bitter, trembling sourpuss bore little resemblance to the young man she'd promised herself to.

"I shouldn't take it personally if I were you," Brooks said, as if he had noticed her dejection.

She dusted her palms down the front of her dress. "Thank you, I shan't. No doubt he'll feel better after some rest. More like his usual self."

Something flickered across his face, nothing more than an ironic twitch. Did he find her optimism *amusing*? She stiffened. With a toss of the head, she made for the door.

"Might I make a suggestion, Miss Fitznorton? Something that might help things along?"

She paused and faced him with her hands behind her back. "Please do." Her tone was less encouraging than her words, but if he noticed he gave no sign.

"Ditch the black."

"I beg your pardon?"

He took a cigarette from the silver case in his pocket; it was battered and dented, as if it, too, had survived more than a few knocks on the battlefield. She hesitated, seeing how his trembling fingers fumbled. Should she offer to help him light it? But she remained where she was, unsure after Eustace's accusation of fussing if he, too, would take such an offer amiss.

He didn't speak until he had succeeded in lighting it and blew out a plume of smoke that curled lazily towards the ceiling.

"The sight of nothing but uniforms each day is tedious enough. But to see a pretty young woman in such dull attire seems a criminal waste. It's obviously been a few months since your bereavement, given the white collar. So, in the interests of cheering us chaps up, put a smile on your face and wear something bright. The last thing we need is to be reminded of death. We've been living cheek by jowl with it since August."

"I wear it to honour my Papa. He died in August, as a matter of fact."

"I see." He flicked a cylinder of ash into the glass ashtray on the desk. "How old was he?" he asked, squinting through the smoke released from his next deep puff.

"He was sixty-eight."

"Then he was a lucky fellow. It seems to me positively fitting to wear something a tad more celebratory, especially six months on. It would help to brighten this old Gothic pile up a bit, that's for sure. But you must do what you think best."

"I shall," she snapped back, cross with him for the implied criticism, and for not offering any condolences for her loss. She was still irritated when she reached the hallway, and made no effort to hide it at the sight of Sharp dressed in a coat and hat and carrying a suitcase.

"Where do you think you're going, Sharp?"

The lady's maid didn't even have the grace to look sheepish. "I've had enough, miss. I put up with coming all the way out here, and being asked to perform duties that weren't in keeping with my position, when I'm sure you were well aware that I would much prefer to be in London. I've assisted you as best I could, in the belief that we were all contributing to the war. But now that I've seen the men you've brought here, I'm not prepared to take any further part in it."

"What are you talking about?"

Sharp took a step closer, her face tight with anger and dislike. "A bunch of raving lunatics, that's what they are," she hissed.

Charlotte flinched.

"I'm going back to London and you needn't try to stop me."

A growing sense of hysteria made Charlotte want to laugh. "Stop you? What makes you imagine I'd want to do that? If you have such a low opinion of men who have risked their lives for their country, then go with my blessing. But don't expect a character reference from me, Sharp. I fear my conscience wouldn't allow me to recommend your services to anyone else."

It gave her a measure of satisfaction to watch Sharp's face fall before she turned away. It would serve her right if no one in London would employ her. Her eyes narrowed as she watched the maid march out through the front door, instead of via the servants' entrance as she should have done. It wasn't worth making the effort to call her back and remind her of her place; let the baggage go, and good riddance, if her attitude to the officers was so harsh. But as the door slammed closed behind her, Charlotte felt her anger desert her in a rush, leaving her deflated.

Why did everyone and everything have to be so difficult? As if the prospect of her stepmother dying so young wasn't bad enough, especially coming so soon after the loss of Papa, and just when there might have been a possibility of them reaching a better understanding of each other. That in itself was awful, but then the challenge of running the hospital and dealing with the officers and staff was proving much more difficult than she had anticipated. She stomped off towards the kitchens, resisting the urge to scream with frustration, but as she passed a mirror she paused, eyeing her black dress reflected in the glass.

Was Major Brooks right? *Could* she start wearing colours again? The idea of it seemed deliciously daring. For a moment she toyed with the idea, longing to don something pretty and bright. No doubt there would be those who would find it shocking after only seven months. Her lips curved upwards as she enjoyed the prospect of rebelling, but only momentarily, for behind her, reflected in the glass, was a portrait of Papa.

I wish you were still here, she thought. *You'd know just what to do.* Would he be disappointed in her if she stopped wearing mourning so soon? She would rather do anything in the world than let him down. And soon she would be wearing black for Rosamund, too. Why did life have to be so unrelentingly awful?

As her steps took her past the wooden kiosk in the hall containing the telephone, she decided on an impulse to call Aunt Blanche. A few minutes passed before she was connected and her aunt's butler had brought her to the receiver. On hearing her voice, Charlotte felt a pang of nostalgia for her carefree time in London.

"Oh, Aunt – everything is going wrong," she said, dropping her voice even though the walls of the kiosk should prevent anyone passing from hearing her conversation. "The officers are not at all what I expected. They think I should stop wearing mourning because it makes them gloomy..." She pressed on, ignoring her aunt's indignant exclamation. "And Eustace has been beastly to me. Sharp has left me in the lurch, even though I warned her she won't get a character reference, but that's not the worst of it. You know, of course, that Rosamund is dying. I went to see her yesterday and she barely knew I was there. But her friend asked *me* to care for her baby. He said you had refused."

"It's a preposterous notion." Blanche's voice was scathing, and so loud in her outrage that Charlotte held the receiver further from her ear. "Why would she or her *friend* imagine that either of us would want to take on a child of hers, knowing it might grow up to be as unbalanced as its mother? And for them to suggest that *you* should do it! Why, you're little more than a child yourself."

Charlotte's conscience pricked her as she thought of baby Josephine's little puckered face, with the grazes and bruises from her traumatic entry into the world.

"She's Papa's child too."

"Allegedly!"

Her eyes widened. She had once impulsively flung just such an allegation at Rosamund, but that had been in the heat of the moment, when she had only just seen Papa's dead body laid out in the dining room and the pain of her grief was still a fresh wound. She hadn't meant it seriously, and Rosamund's recent assertions had made her begin to doubt her previous assumptions about her relationship with Papa.

"We don't really believe that Rosamund would have betrayed him, though, do we? She was always such a cold fish. Baby Josephine is a Fitznorton, as much as we are, whatever our feelings towards her mother."

"Well, I have no intention of rearing that woman's child, and if you have any sense, you won't either. You owe her nothing."

Charlotte hung up the receiver, more confused than ever. She should have been relieved by her aunt's confirmation that Josephine should not be her responsibility. Yet there was a heavy, sick feeling in her stomach that suggested her feelings were much more complicated.

TWENTY-SEVEN

Charlotte

Early that evening, shortly before dinner, Doctor Sheridan arrived. He and Charlotte followed Mrs Longford to the housekeeper's sitting room, the only room where they could be sure to be undisturbed by one of the officers, who were permitted free use of the drawing room, morning room and library. The doctor's steps were slower than usual, his shoulders slightly stooped. Under his bushy eyebrows, his eyes were solemn. Mrs Longford ducked out quietly to fetch some tea, closing the door softly behind her.

"I'm afraid I bring sad news, Miss Fitznorton."

Charlotte swallowed hard and sank into the soft armchair opposite him. It wasn't difficult to guess what he would say: she had been expecting it, keeping herself busy with tasks for the officers in a vain attempt to stop herself dwelling on Rosamund's suffering and imminent end. Now she dreaded hearing the words the doctor was about to say.

"My stepmother?"

"I'm afraid so. She passed away late this afternoon. There

was nothing more that could have been done. Please accept my condolences."

Even though she'd been expecting this news, hearing it now made Charlotte's stomach drop. "You mustn't blame yourself," she found herself saying, struck by his regretful expression. It must be difficult for him, as he had delivered Rosamund's baby.

He scowled. "I assure you, I do not. Regrettably, childbirth is not without its risks, and especially at Lady Fitznorton's age. If not for my intervention, the child would likely have died, as well as the mother. No, I don't blame myself. Not at all."

There was an awkward silence. Charlotte felt a sudden chill, as if a draught had passed through the room. Doctor Sheridan might not blame himself, but she felt a heavy sense of regret. Even though she had never felt close to her stepmother, she'd been the nearest Charlotte had ever known to a maternal figure. Now, just when she had started to gain some insights into Rosamund's point of view, and a more adult understanding of her situation, the opportunity to see if their relationship might change had been denied them.

Since leaving her bedside the day before, the question of whether she should have tried harder had crossed Charlotte's mind several times, causing her to toss and turn during the night, hardly able to sleep. There had been times in the past, she knew, when she had been deliberately unkind, finding Rosamund's nervousness embarrassing. As a small child, her almost idolatrous love for her father had left no room for rivals for his attention, and there had always been something about Rosamund that made her uneasy: a child's instinctive mistrust of adult weakness, perhaps; a deep sense that the woman would rather be anywhere than at Plas Norton.

"I imagine you are aware of her last wishes?" the doctor asked, rousing her from her reverie.

She gulped, hoping he would not expect her to take responsibility for the child.

"I met with one of the executors of her estate, an American fellow…" He paused, frowning, as if unable to recall the name.

"Mr Rutledge?"

"That's the fellow. He told me she wished to be buried with her parents in Yorkshire. Somewhat irregular, I feel. I'd naturally expected that she would be laid to rest in the Fitznorton tomb in the churchyard at Pontybrenin."

"Will Mr Rutledge make the arrangements?"

"I believe so, provided you are willing for him to assume responsibility."

She nodded, glad to pass on the burden of arranging a funeral when she already had so much on her mind and relieved to be spared the prospect of having Papa's tomb reopened so soon.

"And… the child?"

"Ah, yes," he said, as if Rosamund's baby was of little consequence. "It's being cared for by the maids, but they will have to find alternative employment now. It will be adopted, I imagine. Rutledge led me to believe that Lady Fitznorton's preferred choice of guardian was unwilling to take on the burden, so an alternative must be found. There are organisations which can help in such cases. Reverend Butts and his wife may be able to make some suggestions. A shame it wasn't a boy, they are always more sought-after by couples wishing to adopt."

Charlotte's cheeks felt hot.

"Well, that's that, then. A pity how it all turned out in the end." He patted his thighs and rose stiffly to his feet, just as Mrs Longford returned with a tray.

The housekeeper's expression of polite interest changed in an instant when Charlotte explained the reason for the doctor's visit.

"That is sad news. I know Mrs McKie will be as sorry as I am. I've been praying for her since I heard she was ill. Lady Fitznorton was a kind soul. A gentle character who'd never hurt a fly. What a shame she won't get a chance to see her daughter grow up."

"Thank you, Mrs Longford," Charlotte said, feeling another twinge of guilt for some of the less generous thoughts she had held about Rosamund over the years. "My stepmother was keen that Dawson should be provided for, and in the light of Sharp's departure I thought I might offer her a position. What are your thoughts?"

"That sounds like an ideal solution, miss, if she'll accept. It would be good to have Miss Dawson back at the house again. A silver lining to a very dark cloud."

Charlotte nodded.

"Should I tell Mrs McKie that you'll be joining us for dinner, Doctor?" Mrs Longford asked, busying herself setting the cups into their saucers and pouring the steaming tea through the silver strainer.

The old man's eyes brightened under his bushy brows. "I'd be glad to," he boomed, settling back into his chair. Picking up his cup and saucer, he sent Charlotte a calculating look. "It will give me a useful opportunity to inspect your little hospital, Miss Fitznorton, and to see for myself what this 'shell-shock' is all about."

By the time she crawled into bed that night, Charlotte felt exhausted. Glad of the warmth of her hot water bottle against her feet, she wriggled her toes and allowed herself to feel a pang of longing for the comfort of her former bedroom. This hard, narrow bed with its rough, darned sheets was so unwelcoming compared with what she was used to; the room so sparse and cold. She hadn't bothered putting her hair into curl papers, as Sharp would have done, but merely twisted it into a long braid ready for sleep.

After the doctor's sombre news about Rosamund, which

had left her spirits low, the evening had been a slog, not helped by Sheridan's attitude towards their patients.

"That was a most illuminating experience," he had remarked as he donned his hat and coat after dinner. He had made no effort to appear sympathetic during the meal, his brows beetling together when he wasn't lifting one of them in a sneering arc of disapproval. He looked crossly at Captain Reynolds, whose failure to respond to the doctor's questions was a result of his continuing inability to speak. Reynolds spent most of the mealtime gazing into the distance in a world of his own. The doctor had to acknowledge his need for help to cut his food, given the state of his hands, which were bandaged and still recovering from frostbite. Sheridan had no such qualms about Second Lieutenant Ambrose, nicknamed Jam by his fellow officers, whose palsied limb jerks and exaggerated facial tics meant he couldn't feed himself without sending forkfuls of food in all directions. Jam had been the recipient of some particularly dark scowls, whilst Eustace and Major Brooks had been subjected to sniffs of contempt when Sheridan noticed the way their fingers trembled and their heads ducked at any unexpected noise.

"I've no doubt their mental and physical conditions will improve rapidly, now that they are able to rest," Charlotte had said with a confidence she no longer felt as strongly as she had done before witnessing the effects of the illness.

"You mustn't pander to these mental cases, you know. They're swinging the lead, the lot of them. It's clear that they're putting on a show to win sympathy. The best way to deal with it, Miss Fitznorton, is to chivvy them along. Don't let them get away with malingering. Remind them that their place is back in the line beside their men, doing their bit. I gather electric shock treatment is being used in France with some success. We should look into it. Perhaps it will be the encouragement they need to pull themselves together."

She reported this to Venetia, who was still awake and sitting up in the adjacent bed as she stuck rigidly to her routine of reading at least one chapter of a book before settling for sleep.

"Do you think it could work, Vee?" she asked at last. Her own instincts were against the idea of a treatment that sounded at best painful, at worst inhumane.

Venetia pulled a face. "I'm no medic, but I fail to see how torturing a chap could cheer him up."

"I know. I feel the same."

"I could ask my cousin about it, if you like? I'd trust his medical opinion over anyone's."

"Would you mind? It's so difficult to know what to do for the best."

"To hear you sigh, anyone would think you have the weight of the world on your shoulders." Giving up on her book, Venetia slipped a bookmark between its pages and snapped it closed before setting it down on her nightstand. She shivered after shrugging off her warm knitted bed-jacket, then huddled under the bedclothes, facing Charlotte. Her expectant expression where she peeped out from under the blankets made it impossible for Charlotte to remain silent for long.

"It's just been such a difficult day. First Nurse Boyle with her demands..."

Venetia tutted impatiently.

"... And of course the news about Rosamund."

"Ah, yes. That *is* terribly sad. But there was little love lost between you, as I understood it?"

"That's true. The trouble is, now that she's gone... I can't help wondering if I misjudged her in some respects." She was trying to express her doubts cautiously, unwilling to make more of it than necessary. Sensitive to how her words were being received, her heartbeat picked up a gear at the way Venetia pursed her lips.

"What are you thinking?" Charlotte asked, anxious to know what her friend's expression meant. So far away from her aunt, and without a parent to guide her, she had come to rely on Venetia's judgement. The sense that she had somehow made a misstep was unsettling.

"Are you sure you want to know my thoughts on the matter?"

"I wouldn't have asked otherwise."

Venetia sniffed and rubbed her face, as if she was tired of holding back. "Very well. Given that my godmother has always been kind to me, I was shocked to hear that she wouldn't take your sister. I had thought that, whatever the difficulties between her and her brother's wife, she would have more loyalty to the Fitznorton name. And then, for you to refuse, too... You're at liberty to do so, of course, and I appreciate that a baby is a daunting responsibility. Yet I find it odd that you're willing to open your house to trained fighting men whom you've never met before and whom some see as madmen, but will allow your only sister, an innocent infant, to be sent away to strangers."

Venetia shrugged, sending an unapologetic glance towards Charlotte's stricken face. "You must admit it is a trifle ironic. But then, your motivation for helping the men is a selfish one, as it will expedite your forthcoming marriage. The only thing you stand to gain from helping your sister is the satisfaction of knowing you've done your duty."

"That's a horrid thing to say," Charlotte whispered, hugging her arms about herself.

"I know, and I feel like an arch rotter saying it to you. But someone needs to have the gumption to remind you of your obligations before it's too late. You've impressed me up to now in the way you've shouldered your responsibilities towards the Chadwyckes, and how you've thrown yourself into hard work, which I know hasn't come naturally to you. You've shown pluck and grit, and surprisingly good organisational skills. You've been unselfish: generous with your time and your resources. You've shown kindness towards the officers and today I was impressed

THE BROKEN VOW

by how patient you were with poor Jam, when you helped him with his meals. If not for you, he'd have ended up with more food in his hair and on the chaps beside him than he could ever have got into his mouth. You did all that with a spirit of helpfulness and good humour that was heartening to see. All of which makes it even more surprising and disappointing that you seem set on avoiding your responsibility towards your own family.

"What would your papa think if he knew that one of his daughters was going to grow up unaware of her true parentage or the place where she truly belongs – here at Plas Norton – while the other uses that inheritance to further her ambitions in the marriage market? Shame on you, Charlotte. A few months ago I believed you to be a vapid, wilful, self-indulgent, silly girl, but since Eustace was wounded I've come to expect better. It's disappointing to find I was deceiving myself."

It was too much. Charlotte sat up, wounded by Venetia's harsh words.

"Why is everyone so determined to be mean? You; Nurse Boyle; Doctor Sheridan; Eustace; even Rosamund's friend Rutledge. None of you consider what it's like for me. None of this easy for me, you know. Sleeping in this ugly, cold room, on this hard bed with these awful scratchy blankets and rough sheets. Sharing facilities, washing in cold water instead of having a proper bathroom to myself. There's no one to help me with my clothes or hair or mending any more. Every moment of every day is taken up with tasks for others. I don't get a moment to myself. My home is full of strangers; I'm working so hard my hands are chapped and rough; and by the end of each day I ache all over.

"And yet you want me to add another responsibility to those which are already weighing me down almost more than I can bear, to help a woman who did little for me when I was a child; a woman whose behaviour embarrassed me and my father in company and made people talk behind their hands, who was so cold she couldn't love me. The only happy times I can recall from my childhood were those I spent with Papa, not my times with her. You've no idea how I long to have those times with him again. The times in London when we attended the theatre or the ballet, and I would hold his arm and he'd look so proud of me, and everyone was smiling and dressed in gay colours, and we could lose ourselves in the play or the music and the chatter. Why does no one understand how much I miss all of that?"

Tears poured down her cheeks and her breaths came in gulps as her shoulders heaved. She hadn't intended to say so much, but she wouldn't be sorry to have bared her soul if it might make Venetia, whose opinion she had always valued, more understanding.

But Venetia lay still, watching her as if unmoved, her mouth shut in a firm line until Charlotte's sobs had lessened and she had dried her eyes.

"Your grief for your father and for the time before the war is understandable. But perhaps it's hard for the rest of us to sympathise as much as you'd like because we know that, unlike so many of the people around you, you have a choice. You could give all this up tomorrow and go back to your former life in London. You could hand over the reins of your hospital to someone else, or even close it down and reclaim your house and your comfortable bed and private bathroom. You can pretend there isn't a war blinding and maiming people and driving them to the brink of insanity, or salve your conscience with easier tasks like fundraising teas. You can forget you ever had a sister, or even that you had a fiancé, if his behaviour is so hurtful to you. You can get another maid; you need never work another day again. But for most of those around you, it isn't so simple. Nurse Boyle, Mrs Longford, Mrs McKie, Mr Cadwalader: they work because they must. Do you imagine they don't ache, or that their hands haven't been roughened by work over the past ten or twenty years?

"Boyle strives to do a fine job, expecting the same high standards from others that she demands of herself. Eustace and the other officers can't choose whether to go back; they must wait and hope their minds and bodies will heal, and then go whither the army sends them, even if it means they are wounded again, or they die. Most of all, Josephine can't choose her future. She doesn't have the luxury of deciding whether to be cared for by her own flesh and blood, in the home that belonged to her ancestors.

"You have it all in your power, Charlotte, and if you would only stop and think for a moment, perhaps you might truly understand. Now, if you'll excuse me, I, too, am aching. I need to rest my leg and get some sleep; you should do the same." She sighed. "Everything will probably seem much better in the morning. Somehow, it always does."

TWENTY-EIGHT

Charlotte

Charlotte awoke to see Venetia's bed was empty, the covers already neatly drawn up and smoothed flat. Squinting against the light streaming in through the thin curtains with eyes sore and puffy after crying herself to sleep the night before, she groped for her watch and gasped when it revealed that she had slept in past eight o'clock. She would miss breakfast if she didn't hurry.

The shock of cold water from the ewer on the washstand was enough to rouse her fully, and she shuddered as she swapped her warm nightgown for a fresh chemise and drawers, her fingers clumsy as she fastened her corset and buttoned her black dress. She pinned her long hair into a chignon that was practical, if not stylish, and trotted downstairs to join the others at the breakfast table.

Venetia wasn't there. Nurse Boyle glanced up from helping Jam with his kippers, which was fortunate else he could have ended up stinking of fish for the rest of the day.

"Ah, Miss Fitznorton at last. Would you mind assisting Lieutenant Hitchens this morning, please?"

She nodded and slipped into the seat next to him. Hitchens only needed his toast to be buttered and spread with marmalade, and his cup of coffee placed within reach. As long as she guided his hands to locate his plate and cup, he could manage the rest without further assistance.

"How are you feeling this morning, Lieutenant?" she asked, plastering on a bright smile to lift her voice, even though she felt far from cheerful. He might not be able to see her smiling, but he would hear it in her voice, she hoped.

His head turned sightlessly in her direction, brown eyes gazing vaguely somewhere past her nose. It was odd that he still couldn't see, for the doctor had said there was no apparent physical injury to account for his blindness.

"Much the same, but thank you for asking," he mumbled. He groped for his toast, apparently unwilling to say more.

Along the table, Eustace wiped his mouth delicately with his napkin before rising to depart the room. Hurriedly, Charlotte pushed back her chair to follow him, but Nurse Boyle had spotted her and called out to remind her to add sugar to Hitchens' coffee. By the time she had done so, Eustace was gone. She sent a scowl in the nurse's direction, but held her tongue. It wouldn't do to argue in front of the men.

Once the officers had finished eating and left the room, it was the turn of Charlotte and the other staff to eat, before clearing up and taking the dishes to the scullery. While drying dishes, Charlotte ventured to question Nurse Boyle about Venetia's whereabouts.

"She said she was planning to take a walk, then pack her things to head off. Apparently she wants to speak to that doctor cousin she's always going on about, to ask him about our officers. It'll be difficult to manage with one less person to help, especially as we've also lost Miss Sharp. You haven't gone upsetting her, I hope?"

Charlotte's mouth fell open at the nurse's temerity. With her cheeks flaming, she mumbled a hasty denial and finished her chores as quickly as she could, hardly able to wait to get away. She had arrived at a decision during her sleepless night, and hoped she could put her plans into action before Venetia left. It was frustrating to find that her friend had gone before Charlotte could speak to her.

As soon as the dishes and plates had been put away, she brushed past Mrs McKie, who was already starting to prepare the vegetables for luncheon, and hurried out through the servants' entrance towards the courtyard.

She stood in the doorway of the motor stable, waiting for her eyes to adjust to the dim interior after the bright spring sunshine outside. Where was Cadwalader? The motor car was there, its navy-blue paint and brass-edged lamps freshly polished and gleaming in the sunlight slanting in from the doorway. Stepping around it, she eyed the empty space between the car and the work bench, but there was no sign of the chauffeur until a movement inside the car caught her attention. He'd been sitting at the wheel all along, leaning his arms over it, and now looked up as if startled.

Without his cap, his greying mop of curls looked untidy, as if he had been raking his fingers through them. Rubbing his face, he sat up. She noticed a scarlet flush sweeping up his neck to his ears; his nose was equally red and his eyes were swollen. Had he been crying? Surely not. She had never seen a man weep. Her father certainly never had, to her knowledge – the very idea of it struck her as impossible. But then, Cadwalader was a rough-bred Welshman, not a gentleman.

He slid across the front seat and emerged to stand before her.

"Sorry, miss – I didn't see you there at first," he said, his voice thick. "What can I do for you?"

"I'd like to go to the Dower House this morning, as soon as you can have the car ready."

He paled, but nodded and gathered up his cap, squashing it down over his hair. Under her gaze, he squared his shoulders. "Certainly, miss. I'll be ready in ten minutes."

She sat in the rear compartment on the short journey to the Dower House, gazing at the view without taking it in, alone with her thoughts and her churning stomach. Her way forward was clear to her now, making her throat constrict with anxious anticipation. Within moments she would see Rosamund's corpse, and she would be unable to avoid dealing with the problem of Josephine any longer.

It was even worse than she had expected. Ethel, sepulchral in her black maid's dress and severe hair style, showed her to the parlour, where a coffin stood on trestles. Its polished oak and brass handles looked dull in the semi-darkness as the curtains had been drawn closed to mark Rosamund's passing. Light from a single candle cast a glow over her stepmother's face, and the powerful scent of hyacinths on the side tables made the atmosphere almost heady. A wreath of hothouse roses and lilies had been put aside, presumably to rest on the coffin when it made its final journey back to Yorkshire. The extravagance of the flowers made Charlotte pause: it seemed Rosamund must have inspired more respect and affection than she had ever realised. Perhaps she should have brought some blooms herself. In her haste to get here, she hadn't even thought of it.

Drawing closer, she peered into the open coffin to gaze upon the stepmother she had once despised. In repose, Rosamund's face was unlined, as if it had been carved from wax; the hollows of her cheeks were sunken and threw the delicacy of her high cheekbones and fine nose into sharp relief. She was wearing more make-up than she had ever worn in life, Charlotte noticed, and the thought made her inexplicably cross. It didn't seem right to go against the way someone liked to present themselves, just because they were dead and unable to have a say in the matter. But then, perhaps the makeup was necessary. Last summer, Papa's sallow dead cheeks had been rouged, too. She pressed her gloved fist to her mouth until the memory had passed.

So much death. So much suffering. There was the war, yes, but here at home, too, people were enduring pain and sorrow that had nothing to do with the fighting. Who knew how much Rosamund had suffered in those last days, not just from the fever, but from the traumatic birthing, and then the knowledge that she would not live to rear her own child? A wave of pity washed over her. For a moment she was tempted to reach out and touch Rosamund's hand, but she found she couldn't do it. Instead, she bowed her head.

"I'm sorry for the way things were for you," she whispered. "The way they were between us. I wish they could have been different."

A tear trickled down her nose and plopped onto the blue silk lining the coffin. Fumbling for her handkerchief, she drew in a shuddering breath. Regret for the things she had said in the past tasted more bitter than her hatred had ever done.

She went on, even though it was too late. Futile now to make apologies or promises, or to seek to understand Rosamund's side of their story. "I realise I let you down in the past. But I promise I won't now. I'll make it up to you."

Rosamund was past help, but there was still time to make amends by helping the living. Straightening, she gazed upon the other woman's peaceful face for one last time, then stepped back, dabbed her eyes and blew her nose.

"I'd like to see my sister now," she said to Ethel, who had lingered like a shadow in the doorway.

Ethel's face clouded. "You can't, miss."

"What do you mean?" Charlotte marched towards her, trusting that her superior height and status must make the other woman reconsider her defiant words.

"It's too late, miss. She's gone."

"Gone where?"

"Doctor Sheridan took her to the vicarage with Mr Rutledge and Miss Dawson about a quarter of an hour before you arrived. If we'd known you were coming..."

Charlotte's heart slammed against her ribs. Her mind returned to her conversation with Doctor Sheridan. Hadn't he said that Reverend Butts would be able to arrange for Josephine's adoption? That must surely be the reason they had taken her to the vicarage.

She was out of the house in a few strides, almost running down the gravel path to the car.

Cadwalader stepped smartly to open the door to the rear compartment.

"The vicarage," she gasped out before he had time to ask where she wanted to go. "Be quick! We have to get Josephine back before they send her away."

Something shifted in his face as he handed her in and closed the door behind her, the dullness in his eyes changing to a gleam of hope. He had the engine running within moments and slid into his seat, swinging the motor into the middle of the road.

The momentum pushed her back firmly against the padded seat, and as they picked up speed she held grimly to the strap hanging beside her. Her free hand flew to her throat when Cadwalader swerved to avoid a dog in the road, the parp of the horn startling her almost as much as those folk who jumped and stared, open-mouthed. By the time they squealed to a halt outside the church, drawing curious glances from a couple of elderly ladies with baskets on their arms, she felt quite sick. Her armpits were damp, and she had to take a moment to steady herself before she could trust her trembling legs enough to step down, with the help of Cadwalader's outstretched hand.

Dashing past the churchyard, she stumbled and would have fallen if he hadn't been at her side to grab her elbow.

"It's alright, miss – they're still here. That's the doctor's car, look."

She nodded, trying not to look at the churchyard where her father lay in the Fitznorton vault. Taking reassurance from Cadwalader's nod of encouragement, she paused to compose herself, brushing a hand over the front of her coat.

"She can't go to strangers. I promised Lady Fitznorton this morning that I wouldn't let her down."

He nodded and gave her an approving smile that made his eyes crinkle. "Very good, miss."

She led the way around the lichen-speckled wall, topped with ivy, which surrounded the churchyard, and along to the vicarage next door. As they approached the front door it opened; she recognised the tall blond man emerging as Mr Rutledge.

He looked surprised to see her. Removing his hat, he gave a polite nod of acknowledgement.

"Miss Fitznorton. I wasn't expecting to encounter you again."

Doctor Sheridan had followed him out into the sunshine, with a mournful Nellie Dawson in a black coat and hat behind them. Charlotte ignored her raised eyebrow and addressed Mr Rutledge, assuming he must be in charge of carrying out Rosamund's wishes.

"I've come to collect my sister," she declared.

The doctor spluttered something about it being most irregular, but Rutledge remained calm, regarding her with unblinking blue eyes.

"We've left her with Mrs Butts," he said quietly. "She knows of a childless family who will take care of her."

THE BROKEN VOW

"You should go home, Miss Fitznorton. Arrangements have already been made." Doctor Sheridan's moist red mouth clamped shut when she turned a fierce glare upon him.

"Then they'll have to be unmade. *I* should take care of Josephine."

Reverend Butts had been peering down his hooked nose at the commotion and now interjected. "You must think of the child. She has an opportunity to be part of a family who will care for her as if she were their own."

"I'm sorry to have to disappoint them," she said. "But the fact is, she isn't their own. She's a Fitznorton, and she belongs with her true family, at Plas Norton. She belongs with me."

It was strange, now that she was faced with the possibility of being denied the chance to care for her sister, how eager she was to do so. A note of desperation crept into her voice, and she turned back to Rutledge.

"You were Rosamund's friend, Mr Rutledge. You know she would have wanted her daughter to grow up in her ancestral home."

"But you told me yourself that you're too young to take on the responsibility."

"I know what I said." A lump rose in her throat. "You caught me by surprise, that's all. I've had time to think about it now. Time to think about what's right. I'm Josephine's nearest living relative, and I can't stomach the thought of her going to strangers who might not even find they can love her, however much they've longed for a child. She should be with me. She should grow up knowing who her parents were, seeing their photographs, and hearing about them. She should have her mother's jewels to wear when she's older, and learn to play piano on the same instrument her mother used to play. She should be able to play in the gardens where her mother used to walk, read the books her mother read."

"Do you know how to look after a baby?" The vicar's cheeks

had turned scarlet, whether with annoyance or distaste at her impassioned outpouring, she couldn't tell.

"I can learn. Even quite stupid girls seem to be able to manage it moderately well, after all. And I'll employ someone more experienced to help. Our father has left us well provided for; she'll want for nothing." She turned back to Mr Rutledge, who was rubbing his top lip thoughtfully. "You know it's the right thing to do."

All eyes were on the American as he pondered his decision. He looked at each one of them in turn, then finally returned his gaze to Charlotte.

"I had my doubts about you, Miss Fitznorton, even before we met. And then, you were determined not to help your sister. You convinced me your stepmother was wrong to believe you loyal and kind…"

Charlotte's heart sank. Tears sprang to her eyes as she gazed up at him. He wasn't going to listen to her; none of them were. She'd left it too late, and now she'd always have to live with the pain of regret. Venetia would despise her, and her baby sister would be gone.

His voice had faded, but she roused herself to listen again. She might as well hear the worst.

"…I'm pleased that her faith in you, however inexplicable it may be, has been rewarded. It seems you do not lack loyalty and kindness, after all, and you are just as determined as she believed."

She swallowed hard. "Then you'll agree to let me take her?"

He nodded. "Would you ask your wife to bring Miss Josephine here, please, Reverend?"

Butts looked doubtful, but Rutledge had the manner of one accustomed to command. Only a few moments after he had disappeared into the house, the vicar re-emerged with his wife in tow, Josephine bundled in a shawl in her arms. With a frown of concern, she handed the baby over to Mr Rutledge, and he cradled her tenderly for a moment before passing her to Charlotte.

"Mind her head," Mrs Butts admonished her in a disapproving tone that made Charlotte's hackles rise. She didn't need reminding that she was inexperienced and clumsy. She would learn. She was doing her best, if only everyone would see it.

"This is a sacred trust, and it's one you have chosen of your own free will," Rutledge said while she adjusted the baby's weight in her arms. "Now, Miss Fitznorton, you must prove yourself worthy of it."

A sacred trust. As Charlotte carried Josephine back to the motor car, the words played over and over like a gramophone record with the needle stuck. Cadwalader followed, carrying a box containing the baby's clothes, bottles, nappies and blankets. She had the strangest feeling, as if she were floating above herself, looking down. The baby's dark eyes gazed up intently from her serious little face. The grazes were fading now and the bruises on her temples had turned olive green and ochre.

What have I done? The question flitted into Charlotte's mind, unbidden.

"Shall I hold her while you get in?" Cadwalader offered, setting the box down and opening the door to the passenger compartment. To her surprise, he reached out without the slightest awkwardness to take the baby in his arms. The gesture was so confident and natural, it was as if he had held a hundred babies and even enjoyed the experience. She climbed into her seat unaided, and as she settled onto the plush grey corduroy, there was a part of her that marvelled at his ease, and the warmth of his smile, the way his features brightened as he murmured and gently tickled the baby under the chin.

It was a reminder that her driver was a father, and a kind one to judge by his doting expression now as he clucked and rocked Josephine in his arms. She reached out to take the baby from him with a pang: she was taking on the greatest responsibility of her life, without the support of her own parents. Did Cadwalader's children know how fortunate they were to have that paternal care in their lives?

Had she bitten off more than she could chew this time? The magnitude of the task ahead was already hitting home, making her almost giddy, as if a train had just rushed past at speed with a great whoosh of noise and swirling air. Bringing up a child, teaching it right from wrong, keeping it safe from harm, ensuring it had an education and a religion, and the right connections and manners, and an understanding of how the world worked… For all her bravado earlier, the task seemed much more daunting than the simple functions of feeding, clothing and housing it.

And then, worse still – what if she managed to do all those things, but couldn't find it in her heart to love the child? It was Rosamund's daughter, after all, and there had never been any affection between them. But every child should be doted upon. Josephine's world should be built on a foundation of solid and unshakeable love. If Charlotte found she couldn't manage this, she would have failed in what might turn out to be the most important task she would ever perform.

She would need help. All the help she could get.

Cadwalader had started the engine and slid into his seat in the front. They set off smoothly, sweeping past the churchyard back towards the vicarage, where Mr Rutledge and Nellie Dawson were climbing into Dr Sheridan's car.

Charlotte fumbled for the speaking tube and called through it to the cab.

"Stop, would you, please? Ask Dawson to come with us."

She held the baby tightly as the car drew to an abrupt halt, almost holding her breath as she waited for the door to open.

Josephine had grown restless, her lips pursing and her head turning from side to side.

Nellie Dawson wore an inscrutable expression as she climbed into the compartment and perched on the folding maid's seat. It was impossible to tell whether she approved of Charlotte's action in taking the baby or not.

Josephine let out a plaintive cry.

"What do I do?" Charlotte asked.

"I expect she wants to suckle. Her bottles are in the box with her other things, but they should be boiled and the milk warmed. She isn't due a feed for a couple of hours. You'll have to crook your finger and give her that, for now. Either she'll settle with something to suck on, or she won't and you'll have an unpleasant time of it until you can get her fed."

Charlotte nodded and popped a knuckle into the baby's mouth. Her frown cleared when it seemed to pacify her.

"I was wondering what your intentions are, Dawson, now that Lady Fitznorton has..." Charlotte stumbled over the word *died*, and settled upon "no further need of your help." Which sounded worse, almost.

Dawson looked guarded. "I'm not sure yet, miss. In the short term, I'll go to my mother. In the long term... I have some contacts in London."

"Ah, now there I can help you. As you can see, Dawson, I shall need assistance."

"I'm not a nursemaid," came the sharp reply.

Charlotte let the interruption pass. "I'm without a lady's maid at present." She pressed on, pretending not to notice the maid's raised eyebrow. "Mr Rutledge specifically requested that I look out for your interests. My stepmother would have wished it. So, we may be able to help one another."

She smiled, pleased with the way she'd handled the situation, and confident that Dawson would be delighted by this opportunity. If Dawson could be prevailed upon to take on both the duties of lady's maid and the care of the child, it would free Charlotte to focus on the hospital again and lift a weight from her burdened mind.

Josephine let go of her finger, screwed up her face and turned puce. It was startling how loud and fractious her cries were, in this confined space. Within a minute or two, the sound had started to grate on Charlotte's already strained nerves. She tried pushing her finger in again, but Josephine refused to be pacified. Really, how could anyone stand this sort of crying for long? It was intolerable.

Dawson raised her voice to be heard over the squalling. "I'm not sure you and I would get along."

"I beg your pardon?" It wasn't that Charlotte hadn't heard above the noise, but that she couldn't believe the maid could be so ungrateful.

"For one thing, I prefer to be addressed as either Nellie or *Miss* Dawson. And you have a certain – history, shall we say – with maids, miss, if I may be so bold as to say so. They don't tend to stay with you for long. Whereas I like to be settled, and to feel that my work is appreciated. Your stepmother was a gracious lady and never said or did an unkind thing to me in all the years I worked for her."

Charlotte stiffened, appalled at the implication that she was less than kind to her maids. "Hush, now," she murmured to Josephine, focusing her attention on trying to stop the crying so that she could recompose her thoughts. It was impossible to think of a suitable response in the face of so much noise.

"Oh, give her here," Dawson said impatiently, reaching out and taking the baby. She held her up against her shoulder, jiggling her and patting her back surprisingly firmly. To Charlotte's surprise, the storm of crying abated.

"Thank you," she breathed, adding "Nellie" as a sign of her gratitude, and to prove she wasn't as unkind as the maid had suggested.

Nellie caught her lower lip with her teeth, as if she was coming to a decision. "I'll come and work for you, Miss Fitznorton, but only under certain conditions."

Charlotte nodded eagerly, so stunned at the way the baby had quietened in Nellie's arms that she would probably have agreed to anything.

"First, you have a reputation for being spoiled, and I have to say I won't put up with any rudeness or tantrums. I expect to be given respect for doing a good job to the best of my ability. Second, I don't mind helping out a bit with this little one, but I'm not a nanny and I won't take responsibility for her, especially at night. You'll need to advertise for someone else to do that, a girl from the village perhaps, until you can get a proper nursemaid. And third, I need every weekend off to visit my mother."

"The whole weekend?" Charlotte stopped, embarrassed by how squeaky her voice had sounded.

"*Every* weekend."

There was a pause. Charlotte wanted to tell her to go and fend for herself if she was going to be so difficult, but she'd heard Aunt Blanche and her friends discussing their servant problems on many occasions, even before the war. It would be even harder to find a good maid now, with the munitions factory offering better pay and more freedom than domestic service. And in spite of these unexpectedly unreasonable demands, Nellie had proved herself to be a loyal and capable lady's maid when handled carefully.

"It's up to you," Nellie said with a shrug that suggested she didn't care how desperate Charlotte was, she could take it or leave it.

Against her better judgement, and with a sense of foreboding at the prospect of dealing with Nellie's outspokenness, Charlotte found herself nodding.

"Very well," she said. "How soon can you start?"

TWENTY-NINE

Charlotte

The movement of the motor car while Cadwalader drove back to the Dower House to allow Nellie to pack her things had, miraculously, seemed to calm baby Josephine. However, she awoke when Nellie got out of their compartment, her puffy little eyes squinting suspiciously into Charlotte's face before screwing up again. It was strange how Josephine could cry so harshly without shedding a single tear, Charlotte thought, propping her up against her shoulder the way Nellie had done successfully earlier. This time, it didn't work.

"Do hurry back to the house, won't you?" she said to Cadwalader as he moved to close the door.

Instead of doing as she bid, to her great surprise he reached towards her.

"Do you want me to try? She looks colicky to me. See the way she's drawing her knees up towards her belly?"

Charlotte looked down at the baby. He was right. A wave of horror flooded over her: how could she not have realised the child was in pain? How irresponsible she must be! Her thoughts had been solely of her own stress at being subjected to the horrible crying, but Josephine's suffering must have been much worse. She didn't know anything about colic in babies, but she remembered her pony suffering from colic when she was a girl. The poor creature had had to be shot to end its misery.

She didn't hesitate to hand the baby over, then got out to stand beside Cadwalader with her arms wrapped around herself. How could she have failed so dreadfully, so soon, in her mission to care for her sister? She'd never forgive herself if... But no, she couldn't allow herself even to think further.

Inexplicably, after joggling the baby and murmuring some soothing words, Cadwalader flipped her onto her stomach and laid her face down along the length of his forearm, his hand cradling her head. Charlotte felt a jolt of alarm and gasped as he proceeded to swing her to and fro. Surely it wasn't safe to treat a delicate infant so roughly?

Her horror must have shown in her face, because he looked startled, then, to her surprise, grinned. While he swung the baby vigorously, he looked unconcerned, for all the world as if colic was an everyday occurrence. It took Charlotte a moment to register that the squalling noise had stopped.

"There we are — that's better, isn't it *cariad*?"

Gradually, Charlotte's heartbeat slowed. There was something hypnotically soothing, she could see, about the way he murmured, and about the swinging. Almost unconsciously, she found she was gently rocking from foot to foot. She stopped herself with a mental shake.

"How did you know to do that?"

"When you've had nine babies, you learn all kinds of tricks." His wry smile was fleeting; without warning, his face clouded. "You'd better have her back now. I'll drive you both home, so you can get her fed and changed." With his mouth set in a grim line, he was looking intently towards the house; following his gaze, Charlotte realised he was staring at Nellie

Dawson, who was watching from the parlour window. There was something in the look they exchanged that puzzled her, but there wasn't time to think about it, as he thrust Josephine back into her arms, gesturing towards the car.

"There, there," she said feebly to Josephine, and was relieved when the jolting of the moving car once again proved soothing to her young charge.

On the way back, she pondered her options. She could advertise in one of the national publications for a nanny, but finding one with suitable qualifications and references would take time. Such a woman could also be expensive, and travel costs might need to be provided if she had a long journey to reach Plas Norton. Perhaps there would be a local servants' registry, but as she had never had to deal with the hiring of domestic staff, she wasn't sure. She decided to consult Mrs Longford, who would be bound to know about such matters even though Plas Norton hadn't required a nursery maid since Charlotte herself was small. By the time the car drew up outside the stone porch of the house, though, she'd had another idea. If Cadwalader had had nine babies, then so had his wife.

"I'll need a temporary nursemaid until I can find someone suitable to look after Josephine," she said when he opened the door. "Given your wife's experience of child-rearing, I was wondering if she might—"

He cut her off before she could even finish the sentence. The colour had drained from his face, leaving his skin ashen; the creases between his eyes deepened, making him look suddenly older.

"She couldn't. I'm sorry, miss."

"Oh," Charlotte said, deflated. What was it with servants these days, that made them think they could be so forthright? "Might I ask why?" she asked, more sharply than she'd intended.

He shifted his weight and focused his gaze on the baby in her arms, looking almost unbearably sad.

"I appreciate the offer, miss, but we lost a daughter not that much older than this one, and she took the loss hard. It was only the year before last. Before we came to Pontybrenin." He cleared his throat, as if trying to control his emotions. "I wouldn't want her to see this little one. It would upset her too much. It's out of the question, sorry."

Displeased, Charlotte turned away and carried Josephine into the house, leaving him to take her box of possessions around to the servants' entrance. Not for the first time, she felt Cadwalader was a puzzle she couldn't solve.

THIRTY

APRIL 1915

Charlotte

The air in the billiard room was cloudy with cigarette smoke when Charlotte poked her head around the door to look for Eustace. They hadn't had a proper conversation since he arrived, and the arrival of Josephine had meant most of Charlotte's time was taken up with the baby's needs. But this morning they were giving Nora, a girl from the village, a chance to prove she was up to the task of caring for the child. Mrs Longford was keeping an eye on things, so at last Charlotte could seize an opportunity to speak to him. More than anything, she wanted to find out from his own lips how he was feeling, now that he had had time to settle at Plas Norton. Away from the violence of the front lines, she hoped he would be much better, and able to focus on their dreams for the future.

"Have you seen Captain Chadwycke?" she asked Major Brooks, who was leaning over the billiard table lining up his cue.

"Not since breakfast," came the terse response.

She looked enquiringly at Captain Reynolds, even though it

was pointless to expect any kind of explanation of Eustace's whereabouts from him, given his inability to speak. Sure enough, he merely shook his head and returned his attention to the game. How he managed to play with half of his fingers and toes missing and said extremities wrapped in bandages was beyond her, but at least he was out of bed.

She walked on past the music room, as the discordant notes muffled by the closed door suggested Lieutenant Hitchens was attempting to play the piano again. He was somewhat limited, of course, by his blindness. Not a lot of point in him trying to play billiards or read a book, Charlotte supposed, and it might be construed as insensitive to ask if he'd seen anyone.

With his palsied movements still as dramatic as when the men arrived at Plas Norton, young Jam was even more at a loss for things to do than his fellow officers. Unable to hold either his head or a book steady enough to read, he was unable to play billiards or cards, or to attempt to play a musical instrument. He was usually to be found wandering the corridors on wet days, or out in the grounds when it was dry. Today was unusually sunny, and a quick glance out of the French doors revealed that he was out on the terrace.

Determined to track down her elusive fiancé, Charlotte headed out to quiz Jam about his whereabouts.

"T-t-t-try the s-s-s-summerhouse," he stammered, waving wildly in its approximate direction.

Her smile drooped. It would take at least half an hour to trudge over to the summerhouse, and she wasn't one for long walks. Still, it would be worth the effort to see Eustace. Once Nellie had helped her into some sensible outdoor shoes and a warm coat, she set off.

It occurred to her on the way that it wasn't entirely proper for her to seek time alone with Eustace like this. No doubt if Aunt Blanche were here, she'd admonish her to wait until he had returned from his walk, instead of following him to the summerhouse, and they'd have to conduct their conversation with either her aunt or a maid in the room. Being alone with him, in defiance of her aunt's rules, would be rather thrilling. She nursed a secret smile. Perhaps he might even kiss her – the idea of it made her stomach flip. Would his moustache tickle her lip as it had her cheek when he'd kissed it after she accepted his proposal?

Despite the unaccustomed exertion of her long walk, and the inconvenience of having to watch her step to avoid the many pellets of sheep dung scattering the fields beyond the ha-ha, the cool country air was surprisingly refreshing. She hoped it would bring a fetching bloom to her cheeks and a sparkle to her eyes. Being away from the frequent noise of Josephine's harsh cries was a relief, too. They always set her nerves on edge and made her feel she should somehow be able to do more to make the child settle. Sometimes Cadwalader's technique of swinging her worked, but not always, and she'd had to resort to all manner of tricks in the past few days, in the hope of allowing everyone a few hours of uninterrupted sleep. Given how much work they all had to do, it was inevitable that they would be grumpy if their rest was disturbed.

Out here, with only the birdsong and distant bleating of sheep to fill her ears, she felt freer than she had in weeks. She pressed on, past the lake with its surface choked by weeds, and the dense thickets of rhododendrons that threatened to overwhelm the indistinct, muddy path in the absence of any gardeners. Once or twice she slipped and clutched at a branch to stop herself falling. By the time she reached the top of the wooded slope near the summerhouse, she was red in the face and impatient to find Eustace. Her shoes and hem were caked in mud, and her earlobes ached from the cold after her walk in the shady woods. The novelty of exercise had worn off.

The air up here was bracing, and she shivered, huddling into her coat and wishing she had brought a scarf. Plas Norton brooded in the valley below, less imposing from up here where the height of its four corner turrets was less obvious. The morning sun threw shadows over the western face of the building, but warmed the stone it touched. Charlotte paused for breath and smoothed her hair below her hat, then blotted her face with her handkerchief, anxious in case the exertion had made her complexion shiny and unattractive. If Eustace was here – and she sincerely hoped he was, after the trouble she had gone to to find him – she wanted to look her best, not like some kind of hoyden.

As she approached the wooden summerhouse, her feet made no sound on the grass. It was a sweet little building, gothic in style, like the main house, with pointed arches on the windows and fancy crenellations along the edge of the roof, which was steeply pitched and topped by a finial. It was almost like a gingerbread house, with its picturesque design and far-reaching views. A perfect spot for a lovers' tryst, she decided.

A movement inside the building, just visible through the dusty panes of glass, lit her face with a gleeful smile. He must be there. What fun it would be to surprise him. The door had been propped open with a stone; she moved to the threshold, hid behind the jamb to avoid being seen, and peered in.

Tracks in the dust on the wooden floor revealed that he had dragged the bench across to sit near the windows, overlooking the view towards the hills and the distant smoking chimneys of Pontybrenin. He was sitting with his back to her, a newspaper in his hands. She could read the headlines over his shoulder, announcing the sinking of a British passenger ship by a German submarine. So absorbed was he, he didn't notice her tiptoeing up behind him.

She held her breath, stifling a giggle, then darted forward and covered his eyes with her hands.

"Surprise!"

The violence of his reaction robbed her of breath and of

speech. The moment she touched him, he grabbed her wrists and wrenched her around, making her stumble headlong over the back of the bench beside him. His breath, hot and shallow, smelled sour in her face, and she stared up in horror at the sight of his teeth bared in an animalistic snarl before he flung her away with a curse, sending a drop of spittle landing on her face. She flinched.

Taking advantage of his almost immediate retreat to the far corner of the summerhouse, she righted herself, dusting herself off and rubbing her wrists. Their brief struggle had dislodged her hat, and she bent to pick it up, her heart still hammering a frantic beat. She hadn't felt subject to the physical power of someone stronger before, never before understood the terror of realising that someone could hurt her if he chose and there would be little or nothing she could do about it. When he had loomed over her, his bloodshot eyes blazing like ice and fire, for a sickening few moments there had been no telling what he might do. The grip of his fingers had bitten into her delicate wrists as if he'd wanted to snap her.

He had his back to her now and was hugging himself, leaning his forehead against the timber wall of the building as if he needed its support to stand.

"Don't *ever* do that again," he growled, his voice ragged as if he, too, was breathless.

She dashed away tears with the back of her hand, realising as she did so that she was shaking. Her legs felt boneless and she plopped down on the bench, at the end farthest from him.

At last he turned back. His cheeks were still pale from the shock of what had just happened, and his eyes looked startlingly blue in contrast, reflecting the spring sky through the window beyond.

"What the hell did you think you were doing, creeping up on me like that?" He spat the words out, gazing at her with an intensity that looked alarmingly like dislike or, worse, contempt.

"I'm sorry," she said, still reeling from the hostility of his response to what she had thought a harmless prank. "I wasn't thinking..."

"Clearly not. Do you even have a brain in that dizzy head of yours?"

Her mouth fell open. "You shouldn't speak to me like that," she began, but her throat closed over as he crossed the distance between them in three strides and leaned his face towards hers.

"After that trick, it's a wonder I can bring myself to speak to you at all."

"I'd been looking for you. Jam said you'd be here. I got all muddy, look..." She gestured pointlessly at her skirt. A tear dripped into her lap, soaking into her woollen coat. "You hurt me," she added in a whisper.

"You're lucky I didn't kill you."

The harshness of his words, reinforced by the coldness in his eyes, made her cringe.

"I just wanted to talk to you. That's all. We've had no time together since you arrived, and I wanted to ask how you're feeling."

His nostrils flared. "Well, now you have your answer."

"I would have thought you'd at least offer me a handkerchief," she said. She'd been hoping this would be a romantic encounter, and it had been anything but.

He cursed under his breath, and she pretended not to have heard the uncouth word. Her pride was smarting as much as her wrists now; she tried to hide it by adopting the simpering, flirtatious manner with which she had charmed him before.

"I admit it was a little silly of me to creep up on you, but aren't you even a teeny bit pleased to see me?" She tilted her head to one side and peeped up at him under her lashes.

"Charlotte, don't do this."

"Don't do what?"

"This. Whatever this is." He waved his hand in a dismissive

gesture. "We're not at a ball now, drinking punch. You can't behave as if nothing's changed."

"But nothing has changed between us. Has it?" The question came out in a whisper.

"Of course it has. Everything has. It's all fallen apart. Everything I wanted, everything I've worked for. Everything I want to be. It's all crumbled to dust, and yet you want me to behave as if I'm the same boy who danced with you last summer. I'm not that fellow any more."

"Yes, you *are*. I know you've been through a lot, but underneath—"

"I'm not. I'm not the man I believed I was, and it's killing me. Can't you see that?" His voice cracked, a dozen expressions fleeting across his face with the strain of suppressing his emotions.

What could she say to make it alright again? She could appreciate that she had upset him by startling him, but this outpouring of negativity was out of character. The boy she'd known was jolly, always smiling. He had to realise that there was no point in wallowing in this kind of misery.

"These are just temporary feelings, Eustace. You still have me. You still have your parents, and your brother and sister, and your rank. As soon as you're well again you can go back and rejoin your men, and as soon as the Germans have been defeated we can be together properly. Maybe even before that – we could marry before you go back to the war, if you'd like to. I know I'd like to. Please don't keep shaking your head like that. It's true, you know it is. You're in a funk, but it won't last."

With a sigh, he sank down at the other end of the bench and buried his face in his hands.

"Just stop. Stop all this talking, this endless prattle that you seem to imagine will somehow buck me up and make everything the way you'd like it to be. It simply serves to reinforce the point that you'll never understand."

"That's unfair. I'm trying harder to understand your feelings than you could ever know. I've even set up a hospital for you. I left London and turned over my home and moved into the servants' quarters and I've worked my fingers to the bone, dusting and sweeping and mopping and dragging furniture about, and arranging things, all to make you comfortable and happy. It's all been for you, Eustace."

"I never asked you to."

How could he be so ungrateful? Now that she had explained everything she'd done on his account, he should have relented and thanked her.

"Whether or not you would have asked me to, I did it anyway, so that you wouldn't have to go home and face all your old friends and your family until you're better. But it doesn't matter, because I know it will all be worth it. You'll soon be well, and you'll look back on this and recognise it for what it is: nothing more than a fleeting fit of the blues." Tentatively, she reached out to touch his arm, but he shook her hand off.

"You haven't been listening." As she watched, increasingly bewildered by his unwillingness to see her point of view, he scrubbed his hands on his thighs and turned, at last, to look her in the eye. "You can't fix me, as if I'm a broken toy that needs mending. If it was that easy, I wouldn't have been sent back to Blighty like some kind of invalid. All these things you say you've done – I don't want you to do any of them. I don't want you, or anyone for that matter, to see me like this. In fact, I'd like you to leave me alone."

"I don't understand."

"Be realistic, old girl: we don't have a future together, not now. I'm of no use to you, any more than I'm of use to the army. I'm no use to anyone."

Charlotte's eyes widened as the full import of his words hit her. Her heart pounded as violently as it had done when he hurt her, and it occurred to her that it might even stop, if he really was calling off their engagement.

"You don't mean it," she whispered.

"I do. I'm sorry if it leaves you in a sticky situation, but it's for the best. Find yourself a chap who doesn't get the shakes any time a door slams. Someone who doesn't attack you if you catch him unawares. Whoever he is, he'll be a lucky fellow."

He lurched to his feet, snatched up his newspaper, and made for the door. Pausing at the threshold, he inclined his head towards her, unable to meet her gaze. His words fell like bombs, mercilessly blowing apart her dreams.

"I'll write to Mater and Pater today and explain to them that we've come to a mutual decision, without any blame whatsoever attached to you. Given the circumstances, I'm sure they'll agree that the best thing to do is to break off our engagement."

Disbelieving, Charlotte sagged against the back of the bench, fearing she might be sick. It was a few moments before the dazed feeling died away, to be replaced with a growing sense of rage. *How dare he?* Everything she had worked for over these past weeks had been for nothing. He'd thrown it back in her face and treated her as if she were nothing more than a silly fool. He had spat upon her father's plans for her future, not even caring that his rejection would make her tarnished goods in London society. Furious, she jumped to her feet and ran after him.

He had neared the head of the slope ready to take the path descending between the trees when she reached him. Unable to help herself, she raised her fists and pummelled his back.

"How could you do this to me? How dare you break your promise? How could you be so ungrateful, after everything I've done?" she shrieked.

THE BROKEN VOW

Catching her by the shoulders, he thrust her away to keep her at arm's length. Frustrated by her inability to reach his face to slap it as he deserved, she tried to wrench away from his grip, but he only held on more firmly.

He panted out his words, straining with the effort to keep her at bay. "Stop this. Let it go, won't you? Just accept that it's over, and once you've had a bit of a cry you'll realise it's for the best."

Her face was still contorted with rage, but at least she'd stopped weeping now. He didn't deserve her tears, a man who could break his vow to her so heartlessly. Dropping her arms, she tugged off the glove on her left hand and slipped the diamond ring she had once adored from her finger before flinging it at his chest. It bounced off and landed in the grass.

His exasperated expression was wasted on her. As he bent to find the ring, she resisted the urge to give him a shove and send him sprawling into the sheep droppings.

"You'll regret this," she said, determined not to beg him to change his mind, however much she feared the future as an unattached girl again. Stomping off downhill, she paused only long enough to shout back at him: "I could take you to court for breach of promise, you know."

She could, but she knew she wouldn't. Her sense of humiliation would be terrible enough without dragging his rejection of her into the public eye. Thank goodness she had never done anything to compromise her reputation, apart from going to the summerhouse today. She'd never even kissed him. Maybe once everyone knew he didn't want her, no one else would ever want to kiss her either.

Why hadn't he ever attempted to get her on her own? Wasn't she pretty enough? Had he ever really wanted to marry her, or had he just been swept along by his family's desire for her father's money? The thought made her pause. Picking up a long twig that lay across her path, she swiped it at the nearest bush. The sound of it whipping through the air was oddly satisfying, so she did it again.

Perhaps, she told herself, Josephine was the real reason he no longer wanted her. Besides the burden of having a young baby in her care, she'd have to share her inheritance with her sister now, making her a less attractive prospect if Eustace had only been interested in the Fitznorton fortune. Fleetingly, a bitter resentment washed over her. She pictured Josephine, the little interloper who had robbed her of several nights' sleep already. Life would have been so much easier if she hadn't taken her on.

But then she thought of those tiny legs drawn up as Josephine cried, and how Cadwalader had said it was because she was in pain. The poor child had lost her mother after all, and would grow up with no memory of her, a sorrow Charlotte understood only too well. How could she blame an innocent infant for what had happened? She tossed the stick away and heaved a sigh before setting off for the house again.

What would she do now? Her limbs felt heavy, aching as if she were laden down by a great weight. It was hard to put one foot in front of the other and move forward, with her future now uncertain. Her aspirations for the past nine months or more had been ripped away. Would Papa blame her if he were here now? Would he insist that she try to convince Eustace to change his mind? Would it betray his wishes if she simply accepted what had happened and let Eustace walk away?

Failure lay like a yoke across her shoulders. All that work setting up the hospital had been pointless. It hadn't made Eustace feel any better, any more than his fellow officers. And soon he would write to his parents, and word would get out that they were no longer engaged. Everyone would know she wasn't wanted.

Emerging from the path between the twisted rhododendrons, she blinked as her eyes adjusted to the sunshine. It glinted off the lake, cruelly cheerful in the face of her misery.

Eustace hadn't descended the hill yet; perhaps he was still hunting in the grass for his grandmother's betrothal ring. She was the only person in this part of the grounds.

At the edge of the lake, she gazed at her reflection. What did other people see? A young woman on the brink of turning twenty, wearing mud-spattered black; alone, with a tear-streaked face and dishevelled hair. No parents; no fiancé. No one in the world to love her, apart from her aunt, who no doubt found her exasperating most of the time and had probably been relieved to let her go off to the country. There was Josephine, she supposed. Perhaps if she did her best to be kind, her sister would come to love her one day, although it was anyone's guess how long that might take. Venetia was her only real friend, and she had gone, disillusioned by Charlotte's initial reluctance to adopt her sister. How had everything gone so wrong?

With her feet dragging, she plodded back to the house, eager to kick off her filthy shoes in the boot room. More than anything, she wanted to slink to her room to lick her wounds.

The sight of a familiar car parked outside the porch made her groan. Frustrating her hopes of passing unobserved, the front door opened, revealing the portly figure of Doctor Sheridan. He made a beeline for her, holding up a hand and hailing her as if she were an omnibus.

"Good morning, Miss Fitznorton. I trust you are well?" He sounded doubtful as he looked her up and down, his brows drawing together at the sight of her muddy skirt.

"Thank you, Doctor. Have you been visiting the officers?"

"Just one of my regular calls, my dear. I must say, I've seen nothing yet to relieve my doubts about this hospital of yours."

He wasn't the only one, but she wasn't about to admit her own doubts to him.

"Have *you* seen any improvement in the men?" he asked, as if the answer was a given.

"Not yet, but we mustn't give up hope so soon, must we? When we are called to serve our country, we must be prepared to devote our whole energies to the task, and not be disheartened if we don't see instant results."

"Hmm. Opinion in the village is somewhat against your efforts here, you know. Given the losses which have already been sustained by several families whose loved ones have been killed or gone missing in action, the resentment against housing malingerers in the comfort of Plas Norton is understandable. There are those who would rather see your chaps in front of a court martial for dereliction of duty instead of being cossetted in such luxurious surroundings."

Charlotte swallowed, uncomfortable with the thought that the local community would not support her efforts. But Sheridan hadn't finished.

"Have you considered my suggestion of electric shock treatment? I'm told it's been used with some success to jolt people out of this 'shell-shock' nonsense. I believe it could be particularly effective with that mute fellow. A few shocks applied to the tongue would soon prompt him to talk, if only to beg for the treatment to stop. It's no good pandering to that type, you know."

The image of Captain Reynolds flitted through her mind: sitting in the isolation of his own silent world, his misery so strong she could almost smell it on him. The thought of tormenting him into speaking chilled her to the bone.

"I'm afraid I've been too busy to think about it just yet," she said. If she could delay long enough, Reynolds might start talking of his own free will and there would be no need to worry about the possibility of the doctor carrying out his barbaric treatment. "Still – while you're here, Doctor, I'd like to ask you for some advice with regard to my sister. She seems to cry rather a lot."

He smiled at her indulgently. "Of course she does. She's a baby. My advice is to put her in a room and leave her to cry it out. Eventually she'll learn that being wilful will avail her nothing. Teach her obedience from the start, that's what you need to do. It doesn't do for a child to expect to have their own way, especially a girl."

She nodded obediently but, as she watched him climb into his car and chug away, she couldn't help the rebellious thoughts that entered her mind. Did she really want her sister to grow up believing that no one would listen to her when she was upset or in pain? Would it really be right to teach her to stifle her voice when she needed comfort?

"Oh Venetia," she whispered. "How I wish you were here." Her friend would surely have her own thoughts about the doctor's advice.

Behind her, footsteps crunched across the gravel, and she turned to see Eustace, trudging with his shoulders stooped and his hands in his pockets.

"Did you find it?" she called, unable to keep the bitterness from her voice. It would serve him right if his family's heirloom had been lost forever.

His response was inaudible: at the very moment he opened his mouth the ground was rocked by a rumbling roar that rattled the windows in the house and made sparrows squawk into flight from the trees. Although she had never heard one before, she recognised it unmistakably as the sound of an explosion. A glance at Eustace told her she was right. He had crouched instinctively, lifting his arms to cover his head; his face had drained of all colour, like a corpse.

In the distance, in the direction of Pontybrenin, a plume of black smoke rose above the trees. For the second time that morning, Charlotte's blood ran cold.

THIRTY-ONE

Maggie

Maggie's working day began as usual, stemming a measure of gunpowder into shells. Just a little at a time, tipping it into the shell casing from a tin and using a broom handle with a mallet to tamp it down. Little by little, bashing and bashing, making sure the case was packed absolutely full.

It was only one of many processes that went into making munitions. Some of the girls used gauges to check the sizes of the casings. Others, on receiving the filled shells once Maggie and her fellows had done their work, would insert fuses, screw them down by hand, then tighten them up with a machine. None of these jobs could ever be described as interesting, or fun; but she found her mind could wander, her hands working automatically, as if the hours of repetition had taught them what to do without her brain needing to pay attention. The noise of fifty women hammering, together with the machines echoing further along the cavernous room, made talk impossible until break time, but she and Jenny could occasionally look up and smile at each other across their benches.

She still worried about Jenny, and wished she knew more about pregnancy and birth, so she could be of more help to her. As frightening as it had been in the end, being present when Lady Fitznorton had her baby had fascinated her. There was something miraculous about the idea that a woman's body could grow another human being, open up to release it to the world, and then provide its nourishment. Maggie had enjoyed feeling useful, especially when the doctor had shown her how to assist him. If she could be anything in the world, she'd be a midwife or a nurse. But it was silly to dream of jobs that were out of reach for a factory girl like her.

It was some comfort to see that Jenny's cheeks were looking less hollow these days. Hopefully she and her baby would be strong, and her experience of birth would be easier than Lady Fitznorton's. Maggie prayed for them every day, and knew her mam did the same. Jenny was thriving now that she was living with the Cadwaladers and eating Mary's nutritious vegetable soups and rabbit stews, with fresh bread to fill up on. Owning chickens also meant occasional eggs: her father and Stanley always had the first claim to these, as working men, but given their physical jobs Maggie and Jenny were next in line.

Getting more food was one of the aspects of working that Maggie liked best, along with the sense of pride that came from being able to contribute financially to the household. They were better off than many she knew, as her dad's position as the Fitznortons' chauffeur was relatively well paid and he wasn't a heavy drinker. Still, given the way prices had risen since the war started, every extra penny passed to her mam for housekeeping was a help.

She didn't allow her mind to dwell on the nature of her work, except to hope that the shells she made might protect men from Britain and the Empire from danger. It would be pointless, and painful, to think about the German lads who might be on the receiving end. She didn't wish anyone dead, merely hoped, when she thought about it at all, that these shells would help to bring the war to a close more swiftly. It was constantly drummed into the munitionettes that the more shells they could make, and the faster they could make them, the sooner victory would be achieved. Perhaps, if she and the other women continued to give it their all, and the war ended soon, Len and Uncle Wilf might never get as far as the front.

The fact that the munitions work paid for a few luxuries like weekly trips to the moving picture house was the icing on the cake. Maggie's thoughts drifted to the film she'd watched on the weekend, remembering how enthralled she had been by the magnificent medieval costumes and the melodramatic story, even with Jenny teasing her because the villain was called Margaret. The heroine had been forced to sacrifice her virtue to save her husband's life, although Maggie couldn't help but wonder how many women would need such an excuse to become a King's mistress. Surely the parties, fine clothes and jewels would be temptation enough for lots of girls, and with a king as handsome as the one in the film it might not be such a terrible life. She smiled at herself, knowing how outraged her mam would be by such worldly thoughts. It wasn't likely that any rich man would ever charm his way into her own bed. Girls like her didn't move in those kinds of circles.

Even if she did, Maggie had never felt the urge to swoon over any man, rich or poor, and she'd laughed in the picture house at the way Jenny clutched her breast during the love scenes. Jenny was a born romantic, and look where it had got her. Pregnant and unwed. Still, they hadn't lost hope that Len would be sent home on leave and make an honest woman of her before he had to head off to war.

The prospect of her best friend becoming her sister-in-law made her look over in Jenny's direction with a smile, but before she could catch her eye, the ground under her feet rocked. The air in the room seemed to disappear, and her ears filled with sound. Her body propelled forwards, slamming against her workbench so hard she was winded. A blast of heat roared over her like a dragon's fierce breath, scorching her back and making her hair crackle.

She was on the floor before she had time to think, landing in a heap along with the shell she'd been filling moments earlier. Powder had spilled out; the sight of it made her heart kick against her ribs. Where she had been able to look up earlier and see the metal frames holding up the roof, now there was billowing, stinking smoke.

Jenny. The blast had come from the room behind theirs, so Jenny would have been facing it. Was she alright? Through the ringing in her ears Maggie's stunned brain was starting to register ghastly screams. An intake of breath filled her lungs with thick smoke. Choking, she folded over and retched. The movement hurt even more than breathing had done.

Somehow, she had to get out. But first, she had to find Jenny.

The foul smoke was making her eyes stream with hot tears and her throat close over. She lifted her arm to cover her face with her sleeve. Instinct told her to crawl. The air would be even hotter if she stood up, and with her head still ringing from the explosion, she wasn't sure she could stay upright. Someone else was doing the same, bumping into her as she rounded the corner of her bench. The other woman's face was scarlet and raw, two dark eyes wide like those of a terrified animal. She grasped Maggie's arm fiercely and said something. Maggie made out the shape of the words, *Get out*, before shaking off the woman's hand and heading in what she hoped was the direction of Jenny's bench. Blood dripped into her eyes, more annoying than painful; she wiped it on her sleeve and kept going. The egg-sized bump on her forehead that must have resulted from hitting the floor would have to wait.

Someone staggered past, stamping on her hand, crushing

her fingers under the weight of their wooden clog. Maggie crouched under the nearest bench, nursing the injured fingers in her armpit until fear drove her to scramble across the dusty floor again. Using her elbow and her good hand, keeping her shoulders rounded, she might guard against further injury until she could find her friend.

She counted the benches as she dragged herself past: *two, three,* then along to the right, in the direction of the door. *This one should be Jenny's bench – shouldn't it?* Splinters from the rough wooden floor had caught in her tunic, making her knees sore, and her streaming eyes could hardly see through the acrid fumes. Her fingers throbbed.

A little further on, after pausing to cough so violently she vomited, she found her. Jenny lay curled up on the floor, clutching her stomach and coughing.

"We have to get out, Jenny! Come on, now."

Somehow she tugged the other girl up onto her knees to face what she prayed must be the direction of the door. Another worker reeled into them, spluttering violently, but Maggie tucked the crook of her good arm under Jenny's armpit and dragged her along regardless. Everything depended on getting out into the air. It wasn't only their own lives that were at stake, but the baby's. How could she ever face Len if she didn't get his fiancée and unborn child to safety?

With her chest fit to burst and barely able to see through scalding tears, Maggie lugged Jenny towards the exit. They hadn't gone more than ten yards when Jenny shook off Maggie's grip and sank to the ground against a bench. Crouching beside her, unable to hear what Jenny was trying to say due to the overwhelming noise in her damaged eardrums, she tipped Jenny's face upwards and blinked harshly to focus on her lips. *Leave me here,* she was saying.

A rush of anger filled Maggie with a new surge of energy. She wasn't having that.

"You're not giving up on me!" she tried to shout, before realising it only made the coughing worse.

With a desperate heave that seemed to take all her strength, she pulled Jenny up enough to drape one limp arm around her own shoulders. She'd damned well carry her if it was the last thing she did. And at this rate, she realised with a terrifying start, it might well be. Flames were licking towards them, fanned by the air rushing in from the open door at the end of the building. She lunged for it with all her might and blundered into someone coming the other way.

It was one of the factory hands, holding a handkerchief over his mouth and staring wildly into her face. He was the last thing she saw before shoving Jenny into his arms and being enveloped by a dizzying rush of lights.

THIRTY-TWO

Charlotte

They spoke of little but the explosion for days. Captain Reynolds took to his bed, hiding under the covers curled into a ball like a frightened hedgehog. Jam's unnatural limb jerks became even more pronounced, and even Eustace developed a strange eyelid twitch. He seemed to have retreated into himself and become even more morose and argumentative since ending their engagement, and Charlotte felt justified in trying to avoid him as far as possible. Seeing him was just too painful.

She craved solitude, wishing she could crawl away like a wounded animal to hide in a hole. Unwilling to risk the embarrassment of being seen weeping on the telephone in the kiosk in the hall, she sent her aunt a tear-stained letter to inform her of the end of her engagement, then had to wait, dreading the reply.

The only way to find privacy in such a busy household was to lurk in the bathroom, leading Nurse Boyle to ask if she had a stomach upset. At night, she crept under her bedclothes and sobbed into her pillow until her throat was hoarse and her complexion covered in blotches. Over and over, she ran through the events of that awful afternoon in her mind, cursing herself for her stupidity in sneaking up on Eustace as she did. Had he already been planning to spurn her, and seized upon her prank as an excuse to blame her?

She contemplated throwing his photograph away, but the faint, desperate hope that he might change his mind meant she merely hid it at the bottom of a drawer, underneath her stockings, so she wouldn't have to look upon his handsome face.

Each morning, after little sleep thanks to the constant whirling of her thoughts, she forced herself to rise, knowing she was needed, and could hardly bring herself to look at her reflection in the mirror when splashing cold water onto her red-rimmed eyelids and sallow, dry cheeks.

On the first evening, when she had slunk to her place at the table, keeping her eyes lowered and silently helping Jam and Hitchens with their food, she had hoped that her misery would remain unnoticed. But she'd looked up to see Nurse Boyle's unblinking gaze resting on her left hand with its ring finger now bare. She'd hidden it under the table at once, blushing, and excused herself as quickly as possible, pleading a headache. To her surprise, the nurse had been uncharacteristically lenient, allowing Charlotte's lack of energy to go unremarked, and if any of the other patients or staff had noticed the missing engagement ring, they, too, were tactful enough not to mention it. On the third day, the conversation over breakfast was still, to her relief, dominated by the factory blast. Major Brooks craved news, poring over the scant details in the local newspaper with an almost ghoulish satisfaction, and even bringing it to the table. Such was the eagerness among the officers and staff to know every scrap of information, no one frowned at this breach of good manners.

"Twenty-one killed and another thirty or so injured," he said, giving the pages a shake before folding them up. "A shame, of course, but hardly a disaster compared with what's happening on a daily basis in France. Anyone would think these few civilians were the first people ever to die in this war."

Charlotte finished spreading butter onto Lieutenant Hitchens' toast and guided his hand to the plate.

He spoke up in response to Brooks' bitterness. "Fortunately, Major, we're not yet inured to the violent deaths of women, especially when it occurs hundreds of miles from the front, in a peaceful Welsh backwater."

Eustace looked up, carefully avoiding sending any glance in Charlotte's direction. "Those women in the factory were feeding the dogs of war, Hitchens," he said. "One should hardly be surprised when the beasts turn and bite them. I'm sure they knew the risks they were taking."

Charlotte's mouth twisted as she fought the temptation to lash out against his unkindness with harsh words of her own. Still, at least statements like this made it easier to bear her humiliating loss. Could she really endure being tied to a man who could be so heartless about the death and injury of ordinary people who'd been trying to do their bit for their country?

"That's a tad callous, Chadwycke," Hitchens remarked. "I for one am grateful for their willingness to risk their own safety to arm our chaps at the front. I'm sure we all long for the day when our factories are making ploughshares instead of swords, but in the meantime we need all the armaments we can get."

Brooks nodded in agreement. "That's true. Until the factory in Pontybrenin can be rebuilt, it's a most unfortunate loss to our war effort."

"Not to mention the personal and financial loss to the town with so many of the survivors injured or put out of work," Hitchens added. "The factory was a Fitznorton concern until recently, I believe?"

"It was sold when my father died," Charlotte confirmed, conscious that many of the casualties would still feel a link to the Fitznortons. It occurred to her that she might visit the cottage hospital where the injured were being treated; now that a few days had passed, it might be appropriate to do so.

The prospect of seeing their injuries was daunting, but she'd heard that the mayor and his wife had already visited. It wouldn't do to be considered unwilling to do her duty towards the local community, especially when she'd been told there had been some unsympathetic gossip doing the rounds about the officers at Plas Norton. Perhaps a visit could be an opportunity to remind people that her intentions were good, and it would be better to go soon, before anyone in town became aware that her engagement had been broken off. Besides, her spirits would benefit from getting away from Eustace for a few hours, if only as a reminder that there were plenty of others worse off than she.

As soon as breakfast was over and she could be spared for a couple of hours, she went in search of Nellie, whom she found in the housekeeper's sitting room with a basket of yarn, darning socks for the officers.

"Could I trouble you to help me dress for a visit to the cottage hospital, Nellie?" she asked, careful to word her request politely. After Nellie's blunt admonishments when accepting the post of lady's maid, she was only too aware of the need to keep her sweet.

Nellie raised a querying eyebrow. "Have you heard about Mr Cadwalader's daughter then, miss? I only heard myself this morning."

"Heard what?"

"His eldest daughter works at the factory. She was injured in the blast, trying to rescue another girl. Mrs Longford was saying she hadn't seen him yesterday, and she asked around, and Nora the new nursemaid said she'd heard about it from Peggy Wilson, who's Mrs Cadwalader's sister."

Charlotte shook her head, unable to connect all these names and relationships. None of that mattered. What was important was to find out if her driver's daughter was badly hurt. She thought of Cadwalader's gentleness when he held Josephine in his arms, and how he'd told her about the death of his baby girl. She hoped he wouldn't have to suffer the loss of another daughter.

"Will she be alright?"

"I don't know, miss, but I certainly hope so. Would you like me to accompany you to the hospital?"

Charlotte nodded gratefully and within an hour they were both ready to set off in the hansom cab Mrs Longford had ordered from Pontybrenin.

At the cottage hospital in town, Charlotte was struck by the quietness and order of the ward, where it seemed every bed was occupied by someone swathed in bandages. The smell of carbolic reminded her of all their preparations for the officers at Plas Norton, before they had realised that their physical injuries were of less concern than their mental state.

It took as much charm as Charlotte could muster to gain entry, with the matron in charge strictly limiting the number of visitors. Nellie was forced to wait outside while Charlotte presented her argument for being allowed in.

"I won't permit anyone to wander around my ward," Matron said in a voice that would brook no opposition. "The last thing burns victims need is to be treated like exhibits, or for infection to spread on the coats and shoes of too many visitors."

"I understand, but I'd like to offer my good wishes to my chauffeur's daughter," Charlotte pleaded.

"She'll need more than good wishes, I imagine. Five minutes, then. But don't tire her."

"Yes, matron. Thank you, matron." Squashing her annoyance at being spoken to in such a peremptory fashion by a woman so far below her social class, Charlotte made her way to the bed the matron had indicated.

A middle-aged woman with greying hair tied up in a neat

bun under a modest hat was seated beside the bed, knitting something in khaki wool. She looked startled when Charlotte appeared, jumping up and fumbling with her knitting needles.

"Miss Fitznorton! What a surprise to see you here. I hope you don't mind that Joseph wasn't at work yesterday or today, but in the circumstances..." Her voice tailed off and they both gazed at the young woman in the bed, her cheeks red and raw and the top of her head wrapped in bandages.

Charlotte nodded and extended a gloved hand for the other woman to shake. "You must be Mrs Cadwalader. Of course I don't mind. I felt I should come to visit your daughter, having heard that she is quite the celebrated local heroine."

Mrs Cadwalader beamed with pride. "How kind of you to come to see her. Maggie saved my son's intended, Jenny Gittins. Please, take my seat. I'll step outside for a bit of air. Matron doesn't like more than one visitor per bed."

Trying to keep her gaze fixed on the patient's green eyes rather than her painfully raw face, Charlotte perched on the hard, wooden chair and smiled. It was hard to tell how old the young woman was, but Charlotte guessed they must be of a similar age.

"I understand you've been very brave, Miss Cadwalader. Your parents must be terribly proud."

"I'm not..." Wincing in obvious pain, the effort of speaking made the young woman cough and gasp for breath.

"Please don't feel you have to talk to me if it hurts. It will only give that formidable nurse an excuse to send me packing."

The sight of an answering twinkle in Maggie's eyes spurred her on. The girl's ability to appreciate the humour in such a desperate situation seemed to reinforce her bravery and made Charlotte all too conscious of her own privileged position. She had worked hard to help the officers, but not at the expense of her safety. And, as Venetia had so bluntly pointed out, her motives had not been entirely selfless, as this girl's had been.

"I hope it won't be long before you're up and about again. However, it's my understanding that it may be weeks or months before the factory reopens. Given your father's loyal service to my family, I'd hate to see you suffer any financial hardship as a result of your unfortunate accident. I'd be happy to offer some assistance until you're ready to return to work."

The girl's eyes widened. Between laboured breaths, she managed to croak out a few words. "I don't want to go back there."

"To the factory?"

A nod. Charlotte fancied she could see fear in those green eyes, and no wonder after what had happened to her.

"Well, don't worry about that now. Just concentrate on getting better." She resisted the instinct to pat the girl's hand where it lay on the pristine white sheet, realising it, too, was bandaged.

"I want to be a midwife," came the surprising reply, followed by another fit of coughing. "I was there when your sister was born. I was so sorry to hear of her ladyship's passing."

Taken aback, Charlotte gaped at this revelation. In the corner of her vision, she saw the matron heading their way like a battleship at full steam. She had only moments to respond, but felt she must say something encouraging.

"I'll do what I can to help," she promised. There was no time for anything else before she was directed out of the ward.

Outside, she descended the short flight of steps to street level with her mind in a whirl. Nellie was waiting: she straightened and pointed across the road, where Charlotte saw Cadwalader and his wife deep in conversation. He glanced up and saw her, then crossed to meet her.

He looked different without his uniform: less distinguished in his ordinary flat woollen cap and a suit that had seen better days than in his chauffeur's navy-blue coat, peaked hat and long, shiny boots. Older, too, but then that could just be the strain of his daughter's brush with mortality. It would certainly explain the puffy bags under his eyes and the deep grooves bracketing his mouth.

"Miss Fitznorton, we're very grateful to you for coming to see our Maggie," Cadwalader said. He licked his lips nervously, and Charlotte noticed the way his wife nudged him with her elbow. "I hope you'll overlook my absence from work. It's just that..."

She cut him off with a gesture. "I don't want to hear any more about it. Now, what's all this about your daughter being present when my sister was born?"

It was an extraordinary tale. She had had no idea of her stepmother's suffering, or of Maggie and Mary Cadwalader's role in helping her. Hearing about the way Maggie had administered chloroform and the brutal manner of Josephine's entry into the world made her feel light-headed. Drawing in deep breaths only made her feel worse, as the air in Pontybrenin still smelled of burning, a grim reminder of suffering and death. She clenched her fists and, with a supreme effort of will, blinked away the pinpricks of light that had made her vision swim.

When she felt able to speak, she brought up the subject of Maggie's other revelation. "I hear your daughter has ambitions to become a midwife?"

Cadwalader exchanged a glance with his wife. "She told us yesterday that she's decided she doesn't want to go back to the factory, and we're glad to hear it."

"I never wanted her to work there in the first place," his wife cut in. "She was wonderful with her ladyship, miss – she stayed calm and did everything the doctor told her, even though she must have been scared. And when you think about it, it's not right for any woman to be without a midwife's care, but there's only one properly trained midwife in Pontybrenin, and she can't be in two places at once. She came as soon as she could, but of course it was too late. The doctor had done his best, I know, but I really think our Maggie could be useful, when she's better."

"I agree. But do you know if it will be possible for her, given her injuries?" Charlotte chose her words carefully. She had no idea whether the damage to Maggie's skin and lungs would be too severe for her to work as a midwife, or indeed whether a woman of her class would have sufficient education to take up such a role.

"She's expected to make a full recovery, thank the Lord. She's a bright girl, our Maggie. She even passed the scholarship examination at school in Birmingham before we moved here, but we couldn't af —"

Charlotte noticed how Cadwalader nudged her arm, deflecting his wife from talk of their finances. She continued, her cheeks pink but still keen to plead her daughter's case while she had the chance.

"I asked one of the nurses, and she'll have to do three months of training. She'll need to study for examinations, and once she passes those, she'll need to register as a certified midwife. We'll need to buy her the equipment and a bag."

Mary Cadwalader had evidently been doing her research, but it was obvious from her expression that she was by no means certain how they would achieve all this for their daughter. No doubt there would be some expense incurred, and it would put a strain on the family's finances, especially now that they had lost Maggie's income from the factory. Charlotte's light-headedness was replaced by a sense of excitement. This was something she could help with, and if anyone deserved help it was Maggie, who had aided not only her fellow worker, but also Rosamund and Josephine in their hour of need.

"I'd like to help by sponsoring her. Doctor Sheridan may be able to suggest a way forward, and I have connections in London. When she's well enough to make a start, come to me. It's the least I can do."

She cut off their effusive expressions of thanks, anxious to get back to Plas Norton in time to help the officers with their luncheon, but their gratitude made a feeling of warmth curl in her stomach. She was beginning to discover that helping people could be surprisingly satisfying.

THIRTY-THREE

Charlotte

Charlotte woke with a start. The soft light filtering past the curtains was the pale silver of moonlight. It wasn't dawn yet, then. But something had roused her. She couldn't recall dreaming, yet her pulse was drumming in her ears as if she'd had a nightmare.

A split second later, the faint sounds of yelling reached her ears. Something was happening in the main house: footsteps hastening past her door confirmed it. Sitting up, she reached for the warmth of her dressing gown and huddled into it, tying the belt tightly around her waist and ensuring her nightgown was discreetly covered before venturing out into the corridor.

As she descended to the main landing and emerged near her former bedroom, the sounds increased in volume. Angry shouts, and someone screaming in terror. Not a woman, though – or at least, it didn't sound like one. But then, she'd never heard a man scream like that. The sound was primal, like an animal in fear of its life. It made the hairs lift on her head and goose pimples rise over her limbs.

Doors were opening along the landing, revealing the pale, wide-eyed faces of some of the officers. Reynolds' silent face was grim, Brooks' angry, and Eustace looked afraid, until he caught sight of Charlotte and turned away back into his room.

Nurse Boyle appeared at the top of the stairs, pausing for only a moment to catch her breath. "Do you think we should telephone the police?" she panted.

"What's happening?" Charlotte asked, frowning.

"Hooligans are attacking the house." Boyle's terse reply made Charlotte gasp in outrage.

From downstairs came the tinkling sound of glass breaking, a discordant note in the darkness. Without stopping to think, Charlotte stormed downstairs and seized a stout stick from the umbrella stand in the hall. Throwing back the bolts on the heavy oak front door, she dragged it open.

Bright moonlight lit the driveway but threw tall shadows around the building and in the gardens. She burst through the arches of the porch and onto the gravel, too angry to be frightened, and ducked instinctively as a stone flew past her head.

"How dare you?" she yelled, brandishing the walking stick.

A boy whizzed by on a bicycle, his legs pumping as he careered across the lawn, jeering at her. She swiped at him as he sped off, but missed, catching her toe in the hem of her nightgown and landing heavily. Her knees stung through the fine linen and her palms burned from the impact of sprawling on the rough stones.

From behind him came several others, haring off in pursuit and away from the house. Mocking laughter and shouts rang in her ears. Some of the words they threw in her direction were unfamiliar, but it was easy to guess they were uncouth and intended to insult her. As the faceless figures receded into the distance, their cackles and jeers fading along with the clamour of their bicycle bells, she looked back at the house and cried out at the sight of large white letters daubed onto Plas Norton's grey stone. One word, stark in the cold moonlight.

COWARDS!

She felt the affront to the officers and the damage to her childhood home like a wound. How could those hooligans have behaved so appallingly, going far out of their way to cause destruction and distress? They must be young boys, as any men who would feel strongly enough about the war to commit this act of vandalism would surely have already joined up and left town.

Crunching footsteps told her someone had followed her outside, and she struggled to her feet, trembling from the after-effect of the rush of adrenaline and wincing from the bruises on her knees. It was Nurse Boyle, whose customary pinched expression grew even more severe at the sight of the graffiti.

"We'll get that cleared up first thing in the morning," she said. "The last thing we want is for any of our patients to see it. We can't prevent them from knowing about the broken windows, obviously, but this..." She pursed her lips.

"I don't understand...Why?" Charlotte said, pointlessly, unable to tear her gaze from this grave insult to the dignity of the house and the men. She knew the nurse could no more have an answer than she did herself, but the word repeated in her mind like a cry. "What could have made them so cruel? How could anyone be so lacking in human feeling or respect?"

To her surprise, Nurse Boyle reached out and caught hold of Charlotte's hand, giving it a comforting squeeze. Instinctively, she squeezed back. Tears pricked her eyes but she lifted her chin and blinked them away, determined not to be cowed by the vile behaviour of the dull and ignorant. For a few moments they stood together, united in spirit. The unexpected kindness and humanity of the nurse's gesture, contrasting so strongly with the cruelty of the vandals and Boyle's usually gruff manner, touched Charlotte to the depths of her soul.

"Thank you," she whispered, letting go.

Out in the woodland, in the direction of the lake, a fox shrieked; both women shuddered at the unearthly sound.

"We'd better go in and get everyone back to bed," Nurse Boyle said. "There'll be work to do in the morning, and the police will need to be informed. You should try to get some sleep before then."

Charlotte knew she wouldn't sleep a wink, but there was no point standing out here in the cold. The two women marched side by side back into the house with their heads held high.

THIRTY-FOUR

Charlotte

Charlotte had thought things couldn't get any worse than they already had in recent weeks, but upon dragging her weary limbs down the stairs to join the nurse, maids and patients at breakfast, she discovered she was wrong. One seat at the table was empty, and when she sent a look towards Nurse Boyle to question why Lieutenant Hitchens wasn't present, the immediate response was a hard stare and a shake of the head.

Rattled, Charlotte applied herself to assisting Ambrose with his breakfast, sawing the tops off his boiled eggs and buttering some toast. Poor Jam's bizarre tics were even more severe this morning, and he missed his mouth several times. When at last his own frustration proved too much and he pushed his chair back so hard it tipped over, Charlotte jumped.

"I've ha-ha-had enough!" he yelled, before storming wildly from the room.

None of them being at ease with such emotional outbursts, an uncomfortable silence reigned for several heartbeats, ending only when Major Brooks reached over and daintily picked up Ambrose's leftover toast with a finger and thumb.

"Shame to waste it," he said, and reached for the pot of marmalade with a hand that only trembled a little.

Charlotte scowled. There were times when Brooks' dry humour could lighten a situation, but this wasn't one of them.

Across the table, Eustace was still avoiding her gaze; she sighed under her breath and finished off her own breakfast. Her anger at his behaviour in the summerhouse had lessened since her visit to the hospital and last night's attack. After all, he could hardly be held responsible for feeling confused and unable to commit himself when he was still melancholy. The sight of so much suffering over the past couple of days had been a reminder that she mustn't expect too much. He needed her patience and understanding. When he was feeling better, she dared to hope he might come to his senses and return to her.

It wasn't impossible that Papa's plans for her alliance with the Westhamptons might still come to fruition. All she had to do was to gradually win Eustace round. She thought about it while chewing her toast: she'd get Nellie to do something nicer with her hair and make her look pretty in spite of her awful mourning garb. She'd make herself find reasons to be near him. If she could be the most feminine and charming version of herself, she might once again recapture his heart. She must exert the same determination she had shown in the face of last night's attack, and use that power to refuse to see his rejection as anything but a temporary hiccup.

Breakfast was a sombre affair: the officers spoke little and departed singly, until at last Charlotte and Nurse Boyle were left alone to finish clearing up the dishes and sweep up the crumbs. Boyle closed the door as soon as Captain Reynolds had limped away down the corridor, leaning heavily on his stick as if his frostbitten feet were paining him more that morning. When she turned around and leaned against the door, her expression made Charlotte's pulse skip.

"You wanted to ask me about Lieutenant Hitchens," Boyle said. "I didn't want to tell you in front of the officers, although they're bound to find out eventually."

"What's happened?" What could be so bad that the other officers shouldn't be told about it? It clearly wasn't good news.

"He was upset by the attack last night. One of the windows in his room was broken by a stone, and of course he couldn't see what was happening. It turns out he'd smuggled a pair of scissors out of the library – don't ask me how. Someone must have been remiss. He used them to hurt himself."

"Hurt himself?" Charlotte repeated, struggling to picture the quiet, subdued Hitchens doing anything remotely violent. Which was silly, of course, because he must have done and seen any number of violent things at the front.

"He tried to cut his own throat."

Charlotte gripped the edge of the table and sank back into her chair, struggling to accept what she'd just heard.

"He's alright now. Luckily the scissors were blunt. I found him in time to stop him doing a proper job of it. Bandaged him up and confiscated the scissors, of course. We must thank the good Lord he didn't find a razor."

Bile rose in Charlotte's throat; the thought of what might have happened was enough to make anyone's blood curdle. Hitchens was the mildest, most unassuming of all the officers in their care. Not cynical like Brooks, not bad-tempered like Eustace, not trapped in his own silent world like Reynolds, and not bordering on ridiculous like young Ambrose. He shouldn't have been driven to make an attempt on his own life by the actions of young villagers who could have no idea what he had experienced on the front line.

Something would have to be done: she couldn't have the officers in her care subjected to such mental strain ever again.

. . .

The local police inspector arrived shortly after breakfast, accompanied by a constable who gave the impression he was trying to appear unimpressed by the grandeur of his surroundings. He looked about him, sniffed, and took out his notebook ready to jot down details of what he described as an "alleged offence".

Charlotte bit back the urge to snap back that there was nothing *alleged* about it. They'd sent the young housemaid out at dawn to scrub the graffiti off the walls as best she could, but the broken glass and stones still provided proof enough, along with the discarded pot of whitewash and brushes. Fortunately, the inspector seemed more respectful, appearing suitably shocked when Charlotte described the stone whizzing past her head and the loutish yelling of the youths who had carried out the unprovoked attack.

Doctor Sheridan arrived in his motor car soon after the policemen, and joined them in the drawing room to discuss the impact of the night's events. Charlotte and Nurse Boyle carefully avoided any mention of Hitchens' attempt at suicide, knowing he could be arrested and imprisoned for it. Quite apart from the humane considerations, Nurse Boyle had pointed out that it would reflect badly upon the Plas Norton Convalescent Home if word got out that they had neglected to protect one of their patients. It sat uncomfortably with Charlotte not to seek medical attention for his injured throat, but the nurse was so firm in her insistence that the doctor wasn't needed, Charlotte felt unable to go against her.

"My prime concern, gentlemen, is for the officers in our care to feel secure and safe," Charlotte said, keeping her hands folded in her lap in the hope that a calm demeanour would help the gathered officials forget her youth and inexperience. "I find it shocking that anyone from the village should persecute our officers in this way, when they've been wounded in the service of their country."

The doctor huffed. "*My* prime concern, Miss Fitznorton, is to get them back to the front line where they can do their duty. One can hardly be surprised if folk in the village are unhappy about what amounts to a lunatic asylum in their midst, especially one for men who plead illness as an excuse for shirking their duties to their country. If they want to be here, they need to face up to it. There's no point in cosseting these fellows like a bunch of namby-pambies. They'll face worse in France than a few pebbles lobbed through the window. Real wounds, not just attacks of nerves."

"Several of our patients have suffered what you would describe as 'real wounds'. Or did I merely imagine Captain Reynolds' missing toes and Captain Chadwycke's lacerations from being buried alive?"

Nurse Boyle cut in hastily, preventing her from saying too much in temper. Charlotte lowered her lashes and focused on the red, roughened skin of her hands contrasting with the black crepe covering her lap. "I'm sure we are all in agreement with the main point, that the culprits who vandalised this house last night and daubed an insult on its walls should be caught and punished."

The inspector sucked air between his teeth. "It won't be easy, I'm afraid, ladies."

Once again Charlotte saw red. "On the contrary, Inspector. There can't be many schoolboys within easy cycling distance with traces of whitewash on their hands this morning. I imagine a policeman of your calibre and experience should have no difficulty tracking them down." She sprang to her feet and gestured imperiously towards the door. "I trust you've seen all the evidence you need here, so we won't delay you any further in your investigations. Good day, gentlemen."

She rang for Mrs Longford to see the men out, and stood

waiting for them to rise. There was a momentary pause in which she thought they might challenge their dismissal by a girl young enough to be the inspector's daughter, but if their pride warred against the idea of it, it lost out to the deference that came naturally to most officials in the face of superior wealth and breeding. They filed out of the room, the inspector first, and the doctor last.

Sheridan turned to Charlotte on the doorstep as he put on his hat. "Your dedication to your hopeless cause is admirable, Miss Fitznorton. However, I wonder if you realise what will happen to these patients of yours if they fail to recover quickly?"

"What do you mean?"

"The military is not an organisation that can afford to wait indefinitely. Men who do not regain their mental fitness cannot be reintegrated into the forces or indeed into society. There are other institutions, if you catch my drift, more suitable as a permanent home for any patients whose sanity might be called into question. I bid you good day, Miss Fitznorton, Nurse Boyle – and I urge you to think carefully upon my words."

THIRTY-FIVE

Charlotte

Charlotte balanced the tray carefully as she climbed the stairs, unnerved by the way the tall carafes of water and glasses wobbled as she almost tripped on the hem of her long black skirt. How on earth did domestic staff manage to do all their fetching and carrying without tripping and dropping things? It was one of the many aspects of work that she'd had her eyes opened to in recent weeks: things she'd never thought about, like how tiring it could be to be constantly at other people's beck and call, or how stripping and re-making several beds could leave one breathless and perspiring. She didn't even do the most physically strenuous tasks like scrubbing, as Mrs Longford had taken on Cadwalader's daughter Dorothy as a housemaid. Known by everyone as Dolly, she had recently turned thirteen so was more than old enough to leave school.

At the top of the stairs, she began delivering the jugs and glasses to the bedrooms where the officers slept. She paused in the doorway of the one which had previously been hers, wistfully eyeing its apricot silk curtains and pretty wallpaper, the plush carpet and the large window with its fine view over Rosamund's rose garden. She missed the comfort and luxury of this room. At least the bed wasn't the large, canopied one she had once slept in: all the beds in the rooms where the officers slept had been replaced by more utilitarian hospital beds with narrow, black iron frames and crisp white sheets emblazoned with large red crosses.

As she reached the fifth doorway, which was Captain Reynolds's room, she almost bumped into Nurse Boyle, who was hurrying out with an impatient expression. The nurse closed the door and barred Charlotte's way.

"Never mind the Germans, that young man is his own worst enemy," she hissed.

Charlotte's heart sank. It seemed Reynolds was still refusing to comply with any of the nurse's requests for him to get up and mingle with the other men downstairs. He'd been at Plas Norton for weeks, and still no one had heard him speak.

"He's no better, then?"

"Better? If anything, he's worse. This afternoon I caught him curled up underneath his bed. Underneath! I ask you, have you ever heard anything more ridiculous? A grown man, yet he's acting like a child. If he doesn't sort himself out before the doctor's next visit, we all know where that old fellow will send him." She ended with a fierce huff and a toss of the head before stalking off down the corridor. "See if you can talk some sense into him, Miss Fitznorton," she called over her shoulder before descending the stairs.

Charlotte stepped inside, leaving the door open behind her for the sake of propriety. Sure enough, the bed was empty. She set down the tray and poured a glass of water before placing it on the nightstand. For a few moments she gazed out of the window, unsure what to say that might persuade the captain to leave his sanctuary under the bed. Nurse Boyle's concerns were justified, given the doctor's warnings on his last visit, she under stood that the other woman's frustrations, which manifested as irritation, were a sign that she cared. But was it any wonder these men wanted to do nothing more than hide away, after the terrors they had experienced?

She stroked her chin, thinking. She needed to find some words to push Reynolds to come out, but as a stubborn person herself she knew that being pushed might just make him push back and refuse even more steadfastly.

A quick peek under the metal bedstead confirmed that Reynolds was still curled up and facing away from her, his long arms and legs tucked close to his chin. On an impulse, she picked up a pillow, dropped it onto the floor beside the bed, and plumped down onto it. She smoothed her skirt over her legs for modesty, and leaned against the wall.

It seemed only polite to explain why she was there.

"Nurse Boyle tells me you're upset, Captain Reynolds. She's asked me to try to convince you to come out from under the bed. Well, I'm not going to do that. As far as I'm concerned, you may stay under there if you wish, or come out, as you please. I'll stay with you, if you like. Or I'll leave you alone. Whichever you'd prefer."

There was no response, so she took his silence as assent and remained where she was. It wasn't as if she had any urgent tasks requiring her attention. The idea of sitting on the floor and hiding from the world was, in a strange kind of way, rather appealing. Embarrassment could almost have driven her to want to do the same after Eustace ended their engagement. She often had to force herself to mix with other people since his rejection.

With the pillow under her, it wasn't uncomfortable sitting on the floor, and the quietness of the room gave it a restful air. She made no further attempt at conversation, but listened to the rich sound of birdsong audible through the tall windows. Occasionally she heard voices, too indistinct to tell what they were saying: the deeper voices of the officers carried better than those of the women, she noticed. Her thoughts wandered, and she let them. It was so rare not to be distracted by anything, not to be busy doing things.

She thought about Eustace, and Aunt Blanche, who had been predictably shocked at her taking on Josephine and disappointed to hear about the ending of her engagement. Not for the first time, she wondered what Papa would have said, and whether he would have blamed her for failing to cement their alliance with the Westhamptons. The viscountess had sent a letter which expressed more grief at Eustace's failure to recover than for the termination of their prospective union.

Was Charlotte sorry to lose Eustace? She wasn't even sure she liked him much, especially since he had become so ill-tempered. In those first moments of rejection she had hated him, but she couldn't hate him now. He wasn't a bad man really, just a man in a bad state.

If she was sorry about anything, now that she had time and space to think, it was losing her chance to become a married woman, which would have meant being seen as an adult as well as fulfilling her father's ambitions. As a wife she would have had influence, and the respect of others. As an unmarried girl, she often felt that other people, especially men, paid her little regard.

Still, that had changed to a degree, since she'd set up the convalescent hospital. Mrs McKie and Mrs Longford seemed to respect her. Even Nurse Boyle had found little to criticise of late, and Nellie Dawson hadn't left her service yet. These reflections made her lips twitch with ironic amusement. Who would have thought that she would ever care about gaining the respect of her servants?

Her thoughts turned to the recent attack of vandalism. It seemed likely that this had caused Captain Reynolds' relapse. He must have been aware of the windows being broken, and the shouting and jeering of the local youths. This bedroom was the closest to the front of the house, where the hooligans had daubed their cruel taunt. She could only hope he didn't know about Hitchens' subsequent attempt at suicide.

What could be done to prevent such an attack occurring again? The attitude of the police hadn't given her confidence. They seemed to share Doctor Sheridan's prejudice against the officers, seeing shell-shock as little more than insanity. How could such prejudice be countered?

People in the village might feel differently if they could see for themselves that the men deserved sympathy, not scorn. But how could that come about, when the men needed privacy and rest to recover? Releasing a sigh, she fidgeted and turned her gaze towards Reynolds. With a start, she realised he had rolled over and was watching her.

"Don't feel obliged to stay with me," he said in a voice that was quiet and hoarse from lack of use.

Her heart leapt at hearing him speak for the first time, but she maintained her composure. If she made a fuss, it might close him down again.

"Thank you, but I'm perfectly content to stay, as long as you don't mind." She supposed she shouldn't really be there, alone with a man in his bedroom; but the nurse and VAD performed much more intimate tasks than sitting with a fellow, and no one thought any less of their virtue as a consequence.

Reynolds said nothing more, but gave a faint nod before looking away, as if reluctant to engage any further.

"It's surprisingly comfortable down here," she remarked after a few moments of silence. "But then, I have a pillow to sit on. Would you like a pillow, too? There's another on the bed."

His dark eyes swivelled back in her direction, as if she had surprised him. He shook his head. He had such sad eyes, big and brown. With his mournful expression, he reminded her of a spaniel that had been kicked. She had the sense that he had been taking the measure of her with that intense gaze. Perhaps if she went on talking, he might say something else.

"I can't imagine being unable to speak for so many weeks. Is it horrid?"

A quick nod confirmed it.

"Gosh, I am sorry. In a way I wondered if it might be a bit of a relief, not *having* to say anything. Having to be sociable can be draining. And of course being in a position of leadership, as you have been, isn't easy. But even so, I daresay *I* shouldn't like it at all to never be able to venture an opinion or share an idea or make a request."

She was about to add, thinking aloud, that there was a power in using one's voice, whether for good or ill, but something made her stop the words before they spilled out. Would a young man, a fighter at that, appreciate being thought of as powerless? Somehow, she doubted it.

"My throat closes over. I want to speak, but I can't," he murmured, so softly that she held her breath to hear him more clearly. He had uncurled his limbs and lay now on his back, staring up at the underside of the bedstead above him.

Charlotte was still considering how to respond when a brisk knock at the open door interrupted them.

"Come in," she called. A glance at Reynolds revealed he had once again turned away and was shielding his head with his arm.

Nora, the new nursemaid, stumped past the bed with Josephine in her arms, swaddled in a white knitted shawl.

"Oh! I didn't expect to see you down there, miss."

"What is it, Nora?" Charlotte found it difficult to contain her impatience. She had felt she was getting somewhere with the captain, but the nursemaid's arrival meant that their progress had been undone.

"Nurse Boyle wants me to help her, miss, but it's time for Miss Josephine's bottle and I can't be in two places at once. She says if you're not doing anything important, you can nurse the baby."

Charlotte pursed her lips at the implication that helping Captain Reynolds wasn't important, but held out her arms to accept her sister and the bottle of warm milk. "Off you go, then, Nora. It wouldn't do to keep Nurse Boyle waiting when she has so many terribly important tasks for you."

She focused on tilting the glass bottle at the correct angle to ensure that the rubber teat didn't fill with air. When at last she looked up, she noted with surprise that Reynolds was smiling.

"What's funny?" she asked.

He shook his head, but the gentle smile remained and he shifted onto his side to watch as the baby guzzled her feed. Her soft gulping noises were the only sound in the room apart from the distant birdsong, until at last the bottle was empty and Charlotte set it down on the floor.

"She'll need winding now she's finished," Reynolds murmured. He looked so wistful as Charlotte propped the baby against her shoulder and patted her back that she wondered if he had children of his own.

When Josephine let out a trio of satisfied belches, Reynolds' cheeks lifted again in another smile. "That's a good girl," he said.

Charlotte grinned. "Make the most of this, Josephine. No one will praise you for belching after meals when you're older."

She propped Josephine against her raised knees and mopped her chin with her embroidered bib. The skin was dented and red where the neck of the bottle had rested. The baby's eyes regarded her inquisitively and she found herself chatting about nonsense, as if Josephine understood everything she was saying.

"You're a bright girl, aren't you, Josie dear? What do you think of sitting down here, then, eh? I don't think we've ever sat on the floor before. But it's quite comfortable, really. Captain

Reynolds is here with us, too. Can you see him over there? You've made him smile, I think..."

Such was her focus on her little sister's intent expression, she didn't notice at first that two more people had entered the room and were watching her. It wasn't until one of them uttered a deliberate "Ahem!" that she paused mid-sentence and looked up. Her face lit up with a beaming smile.

"Venetia! You're back. How completely marvellous. Look, Josephine: Venetia is here..." Charlotte stopped, noticing her friend's companion, but unsure who he was. This was awkward: she should have addressed Venetia more formally in front of a stranger.

The thin, raven-haired man, who stood perhaps an inch taller than Venetia, returned Charlotte's gaze unblinkingly through wire-rimmed spectacles. Square-jawed, with sharply defined cheekbones, there was a delicacy to his face, as if it had been sculpted by a craftsman with a keen eye for aesthetics.

"Miss Fitznorton, may I introduce to you my cousin, Doctor Christopher Havard."

So this was Kit, of whom Charlotte had heard so much. He wasn't at all as Charlotte had imagined him. Far from being a stooped, balding academic, he was actually rather handsome. His frank gaze made a little tremor slide over Charlotte's skin.

Venetia's smile had a triumphant air, unsurprising given that she had often remarked on how busy her doctor cousin was. Who knew how difficult it had been to bring him here to Plas Norton?

Charlotte fumbled with the baby in an attempt to rise, but Dr Havard spoke first.

"Please don't get up on my account, Miss Fitznorton. I can see you're busy."

"Thank you, Doctor. It is somewhat tricky." She found herself blushing under the intensity of his gaze. "I've been sitting with Captain Reynolds for a little while, and my sister Josephine has been entertaining us."

Under the bed, the captain's troubled expression had returned. She addressed him quietly. "Captain Reynolds, would you be willing to allow Doctor Havard to examine your hands and feet? Miss Vaughan-Lloyd has a high opinion of his medical skill."

There was a tense few moments while everyone awaited Reynolds' decision. Charlotte sent him an encouraging smile and a nod, and at last he slid out from under the bedstead, head first and crawling on his elbows, emerging carefully as if his bandaged hands and feet still gave him considerable pain.

"May I help you up, Captain Reynolds?" The doctor had stepped forward; Reynolds held up an arm and in an instant had been heaved up onto the mattress.

Clutching Josephine, Charlotte scrambled to her feet, then picked up the empty bottle.

"We'll leave you to your examination," she said, disconcerted by her proximity to the doctor. Those eyes, she could see now, were a deep blue-green, with straight brows and thick, black lashes any girl would envy. Under his direct gaze, her cheeks felt warm. She turned back to Venetia.

"Shall we take Josephine back to the day nursery?" she suggested. "I've been simply longing to catch up on all your news."

THIRTY-SIX

Charlotte

Later that afternoon, over tea in the housekeeper's sitting room, Charlotte gave Venetia a summary of the events since she had been away: how she had taken Josephine into her care and been spurned by Eustace, and then about the explosion in the factory and the attack by the local vandals.

"Cripes!" Venetia commented, setting her cup and saucer down. "I wasn't away for all that long, yet you seem to have crammed a lifetime's worth of adventures into a remarkably short period. It seems you can't be trusted to be left alone."

"I wish you'd been here. Especially as we didn't part on the best of terms."

"I may have been a trifle harsh..." Venetia scratched the back of her neck, as if she were embarrassed.

"Don't worry about that now. I'm just glad you're back."

"Quite. The main thing is, you did the right thing. Josephine is adorable, even by the odd standards of those of us who don't get sentimental about babies. And Eustace is an idiot, as are those dolts who think it's fun to persecute the afflicted,"

"I've been thinking about them, Vee. We need a way to make people in the village and Pontybrenin see that our shell-shocked officers deserve support, not hostility. But I don't know where to start."

"My dear girl, have I taught you nothing? Always start with the people who have influence. Get them on your side, and the rest will fall into place."

"Well... there's Doctor Sheridan. He has influence, but he isn't exactly on my side. He'd have the officers bundled into straitjackets and sent off to asylums to be electrocuted if he had his way. He'd deem that to be a somewhat generous alternative to a court martial."

"He isn't the only person of influence in the town. Perhaps the women would be easier to sway towards sympathy...?"

Charlotte tilted her head, thinking. "Hmm. You may be right."

"Before you get too absorbed in making one of your lists to enumerate the great and the good, I want to talk to you about my cousin."

"Doctor Havard? I don't think he likes me very much."

"Whatever gave you that idea?"

"Didn't you see him staring at me earlier?"

"And you think that means he *doesn't* like you?" Venetia's lips twitched; she seemed to be struggling not to laugh.

"I imagine he disapproved of my sitting alone with Captain Reynolds. I suppose it wasn't strictly within the bounds of propriety, sitting on the floor in his bedroom like that. But the door was open, and he was hardly a threat to my virtue, given that he was hiding under the bed. And I wasn't there long before I had Josephine with me. He'd have to be the most frightful brute to go pouncing on a girl with a baby in her arms."

"Charlotte, are you in earnest? Kit is positively the last man in the world who would disapprove of you sitting on the floor with a man who is so obviously suffering. If indeed he *was* staring, it's probably because he was bowled over with admiration. Especially as your unconventional tactics succeeded in persuading the captain out from under the bed. Perhaps we should all take a leaf out of your book, and spend more time just sitting with the poor chaps when they're in a funk, instead of trying to jolly them out of it."

Charlotte felt her cheeks grow warm at the idea of earning Dr Havard's admiration.

"However did you persuade the doctor to come here?"

"It wasn't easy. He's frightfully busy in his work, and with the war on it was a struggle to find another doctor to take over so that he could be released. It was lucky that Plas Norton isn't all that far away…"

"He isn't from London, then?"

"Good heavens, no. He works in a mining town near Merthyr Tydfil. A ghastly place, in all honesty, but he feels it's his calling to work with the poor and one must admire that, I suppose. He'd be a great success as a society doctor, I'm sure, but that particular calling isn't for him. The consequence of his upbringing, I daresay."

Curious to know more, Charlotte poured more tea into Venetia's cup, then added a splash of milk. "Go on," she urged.

Venetia lowered her voice. "May I speak candidly, in the strictest confidence?"

Charlotte nodded, trying not to look too eager. Venetia wasn't one for gossiping as a rule. She felt a small glow of pride at being trusted with details about her family.

"His mother, my aunt Lavinia, married beneath her. Grandfather threatened all manner of dire consequences, but she wouldn't be deterred and simply declared that if he wouldn't let her have her charming Welsh doctor, she would elope and cause a far greater scandal. The women in our family never were fainthearted." A smile played about her lips as she sipped her tea. "Kit followed in his father's footsteps by becoming a medical man, and his elder sister has gone off to work as a nurse in France. Kit would have gone too, but the army wouldn't have him."

"Why not?"

A shadow crossed her face. "Rheumatic fever when he was a boy. It left his heart weakened, so he has to take care not to overexert himself. But whatever you do, don't tell him I've mentioned any of this. He'd be mortified to know we'd been discussing him like one of his medical cases."

There was no time to respond as a knock at the door heralded the arrival of the subject of their conversation. Charlotte shifted uncomfortably in her seat at the thought that he might realise they'd been discussing him, but Venetia greeted him airily, as if nothing was amiss.

"Do come in, Kit, and join us for tea. Mrs McKie's egg and cress sandwiches are scrumptious."

There were two seats for him to choose from, and Charlotte felt inexplicably disappointed when Doctor Havard took the one nearer the door, facing her, instead of the one beside her. Still, it meant she could more easily steal glances at him – and she did, over and over, although she found that she felt awkward looking at him for more than a few moments at a time. The refined beauty of his cheekbones and jawline, and the faint hint of his rare smile, gave her a flustered feeling, like a fluttering bird in her tummy.

She fussed with the teapot, finding her hand trembled as she balanced the silver strainer and poured the dark brew into his cup. Venetia caught her eye with a knowing glance, and she hoped her friend hadn't noticed her sudden bumbling ineptitude, and that Doctor Havard hadn't seen how red and rough her hands were. If only she had worn a prettier dress today, and made more of an effort with her hair. She patted it self-consciously while Havard was focusing on Venetia's quizzing.

THE BROKEN VOW

"What are your initial impressions of the officers, now that you've had an opportunity to speak to a couple of them?"

He sipped his tea thoughtfully before replying. She couldn't help noticing how slender his hands were, with long fingers a pianist or artist might envy. There was a delicacy to those hands, a gentle care in the way he touched things that made her shift in her seat, overcome by a sudden flush of heat she couldn't explain.

"They are as you described," he said. "Their physical wounds, in the main, are less serious than their symptoms of mental debility. I've seen similar cases with men who were caught in a coal mining accident. Tremors, sleeplessness, oppressive melancholy... There are those in my profession who believe that the symptoms of war neurosis – the condition popularly known as 'shell-shock' – are the result of a form of concussion, but I'm not convinced. I suspect they're the natural consequence of enduring a situation so terrifying and unnatural most of us can't begin to imagine it. There are limits to what the human mind can tolerate. The ancients recognised that a healthy body is necessary for a healthy mind, so it's only logical for the reverse to also be true."

There was a pause while both women absorbed this possibility.

"If the injury is primarily mental and not physical, does that mean you would support Doctor Sheridan's suggestion of applying electrical shocks?" Charlotte asked quietly, praying inwardly that he wouldn't.

For a long moment his gaze locked with hers; she hardly breathed until he glanced back to his plate.

"There is evidence that the therapeutic application of electricity may be beneficial in some cases. But there are alternatives."

"Such as?"

"One colleague is using hypnosis with some success. It

enables neurasthenic men's suppressed fears to be released. Others advocate complete mental and physical rest, with nothing in the environment to stimulate the senses: no pictures on the walls or other ornamentation, no activity or interaction with other sufferers..." He screwed up his face.

"You have your doubts?" Venetia prompted.

"I don't presume to disparage it. It may work in some cases. Any approach is, essentially, experimental. But my instincts are that men benefit from being useful. Such a numbing and purposeless existence, even for a short period, may cause more harm than good. Here at Plas Norton, you offer diversions such as reading, billiards and cards, and the opportunity to engage in a little light exercise. But none of those pleasant activities offers these fellows the chance to produce something worthwhile, which might replace paralysing fear with a sense of self-respect."

Charlotte frowned. "What would you suggest, then?"

"Gardening; woodworking; creating and repairing items that are useful. Keep them busy. Occupy their hands and minds, and give them something to feel proud of. That, to me, would seem a better course of treatment."

"But they're officers, not working men. We can hardly expect them to take readily to manual labour."

He raised one dark eyebrow. "Miss Fitznorton, you speak as if they're a separate species, not merely a more privileged rank and social class."

Venetia leaned back in her chair and chuckled. "I daresay they've been brought up to believe they are."

"I see you have doubts, Miss Fitznorton." His tone was gentle, but there was a challenge there that made her feel she should choose her words carefully. His knowledge was as impressive as his sincerity and passion for his work, and she didn't want to disappoint him.

"Not doubts. I find it easier to put faith in the approach you propose than in Doctor Sheridan's... I'm just unsure whether the officers will be willing or even able to do menial work. Especially poor Reynolds and Hitchens, who might be too crippled to perform physical labour."

He had been drawing circles on the tablecloth with his index finger, watching her while she spoke, but now shook his head as if she had spoken in error.

"Not 'poor' Reynolds, or indeed 'poor' anyone among your patients. Reynolds is perhaps the luckiest of the bunch, as he won't be going back to the front – not with fingers and toes missing. And Hitchens won't benefit from your pity, any more than the others. If you'd ever witnessed the conditions of those who are truly poor, believe me, you wouldn't apply such a word to the fellows you've so generously and comfortably accommodated here."

"Now, now, Kit," Venetia interjected sternly, laying her hand over his. "There's no need for your proselytising here. Please forgive my cousin, Charlotte. He's apt to let his passion for his work get in the way of his manners."

The doctor removed his spectacles, laid them on the table and pinched the bridge of his nose. "If I sound churlish, Miss Fitznorton, please accept my apologies. My cousin is well aware that I only came here because she refused to take no for an answer. My preference is to work where I can make the most difference, amongst people who will truly benefit from my help. The town where I work is still suffering the effects of a measles epidemic, and with the cost of food rising higher than wages, there's a great deal of hardship. By contrast, I feel your officers have little need of me... primarily because they are already supremely fortunate in having you on their side."

THIRTY-SEVEN

Charlotte

Charlotte looked around her drawing room at the assembled ladies, keen to catch the eye of each one before making the speech she'd had worryingly little time to prepare. This, she had no doubt, was her most important chance to improve the lives of the officers since she first opened the hospital. Beside her, on her left, sat Venetia, whose usual masculine style of dress was softened today by a high-necked lace blouse and cameo brooch. Charlotte sent her a grateful smile, recognising that her friend was making a special effort to charm the local ladies on her behalf.

To Charlotte's right sat Doctor Havard, whose presence seemed to have caused something of a stir. Charlotte supposed she could hardly blame them for looking a little discombobulated upon meeting him, when sitting beside him was leaving her feeling strangely unsettled too. It wasn't only his fine looks that affected her equilibrium, but also his odd mixture of reserve and confidence. He didn't seem the sort to be overly jolly or to make a brash show, like many of the young men she had met during her London season. Indeed, he didn't seem concerned about whether or not he was making a good impression on others: he was unselfconscious in a way Charlotte rather envied. Since his arrival at Plas Norton, he had devoted his energies to spending time getting to know each of the officers, talking with them and listening, leaning towards them as if deep in thought, absorbing every word. She couldn't help but wonder if they, too, felt as if his undivided attention had cast a spell over them.

Their guests today were a carefully selected group, chosen for their influence and knowledge of the local community. Mrs Butts, the vicar's wife, had arrived first. Still wearing a faintly disapproving air following their recent encounter, she regarded Charlotte and her companions with open curiosity, as if hoping to see how Charlotte fared since taking Josephine. Beside her sat Mrs Grundy, the ample-bosomed wife of the local mayor, resplendent in a hat that trailed puffs of marabou whenever she moved.

Next was Mrs Cleeves, the elderly wife of the Methodist minister. She peered at the fruit punch suspiciously, as if it might contain some kind of hidden alcohol, and, frowning, accepted a glass of lemonade instead. The last was Miss Hollett, headmistress of the Pontybrenin and District School for Girls. Aged around forty at a guess, her lively and dynamic air left Charlotte in no doubt that her support would be invaluable if she could be persuaded to give it.

Rising to stand before this group, Charlotte gave a nervous cough and surreptitiously wiped the palms of her hands on her skirt. She felt all too aware of her comparative youth and inexperience, but she had come this far in inviting the ladies, and as they had done her the courtesy of coming to visit, she must see her plan through.

After stammering over some thanks for taking the time to come, her mind went blank. She shuffled her notes on the table;

she'd scribbled them down in a hurry, and now that the moment to use them had arrived, her brain seemed unable to process her own handwriting. With a gulp, she realised she would stumble over her words more if she tried to rely on them than if she just dived in. She looked up with a tremulous attempt at a smile and took a deep breath.

"As you will be aware, ladies, my family home has been operating for several weeks as the Plas Norton Trust for Convalescent Officers. In the light of the sufferings inflicted on our fighting men by our enemies, it became apparent to me that I could not, in all conscience, leave the house standing idle. It would have been remiss of me to leave such a large house vacant when there are those in need of a sanctuary in which to recover from their wounds."

She paused and took a sip of water to steady her nerves, then glanced around each of the women in her audience. So far they looked interested, but she knew she had not yet engaged their emotions. Remembering Mrs Pankhurst's rousing speech, she felt nauseous. How could she, a girl just turned twenty, ever hope to capture the hearts and minds of this group?

Venetia nodded and sent her the merest hint of a wink. It was a reminder that she had allies at her side.

"Of course, it isn't only our troops who are suffering as a result of the war. The explosion at the munitions factory has been a terrible blow to our community. Each one of those men and women who died or were injured had given their labour for the greater good of our nation and the Empire, in the fight against tyranny. They deserve our support, as much as the soldiers who are convalescing in our midst after enduring the horrors of the front."

The mayoress nodded at that, and murmured agreement, quickly followed by Mrs Butts. Their approval gave Charlotte a spark of energy, as if a momentum was building: she continued with greater enthusiasm and conviction, feeling it was now safe to take a risk.

"I've come to realise in recent days that I made a grave mistake in inviting our small band of officers here without consulting the local community. Blame my youthful inexperience and over-enthusiasm for our nation's cause, if you will..."

Miss Hollett's eyebrows had flown up; she fidgeted with her handbag and glanced at her neighbours to see if they were equally surprised by Charlotte's candour.

"As a consequence, our loyal officers have suffered the indignity of being attacked by the very people they sought to protect. They went to war in defence of our freedom, and we have betrayed them. No, *I* have betrayed them: by failing to ensure that everyone in Pontybrenin and the villages nearby understands why they are here. I wanted to create a haven for them, a space where they could come to feel safe and heal before they return to the fray. In my arrogance I tried to do it alone, without involving you, or indeed anyone from the town – apart from Doctor Sheridan, of course. I should have realised that pride comes before a fall, and indeed in my case it has.

"To my shame, others have paid the price for my hubris. Last week, this building – my family's home – was damaged by vandals from the local area who threw stones through this very window. They jeered and insulted our brave men. Not content with that, they daubed a grave accusation on the walls. Boys, who have no understanding of what these men have suffered, have in their ignorance attempted to destroy the sense of sanctuary and peace I've been trying to create.

"Their actions, as you might imagine, have caused inconvenience and expense, but more importantly – *much* more importantly – they have caused pain and distress to men who deserve sympathy and support in their efforts to heal from their wounds. And let me assure you, ladies, our officers want nothing more than to heal, and to continue to serve this great country of ours."

She paused as her voice wobbled, as much from anger as from distress. The ladies were frowning now, and tutting sympathetically.

"You shouldn't blame yourself, Miss Fitznorton," insisted Mrs Grundy, accompanied by a murmured chorus of "Hear, hear" and "Quite so" from her companions.

"Oh, but I do. I realise there is no point in my being proud of offering a sanctuary to these men, if the community is against them. And so, in a spirit of humility, I ask you ladies to help me do better from now on. My plea to you, as women of importance in the town, is to help me take action, not only to help our brave officers, but to bring the community together. To do all we can to show our support both for the wounded men here and also for those local people who suffered in the accident at the factory. I have Plas Norton; you have influence. Together, as a united body of women, I believe we have the power to achieve the most marvellous things for everyone who needs our help."

Charlotte's cheeks flamed as Venetia broke into applause, quickly followed, albeit with more restraint, by Doctor Havard. The assembled ladies had little choice but to follow suit. Charlotte dared to hope as she resumed her seat and drained her glass of water that they had joined in out of conviction as much as good manners.

Mrs Butts was the first to respond. "I, for one, have sympathy for your intentions in setting up your establishment here. But there have been rumours, you see. About the nature of the men you have brought to Plas Norton. You describe them as wounded officers, but I must tell you, that is not what has been said in certain quarters."

"Thank you, Mrs Butts. I appreciate your honesty. This is why I have asked Doctor Havard to join us this morning. His opinion as a medical man must carry much greater weight than mine."

All eyes were on the doctor as he explained the nature of

shell-shock, not as a nervous complaint or madness, but a hidden wound as genuine as any visible injury. He explained that some of the greatest minds of the medical profession were seeking to understand it, not only on the British side but also on the French, and that the convalescent home at Plas Norton could play a vital part in finding a cure, if the community would get behind it. "Such are the numbers of men suffering, finding a cure could be instrumental in achieving a swift victory," he added.

By the time he had finished, his audience was raptly attentive. They could hardly tear their eyes from him to focus on Venetia, who added her own plea, leaving Charlotte blushing and twisting her hands in her lap.

"Despite suffering her own personal sorrows in recent months, with the loss of both her father and stepmother, I can assure you that my dear friend, Miss Fitznorton, hasn't stinted for a moment in her endeavours. She hasn't asked the community for a single shilling, but has undertaken to raise the funds for this vital war work from her own pocket and from the efforts of our connections in London. And in addition to her work here, she has shown herself eager to help individuals who find themselves in financial hardship after the accident at the factory. Such is her selflessness, she has even offered to sponsor one young heroine to fulfil her dream of training as a midwife. Knowing her as I do, I am convinced that her greatest reward would be to see Plas Norton and the community helping each other. Is there a way, do you think, that we can help the town, and in turn the town can help our officers?"

It was Miss Hollett who came up with the most popular suggestion, which happened to be an idea Charlotte and Venetia had already thought of: a fête, to be held in the grounds of Plas Norton, and involving the local townsfolk and villagers. Miss Hollett suggested staging a revue, with local schoolchildren and teachers performing songs and skits to amuse the officers and survivors of the explosion. Mrs Butts and Mrs Cleeves were keen to lend the support of their churches' choirs and musicians. Mrs Grundy suggested stalls, including a lucky dip, puppet show, and a coconut shy if coconuts could be found while the Germans were blockading the ports and sinking so many supply ships. Finally, Mrs Butts added a suggestion to use the event to help the town's small population of Belgian refugees, and Mrs Grundy promised to ask her husband to present medals to those who had rescued their workmates from the factory blaze.

"Thank you, ladies, for your excellent ideas and your offers of assistance. I imagine some of our officers may not feel well enough to attend the fête themselves, but if we set up the stalls at a discreet distance from the house, it will enable them to maintain their privacy without spoiling the gaiety for the participants and attendees. I'm sure it will be the most tremendous fun, as well as supporting excellent causes."

Charlotte shook each lady's hand as they left, chattering with enthusiasm about their plans for the forthcoming fête. Fizzing with excitement, she hid a smug smile.

Venetia gave her shoulder a jovial slap. "Jolly good show, old girl. You had them eating out of your hand."

"Thank you, Vee. Let's hope I can as easily charm Mrs McKie when I break the news that she'll be catering for a fête a few weeks from now."

Chuckling, Venetia limped away to write some letters, leaving Charlotte alone in the hallway with the doctor. He had waited with his hands in his trouser pockets, his expression thoughtful.

"That was impressive, Miss Fitznorton. It takes courage to admit to having been mistaken, and especially in front of those whom one is trying to win over."

She put a hand to her throat, suddenly awkward. His approval was like fresh air and sunshine: it made her lift her face and glow. But she had made herself vulnerable as a stratagem more than a display of modesty. Pleased though she was that it had worked, she didn't want him to get the wrong impression of her.

"Thank you, Doctor. But what I did wasn't brave. Real courage is going off to fight for one's country, or risking one's safety to make weapons for our soldiers. Courage is saving a friend from a factory fire, or even coming out from under the bed when every fibre of one's body longs to stay there." She wanted to add that courage might also be a man with a damaged heart choosing to work as a doctor among the poor, instead of taking an easier, safer route in a comfortable office on Harley Street. But she held her tongue for fear of betraying Venetia's confidence.

"I'd have to agree with you that courage takes many forms," he said. "And today you proved that it would be a mistake to underestimate yours."

He paused, as if he, too, wanted to say more, then simply nodded and strode away, leaving her to bask in the warmth of his approval.

THIRTY-EIGHT

Charlotte

A sharp rap at the bedroom door made Charlotte sit bolt upright. Venetia stirred in the next bed, mumbled something, and then turned over heavily. Tiptoeing to the door, Charlotte opened it a crack, revealing Nora in the corridor wearing a threadbare dressing gown and slippers that had also seen better days. She looked exhausted, as if she had been awake for hours.

"You need to come, miss. It's Miss Josephine. She's not well."

"I know she has a cold, but she was fine at bedtime."

"Well, she isn't fine now."

Charlotte frowned. Josephine had been snuffling for a couple of days, with a blocked nose that had made suckling from her bottles of milk difficult, but there hadn't been anything seriously wrong. Had she missed important signs of illness? Or was Nora exaggerating and summoning help only because she resented her sleep being disturbed?

Leaving the door open to allow light to spill into the room from the corridor, she fumbled into her own robe and slippers, then closed the door to avoid disturbing Venetia. Exhaling an irritable huff to make her displeasure known, she followed Nora to the night nursery.

Josephine was lying in her cot, her squalling cries interspersed with high-pitched gasps. As Charlotte entered the room, the baby started coughing: a hoarse, barking cough that made her sound not unlike one of the sea lions Charlotte had seen on visits to the zoo. The sound made Charlotte's heart rate quicken.

"Told you," Nora said.

Charlotte rounded on her. "Go and fetch the doctor."

"Doctor Sheridan? I don't know how to use the telephone."

"No, you silly girl. Why would you telephone him when Doctor Havard is staying here?"

Grumbling, the girl slouched out of the room.

Charlotte rubbed her tired eyes to make them focus, then reached into the cot to pick Josephine up. The baby's nightgown was wet with perspiration, and her face smeared with green snot. Grimacing, Charlotte held her close against her shoulder, then hunted in the chest of drawers for a muslin cloth. Her cries were so forlorn, and the cough so dramatic, Charlotte didn't know what to do. Helplessly, she began pacing the floor, gently jiggling her sister and murmuring reassurances to her in a voice that became increasingly anxious and high-pitched.

"It's alright, Josephine. I'm here. Doctor Havard will take a look at you. He'll know what to do."

Josephine's coughing and gasping breaths were no better by the time the doctor entered the room, just ahead of the surly Nora. He looked surprisingly alert for someone who had been woken in the middle of the night, but his hair was still rumpled from sleep. His shirt buttons had been fastened haphazardly, and one of his shirt tails stuck out of his trouser waistband. The sharp angle of his jaw and the hollow below his cheekbones were darkened by stubble.

"She has croup," he declared as soon as he heard the baby's coughing.

"Is it dangerous?" Charlotte asked. It was impossible to tell from his customary serious expression whether he was concerned.

He had placed a hand on Josephine's forehead where it rested against Charlotte's shoulder; Charlotte kept her gaze downwards, looking at the baby, embarrassed in case he saw how his proximity affected her.

"She has a slight fever, but in spite of the cough she's a good colour."

Charlotte's anxiety rose. "You didn't answer the question."

Their eyes locked, hers wide with fear and his soft with compassion, the pupils large and black in the half-light.

"It's very common. She should recover within a couple of days. Warm mist should help to ease her cough, if we can take her to a bathroom with a shower. At least, it's worth a try. Some babies respond better to cool air, so if it doesn't work we can try taking her outside."

She nodded eagerly. "My late papa's bedroom has its own adjoining bathroom, with a shower cubicle above the bath. We can use it without disturbing anyone." The room hadn't been allocated to any of the officers as Charlotte hadn't been ready to allow anyone else to use it yet.

Havard paused before following to give some brief instructions to Nora, who nodded sullenly and headed in the opposite direction, towards the kitchens. Charlotte noticed he was slightly breathless by the time he caught up with her. She paused at the panelled oak door of her father's room to allow him to open it for her, waiting while he fumbled for the light switch so that she could safely cross to the bathroom. His faintly raised eyebrows at the sight of both rooms suggested their size and luxury had surprised him.

"Just the ticket," he said as he turned on the bathroom light and saw the tall shower cubicle. It stood over the bath taps, great silver-coloured pipes towering at least seven or eight feet higher than the luxuriously deep bathtub. Doctor Havard turned all four taps on at once, making water burst from the pipes climbing the sides as well as the central, wide shower head which crowned the cubicle like the rose of a giant watering can.

Soon billows of steam filled the area nearest the bath, and he pulled a wooden chair over from the corner to enable Charlotte to sit near the wood-panelled tub with the baby on her lap.

"Keep her upright, and try to relax," he said.

"I think I'm too worried to relax," she confessed. The barking cough sounded as alarming as ever.

"Try not to be. The thing is with babies: they're little animals, you know. They smell our fear. It makes them uneasy. And even though she senses how much you care for her, she can tell that you're frightened of her, too."

"I'm frightened *for* her, not frightened *of* her."

He remained silent, watching Josephine where Charlotte held her upright in her arms.

"Why should you imagine I'm scared of her? She can't hurt me."

His voice was gentle. "She does threaten your equilibrium, though. And not only when she's unwell."

Her grip on the baby tightened. "We're fine. Really."

"Of course." Putting his palms on his thighs, he moved as if preparing to leave.

"Don't go," she said, so quickly she surprised herself. "That is, could you please stay a bit longer, if you don't mind? Just to be sure she is going to be alright. There seems to be less steam coming out now."

He reached out to the cascade of water, then frowned. "Hmm. You're right. The hot water must be running out. I'll see where the nursemaid has got to."

She ruminated over his words while he was out of the room. "What did he mean, Josie? I'm not frightened of you."

But as the coughing became fiercer, and the whistling in-breaths more laboured, she was less sure that this was true. The weight of responsibility for keeping this helpless little creature alive suddenly felt too much: by the time Doctor Havard returned with Nora, she was on the verge of tears. But she wouldn't surrender to them; she couldn't let anyone else see her as weak.

Nora gazed around at the splendour of Sir Lucien's rooms, her mouth gaping. She was carrying a kettle, and Doctor Havard had brought a paraffin stove which he set down on top of a cupboard and proceeded to light.

"Would you mind filling the kettle, Nora? We need more steam to relieve Josephine's cough."

Nora did as he asked, then stood back, yawning.

"You look done in," he said to her. "Why don't you get back to bed, get some rest while we look after her? In the morning you can take over again while Miss Fitznorton catches up on some sleep."

The girl didn't give him a chance to change his mind, but headed at once to the door. Charlotte noted her insolent arch look as she left, and supposed she would be exposed to gossip now for being alone in a bathroom with a man.

She tutted crossly. It should be obvious that he was keeping a respectful distance, sitting across the room, and that a doctor would hardly be about to commit any impropriety with a woman nursing a sick infant. How silly the world was, to cast doubt on a woman's morals simply for being on her own with a man who was not her husband. Admittedly she was in her nightclothes, and he might be deemed only half dressed, as he had not delayed dressing long enough to fasten a collar to his shirt, or to don a tie or jacket.

Her mouth went dry as she took in how attractive he looked

with his shirt open at the throat and his dark hair tousled, but her thoughts were quickly diverted when Josephine suffered another coughing fit. Charlotte paced the floor, patting the baby's back and murmuring soothing words until the hoarse barking had subsided.

"What did you mean earlier, when you said I'm frightened of my sister?" she asked.

He tipped his head, regarding her thoughtfully. "Only that for such a young woman, recently orphaned and with little experience of young children, it's a daunting task to have to be mother, father and sister to a new baby. It would hardly be surprising if you felt anxious when you had so little time to prepare yourself for the task. A mother usually has months to ready herself. You can only have had days at most, perhaps even hours. My cousin told me you were reluctant to assume responsibility, and yet when we arrived it appeared that Josephine was already settled with you. Forgive me if I've been presumptuous; I merely imagined you might feel some strain now that you have her needs to consider as well as your own and those of the officers you've done so much to accommodate here."

His tone was kind, but she still felt defensive.

"I'm not complaining."

"I know."

She plumped back onto her chair, her head beginning to ache. She put a hand to her forehead, but quickly resumed her patting of Josephine's back as the baby's fitful crying began again.

"Is my lack of knowledge so obvious?"

He smiled. "You must be tired. Would you like me to hold her for a while?"

She nodded gratefully and he rose to meet her in the centre of the room. As she passed the baby to him, she caught his smell, sharp and clean like soap. His arms were warm where her hands brushed against them, making a jolt thrill through her

"You have to support her head," she said, then realised how foolish she must sound.

With a patient nod he started a gentle swaying, keeping Josephine's head cradled against the base of his throat. Moving a little closer to the kettle, though still keeping a safe distance from it, to Charlotte's surprise he started to sing in a soft, low voice. She didn't recognise the song, which wasn't in English, but its simple, tender melody worked like magic on Josephine, whose fractious crying died down to nothing more than a whimper.

"What a beautiful song," Charlotte murmured when he stopped singing.

"*Diolch,*" he replied, thanking her in Welsh.

Their eyes locked, both thankful for the moment of calm as Josephine snuffled sleepily against his shirt.

"It's a Welsh lullaby called 'Suo Gân'," he explained quietly, still gently swaying. "I heard it many times growing up, as my parents sang it to my siblings. Now my sister Lucy sings it to her children."

She couldn't imagine her own father singing, and certainly not in Welsh. Despite living in Wales for most of her life, she didn't think of herself as Welsh at all, and had never had any interest in the culture of the working-class Welsh people living and working around Plas Norton. Yet the song had been so beautiful, it made her feel she had missed out.

"Do you have many siblings?" she asked, keeping her voice low. "Growing up as an only child myself, I imagine it must be wonderful to have brothers and sisters."

"I'm the second of six children. My elder sister Victoria has gone to France to serve with the Scottish Women's Hospital. Then there's Lucy, who has two little boys, and Alexandra, who is at Oxford, as is my brother William. Timothy is the baby of the family, although he would hate being described as such. He's still at school. As for whether it's wonderful... I suppose it is, mostly, but there are moments when tempers fly. We Welsh are a proud and passionate people."

She took a moment to absorb this, imagining a houseful of siblings, and what it would be like to be this man's reason for pride and passion.

"Have you always wanted to be a doctor?"

"Always. I can't imagine ever wanting to do anything else. My father is a doctor, too. For as long as I can remember he's worked with miners and steelworkers and their families. Men and women whose bodies are broken and bruised by toil, who grow old prematurely and die younger than those born more fortunate. Workers labour in the direst conditions, lacking even the most basic hygiene to keep themselves healthy. Even if they manage to avoid accidents and serious injury underground, the dust gets into their lungs and kills them. Boys follow their fathers into the pit and rarely see daylight; girls pick over the coal tips for fuel to keep their families warm. Their education is of the most rudimentary kind, and yet they thirst for knowledge and music, and the things of the Spirit. They pool the few resources they have, to build institutions for the common good: welfare halls, rugby pitches, chapels and libraries.

"The men whose lives depend on their butties underground share a bond it's difficult for outsiders to comprehend. And every day I saw their gratitude and respect for my father: it practically shone out of these hard-working people. When sickness prevents them from working, or their children fail to thrive, some of them are so poor they can't afford to pay a doctor. Imagine that, Miss Fitznorton: imagine a baby with croup like your sister, or whooping cough, or tuberculosis, and being prevented by circumstances over which you have no control from having access to medical help."

Charlotte swallowed hard. She had been frightened enough, even with a doctor in the house and a nursemaid to share the care of the child. How desperate she would have felt without the means to obtain expert assistance.

"My father's principles are far greater than his desire for wealth or renown. He would never refuse to treat anyone, but will let them pay what little they can. If they can't pay him in coin, nevertheless gifts will find their way to our doorstep. Many's the time Cook has opened the back door to discover a brace of pheasants on the step. Poached, I daresay," he added with a low chuckle.

She raised an eyebrow, remembering how her father would rage against poachers stealing game from the estate. How odd it was to hear a man of her own class finding such theft amusing. But then, he wasn't a man of her own class. She recalled what Venetia had said: his mother had married beneath her. This was a man who had grown up cheek by jowl with the poor. His respect for the rough working folk whose lives he had observed while growing up seemed heartfelt. He had been exposed to the realities of lives from which she had always been shielded.

Josephine was sleeping now, still held upright against his chest. Charlotte couldn't help a pang of envy. What would it be like to be held in his arms, cradled tenderly by those sensitive hands against the warmth of that slim body? She allowed her gaze to linger on him, savouring the lines of his shoulder blades under his shirt and the way his narrow hips moved when he rocked Josephine, making the woollen cloth of his trousers cling to the soft roundness of his buttocks.

"As I understand it from my cousin, you were not close to Josephine's mother?"

He had spoken gently, as if he sought to understand, not to judge, but she hesitated, unsure how much she wanted to reveal. She found, suddenly, that she would hate for him to think badly of her.

"I regret that now. When I was a child, I didn't understand why she was so cold. I sensed that she couldn't love me, and it made me dislike her. Recently I learned that she was terribly unhappy during those years. It's made me question many things I thought I knew, and left me wishing things could have been different. But the past is over and done with. I must focus on the future, and do the best I can for my sister."

"And what are your other ambitions?"

"My ambitions?"

"You've set up your convalescent home, and organised your spring fête to help the officers and factory workers and refugees. What next?"

Her face fell and she gazed down at her hands, fidgeting in her lap, wondering how much Venetia had already told him. She hadn't wanted him to know about her humiliating rejection by Eustace, yet the words tumbled from her mouth.

"Truthfully... I don't know how to answer. I have no other ambitions left; no plans beyond the fête. I was to be married. It was arranged before my papa died, last summer. He was so proud of me: the marriage was to ally the Fitznorton name with the Viscountcy of Westhampton. I was proud too, of the prospect of my grand society wedding and a honeymoon on the Riviera; of the idea of being a wife and mixing with the best people in London and in the country. It was all I'd ever wanted: a dream come true. But my fiancé has changed his mind. None of the plans Papa made for me will come to pass, and although I miss him terribly, in a way I'm glad he isn't here because he can't see how I've failed."

The bitter words seemed to hang in the air; she bit her lip, wishing she could take them back. "Forgive me, Doctor. I shouldn't have said so much."

"Please, call me Kit. All my friends do. And believe me when I say there's nothing to forgive."

Pleasure rushed through her at being counted among his friends. "Thank you, Kit. You may call me Charlotte."

They lapsed into a companionable silence. Kit gently

passed Josephine back to her, making soft hushing sounds as he did so. Seeing the patient settled and still deep in slumber, he padded over to the window, lifting the blind to reveal the earliest glimmer of dawn gilding the horizon with rose gold above the dark silhouetted hills.

"Your fiancé is a fool, Charlotte," he murmured, half-turning from the view. The light behind him threw his face into shadow, making it impossible to read his expression, but his voice was as golden as the daybreak. "The most basic principle in medicine is to observe, and from what I have observed of you since I arrived, I have no doubt that he has cast aside a jewel."

He stroked his chin thoughtfully, then strode to the stove and extinguished it.

"You should rest while the baby sleeps," he said, his pleasant voice gravelly with fatigue. "I'll send Nora to you. Good night, Charlotte. I'll see you in the morning."

THIRTY-NINE

MAY 1915

Charlotte

It was disconcerting in the extreme to be the subject of three people's attention, and Charlotte was making a special effort to focus on helping Jam and Hitchens with their dinner.

Eustace's pale blue eyes slid surprisingly frequently between her and Doctor Havard, as if he had suddenly noticed there was a handsome man in their midst who could be a potential rival for Charlotte's affection. It was irritating: it made no sense for him to be jealous, given that he had gone to great lengths to avoid any interaction with her since terminating their engagement. Perhaps the imminent arrival of his parents for the opening of the fête was making him worry that they might urge him to change his mind. In one of their weekly telephone conversations Aunt Blanche had led her to understand that the Westhamptons were no less in need of funds than they had been last summer. Charlotte wondered if she held the same attraction as a match now that half of the Fitznorton inheritance must go to Josephine.

Next to Eustace sat Venetia, whose gaze also swung

between her cousin and Charlotte. At a guess, the humorous quirk of her friend's brow and her occasional irrepressible smile must be due to her suspicions about Charlotte's feelings. Since the night of Josephine's frightening attack of croup, Venetia had developed a habit of teasing her every time she mentioned Kit in conversation, which was embarrassingly often. But what if Charlotte talked of him a great deal? It was only natural after he had been so generous as to offer his assistance with not only the officers but also the baby. It didn't have to mean anything except that she was grateful to him. He'd been so kind, and had shown a surprising and flattering level of interest in her thoughts and plans. Surely it was only natural to feel a certain amount of pleasure in returning to the memory of that evening: of his melodious singing, his gentleness, his patience with Josephine and consideration for Nora and Charlotte...

The object of these thoughts was the third person who seemed to be paying as much attention to Charlotte as to the food on his plate. Tonight would be his last evening at Plas Norton. His serious eyes rested on her at intervals throughout the evening meal, a painful reminder that soon he would be gone from their midst. Mealtimes would seem dull without his conversation – especially his and Venetia's humorous shared recollections of childhood escapades. When he was in the room, she always felt all was well. She remembered the first time she ever made him laugh by recounting something amusing that she'd done, and how she had hugged the memory of his appreciation to herself for days. Without him, there would be a void in her life.

She mustn't dwell on that now. If she allowed herself to think about his departure, instead of focusing on the mechanical task of cutting up Jam's mutton chop, she might end up on a path too emotional to navigate.

She was being silly, really. Given that Jam's palsied limb jerks had lessened during Kit's month-long sojourn at Plas

Norton, and Eustace had been less prone to angry outbursts, and Brooks was now deemed almost fit enough to return to active service, she should by rights be celebrating that they had had him here at all, instead of mourning the imminent loss of his calming presence. She should be able to bid him goodbye with a polite handshake and think little more about it, instead of having this ridiculous lump in her throat every time she stole a peek across the table and considered how much she would miss seeing him there.

It wasn't as if he had ever said anything to encourage her to harbour affectionate feelings. On the contrary, over the past few weeks he had offered nothing more than friendship and dutiful medical care. She would be foolish, maybe even misguided, to expect more. After all, he was not the sort of man to whom Papa would have wanted her to develop an attachment: while Kit's mother was of a good family, warmly acquainted with Aunt Blanche, his father was only middle class, a professional man like Kit himself. Papa, an industrialist descended from merchant stock, had raised Charlotte to aim higher in the marriage market. Wealth would open doors, he had insisted, but it wouldn't give their descendants a title or any of the privileges attached to such. She'd always striven to please him, so she had better put aside any absurd notions of romance with a mere doctor.

When the time came for Kit's departure, shortly after the meal had been cleared away, they gathered in the hallway. Venetia, Mrs Longford and Nurse Boyle all seemed as keen as Charlotte to bid him farewell.

"Safe travels, Doctor, and come back soon, won't you?" Nurse Boyle shook his hand with enthusiasm, holding on to it for perhaps a few seconds longer than strictly necessary as he thanked her.

"Goodbye for now, cous. Make an effort to write. And you'd jolly well better come to our fête, or I'm quite sure I shall never hear the last of it." Venetia directed an impish look at Charlotte which left her blushing.

"It would be lovely if you are able to come, but we'll quite understand if you can't. The officers would be glad to see you, I'm sure..." She broke off as Venetia snorted.

"The officers! Well yes, it's true that they'd be delighted to have you around instead of old Sheridan, but..." Charlotte's fierce glare finally put a stop to her mischief. "Oh, alright Charlotte – keep your hair on. Nurse Boyle, Mrs Longford – might I trouble you both for a moment of your valuable time?" She shepherded them out of the hallway, leaving Charlotte and Kit alone.

"You've been such a great help, Kit. The officers *will* be pleased to see you if you can find time to return soon, and so would Venetia, although I'm not sure how long she plans to stay."

Inexplicably, his face fell. "It will be a pleasure to see them again."

There was an awkward pause in which she dared not say more. He had been turning his hat in his hands, but now put it on. Opening the door, he stood aside and motioned for her to go ahead of him, then came to stand beside her under the shelter of the porch. Rain splashed into puddles on the gravel driveway beyond.

"I think I can hear the car," he said.

At last she dared to look at him. There was something more in his eyes than his polite small talk had suggested, something that made her reach out without thinking to touch his arm.

"Josephine and I will be awfully glad to see you again, too."

He nodded, a slow smile softening his features. "I'm glad. I shall look forward to seeing you both again. Very much."

He added the last with a fervency that made her take an involuntary step forward. For a delicious, thrilling moment they stood only inches apart, drinking in the sight of one another.

She took in the way he looked at her, the unspoken longing in his eyes. No one had ever looked at her like that before. Eustace certainly never had. She realised, suddenly, that she wouldn't care if no one else ever did. No one else, however aristocratic or wealthy, could ever compare, or even come close, to this man's qualities.

But she couldn't allow herself to indulge such fantasies. Not when she laboured under the weight of expectation from the stern Fitznorton ancestors whose portraits lined the walls in the hallway. She stepped back and watched the motor pull up beside the porch.

"I'd better be off," he said. "It wouldn't do to keep Mr Cadwalader waiting."

He seized her hand and kissed it, then made a dash for the car with his shoulders hunched against the rain bouncing off the shiny blue paintwork.

She flexed her hand, wishing she could have stopped time at the moment it had been held in his and felt the warmth of his lips. This was the man who had once called her brave. Watching him leave, she wanted to scream at herself for everything she hadn't had the courage to say.

FORTY

Maggie

Maggie pulled her hat further down over her ears and examined her reflection from all angles. She didn't look too bad, now that her eyelashes were growing back, the straggly, singed ends of her hair were covered and the cut on her forehead had healed. The skin on her face and hands was dry, rather than red raw, and the livid bruises on her ribs had faded. Although she still had a cough, she could breathe more comfortably than she had done in weeks. Hopefully her appearance was normal enough now to avoid attracting unwelcome attention.

"Are you ready yet, Maggie? It's time to go."

"Alright, Mam. I'll be there now in a minute."

Maggie slipped her arms into her coat sleeves. Her mother had left the bedroom door open, and her voice drifted up the stairs as she herded the younger children into order, ready to walk up the lane to the big house. Dad would already be there, preparing the car for locals to pay sixpence a go for a few minutes of riding in luxury around the grounds. He'd looked in on Maggie before leaving for work earlier that morning, planting a kiss on her forehead.

"Proud of you, beaut." He'd whispered the words to avoid waking five-year-old Miriam, then paused to send a wink her way from the doorway.

She knew her parents had worked hard to conceal their concerns from her after the incident at the factory, plastering on smiles and heaping cheery words upon her as if she were a child again, not a woman of nineteen. Her birthday had been spent in hospital, and they'd made more of a fuss than they usually would, bringing in a cake Mam had baked and sharing it out among the patients on the ward, getting everyone to join in with a hoarse chorus of *Happy Birthday* and giving her the hat she was wearing today, in its own box with a ribbon tied around it. And since she came out of hospital they'd let her laze about in bed in the mornings, catching up on sleep, which was frequently disturbed by terrifying nightmares. It made her conscience prick to be so indulged, given that Dolly wasn't around to help with the housework now that she'd left school and gone to work as a housemaid at Plas Norton.

It was a state of affairs that couldn't continue. Mary's protectiveness had been comforting at first, but since Maggie's energy levels had started to improve, the constant fussing had started to grate on her nerves. She knew her mother must be struggling to manage all the tasks of such a busy household, even without Len and Dolly at home. It was time to insist she let Maggie get on with living again. If she could manage at the fête today, walking there and back and wandering around the stalls, then as a minimum Mary must accept that she could chop vegetables and stand at the stove, and maybe do a bit of washing up.

Mrs Gittins had pestered Jenny to move back home once she knew she'd lost her "little bastard", as she'd harshly referred to Len and Jenny's baby. Poor Jenny's cough was as bad as

Maggie's, if not worse, and she'd been recovering from the upset of her miscarriage. Even so, Maggie doubted she'd been cosseted by Mrs Gittins, who would have had her cleaning and cooking and looking after the little ones in no time, glad to have her eldest daughter back as an unpaid servant now that there was no chance of her bringing shame upon the family. Maggie hoped to see her friend at the fête, as everyone who had survived the blast at the factory had received an invitation to attend.

"You look a picture in that hat," Mam said with a glow of pride as they guided the younger children out of the front door.

A picture might be overstating it, but at least she no longer felt she looked like a freak.

The hedgerows were bright with lacy cow parsley and hemmed with pink campion and occasional comfrey. Wild garlic flowers filled the lane with their pungent scent, making Maggie sniff appreciatively, her senses relishing the stimulation all the more after so many weeks confined indoors. Clumps of bluebells nestled under trees, along with golden primroses, their cheeriness lifting Maggie's heart and making her glad to be outside again despite her occasional moments of nervousness.

Teddy and Jack ran on ahead, and Maggie felt a flutter of anxiety seeing them disappear beyond a bend in the lane. Since the accident she'd been more alert to dangers than ever before, flinching at any unusual noises and forever worrying about her loved ones. She held Miriam's small hand tightly as she hopped, skipped and bounced along the path. Telling herself over and over that there was no risk of her siblings coming to any harm, she was nevertheless relieved to spy her young brothers up ahead when they rounded the bend.

The neighbours who passed in their Sunday clothes, also heading for the fête, nodded and smiled and, to her relief, didn't stare. *It doesn't look that bad after all*, she told herself, glad of her new hat concealing the damage to her hair. Nothing was said about the explosion or the war, although some of the townsfolk wore black to honour lost loved ones. It was as if everyone wanted to fix their minds on the clement May weather, and the chance to see the changes Miss Charlotte had made at Plas Norton.

At the far side of the lawn, even the big house looked less forbidding than usual, with sunshine making its windows sparkle. Cotton bunting in patriotic red, white and blue festooned the stalls which had been set up a hundred yards or so away from the house, on the expanse of lawn. At the side farthest from the building, next to the gathered brass band, was a low platform faced by rows of folding wooden chairs. A hand painted notice promised a varied programme for the day, to include a tug-of-war competition, a boxing match, a revue by the local schoolchildren, and choral performances.

"How are you feeling, Maggie? Do you need to sit down for a bit?" Mary indicated a bench in a sunny spot where an elderly lady was taking a rest, huddled under a shawl and warm coat as if it were still February or March.

"I'm fine, Mam," Maggie snapped, feeling immediately guilty for failing to keep the impatience from her voice. Seeing her mother's hurt look, she relented. "The boys are itching to see the Punch and Judy stall. Why don't you take them? I'll take Mim to the Lucky Dip."

As Miriam crowed with delight at this suggestion and Teddy and Jack were no less enthusiastic at the prospect of watching the puppets, Mary had little choice but to acquiesce. Beyond the far end of the row of stalls, the Temperance Band had just struck up a rendition of *Myfanwy*, sung by a somewhat depleted male voice choir comprised mainly of middle-aged and old men.

With a shiny copper penny in her pocket, Miriam had little interest in the singing which was drawing most of the crowd. Her eyes were as round as the coin as she delved into the tea-chest filled with sawdust, her concentration so fierce the pink tip of her tongue stuck out of the side of her mouth. Maggie grinned when she gasped with delight and pulled out a small prize wrapped in brown paper, which was torn off in a trice to reveal a little wooden boat just the right size to nestle in her palm.

"Can I show Mam?" Miriam pleaded, bouncing with delight and waving across the lawn towards their mother, who waved back.

"Go on," Maggie agreed. "I'll follow in a few minutes." She watched until the little girl had reached their mam and was showing off her new acquisition to their brothers before turning away from the stalls in search of somewhere quieter. Being surrounded by large numbers of people was making her feel self-conscious, even though no one was paying her any attention. She needed a few moments to herself, to gather her thoughts. If she wandered closer to the house, she might avoid most of the townsfolk and get a glimpse of Dolly in her new maid's uniform.

The music and chatter receded as she drew closer to the building, until all she could hear was the twitter of birds coming from the neatly clipped hedges and the creeper clinging to the grey stone walls. Rows of late scarlet and yellow tulips swayed in the flower beds, beckoning her closer. Captivated by the glorious shades of colour, she strolled along the gravel path beside them, then around the corner of the house where the path led towards the promise of more gardens. It was so rare an opportunity to glimpse the place where Dad and Dolly spent their days, she couldn't resist pressing on. Hopefully no one would see her and tell her off, as everyone's thoughts today would be on the fête.

A gap in a hedge tempted her forwards. Passing through it, her attention was caught by the sight of a large perambulator standing in the sunshine. From within came the sound of fretful crying. She hastened towards it and peered under the hood, her heart constricting at the sight of a baby whom she guessed must be Josephine, grown a little bigger now, forehead as red as the tulips and waving her fists in rage. Her kicking had moved the spotless white blanket to cover her mouth; automatically, Maggie reached in and tucked it down, noting as she did so that the child was uncomfortably hot. No wonder she was distressed. Where was her nursemaid? Dad had mentioned that Miss Fitznorton had hired Nora Jenkins, a girl from the village whom Maggie vaguely knew, but there was no sign of her anywhere.

In fact there was no sign of anyone at all. Maggie pursed her lips in annoyance. Who could be so irresponsible as to leave a baby to overheat in the sun? Without hesitating, she reached into the perambulator and lifted the child into her arms. With the comfort of Maggie's rocking and murmured soothing words, Josephine soon calmed. In the quietness that was left, the unmistakable sound of giggling drifted over from a nearby arbour, inflaming Maggie's temper. Without pausing for thought, she marched across the lawn ready to remonstrate with the girl, but the sight that greeted her as she looked into the arbour made her squawk and turn her back.

"Nora! Is that you?"

A squeal and a deep-voiced curse indicated that the couple cavorting within had heard her.

"Who's that?" Fumbling with her petticoats and skirt, and smoothing her hair back into place, Nora emerged with her freckled face crimson. "Oh, it's you, is it? What are you doing with Miss Josephine?"

Maggie ignored the girl's outstretched arms and kept hold of the baby.

"What did you think you were doing, leaving her out in the sun? And who's that in there with you, you silly girl? Do you realise how much trouble you could be in now if someone other than me had found you?"

Scowling, Nora folded her arms. "The hood was up on the pram. She was asleep, she would have been fine if you hadn't stuck your nose in."

There was a low cough from within the arbour, and out stepped a tall man with slightly rumpled dark hair and a luxuriant moustache. As he emerged he quickly fastened the buttons on his khaki jacket and straightened his tie. Seemingly satisfied that his appearance had been restored to order, he pulled a slim silver case from his pocket and took out a cigarette.

"I'll leave you two charming ladies to your discussion," he said, and stalked away towards the house.

"Oh, but Major, it's only Maggie Cadwalader," Nora called after him, then huffed at Maggie, reaching for the baby again.

Maggie scowled at her. "Do you really think I'd give her back to you, when it's obvious you don't care a fig for her welfare? You don't deserve to look after her."

"Who d'you think you are, coming here trying to tell me how to do my job? Give her back to me, or I'll... I'll call the police on you."

To Maggie's indignation, the girl tried to seize the baby from her arms, leading to an undignified tussle. Josephine started crying again as Nora's attempt to grab her startled her just when Maggie had calmed her down.

"What the devil is going on here?" a voice boomed at them from across the lawn.

Clutching Josephine close to her breast, Maggie looked up in alarm. An Amazon of a woman was striding towards them – if such a strange, limping gait could be called a stride. It was certainly purposeful enough to be, and the woman's strong face was equally determined. Tall and broad-shouldered in her mannish jacket and plain hat, the woman's eyes seemed to shoot fire across the lawn as she approached. Maggie had never seen a woman so awe-inspiring before. She'd sallied forth from the house like Boadicea marching to face the Romans.

"An explanation, Nora, if you please." It was an order, not a question.

In the face of the woman's obvious authority, Nora had paled, and Maggie could understand why. Whoever she was, she was impressive. Rooted to the spot, Maggie couldn't tear her eyes away.

"Miss Vaughan-Lloyd, she was going to take the baby," Nora blurted out, making Maggie gasp.

"I was not!"

Maggie thought quickly. She couldn't allow this accusation to go unchallenged, but if she told the whole truth to this formidable woman then Nora would more than likely lose her job. As much as the girl had been irresponsible, and probably didn't deserve to be allowed to care for a vulnerable child, there had been no lasting harm done, and Maggie didn't want to be the one blamed for getting her the sack.

"You can see she's picked her up without permission. Give her to me, Maggie."

The tall woman, whom she now knew to be called Miss Vaughan-Lloyd, turned the full power of her gaze on Maggie. Hurtfully, she read disappointment there. Her mouth opened as she longed to tell what had really happened. But what was the use? After all, it was true that she *had* picked up the baby without permission. Her head pounded painfully.

"I'll give her to you, miss, but not to Nora," she managed to say, thrusting the baby into the arms of Miss Vaughan-Lloyd, who gave a startled exclamation.

Maggie didn't wait to watch her fumbling with the baby, but took to her heels. She ran back around the corner of the house, fighting for breath as the unaccustomed exertion made her lungs burn again. Having dashed across the expanse of lawn to reach the relative anonymity of the shadow of a stall, she bent double and succumbed to the coughing fit, almost retching into her handkerchief.

"Maggie, are you alright?" She'd never been so glad to hear her mother's voice.

"Yes, mam. It's just my cough. I'll be fine if I can just get a glass of water and sit down."

"There's no time, love. The presentation is in five minutes. I'll find you some water on the way."

She took her mother's clean handkerchief and used it to wipe her streaming eyes. "What presentation, mam?"

"Oh, Maggie – I'm so glad I can finally tell you. Your dad and I have known for weeks, but we were sworn to secrecy. Miss Fitznorton has organised medals for those of you who helped others escape from the accident. That's what the platform is for, love. You're being presented with a medal for bravery."

FORTY-ONE

Charlotte

As she mounted the steps onto the platform to introduce the gathered crowd to the mayor for the medal presentation, Charlotte was by no means convinced that her limbs would support her as far as the lectern. She'd never addressed so many people before. What would they think of her, a girl of twenty, dressed in severe black, trembling with nerves and a thin little voice that she would have to strain to make heard? She was no Mrs Pankhurst, to rouse a crowd.

But her nervousness at public speaking wasn't the only reason for the anxious roiling of her stomach this morning. It had started earlier, when Lord and Lady Westhampton arrived to cut the ribbon and officially open the proceedings. Lady Westhampton had taken an opportunity to draw Charlotte to one side in the parlour before the ceremony.

"I hope you will be willing to overlook my son's recent ill-judged words," she had said, managing with remarkable tact, Charlotte noted, to avoid using words like *rejection* or *spurning* or *breach of promise*. "He's had time to reflect since then, and of course he's so much better now, thanks to the good work of your convalescent home here. A *rapprochement* is assured very soon, my dear."

Charlotte had nodded and given a little smile that probably suggested a willingness to obey. She'd been relieved when Lady Westhampton nodded graciously and swept away to address Reverend and Mrs Butts, who were drinking coffee with Mayor Grundy and his Mayoress.

Venetia had been watching; she hastened to pull Charlotte aside.

"Am I to take it that Eustace's intentions have changed? What will you do if he proposes to you again?"

It was a good question, one that Charlotte had to pause before answering. She supposed she should be delighted.

"I'm not convinced he will. But Papa would want me to accept him."

Venetia snorted. "And will you sacrifice your future happiness for your father's dream, when he'll never even know what you've given up to achieve his ambitions?"

"I won't have given up anything. It's not as if anyone else has made me an offer."

"If they haven't, it's more than likely because you've been so set on joining the Fitznortons to the aristocracy that they'd never believe you'd accept anyone whose veins flow with ordinary red blood."

Charlotte hoped her scowl would be enough to silence her friend, but it seemed Venetia hadn't finished.

"Could you really be happy with that chinless wonder Eustace? To bind yourself to him for a lifetime, to fulfil the marital ambitions of a man whom everyone agrees was downright cruel to his own wife?"

Charlotte's jaw dropped. "What do you mean?"

"Oh, come now. Your stepmother told you herself. Her

driver confirmed it, and if you won't believe them, then ask Nellie Dawson."

"I think you've said enough." She attempted to move past her towards the table where the coffee pot still stood, but Venetia had seized her arm and she couldn't shake her off without causing a scene.

"Perhaps I've gone too far. But if the Westhamptons are still set on using you to reverse their dwindling fortunes, then you might not have much more time to think about your options. To consider what *you* really want."

It had hurt to hear her situation being described in such a way. Did Venetia really think the Westhamptons thought so little of her, that all that mattered to them was her inheritance? She'd liked Eustace when he proposed last summer, and had been happy at the prospect of being his wife. If he did intend to ask her again, it wouldn't be right to throw such an opportunity away just because the war had changed him. And if her thoughts had turned automatically to Kit, and how differently she felt about him, it was probably just a passing infatuation. Given time, she would forget him. Probably. She'd have to, wouldn't she? Venetia was wrong: she had to consider what would be the right course of action. What she wanted was hardly relevant.

On reaching the lectern, she took in a deep breath and surveyed the gathered crowd. Somehow she summoned a smile and a nod, and addressed them from her notes with a pretty speech about the bravery of the men fighting at the front, and the courage of the factory workers who were also working valiantly to defend the Empire.

"Now, My Lord, My Lady, ladies and gentlemen, boys and girls, I am pleased to welcome The Worshipful, the Mayor of Pontybrenin and district, Councillor Arthur Grundy, who will present medals to those who performed courageous acts at great risk to their own safety in order to save the lives of their fellow workers."

It was a relief to take her seat and allow the Mayor to give his own address before the medal recipients were invited to file along the platform. Each one shook hands with the viscount to receive their medal, presented in a small velvet box. Some of those who passed looked pleased to have been recognised, and gave a grin and a wave to well-wishers in the crowd, while others looked awkwardly at their own feet and almost raced across the platform to descend the steps back into relative anonymity.

Charlotte looked up as Margaret Cadwalader's name was called, momentarily diverted from her own thoughts by pleasure at seeing the girl looking so much healthier than the last time she'd seen her, in the hospital. The chauffeur and his wife clapped harder than anyone, their faces aglow, and the children beside them cheered and applauded with no less enthusiasm. Charlotte was gladdened to see their obvious pride. Yet her downturned mouth and demurely lowered head suggested Maggie wasn't nearly as excited; so focused was she on getting back to her family, she almost stumbled on the steps. By the time her feet were back on the grass, she was blushing scarlet.

When the presentations were over and the local schoolchildren had finished performing their revue of patriotic songs and skits, the crowd began to disperse back towards the stalls. Charlotte slipped away from the notable personages on the dais for a moment of solitude.

The day had gone almost as well as she could have hoped, except for the disappointment of Kit's failure to attend. He'd sent his apologies in his most recent letter, expressing his regret and lamenting the difficulties of finding a locum in time. They'd been corresponding for a few weeks now, a discourse which had begun when she wrote to thank him for his efforts on behalf of the officers and his help with Josephine, whose condition she happily reported had much improved. She'd come to look forward to his letters and had anticipated his attendance at the fête with some excitement, so the change in his plans had come as a blow.

Still, she reflected that there was still much to be pleased about. The event had been a success in honouring the factory workers. It had also provided a few hours of brightness and some much-needed funds for the refugees in the town, who had been on the receiving end of some resentment recently, since rapidly increasing casualty rates caused some to question whether the war to free Belgium from the Germans was worth the enormous cost.

Best of all, it had built bridges between the community and the Convalescent Home. Most of the officers had chosen to stay inside the house, unable to face the noise and crowds, but dear, blind Lieutenant Hitchens had ventured out on Nurse Boyle's arm to hear the singing, and Eustace had briefly felt able to stroll around the stalls with his parents. Confronted by the sight of them in their uniforms, most of the crowd had shown respect. She'd only seen a few people turning away or whispering behind their hands. Hopefully the townsfolk would now support the work being done at Plas Norton, or at least do nothing more to oppose it, and there would be no more acts of hostility from the youth of the district, especially as the boys who had carried out the vandalism had since been caught and punished.

She'd achieved what she had set out to achieve. Why, then, did she feel so flat? It shouldn't be an anti-climax. She should be experiencing a glow of pride to match that displayed on Cadwalader's face earlier when his daughter's achievements were given the recognition they deserved. It wasn't that Charlotte was dissatisfied, exactly. None of today's achievements would have happened if not for her, and the results were, overall, positive. But what next for her?

If Eustace proposed, it would put an end to her feelings of humiliation after being so cruelly rejected. It had taken every ounce of courage to hold her head high, having to see him every day over the past few weeks since he had spurned her, knowing that everyone around them was aware he no longer wanted her. Not even Venetia knew how many times Charlotte had wept, as she'd saved her tears until she was alone to avoid further blows to her pride. Should he relent, that wound could finally heal.

As his wife, she could look forward to a future undertaking more charitable works such as this. Committee work, using her status to influence others, organising events and making things happen. She'd get better at using gracious smiles and offers to put a word in here or there, achieving results without ever again having to dirty her hands with such menial tasks as dusting, making beds or feeding people who couldn't manoeuvre a knife and fork. She had no reason to believe that it wouldn't be an interesting and purposeful life. So why this awful feeling of dread in the pit of her stomach? Why this desire to skulk in the gardens avoiding people?

Squaring her shoulders, she gave herself a mental shake. There was too much to be done to allow herself to wallow in doubts or self-examination. Her thoughts turned to Maggie Cadwalader's solemn, shy face and stooped shoulders. She would seek her out, perhaps offer her a job working with the officers until she was ready to commence her midwifery training. Charlotte was fairly sure that both Eustace and Major Brooks would be moving on soon, as they were fit enough to return to their duties, but with the war showing no signs of abating there would be other patients, and no doubt many of them. Caring, resilient young women like Maggie would be invaluable to Plas Norton, especially if... She tested the thought... Especially if Charlotte might be taking on a new role in London as Mrs Chadwycke.

It took her a little while to locate the Cadwaladers, who

were playing hoopla at one of the stalls. The crowds milled about, most of them brightly dressed and enjoying the chance of a little gaiety. Several touched their caps or nodded as she passed; some murmured greetings or herded their children out of her way, and she made sure to offer acknowledgement, aware that the old Charlotte would have sailed past without caring what they thought of her. Now, she recognised that it mattered: Plas Norton would function more effectively if she could keep these ordinary folk on its side by exercising a little charm.

Mrs Cadwalader thanked her profusely for the fête and for the medal, and was only too pleased to agree when Charlotte requested a few moments with her eldest daughter. Maggie, on the other hand, turned pale.

"Are you alright, Maggie?" Charlotte asked, drawing her aside under the boughs of an elm tree. Its cool green shade made Maggie's complexion take on an even more bilious tone, and Charlotte frowned at the way the other girl avoided her gaze, looking alternately at her feet and at the grounds beyond.

"I'm fine, thank you, miss..." Her voice broke off and her eyes widened as a familiar, strident voice addressed them from several yards behind. They turned as one to see Venetia's formidable figure bearing down upon them. Holding onto her hat, she stooped to duck under the branch and join them under the tree.

"Is this a private meeting, or might I join?"

Do we have a choice? Charlotte thought. "Of course you may," she said a little frostily, still stinging from Venetia's forthright remarks earlier.

Maggie tugged at the neck of her blouse and exhaled audibly, as if resigning herself to some awful fate.

"This is Margaret Cadwalader," Charlotte began, but Venetia cut her off in a voice that was even more brisk than usual.

"We met earlier. Miss Cadwalader had picked up Josephine

from her perambulator without Nora's permission, which caused the chit no small measure of alarm."

"Really? Good heavens."

One of Maggie's hands groped behind her to grasp the tree trunk. She leaned against it as if she were dizzy.

"Indeed. And it was fortunate that she did, because Nora's attention had been comprehensively distracted by the dubious charms of Major Brooks. With her actions, Miss Cadwalader here saved Josephine from sunstroke or worse."

Maggie's chin had snapped upwards; she stared at Venetia as if a sentence of execution had been lifted.

"You knew?"

"I saw you from the window. Naturally I was alarmed to see you pick up the baby. My heart was in my mouth; but when you went over to the arbour and Nora and Brooks emerged it was obvious that you weren't a dastardly kidnapper after all. Any fool could see what had really happened."

"But... Miss Vaughan-Lloyd... you looked so disappointed in me."

"You had the chance to tell me that Nora had forgotten her duties, yet you didn't. You would have allowed her to go on neglecting the child. And then, before I could confront her with her lies, you went running off."

"I couldn't be the one who cost her her job."

Charlotte had heard enough. "Never mind all that. Where's Josephine now?" The idea that any harm might have come to her sister made her want to run and clutch her to her heart. She should have done more, should have advertised for a trained nanny as she'd planned to do, instead of allowing her own attention to be consumed by the officers and the fête. She was as neglectful as Nora, in a way.

"She's with Nora, of course. It wasn't my place to dismiss her. I've offended you quite enough for one morning."

Charlotte put a hand to her forehead and groaned. "I'd better go and find them."

"Wait – one more minute won't make a difference. There's an obvious solution right under our noses. Miss Cadwalader, I understand you are without a position at present?"

"That's right," Maggie said, looking bewildered.

Venetia threw up her hands as if everything was settled. "There you are, then. She's already proved herself more responsible than Nora. She settled the child even when it wasn't her job to do so, and she was discreet to a fault. And we know she's brave. Brave enough to risk physical harm or to be misjudged in order to protect another. Why, she even has a medal to prove it."

Maggie stared at her, transfixed, as if she had never encountered anyone like her before; Venetia appeared equally spellbound.

"A perfect candidate for the post of nursemaid," Venetia added with an awkward cough and a sudden flush of colour on her cheeks. She tore her gaze away and fixed it on Charlotte, who gave in with a sigh.

"Very well. Maggie, I'd be more than happy for you to replace Nora as nursemaid. The size of your family suggests that you have experience of dealing with young children. However, I'm aware that your ambition is to become a midwife, and I wouldn't want you to feel pushed into accepting something that doesn't suit you. I had been intending to offer you temporary work to support our nurses here. You're quite free to take either post, or neither. Whatever suits you."

A slow, mischievous smile lit Venetia's face, making it almost handsome. "I do love it when a woman gets to choose the path that suits her best. The one which will make her happiest. Come, Miss Cadwalader. Which will you choose?"

Maggie's eyes narrowed as if she sensed an undercurrent. She pressed her index finger to her top lip, and Charlotte found she was almost holding her breath as she awaited the answer, veering between impatience to see Josephine and admiration for the way Maggie took time over her decision.

"As I was there when she was born, and it would give me the chance to care for a baby... I'd rather look after Josephine," Maggie said at last.

Relieved, Charlotte exhaled loudly, ignoring Venetia's crow of triumph.

But Maggie hadn't finished. "I still want to be a midwife, though. I'll take over from Nora, if you really are planning to dismiss her..."

It was obvious from her troubled frown that she wasn't entirely comfortable with the idea, so Charlotte gave a determined nod to spur her on.

Maggie straightened, lifting her chin as if she had plucked up the courage to go further. "If you need someone to help with the soldiers, would you consider my friend Jenny Gittins? She's the one I helped at the factory. She's suffered worse than me, and I know she'd be kind and patient with your officers. And I hope you won't mind me asking, but will you still be willing to sponsor me for my training, Miss Fitznorton? I'll have to spend any free time studying, when I'm not caring for Josephine, so I'll need at least an afternoon each week to go to the library, as well as an afternoon to visit my family."

"Oh, brava!" Venetia exclaimed before adding, annoyingly, "A woman who stands up for her own needs as well as those of her friends, Charlotte. What better example could your sister, or indeed any of us, follow?"

FORTY-TWO

Charlotte

The fête had gone well, the rubbish had been collected into sacks for burning later, and Cadwalader and the housemaids had dismantled the trestle tables on which the stalls had been set up. By the time dusk fell everyone was exhausted.

Charlotte had decided not to risk a scene by dismissing Nora during the fête, worried that the girl might spoil the proceedings by kicking up an embarrassing fuss. There would be time for that tomorrow, and then Maggie could take up her post on Monday, along with her friend Jenny Gittins. She could only hope that Maggie's faith in her friend's kind heart and willingness to work hard would prove well founded: such qualities were worth their weight in gold, and as the girl was engaged to Maggie's brother she would hopefully resist any temptation to fraternise with the officers. Charlotte was pleased to be able to offer jobs to young women who had suffered in the disaster at the factory. It might not be as well paid as munitions work, but at least both girls would be well fed and safe from harm at Plas Norton.

She reviewed the day's successes. Of particular note had been the outstanding performances by the choir of soldiers' wives and mothers, organised by Mrs Butts. After singing their repertoire of songs, they'd joined with the men's choir for a rendition of 'David of the White Rock' and 'It's a Long Way to Tipperary'. They'd ended with 'Keep the Home Fires Burning', leaving all eyes moist: even Lord Westhampton's chin had been seen to wobble below his stiff upper lip.

Best of all had been the way Lieutenant Hitchens surprised everyone by joining in with his remarkably deep bass voice. Even now, thinking of it, goose pimples rose on Charlotte's arms.

She plumped down onto the piano stool in the music room, wishing she had practised harder on the piano as a child and could play something now. Rosamund had spent hours at the instrument, but Charlotte had resisted her urgings to practise, partly to spite her and partly because she'd had little self-discipline back then. Even now, her attention was liable to wander, although she had focused surprisingly easily on the tasks required to organise the convalescent home and the fête. Passion projects, Venetia called them, and perhaps she was right: she needed a strong cause in order to throw herself completely into a task.

But what would she do next? She lifted the lid that covered the keys and allowed her fingers to drift across them in the half-light coming from the window, thinking about what the future held for her and for the officers. The recent visit by an army medic who had passed Major Brooks and Eustace as fit meant that they would bid farewell to them both in the morning. Captain Reynolds' frostbitten hands and feet meant he would forever be spared the rigours of war, and she hoped he would improve sufficiently to go home soon. He hadn't hidden under his bed for a few weeks now. Hitchens and Jam were still far from recovered. To her dismay, the medic had expressed his concern that they might both be committed to institutions if Hitchens didn't regain his sight and if Jam's erratic limb movements weren't further improved within the next couple of months. She'd do whatever she could to help them avoid such a fate.

She had set up her little hospital for Eustace's sake. Now, he was about to depart for London with his parents before returning to the front, but there was no question of closing Plas Norton. The wheels she had set in motion would continue to turn for as long as there were soldiers being wounded. Fundraising would continue, and there was no shortage of local committees eager to recruit her organisational skills and financial support. Even so, she didn't really feel needed in the way she had over the past few months. The Plas Norton Convalescent Home could probably go on now without her.

She was still pondering this when some sixth sense, a prickling across her shoulders, told her that she was no longer alone. Looking up, she saw a man silhouetted in the light at the doorway, and her heart leapt as her mind jumped straight to Doctor Havard. Had he returned after all, without her realising? But no – it wasn't possible. This man didn't walk like him, didn't have the same footstep or bearing. He came closer, and she let out her breath as she realised it was Eustace.

"I wanted to congratulate you," he said, sounding uncharacteristically unsure of himself as he moved to stand beside her and laid an index finger on one of the piano keys. "Your little fête was a great success."

"Thank you." She lowered the lid of the piano, just giving him time to pull back his hand. Uncomfortable with his proximity in a way she had never been before the incident in the summerhouse, she slid off the stool on the opposite side and moved so that the piano stood between them. It was strange: she'd never noticed before that the scent of Penhaligon's cologne failed to mask an odour of slightly stale sweat that hung about him. Havard had smelled quite different, a sharp, clean smell that had been much more inviting.

"Charlotte, there was something else I wanted to say." He paused, and her heart thumped with the oddest mixture of hope and dread.

"I owe you an apology for the way I spoke to you... in the summerhouse, I mean." His fingers drummed on the lid of the piano, as if he was nervous, and his feet shifted. "I was wrong to end our engagement. It was an overreaction on my part, due to my... my... erm – infirmity at that time."

She swallowed hard. Was he ever going to look at her, or was the prospect of this conversation so awful that he wanted to avoid it almost as much as she found she did? Could he have made it any more obvious that his parents had put him up to this? If they were both so uncomfortable near each other, what would be the point in marrying him?

"The thing is, old girl, I've had time to reconsider. To reflect on the future. And what it boils down to is..."

He moved so quickly to kneel before her that he bashed his shin on the piano stool on the way and couldn't help rubbing it and wincing even as he held the ring box out towards her. Hysterical laughter threatened to bubble out of her throat, but somehow she kept it in, hoping that he would interpret the hand across her mouth as surprise.

"Will you...?"

She cut him off before he could make the situation any more uncomfortable. Since her discussion with Venetia earlier, she, too, had had time to reflect. She'd tried to imagine life as Mrs Eustace Chadwycke, living under his parents' roof while he was away at the front, and realised it would probably be rather empty. She'd realised that she couldn't recall a single conversation with Eustace that had held any significance to either of them. Oh, he was nice enough, or at least he had been before the traumas inflicted by the war had soured him; but he'd never gone out of his way to help her the way Doctor Havard had. Every time she compared Eustace with Kit, Eustace came out the loser. His desire to serve his country was admirable, but he had never given any indication that he cared about his countrymen, or even for the men with whom he fought. He was quick to criticise others and to judge them for their human weaknesses, without ever considering that he had frailties of his own. He'd written her affectionate letters in the early days, but since coming to Plas Norton he hadn't given her any indication that he cared about her. Even at the start, he'd never thought to ask her about her ideas or ambitions. To be fair, she hadn't really had any when they met, beyond snagging someone like him to assure her future position.

The first time he had proposed to her, it hadn't mattered that she didn't have any depth of feeling for him. Back then, her main concern had been to please her father and become the kind of woman he believed she should be. Now, she had begun to experience a different way of life: one that could satisfy her energy and her mind; and in her rare opportunities to daydream, it was Kit's face, Kit's smile, that came to mind, not Eustace's. It was his lips she wanted to kiss, if she was to kiss anyone. Whatever she'd once believed, whatever her papa had wanted, she couldn't possibly marry Eustace when there was a possibility that she might have fallen in love with someone else. Even if she could bear to do it, it wouldn't be right.

"Eustace. Dear Eustace. I'm flattered, I really am. But I don't think—"

"Don't say no yet. I know what's troubling you. You think I'm still not well, but honestly, I'm so much better. I won't show you up. I'll make a good husband, and we can marry as soon as you like, or when you're out of mourning, which is only a few months away now isn't it, or whenever you think would be most appropriate." He was babbling, and she grasped him by the shoulder.

"Please, Eustace. Put the ring away."

He stopped at last, crestfallen, and slipped the box back into his pocket before using the piano stool to lever himself back to his feet. He stood before her, his shoulders drooping.

"But why?" he asked, with a sullen pout that made him look like a spoiled child.

"It's complicated. I'm not even sure I can explain it myself. You're a fine fellow, and you'll make someone a wonderful husband. But I'm too wrapped up in everything here to contemplate marriage just now." It was only a half-truth, but far kinder to do it this way than to say outright that she didn't want him.

Squaring his shoulders, he gave a curt nod, and she hoped her excuse had been sufficient to allow him to salvage his pride.

"I'm glad you found the ring. It was a bit spiteful of me to throw it away. I blame the heat of the moment. You probably deserve a wife who is less intemperate."

"I hunted in the grass for hours," he grumbled.

"Well then, bravo," she said, in an ironic echo of Venetia's words earlier. "Jolly good show for finding it in the end. No hard feelings?"

She extended her right hand, judging it safe to do so now that the ring was safely back in his pocket, and he shook it briefly before bowing and marching towards the door.

"I'll see you at breakfast, I expect. And Eustace – I truly do wish you all the best. Stay safe, Captain Chadwycke."

As she turned back to the piano, her elbow jostled against a photograph, knocking it face down in its frame. She picked it up, holding it in both hands to gaze at the image of her father in his shooting jacket and plus fours, a shotgun in his hand and several brace of game birds displayed at his feet. Propping it up carefully, she rested her fingers against the picture, trying to ignore the sudden dryness in her mouth. Once, she would have done anything to make Papa proud. She would have willingly made marriage vows to any man he chose. But today, for the first time, she understood that she wasn't the same girl who would have been satisfied with that life. Whatever social standing a marriage to Eustace could bring her, it couldn't be enough.

FORTY-THREE
AUGUST 1915

Charlotte

Charlotte eyed her reflection in the cheval mirror. She'd had it moved from her old bedroom into the attic room she still shared with Venetia on her friend's regular visits to Plas Norton. More than a year after the trauma of Papa's death, it was still such a relief to have finally put aside her half-mourning clothes and wear pretty things. Today she had chosen a white pintucked blouse teamed with a pleated pinafore skirt in jolly mauve and white checks, with decorative buttons at the waist. Her eyes sparkled at the way the bright colour and feminine details of these new clothes never failed to lift her spirits and bring a healthy colour to her cheeks, serving as a visual reminder that her life was moving on. Naturally she would never forget her father, or what he had meant to her, but she had proved she was growing into a mature young woman who could do well even without his guidance.

Plas Norton was a quietly bustling community, with more officers than ever housed within its grey stone walls. Nurse Boyle ruled over two nurses now, and several auxiliary staff.

THE BROKEN VOW

Things were changing as the war progressed, and Plas Norton no longer received severe cases of shell-shock straight from France, but rather men who had already spent several weeks in hospital. The aim these days was for their patients to spend around six weeks convalescing before returning to active service. Such were the numbers suffering from shell-shock a whole year into the war, the ballroom had been turned into a ward for the most recent arrivals, who couldn't be left entirely alone, while the upstairs bedrooms were a privilege reserved for those who were becoming more independent and gearing up towards their return to the front.

Outside, Cadwalader had set up a carpentry workshop and expanded the kitchen garden with the help of some old men from the village who had formerly worked on the estate. They encouraged the officers to help them in digging and sowing, together building a chicken coop and tending a flock of hens. In a few weeks they would celebrate their first harvest of vegetables, which would come in useful given the frequent shortages of food resulting from German attacks on merchant shipping. Some of the officers seemed to take great pleasure in tending Rosamund's neglected rose garden, and here, too, their efforts were beginning to pay off, with a new flush of blooms rewarding them for their efforts.

It had been a pleasure to see the officers change as they settled into life at Plas Norton. Many were wary at first, suffering sleepless nights in a twilight world of sorrow and pain. Improvements came gradually, fostered by gentle exercise, communal activities, and the kind of productive physical tasks Dr Havard had recommended during his visit. As well as helping to restore the physical fitness of men who had in some cases had long and difficult journeys from the fighting – or who had been wounded in body as well as in spirit – working with nature and caring for the fowl seemed to help them regain a degree of mental equilibrium. More than once a man had remarked on the greenness of the hills surrounding Plas Norton, and on the peace to be found walking in the deer park.

In good weather the patients played quoits, bowls and croquet on the lawn, fished in the lake, or went for long walks. The music room, billiard table and library were popular when the Welsh weather was less hospitable and grey clouds rolled in from across the Irish Sea to the west. The house even smelled different these days, of a mixture of carbolic soap and cigarette smoke, quite different from the atmosphere Charlotte remembered from her childhood, when the odour of Papa's cigars mingled with lavender and beeswax polish, and flowers filled vases in every room even in winter.

Josephine was doing well under Maggie's competent and conscientious care, and Charlotte looked forward to her daily visits to the nursery and the two afternoons each week when Maggie took time for studying. She would take her sister out in the perambulator for a stroll around the grounds, making sure to call in at the motor stable or carpentry workshop to see Cadwalader, as he would always stop whatever he was doing to speak to the baby. By pulling funny faces and making nonsensical sounds he invariably managed to make Josephine laugh, and it was impossible not to feel lifted by the babbling and chortling noises she made in response to his chatter. Charlotte had noticed that many of the older officers liked to speak to the baby or hold her on their laps, some of them with tears in their eyes as they thought of their own children at home.

"It makes me remember why I did it," one of them murmured to Charlotte once, pressing a kiss onto the crown of Josephine's yellow bonnet as her little fists grasped the brass buttons on his khaki jacket.

Venetia had taken Maggie under her wing, confiding in Charlotte that the girl would struggle to qualify as a midwife due to her lack of Latin. Having taken it upon herself to teach her, Venetia had even given her a primer and spent hours in a quiet corner with her, teaching her the rudiments so that she might have a chance of understanding medical terms. When asked about their lessons, Maggie would blush and say little except that she was very grateful for the help, and Venetia was similarly close-lipped.

"It keeps me out of mischief, and if it gives the girl a fighting chance in a world which stacks the odds against women of her class, then I'm glad," she said.

Still, Charlotte sensed that there must be more to it than that. "I admire your sacrifice," she'd said to Venetia once, thinking about the hours of travelling and the expense of her frequent train journeys between London and Plas Norton.

"It's no sacrifice. She's special, Charlotte." Venetia's cheeks had taken on a pink glow and she'd looked away, fiddling with an imaginary speck on her skirt.

Charlotte wished her friend's cousin would make similarly frequent visits, but unfortunately the needs of his patients had kept Doctor Havard away. Their correspondence had become a pleasure. She treasured his letters for their insights into his thoughts as much for his descriptions of his work in the mining community, where there had recently been a strike that had even forced Mr Lloyd George, the Minister of Munitions, to come to Wales to negotiate.

Kit wrote to her about his patients, like Mrs Saunders whose scoliosis was so bad she could no longer stand upright, and Mr Evans whose lungs had been wrecked by his work in the mine. He'd shared his dreams of setting up a Medical Aid Society like the one in Tredegar which had established a cottage hospital and provided medical and dental services to members who paid in a penny a week. Through his letters, she'd gained an opportunity to learn more about a world she had rarely had opportunities to encounter before: a world in which poverty bit cruelly and hard, often striking at random or unexpectedly when a working man suffered an accident, or a mother or child fell ill.

More than this, she felt she had been granted the privilege of gaining glimpses into his soul. She had come to understand why his sense of vocation burned so brightly within him. Recently, she had felt honoured when he had even confided in her about his regret at being unfit for military service. Worried that she might believe him reluctant to do his bit, he'd told her about the months he spent in hospital as a child, and the debilitating effects of his bout of rheumatic fever. It worried her to think of the physical toll his work must take on him, and for weeks she had wished he might visit her again soon, so that she could see for herself that he was alright.

In return, she shared stories of her work with the officers, asked his advice, and used it to combat Doctor Sheridan's antiquated views. Kit had taken the trouble to write to Sheridan, convincing the old man that electric shock treatment was more likely to be harmful than beneficial. She knew the outlook for the officers might have been very different if not for Kit's wise and insightful contributions. He had changed their lives, and in doing so he was also changing hers.

She felt she had come to know him well through his letters, understanding his desire to improve the lives of others. She had found similar satisfaction through her own tentative efforts with the convalescent home, fundraising efforts and committee work. As soon as she was twenty-one, and no longer needed Aunt Blanche's approval for major financial outlay, she would be free to do more, and she couldn't help hoping that Kit would approve.

Today was to be a special day, giving her all the more reason to want to look her best. She'd taken to wearing her hair in a plain chignon, but this morning Nellie had done a fine job of a softer, more elaborate hair style. Her bright, summery clothes suited her fair complexion far better than her mourning garb had done. Gazing at her reflection, she couldn't help hoping that Kit would be impressed. More than anything, she wanted him to think well of her.

In her heart of hearts, she wanted still more, but she hardly dared admit it to herself. It was too much to hope that her own growing feelings for him might be reciprocated. To him, she probably seemed like a spoiled and silly girl, dabbling in attempts at good works to keep boredom at bay. He knew so much more of the world. Whilst her experience was limited due to the conventions of her sex and class, he had chosen to live among the working classes and to devote himself to caring for them. His letters made it obvious that his sympathies lay more with his patients than with his own class; his attitude to the miners' strike had been enough to indicate that her father would have despised his politics. The two men would clash if Papa were still alive.

Was it disloyal to her father's memory to admire Kit the way she did? She had a pretty good idea of what Venetia's response would be if she ever dared to pose that question aloud. And perhaps Venetia would be right, that it was more important to be true to herself and the satisfaction that could be gained from making a difference, instead of clinging to views and promises that seemed outdated in a rapidly changing world, with the war creating unprecedented opportunities for women to show what they could achieve if they were only given a chance.

A soft tap at the door interrupted her reverie. She hastened to answer it, and found Maggie waiting in the corridor, carrying Josephine on her hip as she usually did around the house, both wrapped in a fringed Welsh shawl to support her weight. The baby crowed with delight at seeing Charlotte, her gummy smile revealing a pair of tiny white teeth. She had been sucking her fist, but now reached pudgy arms towards her sister, stretching out plump, wet fingers and making both women smile.

"Miss Vaughan Lloyd asked me to tell you that her cousin

has arrived, miss. She thought you might want to give him a tour, to show him the changes since his last visit."

Charlotte's hands fluttered to her hair before fussing with the collar of her blouse to ensure it stood up properly. She glanced down at her skirt, hoping Kit wouldn't think the fabric too bold, suddenly nervous at the thought of seeing him again.

"You look lovely, miss. Bright colours suit you," Maggie said. A smile played at the corners of her mouth and there was warmth in her eyes, as if she understood Charlotte's sudden attack of nerves. The old Charlotte might have taken offence at such familiarity from a servant, but today she felt she could almost hug her for offering reassurance.

"Thank you, Maggie. That's very kind. Will you be alright with Josephine this afternoon? I know you'd usually be studying, but if it wouldn't inconvenience you too much to put it off until tomorrow...?"

"Don't worry, miss. Miss Vaughan-Lloyd will be too busy this afternoon to help me, anyway. Tomorrow will suit us both better."

Nodding gratefully, and pressing a kiss onto Josephine's chubby pink cheek, Charlotte closed her bedroom door and ran down the back stairs to greet her guest.

FORTY-FOUR

Charlotte

Charlotte arrived in the hall to find Venetia chatting animatedly with her equally tall, but much quieter cousin. He had removed his spectacles and was polishing them with his handkerchief, but glanced up with a sudden smile as Charlotte approached.

"Doctor Havard, what a pleasure to see you again," she murmured, extending her hand with her heart drumming as if she had run up the stairs, not down.

"Miss Fitznorton, I'm delighted to be back." He shook her hand, then didn't let go, and there was a delicious long moment in which they gazed at each other, reading each slight alteration since they last met.

Venetia cleared her throat. "Given how hungry you both look, you'll be pleased to know I've sent Dolly to bring tea to the parlour. Shall we make our way there before your tour, Kit?"

Venetia busied herself pouring the milk and tea while Charlotte served the dainty sandwiches, almost dropping Kit's plate as she passed it to him and his long, slender fingers brushed against hers. She sipped at her tea and nibbled the edge of a cucumber sandwich, but barely tasted either. She had little need of refreshment, when the sight of Kit was enough to make every one of her senses spark with energy.

Never had she been so acutely aware of another person's physical presence as she was while guiding him through the new ward and around the carpentry workshop that had been set up at his suggestion. She avoided looking at him too much in front of the officers, afraid to be seen staring. But her attention was caught by small details of his appearance: the weave of his brown woollen suit; the flat brown mole on the hollow of his cheek, below the sharp rise of his cheekbone; the faint shadow along his jaw and top lip, and the nick on his chin where he must have cut himself shaving that morning. The delineation of his cupid's bow and pillowy lower lip struck her as exquisite, making her belly perform absurd acrobatics whenever she dared risk a glance at their perfection.

They paused at each bed or chair for him to speak quietly with all of the officers. Unlike Doctor Sheridan, Kit leaned forward to shake hands with each man, excepting one whose hand was bandaged, instead reaching out to pat his arm. He looked them unflinchingly in the eye, nodded and smiled, treating them as men worth his notice, not shameful mental cases. Once or twice, when he passed close to her, she caught the clean, warm scent of him, and had to resist the urge to take an unladylike sniff to fill her nostrils.

Venetia followed them outside to the workshop, waiting patiently while he conversed with the trio of men who were sawing and whittling under the supervision of one of the old gardeners.

"I expect you'd like to see the officers' vegetable garden as well, cous," she prompted when at last he thanked the men for their time. But when they rounded the corner of the house, she plopped down on a bench.

"This dratted leg," she grumbled, brushing off Kit's concern with an imperious wave of her hand. "You two go on, I'll catch up in a moment."

Charlotte could have sworn she winked before bending to fiddle with the brace on her ankle, but decided she must have been mistaken.

"We'll walk slowly. Call out if you need us," Kit said, then bent his elbow out towards Charlotte. She tucked her hand into the crook of his arm and pointed towards the longer path, through Rosamund's rose garden, so that she would have a precious extra few minutes alone with him.

The roses were a riot of blooms, pinks and yellows vying with apricot and scarlet to charm the eye. Their fragrance was almost heady in the sunshine, filling the air with a rich perfume of fruits and myrrh. Low-growing lavender at the edges of the path hummed with bees and supplemented the glorious scent whenever Charlotte's skirt brushed against it.

As enchanting as it was, Charlotte wanted more than anything to fill her gaze with Kit after so many weeks of having only his letters to connect her to him. To look at him without wasting even a moment to admire the flowers that couldn't compete with him in captivating her senses. To let her eyes feast on him, to gorge her senses on every tiny aspect of him and store it up for the future, when he would have to leave and she would only have her memory of this perfect afternoon. She knew she would cling to her mental picture of the tilt of his head; the jaunty angle of his hat, and the way his spectacles sat slightly crooked on his face; his luxuriant lashes and the depth of feeling in his gaze; the sharpness of his jawbone below the softness of his earlobe. She absorbed it all as if the sight of him could sustain her.

"What do you think of the changes we've made?" she asked, hoping he would be impressed by her efforts. More than anything, she longed for him to be pleased with her.

He paused and squinted up at the sky, deep blue and cloud

less. "Oh, I suppose they're alright," he murmured, then laughed softly at her crestfallen expression. "They're perfect," he said, relenting. "As are you, Charlotte."

It wasn't the summer sunshine that made her feel suddenly overwhelmed by the heat.

"I'm far from perfect," she said, all too aware of her own failings compared with her vision of his kindness and intelligence.

"But you are, to me. It can't have escaped your notice how much I admire you. I did, even the first time we met, but since then that admiration has grown. You've changed, I believe, even more than Plas Norton. You've gained more confidence since I last saw you. I knew it from reading your letters – which I treasure, by the way."

"As I do yours. The insights into your life and work sometimes astound me. They remind me of how much I've yet to learn."

"We all have. But it seems you've found your niche, working with the officers and serving on your committees."

She tilted her head to one side, thinking. "I've realised the satisfaction to be gained in feeling one is making a difference. Not just dabbling with charitable efforts, but diving in. Getting one's hands dirty, so to speak. Making things happen. Earning someone's trust when they've been hurt so badly that it's difficult for them to trust anyone at all. So yes, I suppose you're right that I've found my niche. Still, my efforts seem paltry compared with yours."

They talked of their ideas and plans, coming to a halt at a stone bench in a corner, where they sat down so close together that his thigh pressed against the length of hers. The warmth was tangible even through her skirt and petticoats. He caught up her gloved hands and held them gently, lacing his long, slender fingers between hers.

"Charlotte, I hope you will forgive me if I'm overstepping the mark. I can't allow my feelings to remain unspoken." The enviable dark lashes swept downwards as he hesitated, stumbling over his words in a way she hadn't seen him do before. He'd always seemed so unflappable, so calm and at ease in himself, even when dealing with situations like a man raving or weeping, or when Josephine was ill.

Her eyes widened.

"You're so far above me. My life is not the kind of life you were born to. My work is demanding, and I couldn't hope to support you in the manner to which you are accustomed. I hardly dare presume to dream..."

She shook her head. "If anything, you're much better than I. I'm wilful, often self-centred, and too often I rub people up the wrong way. I rush into things and often overreach myself. *I'm* demanding, probably even more so than your job. I'm not sure it would be easy for anyone to put up with me. And then, there's my sister: I'll always take care of Josephine, for as long as she needs me."

He nodded gravely, then his chest rose visibly with a deep indrawn breath and he licked his lips as if he needed to pluck up sufficient courage to speak.

"Charlotte, do you think you could ever contemplate a future as a doctor's wife? To be more than a wife, to work together with him to build a better, fairer world?"

Her heart thumped. She'd hoped for this moment, but hadn't dared to expect it. The tension radiating from him was palpable, making her mouth go dry. The sound of her name on his lips was as delicious as a caress.

"I might be able to," she murmured. "But I suppose it would depend on the doctor. If it was Doctor Sheridan, I don't think I'd like it."

The tension broke, a sudden bark of laughter illuminating his face from within. "And if it were someone younger than Sheridan? Someone who admired and adored you, whose future would be empty and bitter without the hope of being permitted to love you as you deserve to be loved?"

"Well, then, in that case I think I could consider it." She peeped up at him under her lashes, feeling a rush of pleasure at the way he gazed down at her, sunshine highlighting the amber flecks in his eyes and a shy smile playing about his mouth in answer to hers. "If it were you, Kit, I certainly could."

He fumbled with his spectacles and laid them on the bench.

Almost holding her breath, she tilted her face up to his, her eyelids fluttering closed before his lips touched hers in a kiss that made her belly turn to liquid.

With a swift movement, he sank to one knee on the path and opened his mouth to speak – but she shook her head.

"Don't ask me just yet."

His face fell. "I'm so sorry," he began, moving to rise until she laid a hand on his shoulder.

It pained her to see his dejection, knowing she was the cause. But she couldn't risk the anguish of another engagement being broken if he should change his mind down the line. More than that, she would need time to adjust to the idea of moving to the rough town where he lived, if she couldn't persuade him to move to Plas Norton. There was so much uncertainty ahead, but she was sure of one thing: she wanted to finish what she had started with the hospital.

Stroking his cheek, she sought to soften the blow. "I only mean to say, let's wait a little while. We should get to know each other better, to avoid any possibility of doubt or a change of heart. You have your practice, and for now I have my work at Plas Norton. I've dedicated myself to seeing it through until the end of the war. You must understand, Kit: before I can commit myself to you, I need to be ready, and to feel worthy of you. You say I'm above you, but that's only in the ways that don't really matter. I'm all too aware that I'm not yet the person I want to be... but I'm getting there, and what I'm doing here can only help me. If you still feel the same – and I do hope you will – ask me when the war is over."

His Adam's apple bobbed. "You know that no one believes the war will end any time soon? It could go on for another year, perhaps even several more."

She nodded, eyes welling with tears she blinked away, determined to be strong. It would be so easy just to say yes. Oh, he couldn't offer her the kind of status that would have been hers if she'd married Eustace. He wouldn't bring a fortune or title to the altar when he slipped a ring onto her finger. But she would be loved, and she knew she could love him wholeheartedly in return. They could build something better and more satisfying than anything she could have had with the Westhamptons. If she could belong to this man, and if he could belong to her, there would be a beauty in the belonging that nothing else could ever match. She knew it instinctively. But she needed time.

He lay his head down on her lap, and she stroked his dark hair where it curled behind his ear. When he looked up, with disappointment and hope warring in his expression, she couldn't resist leaning forwards and kissing him. The first time hadn't been enough: she wanted to know that tenderness, that connection and trust that made her feel complete joy, again.

They were still in each other's arms when Venetia clumped around the corner.

"Oh, how marvellous," she said, clapping her hands. "I was hoping I'd given you long enough, and I obviously did. Bravo, Kit, old chap, and congratulations."

With a patch of colour high on each cheek, Kit got to his feet. "Hold your horses, old girl. Charlotte is determined to keep me waiting awhile yet. She has important work to do here first. But I'm happy to say she has given me hope."

Venetia's raised eyebrow and quizzical glance made Charlotte feel a fleeting pang of guilt. It vanished as her friend limped over and enveloped her in a hug.

"I'm delighted to hear it. She'll be worth waiting for, Kit."

"I don't doubt it for a moment, Vee." To Charlotte's relief, the corners of his mouth lifted in a wry, gentle smile.

Venetia linked arms with them both and turned towards the house. The windows sparkled in the sunshine, and as they followed her gaze upwards they noticed Maggie watching from upstairs. She was holding Josephine in her arms, pointing down to them and smiling. All three returned her cheery wave enthusiastically.

"It was most awfully remiss of you not to go and admire the veggies, cous. You might have seen those before attempting to sweep this dear girl off her feet..."

Venetia and Kit teased each other as they strolled back towards the house, and Charlotte laughed along, feeling she could almost float on air. The war might rage on, and suffering would continue, but in that moment the future was ripe with hope. With her sister, and Venetia and Kit, on her side, she could take on the world.

A LETTER FROM THE AUTHOR

Dear reader,

Huge thanks for reading *The Broken Vow*. I hope you were hooked on Charlotte and Maggie's journey. If you want to join other readers in hearing all about my new releases and bonus content, you can sign up here:

www.stormpublishing.co/luisa-a-jones

If you enjoyed this book and could spare a few moments to leave a review that would be hugely appreciated. Even a short review can make all the difference in encouraging a reader to discover my books for the first time. Thank you so much!

In this story I wanted to explore Charlotte and Maggie's characters in more depth. Charlotte was such a spoiled brat in *The Gilded Cage* – I wanted to consider what had made her that way, and to throw her into situations that would change her for the better. Women's options were severely limited in early twentieth century Britain, but the First World War created opportunities for them to step outside the domestic sphere and discover new talents and skills. By writing about Maggie as well as Charlotte, I was able to indulge my curiosity about how life might have changed for working class women and girls, as well as for the rich.

Thanks again for being part of this amazing journey with

me and I hope you'll stay in touch – I have many more stories and ideas to entertain you with!

Luisa

www.luisaajones.com

facebook.com/Luisa-A-Jones-232663650757721
x.com/Taffy_lulu
instagram.com/luisa_a_jones_author
bookbub.com/profile/luisa-a-jones

AUTHOR'S NOTE

If asked to sum up the First World War in just a few mental images, most of us would probably picture soldiers waiting to go 'over the top' into battle; the battle-scarred mud of Flanders and the Somme; rows of immaculately kept graves; the VAD nurse in her nun-like veil and apron with its blood-red cross. As well as these, many would consider the shell-shocked veteran to be one of the most haunting figures of the conflict. It's easy for us to imagine that most of the men who struggled in the dire conditions of trench warfare or in naval or air battles must have suffered the cruel effects of what we now describe as PTSD. They probably did, but statistics suggest that only around four men out of every thousand suffered severely enough to be hospitalised for what came to be described in early 1915 as 'shell-shock'.

In the early stages of the war, attitudes towards the varied symptoms of this condition were mixed. Not all sufferers were seen as being genuinely ill, and the causes of their symptoms were not fully understood. It wasn't until late 1916, more than two years into the conflict, that the British Expeditionary Force had established a network of psychiatric centres and 'mental

AUTHOR'S NOTE

wards'. Sadly, in what we would now view as a grave miscarriage of justice, some men were executed for cowardice or desertion after suffering severe symptoms.

Early in the war, those in the medical field who were more sympathetic to shell-shock tended to see it as a physical condition caused by concussion from shell blasts, fatigue or hunger, rather than a psychological condition. Common symptoms included vivid recurring nightmares, memory loss, shaking, nervousness including nervous tics, depression, obsessive thoughts about their experiences, limb weakness, and headaches. Sometimes sufferers would be dazed; some experienced paralysis, blindness, or deafness; others found themselves unable to speak. The British public, and indeed some in the military, found it difficult to understand or sympathise with such symptoms, many believing they indicated a lack of character or fortitude. They were sometimes even described as examples of lunacy or hysteria.

Once shell-shocked soldiers had been sent back to Britain in unmarked carriages on hospital trains, the aim of those treating them was to get them back to the front as quickly as possible. Every fighting man was needed in the effort to bring the conflict to a victorious conclusion. At home, some men found it difficult to sustain relationships or employment, and became isolated, as it was difficult for them to relate to people who had not experienced conditions at the front. They risked being sent to lunatic asylums if they could not recover quickly.

Those men who did not fully recover often felt emasculated as they had been brought up to view 'hysteria' as a feminine complaint (the word itself comes from the ancient Greek word meaning *womb*). Edwardian Britain was a more militaristic society than ours, and for a man to show fear was considered shameful. Officers, in particular, who had often been brought up in the public school system where stoicism was encouraged,

AUTHOR'S NOTE

felt that they had failed to live up to a heroic ideal if they succumbed to feelings of fear.

In early 1915, when this book begins, weather conditions where the British Expeditionary Force was entrenched on the Western front were very bad. Rain and snow caused severe flooding in the trenches, which were shallow, rat-infested, and in some places only yards from the enemy's position. Constant shelling and sniping caused a high casualty toll, and soldiers were surrounded by danger, death, and the sight of those around them receiving horrific injuries, in a way that their training could never have prepared them for.

With growing numbers of working men volunteering to join the armed forces, the women of Britain stepped up and held the line on the home front. By the end of the war they had made a vital contribution to the economy and society in ways that had often previously been denied them. Married women were temporarily allowed to work as teachers. Women worked on railways, buses and trams; as welders and sandblasters; on farms and in construction work. They worked in hospitals and in the police force; in printworks, brickworks, tanneries, paper mills and glazing factories; in foundries, flour mills and breweries.

The military discouraged women from active service in the early days of the war. Scottish doctor Elsie Inglis offered to set up a Scottish Women's Hospital Unit with female doctors and nurses, and was told by a man in the War Office, "My good lady, go home and sit still." Needless to say, she didn't: she went on to set up hospital units in France and Serbia, and even suffered imprisonment by the Germans for a time.

The greatest number of opportunities for women arose in munitions work, from 1915 onwards. The war effort required the setting up of munitions factories, and in the spring of 1915 the running of these was taken over by the government to ensure a reliable supply of ammunition for the front. 46,000 women signed up to work as munitionettes within a

AUTHOR'S NOTE

week of the Munitions of War Act being passed. Factory work paid more than domestic service or shop work, making it an attractive option for many working-class women, despite the long working hours and often dangerous conditions. They were not always welcomed by their male colleagues, especially if they were married to working men, as it was felt that they were taking up jobs that should be held by breadwinners.

There were government-run National Shell Factories all over Wales. The best factories provided canteens, changing rooms, washrooms, welfare and recreation facilities; but as the health and safety rules of the Factory Acts were put aside during the war to accelerate production, inevitably many women ended up working in poor or even hazardous conditions.

Work using TNT, which smelled awful and could rot clothes and handkerchiefs, could cause a wide range of health problems. These included nosebleeds, eye irritation, headaches, sore throats, a tight chest or cough, stomach pains, loss of appetite, nausea, bowel problems and dermatitis, as well as swollen hands and feet, dizziness, drowsiness and even death. Some women found their skin would turn yellow, staining their pillowcases and clothes and earning them the nickname 'Canary Girls'.

We shouldn't forget that soldiers were not the only victims of the war in terms of trauma and injuries. In the munitions factories, accidents and workplace injuries were commonplace, including acid burns and wounds to eyes. Fumes and particles of acid could land on skin and clothes, and enter eyes and nasal passages. Hair and clothes could be caught in machinery. One of Wales's biggest factories was an explosives works situated at Pembrey, where TNT and dynamite were produced. It was hit by a disaster in July 1917 when four workers were killed in an explosion, including two teenagers, Mildred Owen and Mary Watson. It was this which inspired the incident in the book

AUTHOR'S NOTE

when Maggie and Jenny are injured in an explosion at the munitions factory.

Many country houses were converted to hospitals and convalescent homes, giving me the idea for Plas Norton's transformation. One example is Llanwern House near my home town of Newport, where part of the house was turned into a Red Cross auxiliary hospital at the beginning of the war. It was owned by the parents of Margaret Haig Thomas (later Lady Rhondda), a militant suffragette who went on hunger strike after being imprisoned for bombing a post box in 1913. Unlike Sir Lucien Fitznorton in my books, her Welsh industrialist father was a strong believer in equal rights for women, and Margaret worked alongside him in his businesses. During the war she helped to settle Belgian refugees in Monmouthshire, encouraged women to take up work in war industries, and even survived the sinking of the *Lusitania* by a German submarine.

Lady Rhondda was not the only Welsh historical figure who helped to inspire my depiction of Charlotte and Venetia in this book. Rose Mary Crawshay of Cyfarthfa Castle in Merthyr Tydfil, who died less than a decade before the outbreak of the First World War, was a great public benefactress who set up a soup kitchen for needy locals when she was only eighteen years old. A supporter of female suffrage and keenly aware of the benefits of education for the poor, she set up dressmaking classes for local girls so they would gain skills which might enable them to earn more money. She held free educational readings in her castle, established an essay-writing prize, and set up no fewer than seven free libraries within a two-mile radius for local people to use. She also created an employment agency for impoverished gentlewomen to help them earn their own money by respectable means, as opportunities for such women were few.

A contemporary of Lady Rhondda, Gertrude Bailey was a wealthy Newport widow who inherited and managed her

AUTHOR'S NOTE

husband's ship repair business. As a philanthropist and public benefactress, she funded a wide range of public causes including scholarships, school library books, a window for the local hospital's mortuary chapel, a chain for the mayoress, hospital beds, and a training home for maternity nurses. From August 1914, when the war broke out, she hosted stitching parties for women to meet and sew for the poor and for patients in the town's hospital. As well as donating money to the Red Cross Society and Belgian Relief Fund for refugees, she funded a crèche for the children of munitionettes who struggled to find childcare during their long working hours (six a.m. to five p.m.). She served on local committees which recruited soldiers, provided recreation for those in the armed forces, sent items to local men who were prisoners of war in Germany, and administered War Pensions. Mrs Bailey also held 'at homes' and fêtes for munitionettes working in her factory and for wounded soldiers. With professional musicians and entertainers, tug of war contests, boxing, tea in a marquee, and fortune telling, these must have been fun events for war-weary folk.

I drew upon the work of these real women who used their fortune and influence to improve the lives of people living in Wales to inspire Charlotte's early efforts in philanthropy, including the Plas Norton fête. I hope you have gained as much pleasure as I have in imagining this wilful girl maturing into the kind of woman who might engage in similar works for the benefit of her community.

The women of Britain were not afforded the recognition they deserved despite taking on an incredibly wide range of roles to support the economy and the war effort, many thousands of them risking their health and their very lives for their country. As soon as the conflict ended, they were expected to give up many of the freedoms they had enjoyed when earning their own money and mixing with co-workers. It was several years before women were allowed to vote on the same terms as

AUTHOR'S NOTE

men, and decades before the law decreed that it was wrong to discriminate against them in the labour market or to pay them less on the basis of their sex. It is my hope that in a small way this story has acknowledged the tremendous contribution made by women whose refusal to 'go home and sit still' during the First World War made victory possible for the men who suffered unimaginable trauma at the front.

ACKNOWLEDGMENTS

As always, I would firstly like to thank my husband Martin. Without his unstinting support, I could not have come this far. My cheerleader, encourager and best friend, and a wonderful dad to our kids, dog and cats, he's also my adviser on technical matters. He listens patiently when I waffle on and boosts me when Imposter Syndrome strikes. He also makes a great cuppa.

I am grateful for my parents, children, and wider family and friends who show their love, pride, and support for my writing career. You'll never know how much it means to me.

My wonderful editor Kathryn Taussig's insights and encouragement have been invaluable. She, Natasha Hodgson and Liz Hurst are a dream to work with. All the team at Storm Publishing deserve thanks and praise for their brilliant work in transforming this story into the book you are reading now and sending it out into the world looking so gorgeous.

The talented and generous authors of the Cariad Chapter of the Romantic Novelists' Association have been amazing. Not only are their books brilliant, but they're the most supportive group imaginable, offering their wisdom, good sense and wit every step of the way. Special thanks to Jan, Jane, Natalie, Rosie, Imogen, Juliet, Anne, Morton, Sue, Georgia, Jessie, Lynn, Kitty, Emma, Evonne, Angela, Amanda, Sandra, Vicki, Lizzie and Pat. I wouldn't have got this far without them.

Anne, Imogen, Rosie and Maddie provided constructive beta feedback at very short notice. I'm deeply grateful to them for taking the time to help me make this a better book. David (recently promoted to Writing Husband) deserves a special mention for helping me brainstorm ideas, reading the first draft, and providing constructive feedback as well as historical notes. What a relief when he said he liked the book!

I'm grateful to Chris in Rogerstone Library in Newport, who has sourced so many obscure history books to aid me in my research into the home front during the First World War, especially the role of women at the time.

Last, but definitely not least, thank you for investing your valuable time and energies into reading this book. Without readers, there would be no writers. You are what makes all that research and all those hours at the laptop worthwhile. I appreciate you.